Praise for
Michael Reynolds

Michael Reynolds' *Songs of the Shenandoah* is destined to become a classic. Third in a series of brilliant historical novels, the last is by no means the least. From the coast of Newfoundland through Manhattan and onto the battlefields of the Civil War and beyond, Reynolds has penned a sweeping epic that will leave the reader breathless. Do not miss this masterpiece!

Kathleen Y'Barbo, best-selling author of *Flora's Wish* and *Millie's Treasure* from the Secret Lives of Will Tucker series

Reynolds winds up his series of novels with one of his best works of fiction and some of his finest writing. By turns romantic, dramatic, suspenseful, and colorful, as well as being rich with powerful prose and dialogue, *Songs of the Shenandoah* is a sweeping conclusion to his Heirs of Ireland trilogy. It will be one of your best reads of the year.

Murray Pura, best-selling author of *The Wings of Morning* and *Ashton Park*

Michael K. Reynolds—what a find! I started reading his debut novel *Flight of the Earls* and couldn't put it down. A gripping family series set during a fascinating time in Irish-American history.

—Dan Walsh, best-selling author of *The Unfinished Gift*

Michael Reynolds has given us a stunning debut novel—a saga that will capture both your heart and your mind as you journey back in time to experience triumph in the midst of crushing—except for Christ—circumstances. A soaring chronicle of immigrant America and beleaguered Ireland that will keep you reading late into the night.

Stephanie Grace Whitson, Christy finalist and best-selling author of historical fiction

From the Irish potato famine to the seedy streets of New York, Michael K. Reynolds takes the reader on a moving adventure. The writing sings, the story thrills, the characters are unapologetically realistic, and the message of hope and trust shines even in the grit. A novel not to be missed!

Sarah Sundin, award-winning author of *With Every Letter*

Michael Reynolds's debut novel *Flight of the Earls*, hauls you into an Irish family at the beginning of the potato famine. Sending their grown children to America might save them all. Clare lands in New York City to find another kind of famine, lack of morals, all encompassed by greed and corruption. Clare's dogged fight to keep her family alive amidst overwhelming odds makes her a standout heroine. I heartily recommend *Flight of the Earls* and look forward to the next. Michael Reynolds is an author to look out for.

—Lauraine Snelling, author of the continuing family saga of the Bjorklunds, the Blessing books, as readers call them, and the new Wild West Wind series with *Whispers on the Wind* and coming, *A Place to Belong*

My ancestors on my grandfather's side immigrated from Ireland during the great potato famine. It's something I knew but didn't really understand until reading *Flight of the Earls* by Michael K. Reynolds. The questions, fears, and hopes of a generation come to life through this novel. I found my emotions wrapped up in the middle of it . . . a sign of good fiction!

Tricia Goyer, best-selling author of thirty-three books, including *Beside Still Waters*

SONGS
of the
SHENANDOAH

An Heirs of Ireland novel

MICHAEL K. REYNOLDS

Nashville, Tennessee

Copyright © 2014 by Michael K. Reynolds
All rights reserved.
Printed in the United States of America

978-1-4336-7821-9

Published by B&H Publishing Group,
Nashville, Tennessee

Dewey Decimal Classification: F
Subject Heading: UNITED STATES—HISTORY—1861-1865,
CIVIL WAR—FICTION \ LOYALTY—FICTION \
FAMILY—FICTION

Publisher's Note: The characters and events
in this book are fictional, and any resemblance
to actual persons or events is coincidental.

Scripture quotations are taken from the New International Version
(NIV), Copyright © 1973, 1978, 1984 by the International Bible
Society. Used by permission of Zondervan. All rights reserved.
Also used is the Holy Bible, King James Version.

1 2 3 4 5 6 7 8 • 18 17 16 15 14

*For my family
who contributed immeasurably
to every word in this book.
You bring sweet melody to my life,
a song which never ceases to inspire.*

ACKNOWLEDGMENTS

As I compose these last words concluding the *Heirs of Ireland* series, I realize countless are those who have assisted me in the joyful labors of bringing these characters and stories to life.

My eternal gratitude goes to Jesus Christ who brings all inspiration and purpose to my writing.

And then there is my beloved wife Debbie, the lead character in my life, who has sacrificed greatly in the writing of these novels, and served as my faithful companion throughout this wild publishing journey. My daughters Kaleigh, Mackenzie, and Adeline have been such a blessing as they've tolerated with grace and understanding my many long nights and weekends in the office as my deadlines approach.

For Sheila, my mother and number one fan, who provided precious feedback and unyielding support. Also, for my father Philip who encouraged his son tremendously as did my sisters Cathy and Jacqueline and my good friend Larry Smith.

I am blessed with the world's classiest and most capable literary agent in Janet Kobobel Grant of Books & Such Literary Agency, whose patience and mentoring has helped craft my career.

My hat goes off to all of my friends at the Books & Such Literary Agency, and my many author friends as well, who promoted my writing and lifted my spirits during challenging times. And to the folks at the Mount Hermon Christian Writers Conference, who have positively impacted the careers and souls of many authors.

Blessings as well to my "inner circle" of Allen Batts, Jim Johnson and Greg Latimer, godly men who keep me grounded in my faith through deep valleys and the highest peaks.

For Julie Gwinn, who gave this writer his first publishing opportunity, and made the dreams of this trilogy come to fruition. And to the rest of the gifted team at B&H Publishing Group including Jennifer Lyell who carried the torch forward, my talented cover artist Diana Lawrence, book designer Kim Stanford, and marketing assistant Patrick Bonner.

Special thanks to my editor, Julee Schwarzburg, who has such a unique talent at bringing out the best in a writer. Not only is she a genius at what she does, but she is a pleasure to work with as well.

And for my Author Insiders and friends on Facebook and Twitter who are so willing to share news about my novels around the world. What you do makes a huge difference.

Thanks as well go out to my staff at Global Studio, who put their heart and talents to work in publicizing the author and his books.

All historical fiction novelists rely heavily on the painstaking efforts of scholars. There were so many excellent resources I depended on for the research of this book, chief among them being: *Gotham* by Edwin G. Burrows and Mike Wallace, *A Thread Across the Ocean: The Heroic Story of the Transatlantic Cable* by John Steele Gordon, *The Library of Congress Illustrated Timeline of the Civil War* by Margaret E. Wagner, *The Untold Civil War: Exploring the Human Side of War* by James Robertson, *Battle Cry of Freedom: The Civil War Era* by James McPherson and *The Civil War* series of documentaries by Ken Burns.

Finally . . . I have tremendous gratitude for my readers, who honor me with the gift of their time and imagination. And especially those who make the effort to thrill me with heartwarming reviews, kindly worded letters and who share me with their friends.

Prologue

THE CABLE

TRINITY BAY, NEWFOUNDLAND
August 16, 1858

The mahogany clock inside the telegraph station ticked brightly in contrast to the unnerving silence in the room, and Clare Royce caught herself similarly tapping the tip of her pencil on her open notebook.

As the storied reporter for her husband's paper, the *New York Daily*, she was rarely far from her pad of paper, and for some reason not clearly understood to her, this story was personal to Clare.

Clare regretted not being here eleven days earlier when Cyrus Field, the mastermind of this wild-eyed venture, first arrived with the telegraph wire in tow aboard the great ship

Niagara. Upon arriving in the early morn, he rode a dinghy to this remote landing in Newfoundland, a place of fog-enshrouded shores of blue waters and seemingly endless woodlands. He announced with glee, "The cable is laid" to all who would listen, thus signaling the beginning of a historic conversation between two continents: the elegant lady of Europe and the nubile beauty of North America.

Upon hearing this news, Clare came as quick as she could from New York, wanting to be at this location when Queen Victoria of England sent the line's first official message to President Buchanan of the United States.

As Clare sat here waiting, her thoughts drifted along the thousands of miles of cable laid across the murky floor of the Atlantic Ocean, which when it descended to depths below no doubt provided a curious distraction to the finned, shelled, and clawed inhabitants of the sea before it reached the bottom, there to rest among waving algae, jagged coral, and soft mud.

What completed Clare's fascination of this glorious line of one man's lofty imagination was its destination, an island off of the westernmost point of Ireland, a nation which had never escaped the most cherished places of Clare's heart.

It was there, in the green-grassed coastal village of Valencia, where the other end of the telegraph wire was connected, laid by the crew of the ship *Agamemnon*. Several weeks earlier, this British vessel had started midway in the Atlantic alongside the American-owned *Niagara*, and after splicing the cable between them, the two ships lay their thread like two spiders heading toward opposite worlds.

Clare imagined the sailors of the *Agamemnon*, with saltwater-drenched pants, carrying the cable through the frothy waves to the sandy beach, then looking up to the craggy rock cliffs of the Irish island. Clare wished she could have been there alongside them to gaze upon the lush hills dotted with stony hovels and foraging sheep and cattle.

Had it truly been more than a decade since she had carried her brothers and sister away from the death clench of the Emerald Isle's potato famine to the richer shores of America?

Oh how the sons and daughters of Ireland floated away like tragic driftwood from that land! Pushed by uncaring tides to distant lands, where there they were plucked from the waters with hands of mockery and scorn.

Still, as forgiving as her people were to the indignities they faced, Clare knew the sailors of the *Agamemnon* would be welcomed ashore with grace and ebullience. She could almost see the orange and yellow hues of the rising morning, and the entire populace of fishermen and farmers out early to cheer, assist, and experience the arrival of the mighty ship and its remarkable cargo.

She looked over toward the telegrapher's oaken desk, who with his balding pate and narrow frame seemed too frail for an assignment of such significance. Hovering around him, in between nervous pacing, was Mr. Field.

Cyrus had a stern disposition that belied his kindly nature, and he wore a short, scraggly beard that sprung out from beneath his chin. His intense eyes were monitoring every detail of the process.

Clare had never met a more fanatically dedicated man in her life, and she saw him as both a heroic and tragic figure in his tireless and failure-weary endeavor to connect the Old World and the new with his cable.

And she identified with Mr. Field's fall from financial graces. For just as his paper empire had collapsed as a result of the great banking crash of '57, the *Daily* and the Royces' place among the wealthy had fallen as precipitously.

Now with great success about to be realized, Mr. Field would be able to make a triumphant return to his good fortune.

Clare panned the room and took in the curious mix of well-dressed financiers and telegraph technicians. Some had nodded off in their chairs, with arms folded and heads tilted. Those who remained awake kept their heavy-lidded gazes upon the brass hammer of the telegraph.

Which is why they almost all became startled when the door snapped open and a tall, blond man with round spectacles entered, escorted by a brisk breeze.

Clare was always lifted by seeing her husband, Andrew. For fear she would miss the precise moment when the queen's message arrived, Clare had fended off all of his pleaded requests that she take a break to sleep in their lodging, or at least walk along the beach to clear her mind. But this didn't take away her appreciation of his care and concern for her.

Andrew stepped lightly on the creaking wooden floorboards and slid into the chair by her side. He unwrapped a handkerchief in his hand, revealing some carefully sliced apples and cheese, and held it out to her.

Clare noticed a few irritated glances by some of the others in the room. She reached out and gratefully accepted several pieces of the food. She bit into one of the apple slices and savored the sweetness of the juice.

Clare leaned into his shoulder, which smelled like ocean air. She was careful not to clip the pin tenuously holding up her hair. Too tired to care what she looked like, she rested in the comfort that Andrew always made her feel beautiful. So many years had passed since her long black hair, fair complexion, and sapphire-blue eyes had drawn the unwanted gaze of many a man. Yet now in her late thirties, even the emergence of a few strands of gray in her hair and lines under her eyes had not tempered his affection for her.

He whispered in her ear, "I hate to be the one to ruin this somber moment, but at great personal risk I have followed the full length of this telegraph cable and have made a most remarkable discovery."

"Oh you have, Mr. Royce?"

"Yes I have, *mon chéri*, and after rowing tirelessly out across these churning waters, imagine my distaste in learning that Cyrus's dear cable has not made it clear across the Atlantic as stipulated."

"It has not?" Clare found it amusing when her playful Englishman tried wooing her in French. She reached out for his hand and wrapped both of hers around it to warm it for him. He had certainly aged as well in their ten years of marriage, but his etched features made him appear distinguished.

"No, I am afraid your Cyrus has deceived us all," he intoned with a mischievous whisper. "As a duty-bound journalist, I must report to you that we discovered the cord wrapped loosely around the fluke of a full-grown gray whale."

Clare snorted out a laugh and covered her mouth when she realized she had attracted hardened glares from many of the serious faces in the room. She squeezed his arm. "Must I send you back outside? You are more trouble than both our two children combined. And not nearly as adorable."

The mention of their eight-year-old son, Garret, and their six-year-old daughter, Ella, seared Clare with guilt. She had no intention of being away on assignment for several days. Not only was it unfair of her to be away from the children for so long, but it was a mistake to have dragged Andrew along. He labored to keep up with his responsibilities at the *Daily*, and being away from his office would only put him that much further in arrears.

"What do you suppose Her Majesty will have to say?" He nodded toward the telegraph.

Clare sat up and tucked a few loose strands of hair back in her bun. "Well, since it'll be passing through Ireland, I am certain it will be something quite eloquently stated." She tried to think of something clever, but her mind was numb from the lack of sleep.

"Something like . . ." Andrew shifted to his fake royal accent. "Had you unsophisticated Yankee minions merely paid your proper tea levies, we would have laid this grand wire decades ago."

She tried to hold back her laughter, but she was unsuccessful. This time it was the bald telegrapher himself who gave her a crooked expression. Clare waved her hand in apology.

For fear she would not be able to contain herself if she looked her husband in the face, she closed her eyes. But her lips sought out his ear. "I love you, Andrew Royce."

He gave her a firm embrace, then she heard his voice turning soft and sincere. "Even if . . . ?"

"Especially because."

Andrew suffered with the knowledge he was struggling to keep the *Daily* at the financial strength it heralded when his father was running it. But since Charles Royce had passed, they both learned unsavory details of how the old man had reaped such success.

Andrew's main shortcoming was not being able to clean up the business dealings of the paper without simultaneously washing away its profits. It pained Clare to come to this conclusion, but it was becoming clear they couldn't blame all of the *Daily*'s suffering on her husband's ethics alone. He just wasn't as gifted a proprietor as his father was.

"You miss it, don't you?" Andrew's expression was one of a sudden discovery. "That's why we're here, isn't it?"

She was about to protest. To tell him it was because of her fascination with the miracles of science. Or due to her journalistic curiosity. These were true, but Andrew always knew deep inside her heart, in places she was uncomfortable visiting herself.

"It was . . . a more simple life." Her thoughts drifted to her days on the Hanley farm in Ireland; of living in tight quarters; of feeding from their soil and cutting turf from bogs for fires; and sweet dances of celebration with the entire village, all of whom were both lovingly flawed and part of an extended family.

But this was a sheltered memory, one that would frame

perfectly as a painting. For Clare's last experience of her home-land more than ten years ago was one of crop failure, starvation, and death. And even on their scarcest of days in America, there wasn't the remotest of comparisons to the poverty she had once endured.

No. This land of opportunity had been their savior. Not only for herself, but for her brothers and sister, who had made new lives for themselves; lives not so dependent on the whims of nature or the cruel provision of fate.

And although her brothers Seamus and Davin had scattered to the far ends of this country, in gold-rich California, she was comforted by knowing she had assisted in their arrival to these nurturing shores, to a place where their bowls would never be empty and through effort and innovation, their dreams were always in reach.

America was a place of blessing where someone like herself, her siblings, and her children could rise above their given stand-ing and declare their own destiny.

Yet something troubled Clare, for she knew in her heart that they left something behind in the ship taking them all from Cork Harbour to the promised land. A memory forgotten. A voice that was silenced.

"What's wrong?" Andrew placed his hand on her arm and looked into her eyes with a yearning to heal.

Clare shook her head. She regretted wearing her concerns so obviously. This was not the time for such a discussion. "I was just thinking of home."

Andrew was about to speak but then paused and turned toward the telegraph as gasps came out of several people, and those who had nodded off to sleep were given heavy tugs on their arms.

All attention was focused in silence on the brass head of the telegraph machine, which now danced with tapping rhythms of change.

Chapter 1

CHRISTMAS IN MANHATTAN

MANHATTAN, NEW YORK
December 1860

Clare had been anticipating this moment for more than a decade.

It was to be the most glorious Christmas dinner of her life, with her cherished guests about to arrive, and she was intent on making every detail of her hospitality an expression of the profound love she felt for her family.

After all of this time and separated by so many distant miles of untamed territories, they would be home at last.

She stepped back, raised her hand to her chin, and considered the placement of the candles that were set in brass holders, tied with golden ribbons, and placed on a red silk runner, which went down the center and spilled over the sides of a long cherry table.

The flames rising from the wicks and those emanating from wood crackling in the marble-framed fireplace combined to light up the spacious dining room and cause shadowy figures to shift on the walls between painted portraits and landscapes.

The pine boughs she had weaved so delicately on the shelving and mantelpiece of the room smelled of fresh-cut evergreen. These scents blended with those from the mistletoe arranged on the table and the potpourri simmering in a copper kettle at the foot of the fire, providing a festive symphony of Christmastime aromas.

Garret, with his black tussle of curls, had his back to her, his knees perched on the bay-window ledge, fogging up the glass as he waited anxiously for the arrival of relatives he had known only through letters and photographs.

Standing beside Clare, her sister polished the crystal drinking glasses around the table with the aid of a napkin. The flickering candlelight splashed delicately on Caitlin's face, who at thirty years with her long, wavy blond hair, high cheekbones, and fair complexion appeared much younger.

"This one is quite chipped." Caitlin held the glass up to Clare.

"If you look closely, you'll see they all have their blemishes, I am afraid. Much the same as me." Clare reached down and picked up one of the china dishes. "Look at these poor fellows. If they survive this . . . last supper, it will be only due to God's mercy."

Clare held up one of the silver knives, tarnished beyond repair, and sighed. "Oh to see what has become of all of this! If Andrew's mother were still with us, she would no doubt have good reason to lecture her daughter-in-law. A sad caretaker of the Royce empire I have proven to be."

Caitlin plucked the piece of silverware from her sister's hand and laid it in its proper place on the table. "These are different times. Troubling times. There is victory in . . . just maintaining our position."

"What I would do to maintain. What a glorious ring that

word has to it. No, we slip further with each day." Clare glanced at her fingertips. "And I have calluses to prove how precipitously we hang on."

The harmonies of well-sung Christmas songs wafted through the window. "What's this I hear?" Clare headed to the window.

"Ma," Garret said, without turning. "There's carolers coming."

"What a welcome sound to our evening." Caitlin nodded to her sister to join them.

"Enough fussing about the cutlery." Clare squeezed her son's shoulder. "I should be ashamed to be bantering about such things on this of all evenings."

The three of them peered out the window, smiles warming their faces as they gazed through the misty veil of the falling snow. There, under the gaslight, was a gathering of seven sharply dressed singers, the women in bonnets and colorful dresses and the men sporting tall hats and tailored coats. Each stood closely together and were wrapped tightly in scarfs as steam rose with each Yuletide verse they sang.

As she savored the words and muted melodies of the song, Clare whispered a prayer of thanks for this neighborhood she lived in and this house, a fieldstone two-story structure that despite sorely needing new paint still rose above the others on her block.

"Should we go outside?" Garret turned and smiled sweetly, but his eye had swollen even more in the past hour, and it was darkening.

Clare had almost forgot about his fight earlier in the day with the boys at the park. "Oh, that looks dreadful, son." She put her hand on his cheek. "If only you had the sense to ignore them and just walk away."

"You know I won't allow them to speak of you and Da so unkindly."

"What did they say to you?" Caitlin asked. "I hadn't heard."

Garret looked to Clare for permission to answer, which she grudgingly provided with a nod.

"They don't like Ma's writing in the newspaper." He turned to face the window, his freckled cheeks reflecting in the glass. "They say she hates her own people and wishes she was a Negro slave."

"Who said these horrible words?" Her eyes wide, Caitlin looked to Clare. "You should have told those . . . dreadful whelps . . . that your dear mother has been the greatest gift to the Irish this city has ever laid eyes on. No one has done more for her people than—Oh my, who is that precious little girl playing in the snow?"

Clare peered outside and her entire body tensed. She tapped her knuckles on the window. "Ella Royce! You come in here immediately."

Garret looked back with his mouth agape. "Ma, you're going to scare away the carolers."

In a few moments the front door snapped open and Clare's daughter entered the dining room with guilty and moist steps, her brown hair flecked with snow and her face ruby red from the cold. Ella was wearing only a blue cotton dress, and she had a latticed apron folded up to hold some concealed items that appeared precious to her.

Clare propped her palms on her waist. "What a sight is this! Your clothes are all but ruined and you most assuredly have caught a chill. And what . . . what are you hiding there?"

The child shook her head and appealed to her aunt Cait with sappy brown eyes for some sort of support, which, as always, she was all too willing to provide.

Caitlin bent over and carefully opened the girl's apron and peeked in. "Well if those aren't the most well-formed snowballs I've ever seen. May I?" When Ella nodded, Caitlin pulled out one of the white frozen orbs and held it up with reverence as if it were hand chipped from marble.

"Do you know the effort we've gone to get this house and you decorated in the spirit of Christmas?" Clare glared at her sister who had her hands to her lips, her mouth threatening to open in laughter. "And you are villain as well for your encouragement." Clare turned to her daughter. "Now what madness would cause you to go out in the storm . . . dressed as such, and bring those . . . snowballs into this home, young lady?"

Ella bit her lip and glanced over to her brother and then Caitlin. "I fetched them for Garret. It will make his eye feel better."

The words pierced Clare's matronly scowl, and she rubbed her hand on her face. Then she bent down with a deep breath of apology and kissed Ella on her head. "And that, my kind heart, is why we named you after your grandmama."

She glanced back out the window to see if the carolers remained, but they had moved on and the snow now drifted down in heavy flakes with the flutter of butterflies. "Oh dear, I hope it will be safe to travel. To come all of the way from California, thousands of miles, only to perish in the streets of New York City on their way from the harbor."

"Seamus, the mountain man turned pastor, and young Davin the famed gold miner?" Caitlin exchanged a look with Clare and they both laughed. "How could they stray? One finds lost souls and the other lost treasures."

"We certainly could use strengthening of both our faith and fortunes." Clare glanced at the clock on the wall. "Andrew, Andrew, my dear husband, why are you taking so long?"

Just at that moment, a clamor came from the front entranceway and both of the children went running for the door.

"Oh my, they are here." Clare fanned her face with her hand, suddenly feeling flush.

Clare entered the hallway just as Andrew walked in through the door, his tall frame bent over while toting two large cases, with a smaller one tucked under his arm. He lumbered over and set them down noisily, then he removed his round spectacles, swept his hand through his blond hair, and shook snow from it to the floor.

Behind him came a woman, who even through her travel weariness, was eloquent with her chartreuse dress, black feathered hat, and long auburn curls draping down.

"You must be Ashlyn." Clare met the woman's large brown eyes, held out her arms, and embraced her. She wanted dearly to kiss the woman on the cheek in joy. Was this not the dear creature who had transformed Seamus's life? Could there be a greater angel?

Clare held her firmly for a few moments, and when she pressed back she saw a young girl in the doorway, who she knew to be almost thirteen, disheveled by the journey and seeming overwhelmed by the attention.

Caitlin stepped up and hugged the girl. "And this is Grace?"

Footsteps could be heard and Clare's heart leapt with anticipation and she began to cry and covered her mouth. Carrying several cases himself was her brother Seamus, and Andrew grabbed the cases from him and set them down with the others.

Seamus stood up straight, dusting off snow from the sleeves of his black wool coat, and he appeared to Clare as handsome as ever with his slender build, long black sideburns, and the effervescent blue Hanley eyes. She tried to avoid looking at the scar on the side of his cheek, which was surprisingly tame considering it had been the result of a branding iron—his punishment for being a deserter in the war with Mexico.

His face erupted in a broad smile, and his arms outstretched. "Come here you, my precious oldest." When Clare came, he pulled her in and lifted her from her feet as she hooted and cried. Then he reached out and drew in Caitlin as well.

There were some grunting noises and then a man's voice. "Where should these go?"

Clare looked up to see two carriage drivers backing in a couple of leather-strapped trunks piled on top of each other.

"Right here, I'll help you with that." Andrew guided them to the far edge of the hallway. "We'll stack them neatly. What do we have? About four or five more trips?"

One of the carriage drivers who was short with silver hair rubbed his hands together for warmth. "At least that and probably more."

Clare laughed. "Well, I suppose you would have quite a bit of baggage."

"Oh no." Seamus pointed to the bags he carried in. "Those few there are the only ones that are ours. We had to hire a separate carriage to bring in your little brother's belongings."

"Davin?" Clare peered out the door as the breeze carried in a flurry of snowflakes. "Where is he?"

"Meeting a bloke of his." Seamus gave Ashlyn a knowing glance, and she pursed her elegant lips and lowered her head. "His business partner as it is. Said he would be a tad late for sup and was hoping it wouldn't be a bother to your plans."

Clare noticed Seamus wasn't wearing a minister's collar. Perhaps it was too uncomfortable for the long voyage. "Of course we won't mind."

Seamus tugged on the fingers of his glove to take them off. "Seeing as my little brudder tabbed our trains, coaches, and ferries, it was no discomfort to carry his bags." Seamus cleared his throat. "Have we been properly acquaintanced?" He bent down and extended a hand to Garret, who along with his sister was standing somewhat in awe of their new guests.

Garret shook the hand meekly and Ella took a step back, subdued with her shyness.

Clare was reminded how deeply she cared for Seamus. Since he was a boy and was tormented so by their father, she was the one who always intervened, who understood his thoughts, and who ached when he did.

Which was why she was concerned as she watched him interact with her children. Something was wrong. He hadn't shared it in any of his recent letters, and he was always capable of covering up his problems with Irish cheer.

But she could tell. There was a sadness behind the curtains of his soul.

Chapter 2

THE DINNER

"Do you think we should send after him?" Clare didn't know whether she was more angry or worried. After all of these years apart, why wouldn't Davin want to come directly to see them all?

They had finished dinner more than an hour ago, cleaned up the table and kitchen, and since moved to the sitting parlor, where they rested in the faded upholstered chairs and couches. Muriel, who appeared the part of an Irish maid, with her young face, red hair, and white apron, served everyone evening tea.

What a gift from God Muriel had been to the Royce family! With their inability to afford to hire any help, they were so fortunate to discover this sharp-witted treasure, who provided her precious assistance with the children and the house chores in exchange for lodging and board. She had only been here for a couple of months but had already become part of the clan.

Andrew glanced up from the fire he was lighting. "Would you like me to go out and about to see if we can find your brother?"

9

"Where would you start?" Clare looked to Seamus sitting on a couch with Ashlyn, who sat with proper Southern elegance. "Did Davin inform you of where he was heading?"

Seamus held out a cup and saucer to Muriel, and once it was filled with the steaming fluid, he handed it his wife. "I wouldn't go fussing about Davin. How old was he when you last saw him? Eleven, right?"

Ashlyn rolled her eyes, dipped a spoon in the sugar bowl, and then lifted it to her cup. "Your little Davin is now quite a dandified man."

"But I quite liked him the way he was." Clare sighed. "Is he that changed?"

"'Fraid so." Seamus smiled. "One day he was this kind, considerate, and innocent boy, and then suddenly, well, you'll find out soon enough."

"How unkind of you, Seamus." Caitlin frowned. "Didn't you say he covered the cost of your travel?"

Seamus lifted Ashlyn's hand and caressed it. "Oh, I love my little brudder well enough, that's for certain. Why, he stowed away on a ship for many thousand miles, just to seek me out. And find me he did." He looked at his wife. "It's just . . . we worry about him. Since . . . you know."

Ashlyn grinned. "I believe my husband is about to preach his most famous sermon. And a most unpopular one in the foothills of the Sierra range."

Seamus lowered his head and clasped his hands. "Thins out the congregation a bit when you preach about the evils of the yellow rock in gold country of all places."

"It seems we're all preaching something unpopular these days." Andrew put his arm around Clare. "My wife pontificates with the pen. She has become the voice of abolition. Must be a Hanley tradition to row upstream as they throw rocks from the banks. Even Caitlin is of service to the Underground Railroad."

"The Underground Railroad?" Surprise laced Ashlyn's tone.

"Yes." Clare looked for disapproval in the woman's face. Ashlyn remained a mystery to her. Was she the source of her brother's melancholy? "Caitlin has been part of the movement for years. Why, even Muriel has taken interest in it as of late."

Muriel shook her head. "I've merely attended a few meetings." She placed the teapot on the table, sat beside Caitlin, and folded her brown cotton dress beneath her.

"And," Clare added, "Muriel's been assisting us at the newspaper as well. Our sweet lady here holds many surprises." She lifted her teacup and eyed her sister-in-law. "What about you, Ashlyn? Seamus boasts about you in his letters. And of your baby orphanage."

Ashlyn withdrew her hand from Seamus. "Yes. But unfortunately that . . . was closed, I am sad to say."

Seamus winced. "The crash in San Francisco was difficult for all of us. Banks closed. Merchants failed. Donations were a wee chore to come by. And this was at the same time that I . . . well, we . . . thought it was time to move closer to the mountains. Seek out a new ministry."

"Yes." Ashlyn took Seamus's hand again and rubbed it. She met Clare's probing gaze. "You would have been proud of your brother. Never has a man put so much braveness in trying to start a church."

Unspoken questions hung in the air as a lull lingered for a few awkward moments.

"And what a wonderful father he has been to Grace." Ashlyn glanced into her husband's eyes with adoration.

Clare had misjudged the woman and instantly felt bonded to their shared mission. "She is a beautiful young lady, your Grace. You've both done admirably in raising her."

"We've had our brushes as well due to the financial crash." Andrew tossed a log in the fire, which was struggling to keep the room warm. He dusted his hands and stood. "You are not alone with that one. Devastated not only our newspaper, but nearly wiped out Clare's favorite paper supplier."

Clare snorted. "Oh, Andrew. You are a terrible tease." She looked to her brother and Ashlyn. "He is referring to a certain fondness I have for Cyrus Field."

Seamus snapped his fingers. "Isn't that . . . man . . . who—?"

"Yes," Clare answered. "The bedlamite, as he has been referred to as well as many other unmentionable slanders. His dream is to lay working telegraph wire from Ireland to Newfoundland."

Andrew leaned against the mantelpiece. "If it wasn't for Clare's stories in the *Daily* urging the poor fellow on with such pomp and bravado about the 'most noble pursuit of the nineteenth century,' I'm sure he would have long ago returned to his proper place in the world of reducing trees to paper."

"As you can see, my husband chooses to join in the easy sport of mocking dear Mr. Field. But one day, Cyrus and I will have our say."

A large clattering sounded behind them in the room and they stood up startled with a few gasps.

"What's that?" Caitlin said. "A thief on Christmas Eve?"

The noise came from the window at the rear of the room. Andrew lifted the poker from the fireplace and held it out before him and stepped forward in the dim lighting.

Chapter 3

THE BREEZE IN THE ROOM

 With a clatter, the window thrust open, accompanied by a cool gust of whistling air.

First, a tall black hat with brown curls spilling around the brim emerged, then the face of a young man with a tightly cropped brown beard and sharp features.

Andrew raised his arm with his weapon poised. But unknowingly, the intruder continued to awkwardly climb his way through the opening, snow flurrying around him.

Seamus had moved over to Andrew and eased down the weapon. With a barker's voice Seamus spoke. "May I introduce to you, kind gentleman and ladies, the distinguished gold prospector Master Davin Hanley."

Now fully entered, Davin slammed the window shut behind him, closing out the wind's howl, and spun with eloquence, revealing an exquisitely tailored lavender jacket with long, swooping tails. He lifted his hat and leaned down into a deep bow, to what now were stares from the numbed assembly.

"What?" He flashed a puckish grin and looked back at the window. "That was always my preferred way of coming inside this house."

Clare, who had seen some pictures of Davin through the years, still was amazed at what few semblances remained of the gentle-spirited, frog-chasing boy who lived here eleven years ago. Instead, before them stood a man, distinguished in his stature and grooming, his brown eyes glistening with confidence.

Davin clapped his tall black boots together to free the clumps of snow and patted away the frozen dust from his clothing. He stepped forward and kissed Clare on the cheek and held her tightly. "Now, now, sister Clare. You knew I would come home, didn't you?"

Clare couldn't hold back the tears that flowed freely down her cheeks and onto his. He was so strong in her arms. "If you had any idea of the suffering you put me through, young man." When he had left home at the age of eleven to seek out Seamus in San Francisco, Davin left no note of his whereabouts. For a long time Clare had believed him lost.

Finally she stepped back and laughed, wiping the tears. Caitlin and the others took turns exchanging hugs and handshakes. During this moment of festive greeting, Clare happened a glance at Muriel. The young woman observed Davin with tender fascination. Clare's heart went out to the girl as she was as plain looking as she was kind.

Andrew drew a chair close to the fire and motioned for Davin to sit.

"May I put together a plate of food for you?" Muriel asked.

"Oh?" Davin said. "Is that not Cassie's job?"

Caitlin dragged a chair close to her younger brother. "Cassie hasn't worked here for several years. She's married to Reverend Bridges, who is pastor of one of the largest black churches in Manhattan."

"Ah, I see." He glanced dispassionately at Muriel. "Is this the new girl?"

Andrew had come alongside Muriel. "This . . . new girl is studying to become a doctor." He nodded to her. "You sit yourself down. I'll get Davin some food."

Davin patted his stomach. "Much appreciated." He watched Andrew walk away and then turned his gaze back to Muriel. "He did mean nurse, right?"

Muriel's expression transformed from admiration to resentment. Davin had ignited a spark they had yet to see burn in their boarder. Before the girl could respond, Clare spoke. "So Davin, tell us of your grand adventures out West. Don't leave out the smallest of details. We want to know all about your gold discovery."

Davin rubbed his hands together. "Yes. I suppose you would."

"Have you left any in California?" Caitlin prodded. "Or did you take it all?"

"Most." He removed his hat, set it on the floor beside him, and eyed his rapt audience. "All right if you must know." He crossed his arms. "It all started on Ashlyn's claim. Well, actually her father's."

"Oh, I didn't know." Clare looked to Ashlyn who shifted in her seat.

"That mine unfortunately didn't have much life in her once we got there." Davin leaned back in the chair. "We pulled maybe enough to purchase our next claim. And then the next one after that. Of course, I didn't have much need of money when I was young. It was all entertainment. Enough to keep fed and help a few out along the way." He gave Seamus a glance.

"But then a few years ago, I met up with my partners. My friend Tristan Lowery—"

"Of the Lowery family, here in New York?" Clare asked with surprise. "I heard they made a fortune in gold. I was unaware you were connected with them."

Andrew returned with a plate of food, which was both overflowing and hastily put together.

"Yes." Davin looked over the food carefully, then picked up a fork and poked it into a large pile of potatoes. "The Lowerys wanted in the game, had cash in their fists, but they needed someone with dirt in his boots and I was their man. Quite fortunate, I must say. Happened to be standing there." He swallowed the forkful of potatoes and then lifted a turkey leg to his mouth.

Caitlin beamed at her brother. "So what did they do? Buy you more shovels?"

"Hydraulic mining." They all turned in surprise to see the answer had come from Muriel.

Davin shook his turkey leg at her and grinned. "Well done, Doctor." He took another bite.

"What . . . is—?" Caitlin laughed, almost as if to break the sudden tension.

"They use large water cannons to clear out whole mountains to get to the gold." Muriel's gaze locked on to Davin with the focus a predator would give prey. "Did they chase you out?"

"Not hardly." Davin narrowed his eyes at her, then he smiled. "Although we did get most of the gold in California. Which is what brings me here." He rested the half-eaten leg on the plate and picked up the fork again. "And I am sorry, dear sister, for my delay in arriving tonight, but I had to console poor Tristan. I owed that to him."

Andrew lifted a pitcher of water off of the table and filled a glass and handed it Davin. "I wasn't aware of any suffering with the Lowerys. Has there been a death?"

Clare knew of Andrew's distaste for the family, one of the wealthiest in all of Manhattan. Was there a touch of envy in her husband for their rise to prominence at the same time the Royce's were descending from theirs?

"Worse." Davin took a large gulp from the glass and wiped his lips with the back of his hand. "We moved nearly all of our investments out of gold and into cotton several months ago, apparently with ill timing."

"Only to hear now that South Carolina has pulled out of the Union." Andrew sat back down next to Clare.

"Mr. Lincoln is going to set all of that straight," Caitlin said.

Clare took it upon herself to avert a conversation of politics on such a day as this. "Well, all I can say is it is an answer to our deepest prayers that you are all here and safe and we are together again. Despite these worrying days." She looked to Seamus and Ashlyn. "And you, of course, must know you are most welcome to stay here as long as you want until you have a chance to settle down."

Seamus's expression sank. He gazed at Ashlyn. "We'll be here in the city for just a few more days."

Clare's stomach roiled. What other bitter surprises would these evening hold? "What is this?"

Seamus spoke with tones of apology. "It was our intention to tarry a wee bit here in New York. But. With the way the news is shaping, we'd best be moving before things get thicker."

"Where to?" Caitlin's voice wavered.

Seamus folded his hands and leaned forward. "Ashlyn learned word a few months back that her uncle had passed on, which means her father's Whittington farm has returned to her name. Our name."

Ashlyn's face beamed. "It's quite lovely. In the Shenandoah Valley. It's very good farmland."

"Virginia?" Caitlin said the word with a hint of contempt. "A plantation?"

"It was . . . years back. But not now." Seamus put his arm around his wife. "This dear lady has supported me through all of my mad pursuits. It's an honor and blessing for me to return her and Grace home." He held out a hand and wiggled his fingers. "Besides, I'm looking forward to using these soft hands again."

Clare tried to laugh but the news was still stinging. "My brother Seamus. Returning to farm life?"

"No potatoes." Seamus turned to Ashlyn. "Right?"

Ashlyn whispered, "No potatoes."

They sat there together in silence as the sound of the fire crackled in the background.

Clare struggled to hold back her disappointment in what had become of this night, the one she had waited for so long. She was grateful for Andrew's touch as he put his arm around her shoulders.

As she glanced around at her brothers and sister, aware of the times they were facing in this country they had adopted as their own, a question pressed upon her.

Was there anything she could do to keep them all safe? All together?

She shuddered and wrapped her arms tightly to fend off the chill in the room.

Chapter 4

WHITTINGTON FARMS

TAYLORSVILLE, VIRGINIA
January 1861

 "Oh, Seamus, it's even more beautiful than I ever remembered!" Ashlyn's face glowed as she stared at the unraveling splendor of the Shenandoah Valley farmland and their carriage rattled down the country road with the Massanutten Mountains rising in the background.

For Seamus, there was little beauty in the weather they had endured during their travels to this western range of Virginia. Not only did they face delays caused by snow and icy conditions, but they suffered contempt as well in the stares and treatment they received on their way down South.

On more than a few occasions, their intentions and allegiances were questioned and their carriage even was pelted by rocks. There was a palpable sense of encroaching war and a rising hatred among the people.

It was a strange sensation for Seamus to actually feel relieved to be arriving in Ashlyn's hometown, and he shared in her joy in beginning this new stage of their lives. Yet when he first crossed the borders of Maryland and passed through large fields of laboring black slaves, he felt an uncomfortable finality about his decision to bring his family here.

But there was an undeniable pleasure as well in seeing his wife's spirits rise with each approaching mile. She had endured so much the past few years in faithful support of his meanderings, so he now felt as if a great debt was being lifted from his shoulders.

Ashlyn rose from the leather seat of the coach, pulled down the window, and leaned her face out in the cool air. "Here, Grace. Come here."

The teenager pleaded with her eyes to Seamus. "Ma. Are you going to show me some more trees?"

Her mother was unaffected by Grace's insolence. "That little building there is where I used to go to school. Oh, how wondrous! Seamus we are so close." She leaned back in and kissed him on the cheek. "I had no idea how much I missed this place. How it was in my blood."

Grace dragged herself up and peered outside. "Look at all those horses. They are so lovely. Will we have one?"

"Of course, we'll get you a horse," Seamus said.

Ashlyn came and sat next to Seamus, her long auburn curls draping his shoulder. "It's cruel to get her hopes up like that."

Seamus combed his fingers through her hair. "She had to leave all of her friends. I think it would be proper for a Southern lady to have a horse."

"Yes, Ma. A horse for all of my friends. Sounds like a decent trade." Grace flashed a grin. "Besides, Da can always steal it."

Ashlyn slapped Seamus on the arm. "See what happens when you tell your daughter such fanciful stories?" She rested her head against him. "Really, we have so little to live on. We'll need seed. We must be prudent."

"It will be all right," Seamus said. "We'll just ask Grace's Uncle Davin for another nugget or two."

"Wasn't it my grandfather's gold mine anyway?" Grace left the window and plopped into the seat facing them.

Seamus eyed the girl who he had raised as his own since she was two years old. With her long curls and smooth skin she looked so much like her mother, only younger, with emerald eyes and light brown hair. Did Grace ever ponder about how little she looked like him? She was so clever. Did she know?

Ashlyn crossed her arms. "Your grandfather deeded the mine to your cousin Cade. He was quite generous in what he intended for us to have."

"Yes. I know. I heard the story. Our share of gold sunk to the bottom of the ocean."

Seamus laughed, which drew a glare from his wife. Although Grace's moodiness irritated Ashlyn, he always found it entertaining. "I am terribly sorry, Grace. God never trusted the likes of me with money."

"But why do we have to be poor? Poor farmers?"

"Believe me, young lady, you don't know a thing about being poor and can be thankful to God that you never will." Seamus raised an eyebrow as if to signal she was pushing the line for even him.

"I know, I know." Grace glared out the window. "Your whole family had one potato to eat for a whole day."

Ashlyn's body clenched beside him. "Child, guard the way you talk to your father. He lost his brother and mother and father during those hard times."

Grace met her father's gaze, and her hard demeanor melted as it always did at some point. She lifted her worn shoes and looked down. "I'm sorry, Da." She raised her eyes to both her parents. "I can be awful at times, can't I?"

Seamus smiled and wondered if he could ever love her more. How would he be able to protect her as she was becoming such a beautiful young lady?

Grace narrowed her eyes and glanced to the side. "Do you think they'll like me here?"

"Who? The other children?" Seamus loved being her father, especially when she was vulnerable. "And how did you get your name?"

She shook her head. "Because . . . I am grace from God."

"And who doesn't want—?" Ashlyn began.

"Yes," Grace smiled begrudgingly, "who doesn't want grace from God?"

"So?" Seamus raised his brow. "What color horse will you get?"

Grace looked up and pursed her lips. "Oh, let's see. Perhaps black. No. Brown. Definitely brown."

"Ahhh." Seamus shook his head. "Such a pity. A true Irishwoman would only fancy a gray mare."

The coachman shouted and veered the vehicle to the right, then the road got decidedly rougher and they bounced about.

"Now I am feeling as if we're in Ireland," Seamus said.

Ashlyn gave a squeal and clapped. "We're here!"

They all crowded around her to peer out, and the carriage drew down a long pathway leading up to a large white home with black shutters and a red-brick base. Although the fields were barren from the season, they seemed surprisingly well kept.

"It's lovely." Ashlyn put her hand over her mouth. "And my old swing is still hanging from that oak tree."

"It's lonely looking."

Seamus couldn't argue with Grace's description. He was wrestling with the strange irony of him, of all people, returning to life on a farm. When he left the Hanley family potato fields more than fourteen years earlier, it was in full expectation he would never lift a hoe or bury a grain of seed again.

It wasn't that he was against difficult labor—Seamus had become a hard worker. The challenge was the fields returned him back to all of those difficult memories and emotions of growing up with his father, Liam. His old man was more a prisoner to his responsibilities on the generations-old Hanley farm, and he took his misery and frustration out on his children. And chief among them Seamus, his oldest son.

As a boy, Seamus's response was to flee whenever possible, and any free moment from his duties on his father's farm, he would spend as far away as possible.

So he felt in no position to argue Grace's response to this decision to return to Ashlyn's home. In some ways, he felt it was some type of divine justice for the poor decisions he made back in California, which had taken his family on such a difficult path.

The carriage halted, and with a few groans the driver labored down from his bench. Before he had made it to the door handle, Ashlyn already turned it and pushed it outward.

"Here we are, folks," the gray-haired man said with more formality than cheer. "Whittington Farms."

"Are you familiar with this area?" Ashlyn received the man's wrinkled hand and stepped down. She straightened her dress, a simple green cotton she chose for the comfort of the ride.

"A neighborhood or two away." He pointed in a direction southward. "Close enough certainly to know of Ryland Whittington."

"I didn't realize you knew of my father." Ashlyn's voice was already changing, as if the air itself was bringing back her sweet drawl that had faded in California.

The man climbed up the side ladder of the carriage and unstrapped the belts tying down their few items of luggage. "He was a hardworking man, Ryland was. Did well enough on this farm, he did. Although your daddy never kept it any secret he would rather be hunting for gold."

"That was Daddy." Ashlyn stood up on her toes and drank in the view of the fields and the mountains as if it were a cool glass of water. She put her hands on Seamus's cheeks and kissed him.

"What happened to him, if I may ask?" The driver threw two of the straps down below, and then tugged on the larger case.

"Let me help with that." Seamus reached up and braced himself to receive them as they were handed down. They didn't have much, but the cases were heavy.

"My mama passed." Ashlyn began in a way that Seamus could tell she was measuring her words. As far as Grace knew, Seamus was her father, and this would be no time to explain to a stranger that Ashlyn left her hometown pregnant. "When she did, my father had nothing restraining him from the golden hills of San Francisco."

The driver stepped down and placed his hands in the small of his back and moaned. He looked to both Ashlyn and Seamus expectantly. "Not to be too particular, as this is a small town and we've got too much time not to meddle in others' affairs. So . . . what about the rumors? Were they true?"

"Pardon me?" Seamus couldn't believe the man had posed such a question. Ashlyn had believed the scandal of Grace's illegitimacy had been kept a secret.

The man stepped back, seemingly surprised by Seamus's sudden shift in demeanor. "The gold? Did he find his gold?"

"Oh." Ashlyn let out a deep sigh. "Yes. He did quite well."

Seamus pulled his billfold out from his jacket. "Which unfortunately for both us and you, never made it in our hands." He thumbed through the dollars and counted out the amount owed. How much would that leave them? It seemed like a fair amount of money, but this would have to last them through the rest of winter and be enough to start a harvest.

The driver flashed an expression of professional disappointment and then took the bills and put them in his breast pocket.

He tipped his hat and, with a few more complaints about some unknown pains in his body, was soon pulling away and his carriage became a shadow in the fading sunlight.

"Where's the barn?" Grace's eyes scanned the grounds.

Ashlyn gave him a "look what you've started" glance, and Seamus smiled and put his arm around his daughter's shoulder. "I told you we'd get you a horse. I didn't say anything about giving your horse a house."

Seamus suddenly laughed.

Ashlyn leaned into him. "What are you laughing about?"

"Tell us." Grace put her head on his other shoulder.

Should he share the memory that flashed before him? "Well . . . you know when I was living in the mountains of Colorado? And I first came across the stagecoach that was carrying mail and had crashed and—"

"Yes, Da." Grace rolled her eyes. "And you found Ma's photograph, the one you always carry in your pocket."

He gave her a playful squeeze. "And the horse—"

"The one you stole."

"Maybe you should tell the story, dear."

"Go ahead. We're listening."

"Well . . . that night." Seamus bit his lip. He was surprised this was making him emotional. "Your father was so lonely without the two of you in my life. I was going to have the horse stay in my cabin with me."

Grace leaned back. "That's weird. Some stories you just shouldn't just tell."

"The point is, young lady, that I love you two very much." The words coming to him were surprising because they were ones he hadn't used in a while. "And I believe we're exactly where God wants us to be. A new start. With my favorite people in the world. And me . . . Seamus Hanley. A farmer!"

"I love you." Ashlyn kissed him on the cheek. "Even when you're lying to me."

This moment was one of the first times they had been alone together for quite some time. Holding each other close was not only intimate, but it fought off the rising chill of the cool air.

Suddenly he noticed something strange, and his pulse spiked. "Ashlyn?"

"Yes, love?"

"I thought you said this farm was abandoned."

"Yes. It is."

Both Ashlyn and Grace followed his gaze and now all three were staring at what alarmed him. The breeze abruptly shifted toward them, the smell clearly evident.

Smoke rose from the chimney.

Chapter 5

THE OWNERS

 Seamus's protective instincts came to life and he stepped in front of his wife and daughter.

"Seamus?" Ashlyn's voice shook.

"You did say there was no one living here?"

"There hasn't been . . . for . . . my uncle died a year ago." Her auburn brows narrowed.

"Either the house is on fire . . . or someone is inside." This whole trip could not be yet another one in his long line of mistakes. "And this is the right house?"

Ashlyn dipped her head and crossed her arms.

He held his palms up and shrugged. "It's just a wee bit strange." Seamus could see the concern rising in Grace's expression, who had moved close to her mother. "It will be nothing. You'll see. There is certainly a simple explanation." *There must be an explanation! Please, Lord, don't have this go wrong.* He moved toward the entranceway.

"Seamus, please be careful."

27

He stepped up to the front window and peered inside. There was furniture in place, but no sign of anyone moving about. And there was a definite flicker of light coming from an adjacent room. He looked back to Ashlyn and shrugged. Seamus came to the large black door and rapped the bronze clapper. Rather than being rusted or worn, it was shined to a bright polish.

Nothing. He knocked again. Seamus tested the handle and it freely opened, the door ajar.

"Should you really enter?" Ashlyn crept forward with Grace at her hip. "Maybe we should just go."

"Where? We'll freeze out here." He didn't wait for a response. Seamus stepped inside. Almost immediately, he thought he saw a shadow flash by at the other end of the hallway.

"Hello? Who goes there? I've seen you. Will you please speak up?"

The home wasn't imposing from the outside, but it appeared rather spacious for a country home now that he was standing on the creaking oak floorboard. A winding staircase led up to a second floor, which was too dark to see clearly. The hallway led in both directions, but it was from the left where the light was flickering against the walls.

In front of him was an empty coatrack, with a wooden cane leaning beside it. Seamus lifted the cane and tested it in his hand for balance. It was too light to serve much as a weapon, but it gave him some comfort to grip it.

Although he had been a minister for several years now, it was his experience from serving in the Mexican War that now pulsed through his veins. And with memories recalled of real terror he had endured, he was able to calm his nerves and move forward.

"Please come out. Whoever you are. There must be a misunderstanding of some sort. My wife is a Whittington, and we have come to reclaim our home."

With cautious steps, he approached the flashing of light in the adjoining room, and as he passed the entranceway, he saw it was well appointed with an elegantly styled couch and cushioned chairs. On the walls were carefully hung paintings, and one of the portraits was of Ashlyn's father, Ryland, and what must have been her mother, Hazel. Her parents appeared young and vibrant, and he was struck in particular by the posture and poise of Mrs. Whittington, who stared at him with Ashlyn's brown eyes.

Would she have approved of Seamus? What an odd thought to have in such a moment.

There in the center of the room was the stone hearth where some freshly placed logs crackled with greenness and appealing warmth.

Seamus heard a sound.

A woman whispering.

Stepping out from the darkness of the room was a black face, barely discernible in the diminished light. It was hardened, scarred, with a gray-stubbled face and tight curls. The eyes glaring through the shadows were proud but worn as well.

"I'm sorry, sir." The voice was graveled, but there was a softness to it that seemed ill-suited to such a mask. "We ain't been expecting no one. Nobody done tell us there were more Whittingtons."

"Come." Seamus beckoned with his curled fingers. "Step into the light so I can see you plainly."

The man did as he was told, wearing jeans, a white cotton shirt, and suspenders. He lowered his head as if he had learned not to look anybody straight in the eyes. At this point, Seamus realized there was another set of brown eyes behind him, these also subdued with weariness. It was a woman whose weathered skin and silvered hair appeared to make her equal in age to the man. And there was a familiarity to her appearance as well.

"It's all right, Seamus." He was surprised to see Ashlyn had come in the house behind him and his anger rose, until she laid her hand on his shoulder. "I know them." Her tone shifted from caution to surprise. "Mavis?"

"Miss . . . Ashlyn?" The woman stepped forward and a curious smile lit up her expression, but then she halted and looked up to Seamus with fear.

He followed her gaze and realized he was holding the cane up, still poised to strike. "I'm sorry." Seamus lowered the cane and laid it against the mantelpiece. "It's all right. Come on out."

Mavis relaxed her shoulders, and her smile returned. She reached a slender ebony hand up to Ashlyn's cheek. "Why . . . you was just a girl."

Ashlyn leaned forward and gave the woman a firm embrace. Then she spun, wiping a tear from her eye. "Seamus. Gracie. This is Mavis. She is Annie's sister."

Of course! She looked just like Annie, the faithful woman who had accompanied Ashlyn and her father on their journey to San Francisco. Annie had become Ashlyn's best friend. She was one of the only ones trusted to keep Ashlyn's secret.

"I didn't know Annie had a sister." Seamus held out his hand to the woman, but she was still looking to Ashlyn for an answer to a question.

"Is she?" Hope lit in Mavis's eyes.

Ashlyn shook her head, her eyebrows raising with compassion. "Annie passed away two years ago."

Mavis looked away. "Oh. I feared I never seen her again when I first say my good-byes."

"She was like an aunt to me." Ashlyn put her hand on the shoulder of the woman's brown dress.

"She sure doted on you a might bit. Annie loved the baby Ashlyn. And your sweet mama too. Just as I did." She looked past Ashlyn. "And who might this be?"

Grace had made her way to join them. Seamus nodded to her that it was okay.

Mavis stared at Ashlyn. She was about to speak but seemed to catch herself.

Ashlyn just nodded and gave Seamus an uncomfortable look.

Of course, Annie would have told her sister Mavis about the reason for Ashlyn having to leave for San Francisco. How many others would know of his wife's shame? Would he be able to shield his daughter from these impending whispers?

The worst was yet to come. There would be no avoiding their past. In response to this revelation, he put his arm around Grace and pulled her toward him. Oh! What he wouldn't do to allow his precious girl to avoid all of the struggles he had to face in his life.

"You are Annie's sister?" Grace looked up with awe as if she was getting another chance to gaze upon the woman who raised her as a second mother.

Ashlyn still appeared uneasy about the subject. "Gracie was very close to Annie. She took her passing quite hard."

"I's surprised about it, that's all." Mavis's lips trembled, and she slipped her teeth over them. "I wouldn't never thought she'd go before me. Annie was the strong one. Since we's both girls. How?"

"Her heart." Ashlyn glanced toward the fire. "She liked to play the role of this tough lady, but as you know, her heart was her softest part."

"That's a true thing there. Hmmm."

Seamus held out his hand to the man whose shoulders and glare remained stiff. "I'm Seamus. Seamus Hanley."

He seemed uncomfortable shaking Seamus's hand but did so limply. "Name's Tatum. We's don't mean no harm any in being here. We ain't looking for no trouble. We can just be on our way. Besides. We've been giving Master Fletch his due. Just as he say."

"His due? Master Fletch? I . . . don't . . . understand." Seamus turned to his wife.

"Are you talking about Virgil Fletcher?" Ashlyn spoke with surprising contempt.

"That be the one," Tatum said. He then looked beyond Seamus and his eyes widened. "That, in fact, be Master Fletch coming now."

Chapter 6

FLETCH

Seamus followed Tatum's finger toward a window with view of the front pathway leading to the house. Although there was little lighting inside, there was enough remaining of the dusk to clearly show a wagon pulled by a large horse, which appeared to be laboring under its load.

In the driver's seat sat a burly man hunched over the reins wearing a plug hat. Next to him was a woman in a large hoop dress who, in contrast to the man, was sitting erect. The rear of the wagon was covered with canvas, and barely noticeable, a young man sat on the edge of the rear gate.

"Whoah." The voice came from outside and was deep and bellowing. The man cranked the brake and lurched his way down, then waddled around to other side where the woman awaited his hand.

Seamus stabbed a glance at his wife.

Ashlyn waved her hand dismissively. "They are harmless enough. Unless one can be mortally wounded by idle prattle." She headed to the front door before he could protest and Seamus had to skip to keep pace.

She pushed through the door and spat out in her newly recalled Southern tone, "Could this be the one and only Mr. and Mrs. Virgil Fletcher?"

They halted as they were approaching on the walkway. "Well, hello there, little lady," the man said in a voice that sounded like laughter. Even in the diminished light, his striking features stood out. He had a large head, almost crookedly placed on his neck, with a bulbous nose and one eye that seemed clouded. "We was a figuring it was you."

"Well . . . I'll be." The woman waved a handkerchief in her hand like a flag. She appeared much younger than the man, and it was now clear it wasn't just the dress that was wide, as her cheeks were broad as if filled with acorns. "Why if it isn't our little Shenandoah Rose, Miss Ashlyn Whittington. That might just be the most beautiful sight these tired eyes have seen."

"Hello, ma'am."

"Don't you ma'am me, little Rose, as you are a grown woman now. I am Coralee henceforth." She held out her gloved hands and pulled Ashlyn's toward hers and then eyed her up and down. "And you have grown well I see. How long has it been?"

Before the question could be answered, Coralee extended a freed hand toward Seamus. "And who might this be?" She winked at Ashlyn and pursed her lips.

"This wonderful man is my husband, Seamus." Ashlyn waved for her daughter to approach. "And this shy lady is Grace."

"I am not shy." Grace wrinkled her brow and shot an embarrassed look toward the young man standing in the background with his hands in his back pockets.

Coralee had not taken her eyes off of Seamus. "Well, I'll say you have done well with this one, Ashlyn child. And I always thought you would be married to Percy all these years, but I can see now why you spurned that unpleasant boy and better spent your affections on this gentleman."

The name Percy made Seamus cringe and his wife stiffened as well.

Ashlyn cleared her throat and straightened. "My husband is handsome indeed."

These words brought Seamus to his youth, back when he captured the gaze of most women, with his tall, fit frame, his black wavy hair, and his Hanley blue eyes. Having spent so many years wearing a collar it seemed odd to be spoken of in this way.

Ashlyn continued. With her melodic, swaying voice, it was as if she had become a different woman. Yet it appealed to him because she sounded happy, something he had missed. "My dear husband is a preacher, a man of God."

"Ohhh." Coralee gave a slow nod of approval.

Seamus shifted his foot. Why did Ashlyn say that? Weren't they here to start anew?

"And a man of God to boot." Coralee paused. "I think this makes a man even more striking. Don't you, Anders?"

The boy pulled out his hands from his pockets and tucked them under his red suspenders. "Yes, Ma." He appeared to be in his late teens and had a nest of dark hair, which seemed more untended than curly. Although almost as tall as his father, he was fortunate enough to share few other features.

Ashlyn put her arm around her daughter, who received it stiffly. "Gracie, this is Taylorsville's pride and joy, Mrs. Coralee Fletcher. If there is anything, and I do mean anything, you need to know about anyone, our Mrs. Fletcher will have your answer."

Seamus outstretched his hand toward Mr. Fletcher, who seemed to have lost his patience in his wife's chatter.

"Virgil Fletcher. Although everybody just calls me Fletch. Now dear. We best be leaving these folks be for now. We was just happening to pass on by, and hearin' the young miss was on her way home, wanted a welcome. Not a wearing out. And it's turning dark on us besides. Anders!"

"Yes, Pa?"

"Get these folks a few items to hold them over for now." He gave a gravelly chuckle. "We'll open an account for them soon."

"Now we thank you kindly, Mr. Fletcher." Ashlyn glanced toward the wagon, where Anders was barely visible in the fading illumination but could be seen carefully unfolding part of the canvas and tucking some items under his shoulder. "But we won't be interested in any of your famous shine."

"No liquor, boy!"

"Yes, Pa."

"Fletch has expanded his enterprise quite a bit since you left here," Coralee said. "Now with these hints of war, his abilities at importing are going to be mighty valuable to the cause."

"Troubling times," Fletch said, in a way that didn't sound concerned. "We should be getting gone."

They all started walking toward the wagon. Coralee put her arm under Ashlyn's. "And with Taylorsville in such a huff about all the goings-on in our state, there will necessarily be some talk of your arrival here."

"What do you mean?" Ashlyn helped the woman climb up to her seat.

"It's the timing, that's all." She glanced to Fletch who had made his way up to his side of bench and lifted the reins. "Everyone's on edge. It's natural to be concerned about people who suddenly arrive from the North. Oh dear, I wouldn't take any of it personally."

Seamus wondered what kind of trouble this could mean for them. Anders reached out to him with a small crate of Mason jars, which appeared to be preserves of several different fruits and vegetables, and a couple loaves of bread. "Thank you, son."

The boy nodded, gave Grace a nervous glance, and then went about lighting two lanterns hung from the front of the wagon.

"I appreciate the kindly greeting." Seamus walked around to extend his free hand to Fletch. "We hadn't even put thought to food yet."

Fletch leaned over with his good eye and saw what his son had gathered. "Just a few items to hold you by." He gave Seamus a wink and spoke with a hush. "Most of my customers ain't supposed to be partakin'. Let me know when you're ready for the good fixings and it'll be between us."

He started to sit up but then nodded toward the house. "And . . . a . . . we can talk about business next time I'm by."

"Business?" Seamus shifted the crate under his arm. He could hear Ashlyn tied up in a conversation with Coralee.

"The Negroes." Fletch rubbed his hand on the back of his neck. "I got the papers on them two from Ashlyn's uncle. He had some debts and wanted to clear things up some before he moved on. Didn't want to burden his niece none."

"I see." Seamus felt awkward holding the food now, as if he had compromised himself. He wanted to give it back to this strange man.

"Don't bother yourself none. We'll come to arrangements." Fletch gave Coralee a nudge and she bade farewell to Ashlyn and Grace who came over to join Seamus.

They watched as the horse spun the wagon and then drew the Fletcher family away from the farm in near darkness except for the lanterns, with Anders staring at them with his legs dangling off of the back.

"What were you speaking about?" Ashlyn squeezed Seamus's arm.

He didn't want to burden her with his odd exchange with Fletch. All he wanted was to see the glow in his wife's eyes, the one she had when they first arrived at Whittington Farms. "We'll speak on it later." Seamus cradled the crate with both hands. "What do you think we have here?"

Ashlyn laughed. "Well, if it wasn't Fletch's Shenandoah Shine, then it must be the possum jerky or some hogs' feet. Who knows what he's running these days?"

They turned and walked toward the house, which was framed in the background with sunset hues glowing behind the mountains. This was indeed bucolic country.

Tatum had come out to the door to greet them with an oil lamp in his hand. "Come on in and warms yourselves up a mite. Mavis has done gone ahead and fixed a fine meal for you." They followed him inside.

But at the doorway Seamus touched Ashlyn on the shoulder and they allowed Grace to go ahead. Something bothered him about Fletch's appearance. "What was with his . . . ?" Seamus point to his neck.

"That," Ashlyn leaned in to whisper, "was when they tried to hang him."

Chapter 7

LINCOLN'S ARMY

MANHATTAN, NEW YORK
April 1861

 "Have you ever seen such a gathering of muttonheads?" Tristan Lowery, with his perfectly coifed blond hair, sat in the open window frame of the five-story stone building his family owned. The flustered shouts of the mob outside echoed up through the room.

Davin got up from the burgundy studded leather chair and joined his friend, the son of one of the most successful traders in Manhattan, in observing the scene below. Quite a distance down, hundreds marched through the paving-stone streets waving American flags and pumping fists and singing songs of patriotism, both of here and Ireland.

"Like sheep to the slaughter." Tristan, who at twenty-six was just a few years older than Davin, had the soft complexion and hands of the favored class, with rosy cheeks and the droopy eyelids of boredom. "What do you think about all of your people now, dear fellow?" He made a poor attempt of bleating like a lamb. "Baaah . . . baaah."

Tristan's most relied-upon form of entertainment was to skirt on the edges of Davin's anger. Tweaking and probing and retreating just prior to the kettle boiling. Davin often wondered why he befriended him, and hoped it wasn't merely for the pleasure of being able to loiter among the city's elite.

For within the confines of this narrow, privileged fellowship, Davin was able to dip into the pools of prestige, excess, and cultural play. He wasn't foolish. There was a part of him who knew his membership was limited and that he would be tossed at some point when his friend grew weary of his companionship. But at least for the time being, it was another adventure for him to grasp before the expiration of his ephemeral youth.

There was an element to pulling riches from the earth through your own risks, efforts, and strains that gave men a certain intoxicating sense of accomplishment and entitlement.

Yet there was also something Davin had learned he could not extract from the ground. Could not draw up with his own hands. For all of his fortuitous discoveries, there was a deeper yearning in his soul for something more than the high society, fine clothes, and attention from women his wealth had attained.

Even from his early days of finding gold, he recognized he was losing part of himself. The boy with the passion to seize life with both hands. The heart he once had for others. It seemed as if the more he obtained, the more numb he became.

Was this all life had to offer? Just another mountain to climb? Another hole to dig? It seemed he had so much more wisdom when he was ten years old, but that was somehow buried in the dust of the Sierra mountains.

And what of Seamus? All of these years Davin had looked up to his older brother, but what value would there be in following his lead now? Seamus had pursued God, and look where that had taken him?

Davin had a sense he wouldn't find too many answers in his peculiar friendship with Tristan. But at least he could be entertained, distracted from the emptiness.

"My Irish . . . lambs . . . have a long tradition of fighting for freedom and country." Even as he said these words Davin had a thickness in his throat. How distant he was from the people below. How could he have spent so many years thinking and living that way?

"Really, young prince?" Tristan leaned his head back and lazily peered down. "The Hiberians have a long tradition of being defeated. We can only hope, for the good of my own dear, sweet hide, that they have learned how to fight since arriving."

Tristan lifted his glass of bourbon to his lips and sipped noisily. Then he swung both of his legs outside of the window and let them dangle.

Davin flinched. "What are you doing?" There was a playful madness in his friend which both irritated and intrigued him.

"Go get them Southerners, boys! Hear, hear, all you brave young lads."

He saw the glass loosely gripped in Tristan's hands and Davin worried he might throw it down.

"Get Fort Sumter back for us, good chaps! Your nation and Abraham need you!"

Davin was relieved to see the clatter below was drowning out Tristan's mockery. He probably appeared as just another of the dozens of women and children leaning out of their sills and waving arms. Davin went back to the chair and sank down.

"Come back in and stop being such a fool. You'll regret this one day when one of those boys takes a bullet for you." Davin glanced around the sitting room, which smelled of cigars and fine liquor. The walls were of dark mahogany, and carefully placed gas lamps brought diffused light to paintings of hunting landscapes interspersed between heads of mounted animals and stuffed birds.

Tristan climbed back in, hopped down, and dusted his vest as if from the world outside. He went over to a table containing crystal decanters of a variety of cordials. "You'll never understand this, Davin."

"Understand what?"

"It's the difference between . . . being golden and finding gold." He poured his glass full and set the decanter down.

"Is anyone fond of you?" Davin had been blunted to most of what came from Tristan's mouth.

"Seriously, dear laddie. It's just the way it's always been." He opened up a wooden box and pulled out a cigar and drew it under his nose. He offered it up, but Davin shook his head.

Tristan cut the end off and then struck a match, giving the cigar a deep draw and exhaling the smoke slowly. He blew out the match and then sat on the couch adjacent to Davin.

"So what does your father say about all of this?" Davin rarely got to see Alton Lowery, but when he did, he was always impressed with the man's brilliance.

"It's not good news for us, I am afraid." The ashes on the tip of his cigar glowed red.

"So this will be a serious war, then? Does he believe that?"

Tristan raised his eyebrow. "The problem, dear friend, is not the war, but the length of it."

"But everyone is saying it will be over soon. The South don't stand a chance."

Tristan pulled out his cigar and pointed it at Davin. "And that is precisely the problem."

"I . . . don't . . ."

"You are new at this, aren't you? I have to keep reminding myself that not too long ago you were pulling potatoes out of the soil. There are few better opportunities to profit than during these times . . . of great strife."

He folded his leg over the other and glanced at the ceiling. "And with such limited time of opportunity . . . well, we'll just have to be . . . opportunistic." Tristan lifted his glass from the table beside him. "What about your dear sis?"

The abruptness of the shift of the conversation caught Davin off guard. "What?"

"Your sister. The fighting sword of the Irish, the defender of the new Black empire, Clare Royce, grafted by marriage into the once-mighty Royce empire."

Davin tensed. "You know. There is going to be a time . . . soon, I think, when this potato grubber is going to clear out a few of your teeth." He didn't mind the barbing when it came to him, but his family was another matter.

"No, truly. I admire your sister. Wonderfully talented reporter. It's just . . ."

"It's just what?"

"Her poor sap husband has really devastated the *Daily*. Fine fellow, dreadful businessman. I . . . we . . . just can't see how it will be able to sustain itself much longer."

Davin clearly noticed that the fortunes of his sister and her husband had taken a turn, but he had no idea they were in such a position. But then again, it was just Tristan. Who could believe what came from his mouth?

"It's a shame, really," Tristan said. "Andrew Royce opens that mission for the supposed downtrodden and squanders all of his father's wealth into it. Only to see it fail."

Davin never before had an unkind thought when it came to Andrew. But now that he was older, he had learned there were many sides to people and that life was complicated. How could Andrew have allowed his fortune to dwindle and leave Clare in this position?

Tristan tapped his cigar and let the ash fall to the carpet. "Of course, they do have you now. Fresh from the Sierra Nevada mountains with gold bulging from your pockets." He raised an eyebrow at Davin. "Problem solved."

Tristan could say many things that would cause Davin to want to strangle him. The difficulty was, there always seemed to be some underlying truth in what he shared. Tristan seemed to have some inner understanding of the dark reaches of man's soul, which seemed to be the source of how he was able to rise above others.

"They haven't asked me for a penny." Davin spoke through clenched teeth.

"You know, dear fellow" Tristan said. "There are many people, friends of my father, who would be willing to swing their . . . patronage . . . back to the *Daily*." He snapped his fingers. "They've drifted into the weeds. But they can certainly find themselves again. We all believe in second chances."

Sounds rose from the window, the crowds stirring again. They blurred in the background as Davin was distracted by his inner thoughts. Was Clare in danger? What a travesty for her to come to America to seek her fortunes, only to have them slip through her hands.

He had believed she was different than Seamus, who he had given up on long ago on that river in the mountains. It was a cruel prank Davin had played that day on his older brother, but it was all with good intentions. To try to cleanse him of his frivolous pursuits. Seamus was wasting his life in trying to save men's souls.

But Clare? She had come to Davin's rescue so many times before.

Maybe this was his chance. His moment to help in the way he best knew how.

Chapter 8

THE DOCTOR

How strange to see men so anxious to participate in war!

It wasn't easy for Davin to tunnel his way through the frantic crowds on the streets leading to Clare's quiet neighborhood, but he was determined to not only speak to his sister, but to escape the clattering.

As he observed the faces of those parading in angry protests against South Carolina's attack on Fort Sumter, he wondered why he didn't share their angst. Was he not proud of his new nation? Did he not have an obligation to stand up for the country that allowed him such a great changing of his fortunes? Perhaps it was because he came from California, where the politics of division and slavery seemed so distant and less important.

And what did he believe in all of this? Was he losing his Irishness? His willingness to fight for a cause? Could it be that he didn't have a cause?

Then again, maybe Tristan had a point. Let the rest of the world be distracted by the madness while the wise among them used the diversion to seek profit.

45

When he arrived at the front of the Royce home, a man was already walking to the front door. He scooted to catch up to him. "May I be of some service, sir?"

Startled, the young man turned. He was wearing a uniform and reached into a pack slung over his shoulder and pulled out an envelope. "A telegram, sir. Do you live here?"

Davin paused for a moment. This was his home, wasn't it? Even after all of the years, he still felt part of the Royce family. "Yes, of course."

The man handed him the envelope and then had him sign a piece of paper. He tipped his hat. "Good day, sir."

Davin watched him go away and then instinctively turned and opened the door and entered. Once inside, he regretted his unintentional impertinence, but it would be foolish to go back outside now.

"Hello there? Clare?" Davin took off his hat and tucked it under his arm. He looked around the hallway and, following his discussion with Tristan, saw things through a more-jaundiced eye. The once-proud Royce Manor was now sagging and seemingly defeated. Gold-leafed paper was curling from the walls, paint was chipped, the wood on the stairway bannister was cracked, and even the ceilings seemed to droop.

A young boy arrived in the hallway at such a speed that when he tried to stop, his feet skidded across the smooth floor. His eyes widened in fear at first, but then he relaxed.

The boy turned and shouted, "Muriel! A man's here."

Davin realized with some embarrassment that he hadn't visited more than once or twice since the Christmas dinner.

Behind him turning the corner came Muriel, dressed simply in the clothes of a housemaid. He hadn't paid much heed to her appearance when he last saw her, but now that she was standing before him, he did. She was not unattractive by any means, pleasant enough with red curls, fair skin, and a gentleness to her demeanor. But Davin's high-society standards had blunted him from appreciating any but the most physically striking of women. Mostly she was one he would normally pass by on the street without giving a second glance.

Muriel dried her hands on her apron. "Why, Garret, that is not just a man, that is your uncle." Her words had a melody to them from Ireland, but also an unfamiliarity to them that made it difficult for Davin to determine from which county she had arrived. She turned to him. "Davin, is that right?"

"Uncle Davin it is." He knelt beside Garret. "Did you know I was your age when I last lived here?" He tapped the top of the boy's head. "Where's your mother?"

"Clare is at the newspaper." There was a strength to Muriel's voice that seemed mismatched with her appearance.

"Yes, of course." Why hadn't he thought of that? With all of the news to cover regarding the president's call to arms, there would be much for Clare to do.

Davin was disappointed, nonetheless. He was anxious to confront Clare regarding the unpleasantness of her finances. "So . . . you are the maid?"

Muriel laughed. "Do I look the part of a maid?" She looked down at her clothes and smiled. "I suppose I do. No, I help the Royces out whenever I can. When I don't have classes."

"She's a doctor," Garret said.

"Your uncle doesn't believe women can be doctors." She raised her chin with a strange confidence, one he was unused to seeing in a woman. He knew many beautiful ladies who were aware of their allure and employed them well, but Muriel's verve seemed to be grounded in the strength of her intelligence. And so oddly placed in the hands of an Irish housemaid.

She turned to Garret. "How about you get yourself to the kitchen and gather for your uncle some of those scones we baked?" The boy nodded and left the room.

Muriel wiped her hands on her apron. "So, is there a message I should share with Clare?"

Davin tugged on his earlobe. What message could he leave? "Oh . . . yes." He reached into his coat pocket and pulled out the telegram. "This came in."

"Yes, I was expecting that." She snatched it from his hands and tucked it in her dress pocket.

He was startled by her aplomb. "Uh . . . how do you know it's for you?"

"They come from my aunt." Muriel narrowed her red brows. Her blue eyes were tinged with both yearning and melancholy. "She lives in Canada. Worries about me and sends them all of the time."

"What about the rest of your family?" Davin found this girl intriguing.

"Just me." She twisted her lip and rested her hand on the banister. "They are all back home. Outside of Dublin a ways."

"Why move here? Why New York?"

Muriel gave him the look again, as if she found his questions somehow insulting. "You already know. It has one of the only medical schools that admits women."

"So all of that about you studying to be a doctor. That's true?"

She tightened the bow on her apron. "I've wanted to be a healer. All of my life."

"And you would see yourself as being capable of . . . something like . . . sawing off a man's leg?"

"I suppose that would depend on whether the rest of him was worth saving."

He gave her a congratulatory nod. She was unnerving him. Had he met a woman like this before who seemed . . . more intelligent than him? What man would ever want to commit to a life with someone like Muriel? Where he would always be made to feel inferior?

His nephew showed up with a plate full of scones.

"Thank you, Garret." Muriel took them from him. "Your

uncle was just getting ready to leave. I will get a small tin so you can bring them with you."

Before Davin could protest, she was gone.

"How much do you have?"

"Hmm?" Davin looked to Clare's son and could see some of himself in the boy.

"How much gold?"

"You know what?" Davin reached into his breast pocket. He curled a finger in there, pulled out a small rock, and laid it out on his palm.

Garret's blue eyes widened. "Can I touch it?"

"Better than that. You can have it. It's one of my lucky ones. It's brought me good fortune wherever I go."

"Really? Can I?"

"A gold nugget?" Muriel held out a small circular red tin to him.

He took it from her, opened the lid, and gave it a sniff. It still smelled as if had just come out of the oven. "Seems like a fair enough trade."

Davin put his hat on and turned to go but then paused. "Good luck with your schooling. I think it's a fine thing for the world to have another doctor."

With that he turned and left, having forgotten the intentions of his visit.

Chapter 9

THE *NEW YORK DAILY*

 "Sounds a bit gloomy, doesn't it?" Andrew slumped back in his office chair.

Clare glanced over his shoulder and read the headline in the paper he was holding, still moist with ink: *War Inevitable.* "Yes. But sadly, it's also true." She rubbed the back of his tense neck, and he responded to her touch with a groan of relief.

"We received a wire from Washington," Clare said. "General McDowell has ordered the soldiers to prepare for departure. The camps are breaking, and the batteries are being prepared to roll. May God forgive us. They are just a few days away from blood being spilt."

Andrew leaned back. "You've taken a peculiar interest in this war, have you not?"

"I . . . still can't believe it's risen to such contempt. Even an eagerness for violence. How can a nation be so broken?" Clare noticed the lines formed under his eyes. He had aged so much

51

since taking over management of the newspaper following his father's death.

"The Irish certainly are no strangers to rebellion." Andrew folded the paper and rested it on his large desk, which was covered with ledger books, ink drawings, and scattered notes.

"At least my people aren't threatening to kill one another." She walked over to the wall and straightened a framed photograph. "What have we become? I never believed I would say this, Andrew, but I sometimes wish we were back home in Branlow growing potatoes."

A firm knock sounded on the glass of the door. They turned to see the newsboy cap of Owen Kavanaugh, who though he was in his early thirties, had the kind of face that appeared much younger. And it was the kind of face that could never disguise bad news.

"Come in," Andrew said, rolling his eyes at Clare.

"Sorry to be disturbing you." Owen stepped in and snapped the door shut behind him.

Clare appreciated few people more than Owen. He had started at the *Daily* when he was a newsboy, selling papers before the sun and most of the city rose. Then he worked his way into the press room and was soon recognized as the best mechanic. Finally, he made the big jump to editorial and had been Andrew's chief editor the last couple of years. He wasn't a writer by any means, but he did seem to have a natural sense for business, much more than her husband.

But what Clare appreciated most about Owen was his character. He was as reliable as they came and as good a friend as Andrew had. Whenever there were grumblings among staff about Andrew's leadership, Owen would quickly douse the flames. More than a few blamed Owen's lack of talent for the demise of the *Daily*, but Clare was not among them.

"Haven't I told you never to visit unless you're bearing good tidings?" Andrew rubbed the back of his neck.

"Yes. But then I would never get to see you." Owen leaned back against the door. His tight brown curls spilled from the sides of his cap.

"Then be about it," Andrew said, "so I can get along with the grieving process."

"It's Mr. Murphy."

"Oh dear," Clare said. "Is he pulling his advertising again? Does he believe we'll shut down without him?"

"Well." Owen took off his hat and scratched his head. "There may be some truth in that. He happens to be our largest advertiser."

Andrew tapped his hand on the desk. "Clare, I warned you that story was going to push our readers to their limits."

"But really, Andrew. This notion that we're going to empty the Five Points of every black soul and put them on ships back to Africa. We have to speak out about such . . . drivel, even if it's coming from the mouths of my own dear people."

Owen rocked on the balls of his feet. "I believe the line Mr. Murphy protested to in particular was the one where you said . . . what was it? Oh yes, that—"

"That we should put every fool Irishman who proposed such an idea on a train headed south so they can trade in their potatoes for Jefferson Davis's cotton." Clare's stomach tightened. "I know what it said, Owen. I wrote it."

Andrew chuckled. Was the man capable of getting angry at her?

Owen held his hands up in surrender. "I am merely sharing the news. That's what I do here. I am a professional newsman. Occasionally, I'll throw in a minor suggestion, you know one like, 'Let's try not to anger our last three customers.'"

"We still have three?" Andrew raised a mocking eyebrow. "And you said you came with bad news." He leaned forward. "Wait. You're still standing here. Please tell me you don't have more to share."

"'Fraid so. It's Ben Jones."

Andrew adjusted his glasses on his nose. "What did he do this time?"

"He packed his desk."

"He's leaving us?" Andrew brought his hands to his face. "Now? He's our last remaining war correspondent. Where?"

"Went to the *Times*." Owen placed his hand on the door handle.

The *Times*? Ben Jones was too good a reporter to work at such a place. Clare wanted to say something to Andrew to console him, but she couldn't think of anything. With the armies of the South and North facing off in a couple of days, it would be ruinous for the *Daily* if they had no coverage of the confrontation.

"We could send Zimmerman," Owen said.

Andrew flopped back in his chair. "We're not doing a theater review. And he is at least a hundred years old. I am afraid the poor fellow's heart would give at the first gunshot. Who else?"

Clare went through the few options that remained in their editorial office, and none of them would be capable. They had counted on Ben Jones to take all of the most difficult assignments. He interviewed the hardest of criminals, went to the darkest of neighborhoods, and as a soldier once himself he was perfect to cover the war.

Almost simultaneously Owen and Clare spoke. "I'll go."

They exchanged equally surprised looks at each other.

"You can't write a decent story," Clare said.

"We aren't sending a woman," Owen responded.

"Neither of you are going." Andrew clasped his hands. "But you're both right. We don't have anyone else. It will have to be me."

"Andrew," Clare said. "You can't go. You're the only indispensable one we have in this building. If you don't replace the advertising I just lost, we won't need to worry about covering the battle."

Owen wagged a finger at Clare. "She's right."

"Of course I'm right." Clare was surprised she was getting excited about the idea of being there to give a firsthand account of the battle. "We can't afford to hire Ben Jones's replacement, and even if we could, there isn't enough time. Besides, everyone is saying there will only be one battle in the war. The Union is going to make short order of this, and we can't be the only newspaper that missed the coverage. The *Daily* needs this story and to do it well. My mind is clear on this now. I am the only one who makes sense."

"I am not sending my wife and the mother of my children to the battlefield to dodge musket balls hurled from Johnny Reb. I would much rather shut this all down once and for all and open up . . . a fruit stand."

"How about we both go?" Owen looked to Clare for her support.

"Brilliant." There was certainly a part of her that would be terrified to take on such an assignment. Having Owen along would quell those concerns.

Andrew started to shake his head, but Clare could see his protest starting to wobble.

"Just for this battle," Clare said. "We'll keep a safe distance. I promise, I won't stab one Virginian with a bayonet."

"Dear, please."

Clare sensed he was weakening and pounced. "No. This will be good. We'll keep a close eye on one of the New York regiments, and I'll do a story on the bravery of the Irish soldiers. We'll win that dour Mr. Murphy back, as well as the whole of the Five Points."

Owen nodded toward her. "That's why she's writing it." He reached over and gave Andrew a pat on the shoulder. "I'll take fine care of her, I will. You know I'd lay my life down for the two of you."

"Yes." Andrew looked up to his friend. "I know you would." He pulled out his watch by the chain in his pocket. "Then if you're going to leave—"

"We'll need to leave immediately." Clare came around and gave him a hug. "I'll stop at the house and pack and say good-bye to the children."

"You know it's gruesome to be this excited about going to war." Andrew raised his eyebrow.

"Oh, dear." She kissed him on the cheek. "My excitement is getting to help you. The *Daily*. To lift some of this burden from your shoulders."

"I better get going," Owen said. "Ben Jones was supposed to ride with a group of reporters who were going to catch the same train. I'll let them know two more will be joining them." He turned and left.

"I should go as well." Clare headed toward the door, then paused. "We're going to make it through this."

Then she scurried out the door and headed home, trying to convince herself of those very same words.

Chapter 10

BULL RUN

PRINCE WILLIAM COUNTY, VIRGINIA
July 1861

 In the distance, the rockets flared with brilliant flashes, accompanied by rising plumes of black smoke. Far away as well were the muffled sounds of explosions, musket shots, bugle calls, and the screams and shouts of men.

But as Clare and Owen approached in their bouncing wagon toward the ridge where most of the journalists had gathered to view the battle, what they saw was more remarkable than the fighting itself.

For several miles along the way, they had passed what seemed to be the entirety of the Washington elite, all of whom had come to take in the spectacle of war as if they were attending a foxhunt.

On either sides of the road, they were strewn out on blankets and chairs, pouring from bottles of champagne and wine and snacking on sandwiches, bread, and cheese.

"Had I known how pleasurable these battle assignments were, I would have petitioned Andrew for this job years ago." Owen guided his wagon off of the road and around a black carriage that had gotten stuck in the mud.

"I believe that is Ben Jones over there." Clare pointed to a ledge where a gathering of men and women stood, dressed more for a presidential ball than the first major conflict of the war.

As they got down from the wagon and walked over to where others were standing, Clare could understand why this particular location was chosen by the other reporters. The ledge overlooked the broad territory surrounding the Manassas River.

"Are those soldiers?" Clare's heart started to pound as she realized the movement of the terrain below was actually many thousands of soldiers exchanging blows. They must have been a good mile away from the confrontation, too far to see the actual hideous details of battle, but the evil of war penetrated through her bones. Maybe this was a big mistake for her to be here.

What a strange juxtaposition it was to see the merry gathering nearby her! Picnicking and cavorting while their sons were dying in the distance.

"Over there." Owen pointed to an area at the end of the ridge where several men were drawing on easels. "At least some of them are working."

They moved their way through the crowd, overhearing conversations splattered with gossip and drunken laughter.

As they approached, they saw the *Daily*'s former war correspondent in an earnest conversation with several other distinguished-looking men. Ben Jones was tall and gaunt, with neatly combed and oiled hair, parted at the center. When they were just a few steps away, Ben glanced over and his eyes broadened. He excused himself from the conversation and came over and greeted Owen with a handshake.

"I promise, I was intending on removing that piece of gum from under the desk." He nodded to Clare.

Her first impulse was to be angry at the man. Andrew had been good to him and deserved more of a notice than he received. At the same time though, she couldn't be too harsh on those employees who had left the *Daily*. Their financial difficulties were not well concealed, and if others had an opportunity to have a more reliable income, how could she fault them for leaving?

Ben nodded over toward their wagon, which had two bales of hay in the back and a tired-looking horse up front. "It's good to see that Andrew provided his new correspondents with such fine transportation."

"And it's good as well to see such excellent reporting coming from the *Times*." Clare always appreciated Ben's wit. "We always wondered how they fashioned such quality stories. Now we know."

A gasp came from the crowd, and many of the conversations halted and some moved closer to the ledge to see what was happening below.

Ben nodded in the direction of the illustrators and they started moving over. "Apparently, this quaint little rebellion won't be dusted away in a day."

"Wasn't this supposed to be a short battle?" Owen asked.

"That's why we have all of this." Ben pointed to the carriages. "Everyone thought they were going to enjoy a lovely day in the park and didn't want to miss the entertainment. We've got senators here, judges, wives, mistresses. Apparently a better ticket than the Washington Symphony."

"All of this while men are dying below." Clare wondered what would come over someone to be so calloused.

Ben leaned in. "And I thought I would have to count cannon blasts. This makes for a much more interesting story."

Clare knew the answer, but she needed to ask. "So . . . why did you leave us?"

He shrugged his arms. "The *Times* offered me nearly double. I am afraid they are sensing the once proud Royce institution is just a few gusts of winds away from toppling."

"Well," she said, "their senses are keen, I fear."

"The *Daily* will be back strong." Owen's eyes narrowed. He never did get along too well with Ben.

"Yes, I'm sure it will." Ben turned to face her. "And just on the off chance it doesn't, you let me know if you need a new job. I'm sure the *Times* would love having the great Clare Royce. Besides, it pays better and I know Andrew could use the money."

"You are a heartless man, Ben Jones. I am so thrilled we fired you."

A loud explosion sounded, and some shouts came out of the group.

"That was dreadfully close," a woman nearby said.

"They are still far away," said another.

The three of them came to one of the illustrators, who had just put in a blank canvas and was sketching away.

"What's happening down there?" Ben asked.

"See for yourself," the illustrator said. "It looks like them Southern boys have us on the run."

"They are retreating!" came a shout.

This was closely followed by howls and shrieks, and in short order people hurried themselves back to their carriages. Anxious horses neighed, and a few of them took off without their passengers. The artists who were drawing the battle scenes scurried to gather up their drawings. Two Union soldiers raced toward them on horses.

A man, who Ben Jones had identified as a senator, stepped up to the approaching cavalrymen. "What is the meaning of all this? Why are you turning and running?"

"Move along, sir!" replied the soldier.

"Do you know who I am?" the senator retorted.

"We're being overrun. It's not going to matter who any of us are in about five minutes."

These words seemed ample enough to silence any further protests. As all were retreating in a frenzy, Clare stepped forward to the hilltop and peered down. The Union army was now in full disarray and in mad retreat. Being pulled up the hill were the large cannons of the North, although some were being abandoned.

Left discarded behind them were the lifeless sons of a thousand mothers, being stepped over like they were bags of flour.

Pouring across the river through pontoons were the victorious Southern troops, with raised sabers and banners, in full pursuit while crying out in shrill screams that were a blend of terror and mockery.

A strange thought occurred to Clare. Was Seamus out there somewhere? Was he fighting for the other side, cheering on the defeat of his own family? How could he have abandoned her again?

A shattered nation. A torn family.

"Clare." Owen's voice was frantic. "We must go."

But she couldn't pull herself away from the display of anger and violence unfolding below. It was as if America itself was crumbling before her, sweeping away the dream she had pursued with such vehemence.

"We can't tarry." Owen's hand clasped her arm.

Almost in a moment slowed in time, she saw something approaching in the corner of her eye. She looked up in time to see something flying in their direction. Suddenly, she was yanked to the ground and Owen was on top of her just as the explosion ripped through her trance. And then they were showered with dirt.

He pulled them up and they were running toward the wagon, dodging carriages and even full-sprinting soldiers. They leapt to their seat as another sound echoed and Clare covered her ears.

Deftly Owen turned the wagon, and with a few steps their horse was pulling them out of danger, seeming equally motivated to retreat. They maneuvered around obstacles and slower vehicles. It was a good twenty minutes before they cleared out of the fray enough to feel it was safe to stop again.

Now she was focused on her obligations to Andrew and the *New York Daily*. It was her job to bring her readers to the front lines of the battlefield, and she would do it with excellence.

The pounding of her heart subsided, and Clare pulled out paper and pencil and scribbled down her thoughts as fast as she could, the tip of the graphite scraping noisily. Even though they had spent such a short time on the ridge, there were so many images she wanted to describe and so many emotions to put to words before they were lost.

Owen knew her well enough not to disturb her while she was about her work, but after a few minutes, Clare had filled several pages and he must have sensed it was the right time to speak. "What shall we make of all of this?"

Clare looked up and saw soldiers approaching, but without haste and frenzy. For today at least, the battle was over. However, their shoulders and disposition slumped in defeat, and she shared their despair with both her prose and her tears.

Chapter 11

THE PAINTED FACE

Caitlin seem terrified of what she was about to see. Muriel worried if this idea of hers was a mistake. Despite both of them having sat on this uncomfortable wrought-iron bench for a tortuous length of time, Caitlin couldn't peel her gaze from the front door of the Blue Goose.

What was so obvious to Muriel was so difficult for Caitlin to grasp. This seemed to be the only way to help her friend come to grips. And what irony! For her to be assisting Caitlin when it came to men. What did she know about them?

"Maybe you should go home, Cait dear." Muriel had been at her side this whole time, trying to lighten the mood with gentle conversation. "It isn't necessary for you to be here, you know. I already told you what I saw. There is no need for you to suffer any more."

"No," Caitlin asserted. "I need to see for myself. I have been engaged to this man for more than a year."

Engaged? Hardly. Muriel had known from the beginning that Martin was only engaged with his work and himself. Maybe that was why Muriel seemed to attract only disinterest and disdain from men. She was on to them. She knew what they were thinking before they did.

But then again, that was her being too kind to herself. Yes, she was a smart lass, but men weren't interested in that. They wanted pretty and quiet and she wasn't good at either. Even her uncle, who along with her aunt had raised her since her parents died on the ship to America, had tried to bring her down gently when it came to her aspirations for marriage.

He told her when she was young that some women could be cared for and others would have to learn to care for themselves. For many years she thought he meant it as a compliment, but the truth became clearer once she was of wooing age and realized few were lining up to woo her.

He foresaw her as a spinster even when she was a child.

But it made no sense to her that Caitlin would fall to the same fate. After all, she had the appearance all men craved. If only Caitlin could crave a finer breed of men. What poor taste she had!

Maybe she was being too difficult on Caitlin. It could be there just weren't that many good men out there. It was no secret that most so-called gentlemen in Manhattan partook in what they dismissed as harmless sport. Prostitution was as common a vice as hard liquor and cigars.

"We've been here for more than an hour and haven't seen him." Caitlin's voice was laced with hope. "Are you certain you didn't make a mistake?"

Muriel grimaced with compassion. "Oh, dear Cait. I wish it weren't so."

"How did . . . how did you find him?"

"I told you." Muriel tucked her red curls behind her ear. "I've always been good at having a sense of people. I knew of his nature the first instance I met him."

Caitlin rolled her handkerchief in her palm. "Well. That certainly is a skill I have been without all of these years."

"It could be worse."

"How? How could it be worse? Do you know how many times this has happened to me? Do you know how many poor choices I've made with the men in my life?"

Muriel lowered her head. "It could be worse . . . if you had never been loved by a man."

"Oh, dear." Caitlin put her hand on Muriel's shoulder. "You are the most beautiful woman I've ever known. Your kindness shows through for all to see."

"And we know how much men favor kindness above all things." Her eyes glistening, she looked up and smiled at Caitlin.

"Many men would wrestle a wild boar for a chance with such a brilliant woman."

Muriel laughed at her friend's choice of words. "Perhaps they consider time with me just as wrestling a wild boar."

"Oh, Muriel. You know what I intended." She gave a mischievous smile. "Why it's a fact I know someone dear to me who is smitten with you."

Heat rose to Muriel's cheeks. "Please don't be speaking about Davin."

"Why not? You know I speak truly. Every time he sees you, his eyes betray it. Believe me. I know my brother."

"And who says having your brother interested in me is something I fancy?"

"Because, my dear Muriel, I know you as well."

Muriel grimaced, but more at the irony of what Cait had said. Oh, how little her friend knew about her. She felt a twinge of guilt about this, the one she experienced every time Caitlin, Clare, or Andrew showed her kindness. And worse of all were those dear children Garret and Ella. What would they think one day when they learned of her past, who she really was? Did Muriel even know who she was herself? She had spent so much time pretending, it was difficult to know. "Well, I suppose your brother is all right. Bearable at least."

The two giggled as sisters would.

They had only known each other for seven months or so, but Muriel had shadowed just about everything Caitlin did. Whether it was joining her at Underground meetings or working together at the newspaper, they spent time with one another nearly every day. Even with Muriel focusing on her studies in medicine. Caitlin and the Royce family had proved perfectly suited to her intentions. Better than she could have ever expected.

But something disturbed Muriel. She had never planned on feeling so loved by this family.

"You are exactly what my brother would need to straighten him out." Caitlin seemed to enjoy the role as matchmaker. If only she could use those talents better on herself.

"So, that's it. Now I'm medicine for your little brother."

"Well, you both are of the same age. He's quite handsome and you are as well."

Muriel waved her hand. "Your brother has tastes in qualities I do not and will never possess."

"Pure nonsense, Muriel McMahon. What he needs is a brilliant Irish girl to get . . . to get him back."

"Back?"

"Oh, I do wish you knew my brother when he was a boy. So precious. Such a perfect gentleman." Caitlin's eyes glanced upward. "Did you know we nearly died in each other's arms? Back in Ireland?"

"How sad."

"I don't know. There is something sweet about it as well. We became close, closer than any brother and sister could be at that moment. When I see him now, I still see the boy."

"You shouldn't be hard on him now." Muriel tapped the point of her worn boot in the ground. "It's natural after him being in poverty for so long to be drawn to wealth. I'm sure it will be a passing phase for him. You'll see the boy again."

As these words came out of Muriel's mouth, she looked across the street and her disposition fell.

"What is it?" Caitlin traced her gaze to across the street and saw Martin, disheveled and swaggering, as he was escorted out the front door by a woman clothed in a silky blue dress, with a feathered boa and a brightly painted face. Martin hugged and kissed the woman with familiarity and then she waved at him as he hailed a cab, completely unaware his fiancée was observing all of this.

"I'm so terribly sorry." Muriel put her arm around Caitlin's shoulder.

Caitlin's eyes moistened but then she seemed angry at the tears.

A carriage pulled up to Martin, obscuring him from their view. They saw his head briefly as he stumbled into his seat, and then the driver gave a sharp crack of his whip and it was away.

"What do I do now?" Caitlin drew her handkerchief to her face.

"You grieve. You get angry. You forgive. And then you find yourself a much, much better man."

Caitlin let out a grunt that was half laughter and half tears. "You make it sound so simple."

"Of course I do. I have no experience myself."

"Oh stop that." Caitlin seemed grateful to have a friend with her. "We'll just have to find those better men together. Won't we?"

Muriel stood. "Come up, you. Let's get you home."

Caitlin rose. "What's with the smile? Now you're mocking me?"

"Hardly. It's just that I've got some news to share and it concerns you as well." What was she doing? It was Muriel's intention to leave the Royces and the Hanleys behind before she got any closer to them, but here she was again, refusing to let them go.

"Oh really? How so?" They started walking toward home, arms locked together.

"I have plans," said Muriel. "Big plans. And now they include you, seeing as you are suddenly quite available."

"Are they exciting?"

Muriel laughed. "Come. I'll let you decide for yourself."

Chapter 12

THE SANITARY COMMISSION

 "Next!"

The old woman's shrill voice caused Muriel to awake from her drifting thoughts. She had been sitting with Caitlin in the cold waiting room for more than an hour and now could hardly believe it was finally their turn.

"It's us, Cait. Are you ready for this?"

"No. I am not." It had been two weeks since her engagement with Martin ended, and Caitlin hardly seemed motivated to do anything. It had taken no little effort for Muriel to drag her to this interview.

"I am Miss Patterson. There are many others waiting. Will you be coming, or should I take note of your indolence?" The lady standing before them in the gray dress lifted her chin, and the many wrinkles of her face seemed to converge to her pursed lips.

"Yes, of course. I mean, no on the indolence. Yes that we're coming." Muriel cast a glare to Caitlin out of view of the pettish woman.

69

Miss Patterson led them out of their waiting room and down a long hallway, which echoed with the angry sounds of the woman's heels striking the hard floor. Caitlin leaned in and whispered in Muriel's ear, "You shall never be forgiven."

"What I am sure you are saying," Muriel gave her an awry smile, "is you will never forget my kindness for including you. Come now. For several months now, your dear sister Clare has been serving the war effort through her brave reporting. Don't you think we should do our part as well, however small?"

"I am quite unclear on how trouncing about a muddy battle-field dodging artillery fragments is . . . any small part."

"Oh, why must you be so maudlin?" Muriel sighed. "I will merely be putting my medical training to good purpose, and you will be able to offer your . . . many talents to our brave soldiers."

"And what talents would I have that would be any help at war? Shall I polish the cannon balls?"

"Oh, Cait, sometimes you are so incorrigible. Don't you feel helpless with the idea that our nation's sons and fathers are defending our beliefs while we're back home, knitting by warm, cozy fires?"

Miss Patterson stopped, turned, and held her hand out toward an open doorway where another woman in a black petticoat, who could have been their escort's sister in dourness, dipped into an inkwell and scribbled on a piece of parchment without bothering to acknowledge their entrance. She was not as old and had a long slender face, with her black hair pulled so taut in a bun it seemed painful.

The two of them entered a Spartan room. Miss Patterson held out a hand pointing to two empty chairs. Then she circled the table and sat next to the other interviewer, who still had yet to lift her head from attending to her notes.

They sat and watched the pen scurry across the paper for what seemed like several minutes, until finally, the last punctuation of what must have been an emphatic sentence was done with both flair and force.

The woman gave her document a read, blew on the ink with puckered lips, and then slowly raised her head and offered a curt smile. "I am Mrs. Jennings. And who do we have here?"

Miss Patterson slid over the two applications. "The redhead is Muriel McMahon and the pretty one there is Caitlin Hanley."

"Pretty one?" Mrs. Jennings gave Caitlin a disapproving glare. "You do realize what the mission of the Sanitary Commission is?"

"Why yes," said Muriel. "It is for us to bring comfort and assistance to our ailing and injured soldiers, to provide healthier and more sanitary conditions at their camps—"

Mrs. Jennings held up her hand. "I was not asking you." She pointed at Caitlin and narrowed her eyes. "I want this one to answer that question."

Caitlin cleared her throat. "It is my understanding . . ." She paused. "I was told there is great concern that our soldiers are dying more from disease than from the enemy's weapons. It is believed a woman's touch would be most useful."

"A woman's touch?" Mrs. Jennings face squeezed into a revolted scowl.

Muriel leaned forward. "What my friend intended to say much more gracefully is women would be most useful in cleaning these military campsites, preparing nourishing meals, and tending to our wounded men. In such dire times, all of our beloved country's assets must be accounted for."

Mrs. Jennings continued her assault of Caitlin. "Are you aware, young lady, that we have been most purposeful in avoiding providing any distraction to our young men on the battlefield? That is why we do not allow for young . . . pretty . . . women to apply."

"Well, ma'am." Caitlin sat up straight in her chair. "I am not quite that young, and I have not been enough of a distraction to any man at this point."

The woman looked down at her application. "Yes . . . I see here you are yet to be married. Answer me plainly, please. Is it your intention during your service to the Commission to find yourself a suitable husband on the battlefield, where your odds will be most favorable and their young soldiering hearts will be most vulnerable?"

Caitlin's cheeks flushed red. "I most certainly have no intentions of the sort."

"Miss Hanley, I am sorry, but we are not interested in your services at this time."

"As for you." Mrs. Jennings eyed Muriel as one would a tomato before buying it off of a merchant's cart. "You are young, I see, but I think you will be less . . . distracting to the boys."

"Yes, much less," echoed Miss Patterson.

Muriel swallowed and tightened her lips. She had been worried about getting passed over for this opportunity because of her youth, and this was good news. But the old woman's bitter words hurt nonetheless. Was it obvious to everyone that she would be single her whole life? She bowed her head, just before recapturing her poise and raising her chin.

"This says you have been trained to be a doctor?" Mrs. Jennings raised a suspicious eyebrow.

"This is true."

The two older women exchanged glances. Mrs. Jennings clasped her hands and rested them on the table. "We have no place in the Commission for any of this cultural . . . experimentation. If you would prefer for us to consider your application with any level of seriousness, you will heretofore use the term *nurse*. Are we clear?"

"Yes, ma'am. I understand." But she didn't. She couldn't think of a more qualified student at her school than herself. What did being a woman have anything to do with being limited in life?

"Very well." Mrs. Jennings turned to the woman beside her. "What do you think of this applicant?"

"Quite favorable." Miss Patterson nodded.

"I agree as well." Mrs. Jennings lifted her pen and dipped it into the inkwell. "As for you, young lady." She glanced up at Caitlin. "I am afraid—"

"Before you say anything," Caitlin blurted out. "Before you announce your decision with me, I would want you to know that I am very intent on pursuing this until I get my assignment."

Muriel was startled by her friend's demeanor. What had come over her? She went from not having any interest in being involved with the Sanitary Commission to now not wanting to be left behind. Wouldn't this be exactly what she would need to distance herself from the pain of her breakup with her fiancé?

"We are not here to find husbands for women," Mrs. Jennings said flatly. "Our only obligation, our sole mission is to serve our soldiers, and we have made a sincere promise to President Lincoln that the Sanitary Commission would in no way be a hindrance to his brave and righteous war effort. With so many of those boys starved for affection and attention from a female, it would be a great injustice to them and their mothers to offer up such temptation. I'm quite sorry, but that is our final decision." She began to write on Caitlin's application.

"Wait." Mrs. Jennings glanced up. "What is this? Are you related to Clare Royce?"

"Yes. She is my sister."

"Clare Royce of the *New York Daily*?" asked Miss Patterson.

"Yes. That would be the one."

The two older women looked at one another. "Well, I wish you would have mentioned that to us from the start." Mrs. Jennings rested her pen down. "Your sister and her husband have been great friends to the Sanitation Commission."

Miss Patterson nodded. "Yes they have indeed. And as a matter of some coincidence, we have requested on many occasions that Mrs. Royce come in person and report on our operations. We're quite proud of them, you know."

"So," Mrs. Jennings continued, "if we were to reconsider your application, do you think you could provide the reporting yourself?"

"Well . . . I don't know. I help out at the newspaper, of course, but I have never considered myself—"

Muriel held her arm out. "Caitlin is overly modest. She is an excellent writer. I have read her stories myself." Caitlin's work at the *Daily* was almost strictly limited to clerical work and assisting with the classified ads. But how difficult could it be to write some stories on the activities of the Sanitary Commission's volunteers?

"Then it's surely settled." Mrs. Jennings returned to writing on the paperwork. "There is a shift leaving in two days. Will this be sufficient time?"

All of the sudden, Muriel realized the finality of all of this. Two days? Was she really prepared to abandon Clare and leave the relative safety of Manhattan to head toward the front lines?

"Absolutely. Will that be all now?" Muriel stood and held out her hand to Miss Patterson. After shaking it, she extended a hand to Mrs. Jennings, who shook it without looking up from her notes.

"Very well, ladies," Miss Patterson stood and straightened her dress. "We welcome you to the Sanitary Commission where we will expect you to serve your country with devotion and diligence."

"Yes, ma'am. Good day. And thank you." Muriel grabbed Caitlin by the arm and led her from the room.

Caitlin glanced back before they started down the long hallway and then whispered in Muriel's ears, "What horrible manners! I hope you did not listen to a single cruel word they uttered."

"Had they been untrue I would have protested. Today I have learned what a virtue it is to be plain and simple. Not a single bullet will go astray on account of my graces." She laughed and leaned into Caitlin. Maybe her poor uncle, bless his soul, had a vision for her larger than merely getting married.

"But," Muriel said, "we must do something about your intolerable beauty. I fear you possess the credentials to single-handedly lose the war."

"Oh, you are a terrible tease."

They exited the hallway and continued out of the waiting room and were shortly on the streets, where the brightness of the midday sun caused Muriel to cover her eyes.

All around on the streets of New York City, they passed by mothers, with babies in their arms, and children playing. Muriel tried to extinguish her thoughts of the humanity of this place. It was difficult as she walked alongside Caitlin, who had become her good friend. Muriel thought of the Royces she would be leaving behind.

And then there was Davin. Was Caitlin right? Had she become emotionally drawn to him?

She needed to rise above these sentiments. Hadn't she learned by now?

First losing her parents. Then bonding with her uncle, as flawed as he was. And look what happened to him?

Yes. She needed to leave all of this before it became too real. Before she got too close.

Chapter 13

THE EMPTINESS

TAYLORSVILLE, VIRGINIA
February 1862

"What hour is it?" Ashlyn pulled Seamus's timepiece from his pocket.

They sat together in the wooden pew of the Taylorsville church as a packed sanctuary of mostly well-dressed women, children, and old men squirmed in their seats and chattered.

"It is time for us to go." Seamus smiled at his wife, amazed that at thirty-five years of age, she still looked as angelic to him as the first day he saw her in a photograph. Her long, auburn hair was fashioned atop her head and tucked under a black, plumed hat, with two curls reaching down on either side of her cheeks. Ashlyn only had one nice Sunday dress—burgundy with white lace trimmings—but she had taken such good care of it and it fit her so well she appeared wealthy, well beyond their means.

"You are not going anywhere, Seamus Hanley." She tapped her finger on his nose.

Seamus sighed. There was so much to do at the farm in order to prepare for planting season. If it wasn't for Tatum and Mavis there would have been no harvest last year, and he felt obligated to assist them as much as possible. He had remembered much from the days of his youth on his family's potato farm in Ireland. Yet there was so much new to learn in understanding the land of the Shenandoah Valley.

Last year's corn crop was rich and bountiful, and it had provided plenty for not only the Hanleys, but for Tatum and Mavis as well who earned a fair share. But they weren't the only ones who received a generous portion of the yield. Seamus glanced toward the front of the church where Fletch sat next to his wife, Coralee.

It was painful for Seamus to agree with Fletch on a "gentleman's tithe" of Whittington Farm's provision in exchange for the services and conditional freedom of Tatum and Mavis. At the time of the arrangement, Seamus could not afford to buy their release outright, although he was hopeful with a good season this year, they would be able to do just that.

Sitting quietly next to his mother and father was Anders Fletcher, whose only attempt at dressing up for Sunday was wearing a clean white shirt under his black suspenders. He turned back toward them, as he did through most of the Sunday services, showing his full-cheeked face with long sideburns, his head topped with bushy, brown hair. When he caught Seamus's protective glare, he turned away.

Seamus looked to his daughter, Grace, who had her mother's beauty but none of her interest in Southern flair. In her plain tan dress, she looked the part of a country girl. Ashlyn was right about their daughter. Farm life had suited her well and taught her about humility and hard work. The cantankerous teenager had given way to a more gentle-spirited young lady. It was even her own idea to postpone her wish of having a horse so they could afford to build a small hutch for Tatum and Mavis under the great oak tree at the far end of their property.

He glanced to the front of the church where the pulpit seemed barren without Pastor Asa Hudson looking down upon them. Pastor Hudson often began his preaching with a measure of insightful challenges to their faith, but he never neglected to finish without heavy measures of unabashed grace. As he would often say, this cruel world provided enough condemnation, he wanted his message to offer spiritual salve to his congregation's wounds.

"Where is the good pastor?" Seamus turned before realizing he had interrupted Ashlyn's conversation with Grace. The two of them had developed a sweet friendship, once again something he credited to their life in the Shenandoah.

Before his question was answered, he heard murmurs from the fellowship and looked up to see Pastor Hudson's wife making her way to the front of the church.

"My dear friends." Ethel was a short woman, her gray hair fastened with a blue bow that matched her dress. Both her voice and disposition were soft and cheerful. She raised her hands to quiet them down, and they acquiesced. "I am terribly sorry to inform you that Asa has chosen not to preach this morning. He fully expects, Lord willing, to be hurling fire and brimstone at each and every one of you next week."

A mixture of responses varying from surprise to consternation ensued.

"That fellow's only gots to work but once a week." Abe Durham scratched at his white whiskers. "I reckon he ought to be here on the Sabbath."

There were grunts of affirmation and protest to what the wheat farmer had uttered.

"Has he taken ill?" a woman piped in from the back.

"No," Ethel said. "He is quite well. Just he has decided not to preach today and wishes you all the best."

Voices rose from the gallery.

"What are we to do without a word from God?"

"In such difficult times as these?"

"We've been waiting all week."

"Not even a verse to meditate on?"

As Seamus heard this, he felt the familiar knot in his stomach. It sounded to him as if sheep were bleating. How quickly they had turned on Asa. Certainly Seamus, of all people, knew and understood the pain a congregation could cause to its pastor. How easily does the faithful man fall!

The widow Nell Turner's deep drawl broke in. "Don't seem right he couldn't spare a kind word or two." She spoke from behind the black veil, the one she wore every Sunday, even though her husband passed away three years ago.

"I am afraid that won't happen today." Ethel gave a strange, desperate glance toward Ashlyn.

"Seamus." Ashlyn grasped his arm and locked in with her brown eyes, the one she brandished whenever she needed a favor or was about to make a demand. "Please do something about this. Surely you can help out dear Pastor Hudson?"

Grace who was sitting on the other side of Ashlyn leaned in with a mischievous smile. "Yes, Da. Do something."

Seamus clenched his hands around his Bible, which was worn from its time in gold country. "Do what exactly?"

"Go up." Ashlyn gave him a playful nudge. "And say a few words."

"C'mon, Da. It's been so long since we've heard you preach." Grace brushed back the long brown curls draped over her beaming smile.

"I will certainly *not*."

"All right. All right." Fletch stood and faced the congregation with his hands held high. "There is no need for us to waste such a fine Sunday, now we're all here. I suppose I could share some, seeing as the good reverend ain't figuring us worthy of his time."

There was a smattering of applause but mostly derisive laughter.

"Finally a sermon I'll wake for," Abe Durham bellowed on account of his poor hearing. "Ol' Fletch is gonna share his shine recipe."

The mere sight of Fletch moving toward the pulpit was enough to cause Seamus to spontaneously rise to his feet. What was he doing? Seamus apologized as he stepped by Lara Banks who was cradling her sleeping baby. Once he made it to the aisle, he was committed. He would appear more foolish by returning to his seat now than pressing forward.

So with his legs beginning to wobble, he pressed forward to the pulpit, without any notion of what he was about to say.

Chapter 14

THE RELUCTANT SERMON

Although he had given up his own ministry life, Seamus had enough pastor left in his soul to know allowing Fletch to speak in Asa's church would not be a good idea. Seamus couldn't permit the man to defile this sanctuary with whatever might spill from his lips.

When Fletch saw him approaching, the bent-over man rested his palm on the wooden lectern and furled his brow in a challenge of wills.

Seamus went around to the other side, slapped his Bible down, then fumbled through the pages, hoping there would be some sudden inspiration. "Sit down, Virgil," he said with a firmness that didn't conceal his anger.

To his surprise, the large man waved his arms in surrender and wobbled his way back to his seat. "Let's hear what the Yank has to say."

The "Yank" was a nickname the town had given him, but never was it uttered so boldly in front of him. Although the town had warmly welcomed Ashlyn and her daughter back home, there

83

was still visceral distrust for him, even though it had been more than a year since they arrived.

He rolled up his sleeves and peered out at the faces now looking up to him, a montage of shock, veiled disgust, and whispers. Then there was Ashlyn, who had pulled out a handkerchief and was dabbing her eyes, her visage lit with pride. Leaning into her shoulder was Grace, who now seemed more concerned than encouraging.

Seamus was determined not to embarrass her in front of all of these people. But the shaking of his knees and his hands were conspiring against him. How long had it been since he was in this position?

The memory of his last act as a minister of God weighed heavy on him. Suddenly, he could smell the fresh spring air of the Sierra mountains, hear the warbling birds, and see the snow melting into newly wrought streams. A setting to behold on any other morning, but not as he marched down the boulder-strewn trail out of the gold mining camp, his clothes soaked and muddy, the laughter of mockery following behind him.

He had sworn he would never preach a kind word to fools again!

Seamus looked down at his Bible, the pages still showing signs of the water damage they suffered that day. But he would never replace this book. It was inscribed by Reverend Charles Sanders, or Brother Chuck as everyone knew the kindly man.

The reverend was the one who saw something in Seamus and encouraged him to pursue the collar. Brother Chuck believed in him. Mentored him. Prayed for him. And although the man was wrong about Seamus being meant for ministry, he still remained a father figure to him.

Seamus saw much of Brother Chuck in Asa. They both were pastors who had a devotion to God that seemed beyond reason. The two of them suffered the indignities of gossip, slander, and ingratitude from the very people they served with such devotion.

Perhaps this was why Seamus found himself on the podium. He was here to defend the honor of both of these men.

Or was there another reason? There was a stirring in his heart as he looked out at those peering up to him. He wanted to be angry at them. He wanted to lash out at their attitude toward Asa. But something else was coming over him. Something he had been missing for so long.

Seamus glanced at Ashlyn and Grace and saw the longing in their eyes for him to be the man of God he once was. How much had he injured them while he had been drifting away? He turned away because he didn't want to cry, but the effect was complete. The hardness in his spirit melted and he felt the weight of his burden being lifted.

What passage could he share? What could he say?

Tell them.

No. Only Ashlyn knew why. He hadn't even told Brother Chuck.

Tell them.

"I'm sure you all are wondering why I am standing before you. No. You all know already. How do I know? Because you all are tireless gossips. In fact, this entire town is full of the most intolerable gossips I've ever endured."

The entire congregation stiffened in their seats. He had them. And he was invigorated with an energy he had not experienced for some time. He expected to see Coralee glaring at him, but instead she seemed distant and sad. Again a glance at Ashlyn revealed there wasn't a trace of worry. She knew and gave him a nod. Had a man ever had a more faithful encourager?

"You all know I left California. From the gold country. You also are aware that I was a minister of the faith, I was. A servant of God. A preacher. A missionary. Did you know this, friends?"

They nodded almost with a sense of guilt.

"And you all have been dying to know why I left the service. Have you not?"

Tell them.

"Today, you are all going to learn the answer. Your curiosity will be appeased at last. Because I am going to speak of something only dear Ashlyn knows. And I am quite certain she did not tell any of you. Shall I speak it? Would you like to know about my failure? All about my disgrace? Care to hear my confession?"

Seamus clasped his hands and brought them to his lips and bowed his head. What was he doing? He closed his eyes and thought of Ashlyn working at *La Cuna* in San Francisco. She was so happy in her ministry to the prostitutes in the city. They were both happy.

His eyes moistening, he lifted his head and smiled at Ashlyn. "My wife. You knew her as a wee girl. A young woman. But she was revered . . . adored . . . beloved in San Francisco. Did you all know my dear bride started a charity, an orphanage for babies? But more than that, one that reunited mothers with their babies. Not any mothers. Painted ladies. The fallen. Imperfect people, like me, and yes, you, dear ones."

Tell them.

"But I stole that all away from her, I did." Seamus opened his Bible and ran his hand over the pages. "God gave me a vision." He laughed. "Or so I believed. Couldn't sleep. Couldn't think about anything else. Just kept hearing this voice . . . telling me I was to preach to men. I was to live in a tent and go where men were living in tents. Out there in the foothills of California, in the mountains, and by the streams, there was no shortage of men living in tents."

He looked to Fletch and saw the man handing a handkerchief to Coralee, who was wiping her cheeks with her bare hand.

"So you know what my dear Ashlyn said when I confided this to her? Hmmm? She said . . ." Seamus began to choke on his words and paused. "She said the three most difficult words a woman can ever tell her husband. Would you know what those are?"

Seamus's gaze moved from person to person and from the old to the very young, each were braced on his every word. "My wife said to me, 'I trust you.'"

"So we passed my wife's sweet ministry onto another, and we took every last dollar we had and built a small church, much like this, in Sacramento City. See I wasn't yet willing to live in a tent. But men were living in tents there. I thought that would do. Appease the voice I was hearing.

"But . . . but nobody came. Hardly anyone. No one wanted to hear about the evils of wealth in a place where gold nuggets were rolling through the streams. Yet I wasn't finished. So I decided the problem was I didn't have enough faith in me. I needed to actually live in a tent. I told my dear wife I was going to get me a burro and take the church to the hills. Where the men were hurting. Where they needed to hear a message of hope.

"And you know what my wife said when I told her this? Even after my church had failed?" He met Ashlyn's gaze. "You remember, dear?"

She nodded back.

"She told me, 'I trust you.' I was not going to betray her confidence this time. I was determined, I was." He slapped his hand on the lectern, which startled many of them.

Tell them.

"So I went off by myself to a very large gold mining camp. I knew they didn't want me there. I knew they didn't want to hear what I had to say. But I was stuck on it. Perseverance. Am I right?"

He closed the Bible and held it up in his left hand. "'Behold, I send you forth as sheep in the midst of wolves: be ye therefore wise as serpents, and harmless as doves.'"

He lowered his arm and set the book back down, then he ran his fingers over the cracks of the leather. "Large camp. Hundreds there. And I would talk to the men when they were working. I'd even pick up a shovel. Swing a pick. Join them at their dinners.

But they weren't off on Sundays. Couldn't come to my service. Hear me preach. So one week, I told them they needed to take the day off. At least in the morning. For a few hours. And they did. A few, not many. And I thought maybe, just maybe, this was meant to be.

"Meanwhile, I was missing my wife and daughter. Visiting some. But we were nearly broke. Something needed to happen. So I spoke to the owner of the camp and asked him if he would support me. I knew him well. And he was a wealthy man."

Seamus looked down the aisle to the entranceway, and the light was shining in brightly. Someone was standing there but off to the side, so Seamus couldn't see who it was. "But this owner. He not only told me he wouldn't give me a flake of gold, but that I needed to be off his site by sunrise. Said I was hurting production, he did."

He could remember that Saturday evening well. Walking alone to his tent in the cool air, feeling broken, desolate.

"'But when they deliver you up, take no thought how or what ye shall speak: for it shall be given you in that same hour what ye shall speak.' Does anyone know the next line in that verse?"

"'For it is not ye that speak,'" the widow spoke through her veil, "'but the Spirit of your Father which speaketh in you.'"

"Yes!" Seamus stepped forward. "So I was determined. That night, by candle and moonlight, I prayed and prepared for the sermon they all needed to hear. I was so anxious I barely did sleep at all."

He looked back up in the doorway, and this time he could clearly see who it was. It was the diminutive figure of Pastor Hudson, leaning against the frame. What was this about? Seamus glanced over to Ashlyn and Grace. Had he been set up?

"So . . . I was sleeping in my tent, which was up on a hill leading down to the river, a fast-moving one. Suddenly, I was awakened by a clamor. I was under attack. Or so I believed. Then I felt my tent starting to give way. It was sliding and I panicked because

I could tell I was heading down the hill. I scrambled to find the opening of the tent, but it was already buckling and tumbling. I crawled. Finally getting my hands out, I clawed at the mud, and it was like an avalanche.

"Next I knew I was out and could see what was happening. Three men were pointing a nozzle and hose at the ground around me. These great hoses they used for mining. And before I could do anything about it, down the slope I went, with the mud and the tent and we all ended in the icy river. Wet. Ashamed."

He clenched his fist and set it against his mouth. The congregation no longer wore faces of condemnation but now were softened with compassion . . . and pity.

"It all happened quickly. Meanwhile, there was the laughter. By now, most of the camp was up and joining in, pointing fingers at the fool preacher with harshness in their voices. And there, holding the hose in his hand, was the owner. A young man. A handsome man. I knew him well."

"Who was he?" shouted Abe Durham.

"It was my brother. My brother Davin."

The people in the church were hushed, many of the women were reaching for their handkerchiefs.

"I left without a word. Found the tent downstream a ways and only retrieved one item." Seamus lifted his Bible. "I went down the mountain and that was the end of my ministry days."

He turned to Nell. "And what else in the passage?"

She had opened her Bible and read from it. "'And the brother shall deliver up the brother to death, and the father the child: and the children shall rise up against their parents, and cause them to be put to death. And ye shall be hated of all men for my name's sake: but he that endureth to the end shall be saved.'"

"So. My apologies for the length of this story. I know I am just a stranger among you. But I wanted you to know who I am. A failed man. Oh, if you only knew how true this was! Unworthy of speaking before you. And not much of a farmer either, if I am being honest. But I just couldn't bear hearing words of unkindness toward our pastor. Not only to him, but to one another. Look at us. All of us. What great shortcomings we possess. But we are family, are we not? I mean, Abe, you have already lost your boy in this war. Nell, you've never healed from the loss of your husband. These are the times that try a man's soul. Should we not spend our time together, encouraging one another?"

As he panned the room, their heads were down. Should he say anything else? Or just let these words soak in. He lifted his Bible and glanced up to see Pastor Hudson coming toward him with an unrestrained smile. It was then that Seamus saw another man leaning in the front doorway of the church. In his brief look he could only see it was a Confederate soldier.

"And I have just witnessed Elijah emerging from his dark cave!" Pastor Hudson reached out and gripped his hand, then put his arm around him, and they both faced the congregation. Asa was a short man in his sixties, but he possessed uncanny strength. "What say you, kind people? Can my brother preach?"

"Pastor Hudson!" exclaimed several voices both in surprise and shame.

"Have you been here alls the while?" Abe Durham asked. "If you was, I wanted you to know I didn't mean no ill."

Then a slow, deliberate clap sounded, and one by one they all turned in their seats to look back toward the doorway. As the soldier stepped out of the bright light, Seamus recognized him as a man he hadn't seen since San Francisco. Immediately, his gaze met Ashlyn's and she shared his terror and concern. He glanced at Grace and could see she had no idea who this man was or what he meant in her life.

"Why it's Captain Percy Barlow," Pastor Hudson said with a strange reservation in his voice.

Many of the older women in the church turned their gazes to Ashlyn.

"Yes, it is I. *Colonel* Percy Barlow." He was a couple inches shorter than Seamus, but he stood erect, with blond hair and a tightly trimmed mustache and goatee. Seamus eyed the man who was dressed perfectly in his gray cotton uniform, his cavalry hat in hand. It was twelve years since Seamus had last set sights on the man, the one who had fathered Grace. The one who had run off when he learned he had a daughter.

"That was a mighty fine speech you just shared," Percy said brashly as came forward. "Seamus Hanley, correct sir? Why I never forget the face and name of a man I saw on a poster."

The words cut through to Seamus's core and his stomach muscles clenched. He glanced at Grace, who seemed confused.

"You know Seamus here?" Pastor Hudson seemed unsurprised by Percy's tone.

"I most certainly do. I met him and his precious Ashlyn back out West. He's the kind of man one won't easily forget." He eyed Seamus from top to bottom, making no effort to disguise his disgust.

"What news do you bring from the war?" Pastor Hudson asked brusquely. "That is why you are here, right?"

"It's been a couple of years since I've been in Taylorsville, having been somewhat engaged in N'Orleans." Percy turned his gaze toward Ashlyn. "I thought maybe I would soak in the welcome of those I haven't seen for some time. Get the opportunity to meet some of my kinfolk." He glared at Grace.

"We are most grateful for your service to our cause, Percy, but this is a church service."

"Colonel Barlow, Preacher. Colonel Barlow. I am not a boy sitting in your pew. There is decorum to maintain."

"What news, Colonel Barlow?" The words were spoken through clenched teeth.

Pastor Hudson must know. Ashlyn must have told him.

"Having just arrived from Richmond," Percy began, with an emphasis seemingly designed for self-import. "General Jackson will be on the move. The enemy is approaching. There will be great war in our area, I am afraid to report."

There were gasps and worried conversations began to spread.

Fletch stood and his face was clenched with anger. "You best take good care of our boys."

The room silenced.

Percy eyed Fletch with contempt. Then he put his hat on and adjusted it firmly. "Yes. We will most certainly take care of your boy, Virgil Fletcher. I was well pleased to see young Anders was drafted to the cause and might finally bring some honor to your family."

Coralee began to cry.

Seamus glanced over to Anders and saw the fear in his eyes. Then he looked to Grace and she was crying as well.

"There are others here who look . . . capable to serve and should be willing to do so." Percy scowled at Seamus. "Then again not all can be trusted." He turned to Pastor Hudson and nodded, then he marched away and out of the door.

"I never did like that boy," Nell Turner said.

Others chorused in.

"Now . . . now, people." Pastor Hudson waved his arms to quiet them. "Let us not forget the words Seamus shared with us. These are dark times. We must encourage one another." He glared at the doorway.

"What about that pearls and swine thang?" someone said.

"Now again. Let us all pray for our brave soldiers. And Percy as well. Then you can be on your way. This news means those soldiers will need to be fed, and if that's our way to serve, we shall, with God's blessing, do it well."

Pastor Hudson prayed, and in a short while they were all filtering out of the building, in a decidedly somber mood. He turned to Seamus. "Don't worry about what was said, son. They'll only remember the part about the enemy approaching. Dark times indeed."

"So," Seamus said, "I suppose this whole bit about me doing the sermon, that was your idea?"

"Oh no." Asa chuckled. "That was your bride. I was worried about what you might say, to be plain. I knew you had a cloud over you and was concerned you'd just drag it over my people's heads. But she's a persuasive woman. She said to me, 'I trust him.'"

Seamus laughed as he saw Ashlyn and Grace waiting for the others to depart before making their way to him.

"And she was right. Ashlyn was right about you. You have a gift, son." Asa looked him in the eye. "In fact, something came to me while I heard you preaching."

Grace came up and put her arms around Seamus and buried her head in his chest. "I am so proud of you, Da!"

He wanted to correct her for interrupting his conversation with the pastor but was too comforted in her arms. His friendship with his daughter had grown so much in the past year. Ashlyn leaned over and kissed him tenderly on the cheek. Since she had returned to the South, it was the first time she had done so in public, but the room was empty except for Asa.

She turned to Pastor Hudson and gripped his hand with both of hers. "How will I ever thank you?"

"Thank me? Thank Him." He looked toward the ceiling. "God spoke through your husband today. And as I was just sharing with Pastor Hanley, there is something quite urgent I need to show him."

Seamus wasn't sure what startled him more. Being called a pastor or the urgency in the man's words. "Is that so?"

Pastor Hudson kept his focus on Ashlyn. "Our job is not complete. Have this young man ready and with a lunch packed. I'll be knocking on your door before the sun rises."

Ashlyn shrugged and grinned. "As you say. We shall tuck the young man into bed early, won't we, Grace?"

"Yes, we will." Grace took her father's hand and tugged him toward the door. "Good-bye, Pastor Hudson."

Seamus and Grace left Ashlyn and the pastor behind and walked out of the door and into the bright sunshine of the day. "Da?"

"Yes?"

"Who was that man? The one in the uniform?"

Seamus feared this question and expected it would somehow haunt their daughter all of her life. And even though he had years to think of an answer, there wasn't one he could bear offering up now.

"Hopefully a man you won't see again." Yet as these words emerged from his mouth, he knew it was unlikely they had seen the last of Colonel Percy Barlow.

Chapter 15

SONGS OF THE SHENANDOAH

"Had I known you were part burro, I would have never agreed to this." Seamus stopped, put his hands on his knees, and took a few gasping breaths of the moist, morning air.

Up ahead of him, Asa continued to churn his short legs up the sinewy trail rising sharply into the Massanutten Mountains. He marveled at the old pastor's constitution.

Asa paused and leaned back against a thick oak just beginning to show green buds on its angling branches. "I am up here as often as I can once it warms. It's rare during summers that I miss a day, except, of course, for Sundays, weddings, funerals, and when Fletch is pit roasting a swine for the town."

"And I thought all of this time you were busy about the good work of the church." Seamus staggered his way up to the man, his boots sinking in the soft soil.

"But Seamus. This is the most important work of my job."

Seamus had been in Taylorsville for a while, but this was the first time he had traveled up this particular path, which now seemed embarrassing considering how close he lived to the foot of the mountains and how spectacular and inviting the scenery was that surrounded his farm.

Their hike had taken them through a forest of maple, birch, and ash, and at higher levels they came upon red oak and cherry trees. The lower trunks of these sky-reaching inhabitants were draped with moss and at the ground around them, mushrooms and fern rose from the moist, dark soil. Already the white blossoms of the serviceberry were visible.

Adding to the dewy freshness of the sights were the vibrant sounds of this warm day. Upon passing ponds and trickling streams they heard the chirrups of bullfrogs, a fluttering of insect wings, and the woodsy gossip between warblers and chickadees. Adding to the chatter were the arguments of gray squirrels and the tapping of woodpeckers foraging for termites in the bark.

At almost every turn, a clear vantage point of the vast farmland below offered insights into why this part of Virginia was the chief food provider for much of the South, which made it a strategic priority of defense by the Confederate army.

The sun was well above the horizon in the east, yet the bending of light remained, casting interesting shadows and shapes on slopes around them. Just when Seamus was wondering if their ascent would ever end, they rounded a corner and came upon a large granite boulder perched on the cliff's edge, which almost appeared to be a couch carved out of stone.

"Ah, my morning respite. Come, son. Have a seat with me." Asa climbed his way onto the boulder and then plopped his backpack beside him, which he opened and began to probe inside.

Seamus didn't waste time in following the pastor up as he was anxious to rest his throbbing feet. He was no stranger to difficult work and labored for many hours each day on the farm, but this steep climb put a strain on muscles and joints he seldom used.

Once he settled, Seamus took in the spectacular valley beneath him. For miles and miles he could see the rich quilt of hundreds of farms weaved together, of corn, hay, barley, and herds of horses, sheep, and cattle. It was a magnificent setting, and with the pain of the climb behind him Seamus now understood why his friend frequented this location.

"This morning should be painted on canvas." Asa took in a deep breath, and it was as if his entire body smiled. He pulled out a knife from his pocket and unfolded it open. Then he sliced into a small block of orange cheese and offered a piece to Seamus, which he gladly accepted.

The pastor carved one for himself and savored it. Then he pointed down below with his knife. "Look. There is the Grimwald farm. And that's where the Simpsons live. Yours is just out of view, but I can see the farms of most of our congregants here. This is where I come to pray as much as I can." His wrinkled face glistened with sweat, which he wiped with the back of his hand. "I pray for you and Ashlyn and Grace. But especially for you."

"Oh?" Seamus laughed. "I suppose I am in need of much prayer."

"Yes you are. As I am as well." A small tuft of his silver hair blew in the wind. He narrowed his eyes, as if he was measuring what he was about to say. "I hope this doesn't come across as presumptuous."

"Go ahead, Pastor." Seamus lowered his eyes.

"I have been through your valley before."

Valley? Of course he has.

"No." He smiled and sliced another piece of cheese. "Not the valley down there." Asa reached out the knife and Seamus pulled off the slice. He had forgotten how much better food tasted when in the wilderness.

"No. I am talking about the valley of shadows. The darkness."

Where was all of this heading? Seamus missed his old mentor Brother Chuck dearly and wondered if Asa could fill that role here in Taylorsville. "I don't know. I believe I left this darkness you speak of . . . back in California. We are doing well now since arriving. Ashlyn. Grace. Myself."

"I'm afraid the valley is not something you can move away from. It comes with you everywhere you go." He pressed his hand against his chest. "It lies in here. And oh, it is painful. Worse than any wound. But I suppose you don't need to be told any of this."

The sun had shifted to where it was beginning to get in his eyes. Seamus put his hand above his brow to block it. "Maybe life was meant to be difficult for us. Some more than others."

Asa squinted. "You believe this?"

Seamus glanced down. He thought he saw a carriage moving on a distant road. "I hope it's not true, actually."

"It doesn't need to be." Asa pulled a handful of strips of dried meat out of his pack and handed one to Seamus. "I have the answer, if you are asking."

"That looks like Fletch's possum jerky." Seamus reached out for it and bit into it, and the taste of salt and smoke filled his mouth.

"Or it could be the skunk." Asa chuckled. "You have to learn to laugh at them."

"Is that your secret?"

"No. That's just so you don't strangle them." Asa took a bite and chewed, then he tilted his head. "The valley. The darkness. No. That's a place we lose ourselves in. We can't blame that on a moonshiner. Or some disappointment in our pasts."

"I don't know what you mean."

Asa lifted his canteen, uncorked the top, and took a drink. "It isn't the people in your church. The neighbors. The crooks. The murderers." He waved his arm around him. "The world, which crushes in on us. The death of a nation. The battles of war. We'll always have those."

Seamus was struggling to understand.

"Those aren't what control us. Those are merely the distractions."

"The distractions?"

"Yes, son. From the gift."

"The gift?" Seamus worried if there would be a point to all of this.

"The ability to listen."

"I am listening."

"No. All you hear are the noises. And you've allowed them to press on you. To wear you down. Just as what happened to me."

Asa had a peace in his green eyes, a stillness in his soul, that Seamus yearned for, but it seemed so distant. Had Seamus ever experienced that? Yes, he had. But so long ago. And the Southern pastor had no idea what Seamus had been through. From the deep disappointment he saw daily in his father's eyes. To his many failures in life.

"You don't like me comparing my life to yours, do you?" Asa jutted his chin out. "No one could ever be in as deep or dark of a valley as you? Isn't that what you think? That's the biggest lie of all."

Who was this man? How was he able to peer deep into the hidden chambers of Seamus's heart?

"I see you struggling against this, son." He pulled up his knee and cradled it in his arms. "Just listen for a moment. Really listen."

They sat in silence for a moment. As they did, the sounds of the mountains rose, the birds, the insects, the creaking of the trees, an unseen creek gurgling, and the humming of the wind.

Several minutes went by. "Hmmm . . ." Pastor Asa smiled sweetly. "I call this the songs of the Shenandoah. This is the music that lifts my soul. It's here where I can hear His voice."

His voice? Ha! Seamus ruined the life of his family by listening to that voice. How much better their lives would have been if he had never taken Ashlyn from her ministry in San Francisco.

"Seamus, I don't know what your life has been about. I don't know all you've been through. And I am not here to say I have faced more hardship or fewer troubles. None of that matters anyway."

"None of that matters?"

"No. Of course not. We all have different circumstances. If we believe we are to measure God's favor through our circumstances, that becomes the greatest distraction of all. You see . . . the hearing. Hearing His voice. It's not with this." Asa pointed to his ear. "No. I come here to quiet my soul. The birds don't speak to me." He laughed. "There is only one way to hear these songs. These songs of the Shenandoah. It's through trust. Through faith. When you do, you know only one voice matters."

"But He lied . . . to me." As the words came out, Seamus wanted to pull them back. It was the worst of blasphemy and he knew this. But it was also what he believed.

He expected an angry retort from the pastor. But what he received was much worse. No response. *Is he judging me?*

Finally Asa spoke. "How did He lie to you?" His eyes glistened with concern. "Go ahead. Speak freely, son."

"My . . . wife. She trusted me. I was called to those mountains. Those tents. I was going to be Paul the tentmaker! It was so clear to me." He picked up a small pebble and tossed it over the edge. "It was just my own arrogance, I suppose. The more I pressed, the more I failed."

"Tell me about your brother. What is his name?"

"Davin. I have already forgiven him long ago. It's not what's doing me harm, if that's what you're thinking." Seamus thought back to the day when he first saw his younger brother in the pub in San Francisco thirteen years ago.

"You're smiling, Seamus. What was that about?"

"Oh, I'm just thinking of my brudder when he was eleven, just a lad. When I first seen him after he stowed away in a ship and sailed for a couple of months. Just to come find me. To rescue his older brudder."

"Did his older brother need rescuing?"

There were hanging posters of him as a wanted man for stealing a horse from the United States Army. Percy had just arrived to San Francisco and was threatening Seamus's burgeoning relationship with Ashlyn. "Yes. I suppose I did."

"Hmmm. Do you think maybe that is what it was about?"

"What?"

"Well, you abandon your thriving ministry in San Francisco. You spend every dollar you've saved. In poverty, you end up in the very camp your brother owns. Do you suppose it was your turn to rescue him?"

Seamus scoffed at the notion. "Some rescue! Rolling down the hill in the mud. Shaming myself in front of my brudder and all of his workers. Only thing I did well was prove what a fool I was. A broke and broken-down fool."

Asa didn't say anything. Those patient, peaceful eyes knew he had more to say.

"Do you know . . . ?" Seamus glanced up, embarrassed his voice was cracking. "Do you know when I decided to give up my wild dreams? My chasing of the wind, as it were? When we found out that Ashlyn's uncle had left Whittington Farms to her. We had nothing. No way of getting home. I had to go back to my brudder, the one who humiliated me, and ask him for the money to bring us back here. I can recall the look on his face. The pity. The shame. There was a time, you know, when I was the boy's hero."

"Can I ask you something?"

Seamus wiped the tears from his eyes. "Sure. What else would you like to know?"

"What do you think about a man who spent his entire life in suffering. In pain. In failure. But somehow, through his misfortune and his struggles, what if he was able to save the life of one other person? Not physically. But spiritually. Eternally. Set one person on the right path. If all he accomplished was to have that impact on another, would you consider that man's life a failure or success?"

This immediately brought up thoughts of Shila, the young Indian who at the cost of his own life saved Seamus when he was about to perish in the snowy banks of the Yosemite Mountains more than thirteen years ago. Shila's display of selflessness and faith changed Seamus forever. If not for the boy. If not for his sacrifice, where would Seamus be? Then his sister Clare came to mind. How many times had she lifted Seamus up when he thought he would never rise again?

"See." Asa reached over and fastened his pack. "Until we can answer that question, I don't believe we can truly serve others. That we can be in ministry." He slid his arms into the straps. "Because there is only one answer, I believe, that makes you worthy of serving."

The question penetrated through Seamus's thoughts. Until this moment, he always believed he needed to save hundreds of souls to please God. He laughed inside at his own arrogance. What if it was only one? Would his life be worth it to him?

"Are we leaving now?" Seamus leapt down and then held his hand up to Asa.

"Oh no." The old man took his hand. "I've got to show you what I brought you up here for."

"I thought it was . . . all of this for me to see." Seamus panned the view.

"No. Come, son. You called God a liar, right? I've got your evidence to the contrary. It's just a ways ahead."

Before Seamus could respond, Asa was on the trail and climbing once again with intensity. Beyond the crunching sounds of their boots on the soil and twigs, Seamus tried to listen to the songs of the Shenandoah.

Was that what had happened? Had he allowed the noise of the world to clutter His voice? Had he sought out the approval of men ahead of the affirmation of God? It all sounded so easy now. He could have preached it a hundred times himself. As they walked together, Seamus's mind filled with comforting thoughts, and he welcomed them as if they were the return of a favored friend.

What Asa had shared as "just a short ways ahead" ended up being a couple miles farther. But the time passed quickly for Seamus and he felt lighter with each step. His senses grew alive. His spirits rose. Where have You been?

I never left.

Finally they had wound their way to another ridge on the mountain and Asa, who had once again made his way ahead, waited for Seamus with expectation.

As Seamus came closer, he saw another valley beginning to unfurl before his eyes. Soon he was at the edge, and around him the wind began to swirl. Stepping gently with his boots, because the ground seemed unsteady and the drop below was several hundred yards, his heart pounded as he witnessed the spectacular setting below.

It had been nearly fifteen years since he had served in the army, first on the side of the United States Army, and then for the Mexicans. His switch to serve in the San Patricios Battalion, an Irish division of the Mexican army, nearly got him hung. Instead, he received forty-nine lashes, was branded with a *D* for *deserter*, and then set free.

The pain of the moment, the smell of his flesh burning, and the ultimate loneliness of abandonment seared through his memory.

"Can you believe it?" Asa gave him a wry look. "There are some thirty thousand men in Stonewall Jackson's army down there. I saw them settling in a couple of days ago. It's amazing how quickly they set up their camp."

"The Union army?"

Asa shook his head. "Can't be far off. It will be a matter of weeks when they clash. A terrible thing this war. A terrible shame."

They were camped alongside a creek, a blur of motion below, a sprawling city of men, horses, artillery and—" Seamus froze.

"You see it?" Asa reached up and squeezed his shoulder. "When I heard your story yesterday . . ." Asa shook his head.

Down below as well were hundreds of rows of tents.

"I don't understand . . ." But this wasn't the truth. Seamus comprehended it all well enough but he didn't like what the voice was saying.

"They came to us last week. A couple of officers. They were asking . . . no begging for chaplains. I was tempted myself because so many of our young men, our boys, are down there. But I'm much too old to be running from battlefield to battlefield."

Seamus ran his fingers through his hair. "I don't think I can."

"I know, son. It's all sudden. But I can tell you this. You'll have one of two choices. You can either obey God's voice, the vision He planted with you. Or you'll be obeying Jefferson Davis's bugle and be drafted into military service. You're of the age still."

"But what will Ashlyn say?"

"She'll be given a choice. A bayonet or a Bible. I don't think that will be nearly as difficult for her as it will be for you."

Seamus couldn't stop staring at the rows of tents. There was no question it was aligning with his vision, almost as if pulled straight from his dreams. Of what he felt called to do. But his stomach wrenched. What an odd sense of humor God had. Bringing him back to the place in his life where he experienced so much pain. The mere thought of being among soldiers again made him nauseous.

"But . . . I don't . . . I don't believe in the cause." Even mentioning this aloud would be enough to sentence him to hanging as a traitor. Especially with the town believing all along he was a Northerner.

"Nor do I." Asa pointed down below. "At least not that cause. The book of Joshua. Chapter five. The words spoken by the commander of the army of the Lord. That is how I answer when asked."

Seamus could vaguely remember the passage. He knew that there were a lot of battles and bloodshed in that book. It had been so long since he spent much time in his Bible. "Then if I don't believe in the cause. What am I to do? How could I be of service?"

Asa shrugged, apparently realizing Seamus didn't recognize the verse. "I imagine you need to merely follow orders. From the One who matters."

Seamus couldn't deny it. Looking down at the camp below, he felt a strange draw. As frightening as it was, Asa was right. It was where Seamus needed to be. "You know. They'll kill me. When they find out who I am." Instinctively his hand went up to the scar on the side of his face, his fingertips feeling the rough edges of his skin.

"Yes. They probably will. And me for recommending you since I won't lie about knowing." Asa nodded toward the trail, and they started to head out, but not before Seamus gave Stonewall's army one last view.

They pressed down the trail as Seamus's mind whirled with questions and doubts. What would Ashlyn say? He reached into his pocket and pulled out the picture he was never without. Then he smiled. He already knew what she would say. It would be after her initial protests. Long after she cried. And prayed. He knew what she would say.

I trust you.

Chapter 16

THE PROMISE

KERNSTOWN, VIRGINIA
March 1862

 Seamus sat in the wagon, bouncing along the rocky road, his mind drifting to the sadness in his heart as he waved good-bye to Ashlyn and Grace.

He felt as if it was the most difficult task he ever faced. Would he ever see them again? No. Now that he was back in conversation with God, he was certain that was a question he did not want answered. It would not serve him at all to know his fate.

His neck felt uncomfortable and he stuck his fingers underneath the white collar and tugged on it to try to loosen it up a bit. How long had it been since he wore one of these?

Asa had provided his clothes as a gift. He insisted for his safety that Seamus look as much the part of a chaplain as possible.

Although the war had caused bitterness to grow deep, both sides had a restrained reverence for men of the cloth. So, Seamus wore black pants, a black shirt, a white collar, and a minister's black hat.

"How handsome you are." Ashlyn had said to him in a whispered voice, tears blending with pride and remorse as she fastened one of the buttons on his shirt he had missed.

"Well . . . we're here." The wagon slowed to a stop, and Seamus's unlikely driver pulled the brake. Fletch climbed out and walked around, and the two of them unloaded Seamus's belongings.

"I appreciate the ride," Seamus said. "That was kind of you to tote me." But he knew something was on Fletch's mind. Seamus waited patiently, as the man with the stoop and the crook in his neck struggled to ask for help.

"There is something. Something I've been aimin' to ask."

"About your boy?"

Fletch sized up Seamus with his one good eye.

Seamus put his hand on the man's shoulder. "You want me to look out for Anders."

"Yes. I do. He means much to his mother and me."

"You'll be pleased to know that my daughter, Grace, has already put in that request on your behalf."

A strange smile came to the man, as if a crack in a piece of old pottery. Then it disappeared. "She fancies him?"

"She does. And I fancy her."

Fletch cleared his throat, then straightened himself. "I'll take mighty fine care of your girl. And Ashlyn too. Rest assured. Just . . . bring my boy safely back home."

This was something out of his control, beyond his capability, but he couldn't think of anything else to do but nod. "Oh, there is another thing to settle between us."

"What would that be?"

"I will do all I am able to bring Anders back safe to you,

Fletch. I'll mind him as if he's my own son. This I promise. And I have a favor to ask in return."

"Yes?"

"I want you to release Mavis and Tatum. I want their freedom."

Fletch turned his head and spit. Then he pointed a finger in Seamus's chest. "You bring my boy back alive, Reverend, and I'll set those two free as the wind. On my honor."

He held out his large, weathered hand, and Seamus shook it, wondering just how valuable the man's word was anyway. But it didn't matter. Seamus now had something he could fight for. He could believe in.

Then he flung his haversack over his shoulder and walked away. From Taylorsville. From the farm. From Grace. From Ashlyn.

But for the first time in a long time, Seamus didn't feel alone.

Chapter 17

GRATITUDE

MANHATTAN, NEW YORK

 Clare was ashamed they had never done this before. All these years and never once! But she supposed they had been victims of their own routines. But now that her mind was upon the task, she was filled with anticipation.

"Where are you taking me?" Andrew craned his neck toward the window of the fast-moving carriage. "And does this coachman plan on bringing us there alive?"

Clare was surprised to hear the humor in his voice. Especially after completing such a difficult task the day before.

Thinking back to yesterday at their church, she recalled the man with his hat in one hand and his long arm reaching down and tracing his fingers over the brass plate that read, "Charles

Royce & Family." He bit his lip as he glanced around the rising expanses of the historic church, with its great stone walls and carefully crafted stained-glass windows. In the front was the altar and podium where the droning voice of the aging Reverend Tannerbaum would bellow out exhortations to the congregants, many of them among Manhattan's wealthiest.

Her heart sunk as she remembered Andrew's eyes glistening behind his glasses. He wasn't enamored of the prestige of church membership and was more embarrassed than anything for their family to have such a prominent permanent seating in the church. But the difficult part for him was the ongoing erosion of his father's empire, something that wore heavily on Andrew's tall shoulders.

"Well," Andrew had said. "We were hoping to get five hundred dollars for it."

"That will do." The man reached into the inner pocket of his long-tailed jacket and pulled out a checkbook and a pen. "Say no more. I won't haggle a fair price. Who should I write this to again?"

Heat rose to Clare's face. How could this impertinent man not know who her husband was? Then she pointed to the brass plate. "Andrew is a Royce. The founders of the *New York Daily*. I'm sure you have heard of it?" Her husband reached out for her hand and gave it a gentle squeeze. She exhaled and smiled. "Andrew Royce. Write the check out to Andrew Royce, please."

Clare had pulled Andrew's hand in and clasped it with both of hers. She looked into his eyes and saw the look that had become so familiar in his beautiful green eyes: failure. These years had taken a toll on him and his once-blond hair was now equal parts gray.

She wished there was something she could do to relieve the pressure he put on himself every day. But what could they do? What was left? They had already mortgaged their home, and if not for the generosity of their landlord, they'd be out on the street.

The newspaper was bleeding dollars each month, and it was only a matter of time before they would have to shut it down.

But today was a new day, Sunday, and remarkably, as he always seemed to do, Andrew had bounced back from this disappointment. Now, all Clare wanted to do was to keep his mind off of his worries.

The carriage jolted and the four of them bumped against one another. "I suppose I shouldn't have told them we were in such a hurry." Clare smiled at Garret and Ella sitting across from them, who were giggling with delight at the turbulent ride.

"Did you dress yourself this morning, Ella?" Clare looked at her daughter's hat, which was badly mismatched with her dress.

"I picked it out for her." Garret fastened the button of his jacket. "Why?"

"She looks glorious," Andrew said.

"Thanks, Da." Ella tapped her shoes together.

"This isn't the way to our church." Andrew gave Clare a querying glance. "We haven't missed church as a family for . . . I can't remember when. But then I suppose we don't have a place anymore."

"Are we going to the new park?" Garret gripped a handle when the coach jumped again.

"Nobody said anything about missing church." Clare looked at her son's uncombed black hair and sighed. He was old enough to watch his younger sister at home, but Garret at twelve still needed someone to take care of him. But Andrew spent most of his day at the newspaper and Clare's schedule was frantic as well. Since Caitlin and Muriel had left for their assignments with the Sanitary Commission, Clare was forced to beg her friends for help. There just never seemed sufficient time in the day.

The coach halted to a stop. Their driver was as unskilled with braking as he was driving in a straight line. Clare was most relieved they had arrived safely as this was all her idea. She had wanted the family to walk here, as they would be taking much fewer carriage rides now, but they would be late as it was.

Garret bolted out the door before the driver opened it and Ella was right behind him.

Andrew looked out the window and then turned back and raised his eyebrows. "You think this is a good idea?"

"Why not? We should have come a long time ago. At least to show our support."

"Are we even allowed to?"

"Let us find out for ourselves."

"All right." He motioned for Clare to get out and then he followed and paid the coachman while Clare joined the children on the side of the hard-packed dirt road.

The driver made no delay in getting back up on his seat and out of this neighborhood, which was one of the poorest in Manhattan. The streets had only a few merchants out this morning, one selling hot corn and another displaying fruit.

Rows of multistoried tenement buildings lined either side of the streets. A couple of them were boarded up, some with broken glass. And those that had windows were mostly covered with clothes hanging precariously from lines and flapping in the wind.

However, standing before them was a large brick building, which seemed oddly out of place because it was architecturally attractive and appeared new, with freshly painted white shutters and doors.

And although the large wooden doors were closed, the sounds of celebration and music could be heard brightly from the street. Chills skittered over Clare at the joyful singing, and she crossed her arms and rubbed her forearms.

"What is that?" Garret seemed intimidated enough by the strangeness of his surroundings that he, along with Ella, stood close to Clare and Andrew.

"That," Clare put an arm on his shoulder from behind, "is a church."

Ella tilted her head to the side. "It doesn't look like a church."

"And what is a church supposed to look like?" Andrew smiled at Clare. He obviously had a change of opinion on her idea.

Clare gave Garret and Ella a gentle shove and they headed down the brick walkway, which was edged on either side by plainly but carefully groomed grasses and flowers.

"This is beautiful." Andrew reached for Clare's hand. "Why haven't we—?"

"Supported them sooner? I don't know. I am ashamed to think why."

There must have been someone watching from the windows inside, because one of the large doors opened before they could reach the handle, and the merriment of vibrant voices chorused together, with clapping of hands and stomping of feet.

> *Can you feel the ground, it's rumblin'?*
> *And there's whispers in the wind.*

A black man greeted them, who was thin and bent, with gray curly hair and a white jacket and pants. He eyed the four of them with both surprise and confusion.

> *Can you feel the ground, it's rumblin'?*
> *And there's whispers in the wind.*

A mulatto woman, wearing a bright yellow hat and dress, pushed past the man, giving him a scowl, and waved them in.

The woman shouted above the music. "Y'all just come inside. I'm Mrs. James. Don't mind Mr. James one bit. Come now."

Andrew smiled at Garret, whose face was blanched with alarm, and reached a hand for Ella. They entered to a large, tall-ceilinged room, and nearly every space was filled with gyrating and applauding and singing black faces, mouths opened and hands raised in glee.

> *For that sweet day is arrivin'*
> *When my Jesus comes again.*

The woman escorted them to the last row of the church, which like the others was a long, crude, backless bench. But for now, these were mere obstacles to the wildly, waving throngs of celebrants who except for a few of their oldest members were on their feet.

For that sweet day is arrivin'
When my Jesus comes again.

"Get on, y'all." Mrs. James shooed others to press farther in, creating some cramped space for the four Royces who stood stiffly and tightly together.

As they were slowly noticed by those around them, the response was the same. The congregants stopped and pointed them out to others, and when the singing ended, they were surrounded by many strange stares.

"Sit yourself down," Mrs. James said, with little effect as more and more folks stood around and murmured to one another. Finally the whispers had taken over any voices until nearly two hundred white-eyed gazes were directed their way.

Ella scooted over to Clare and buried her face into her stomach. Garret pressed up against Andrew.

"What is it?" came a familiar booming voice from up front. "Now what's going on back there? C'mon, my brothers and sisters. Seat yourselves down."

One by one, they followed the man's directions and soon, like a tumbling of dominoes, they had all folded their way into their seats, leaving the Royces as the only ones in the congregation still standing.

Except for the large, broad black man standing on the podium looking at them. His expression of irritation soon gave way to a toothy smile, and then he started to laugh, at first deep and slow, but then it graduated to a full hearty roar.

His mirth proved too hard to resist, and soon the laughter spread from one congregant to another until nearly the entire room was convulsed with cheer and pointing fingers at the Royces.

Clare should have been more bothered by having hundreds of these strangers laughing and pointing fingers, but she knew the man at the front too well, the good Reverend Zachary Bridger. There wasn't an unfriendly thought in the man's character.

He was married to Cassie, the woman who for many years was a maid to the Royce family but who ended up being a prominent participant in the Underground Railroad. Still, even with important responsibilities, she still served as an occasional volunteer nanny for Andrew and Clare, just because she loved them and the children.

A scream arose from the front of the church, and soon Cassie, with her arms raised and waving, moved as quickly as her body would allow her down the aisle toward them. "Oh, dear Lord! Look who's come!"

When she arrived at the back of the church, her full brown cheeks brimming with cheer, she clasped her plump hands on Andrew's forearm and tugged. "Come now. We're gonna bring you up front."

Andrew's face reddened, but he knew their friend Cassie was an undeniable force and that whether they walked on their own powers or were dragged by virtue of her strength, they were moving forward.

Now that Garret and Ella recognized the woman who had helped to raise them, they showed signs of relief and followed Andrew out with less reticence than he was displaying.

The laughing had died down and there were no remaining signs of trepidation on the gazes of the congregation as Clare and her family walked toward the pulpit, but now there was a gentle curiosity. Clare could only imagine the questions they all had. Who was this white family invading their church?

The reverend beckoned them up to the podium, which wasn't much more than a crudely constructed platform with a couple of steps. Now it was Clare's turn to feel embarrassed, but they were no longer in control of the situation, and surrendering to the moment they moved to the reverend's side.

They stood close to one another, facing the large gathering. Although it was clear that the members of this church weren't affluent by any means, Clare was struck by how well they were all dressed for their Sunday service. She could only imagine how much of their monthly earnings had gone into the clothes they were wearing.

Clare recognized a few of the people gathered, ones who had been at Zachary and Cassie's wedding. Ten years ago they had gotten married in a small ceremony. This was before Zachary started his church, and not too long after he had escaped from a plantation in Savannah.

"Y'all may not know who these folks are." The reverend put his arm around Andrew and pulled him so abruptly, it made his glasses tilt on his face. "This good man right here is the publisher of the *New York Daily*."

A gasp burst from the group and they exchanged glances.

Andrew pressed his glasses back on the bridge of his nose and glanced nervously at Clare.

"Now I know many of you aren't readers yet, but there are enough of you to know there isn't a greater friend to our cause than the *Daily*."

Clare could see by the responses that many of them were not only aware of the *Daily*, but of the stance it had taken on behalf of the abolition movement and the treatment of blacks in Manhattan. The work she and Andrew had done was never for recognition. It was always about saying what was in their hearts and minds. The only feedback they had received to date was having angry customers pulling their advertising.

"And this lady here." Zachary walked over and released his deep chortle. "This fine woman. This is Clare Royce and I think you all know—"

Before he could finish his sentence, his loud voice was drowned out by spontaneous cheers and shouts from the audience, and they rose to their feet and applauded and some hopped and raised their arms.

This continued for so long that Clare realized they weren't only honoring her family, but they were celebrating their victories, their advances. How many of these standing before them had suffered in their road to freedom? How many had struggled to persevere not only against those who wished to enslave them, but those of her own people, the Irish, who had made them feel most unwelcome?

Clare began to cry, and though many emotions surged through her, disappointment drove to the surface. They could be doing so much more. More stories. Pressuring the community's leaders with their commentary. She looked over to Andrew and knew he was sharing her thoughts.

Forgive me, Lord. Here I have been thinking we've been struggling and suffering, yet we haven't even started. We haven't even begun the fight.

Once the cheers and shouts died down, Cassie guided them down the steps, and several of the congregants gave up their seats so the four of them could sit front and center. It was the last thing Clare wanted to see happening, but there was no use in turning down this act of kindness and generosity.

"I feel as if we should all sing again, our deepest thanks for our Lord's provision. For His deliverance. What say you, my brothers and sisters?"

The answer came in a burst of singing, first a few in the back rows, and then within moments the entire church was shaking at its beams, clapping and stomping.

Can you feel the ground, it's rumblin'?
And there's whispers in the wind.
Can you feel the ground, it's rumblin'?
And there's whispers in the wind.

Clare's family didn't know the words, but they joined in the best they could, and although they had never done so in a church before, they clapped their hands as well while many sitting behind them patted them on the shoulders and heads.

What was most remarkable to Clare was the expression on her husband's face. He had taken off his glasses because they were fogged up with tears. It reminded her of the day she had first met him, when he was singing hymns of praise under the evening sky.

For that sweet day is arrivin'
When my Jesus comes again.
Yes that sweet day is arrivin'
When my Jesus comes again.

So many years had gone since she had seen so much joy in the man she loved. Even Garret and Ella were swept by the spirit of the moment, and this made Clare profoundly happy.

As she glanced around to those around her, she saw something here so powerful, which was unfathomable. Here gathered in this room were some of the poorest, most oppressed people in the entire city. But rather than hearing the cries of bitterness or anger, she heard something so rare to behold.

The sweet sound of gratitude.

Chapter 18

SOUP KITCHEN

 "It's Father!" Ella exclaimed in response to the sudden noise in the front hallway. She leapt up from the bay window and sprinted toward the door.

"Don't tell him our surprise," Clare hollered after her.

"Don't tell me what surprise?" Andrew entered rubbing his hands. His old black wool jacket was crusted with snow and his cheeks glowed bright red.

"You didn't walk all of the way home from the office, did you?" Clare stood up from the fireplace she was tending and grabbed his coat and hung it on the brass rack. "You poor soul. What a dreary day to be out in the cold."

"The snow in March is lovely. I wanted to enjoy it with a brisk tour of the city."

"That's quite a long tour, Mr. Royce." Clare felt his cold face with the back of her hand. "You should have hired a cab."

"Nonsense. Other than the fact it delays me from coming home to my family, it truly is a wonderful way to get a feel for the heartbeat of this town."

121

"Ma is fixing something special." Ella clasped Andrew around his leg.

"Come on, Da." Garret grabbed his father by the hand and dragged him toward the warmth of the hearth.

In the fireplace, a crackling fire was raging, with sparks flying and the embers at the base appearing as glowing red worms. Hanging over the fire by an iron hook was a large black kettle.

"That's Grandmother's!" Andrew's face lit up with childish glee. He unwrapped a scarf from around his neck.

"Have a seat, Da," Garret said. "We put the chairs close to the fire. We're going to eat dinner here like a picnic."

"Strange weather for a picnic." Andrew plopped down in the leather chair and lifted his legs as Ella slid a footstool under his ankles and then took her father's shoes off.

She giggled. "Da's got a hole in his sock!"

Andrew wiggled his big toe. "This one has broken free from jail. Call the coppers!"

"Ella, are you forgetting something?" Clare propped her arms on her hips.

"Oh yes!" Ella skipped off.

Garret chased after her. "I'm going to get it first."

"Garret," Clare shouted. "Let your sister do it." But they both scurried out of the room with a pounding of feet and playful screams. She let out a deep sigh and slid her chair next to Andrew's and held his hand.

"What is all this?" Andrew looked tired.

"You don't remember?"

"Hmmm." He pursed his lips and traced his eyes to the ceiling. Then he raised his hands. "Don't know."

"It's your birthday." She squeezed his hand.

"Oh that. I thought we both agreed to stop celebrating those."

"I never agreed to such a thing. Besides, we could certainly benefit from some celebration." She placed her hand on his cheek, rough with stubble. "I am so proud of you, Andrew. You know that, don't you?"

He grimaced. "What for? What is to be proud about?" He panned the room that had lost so much of the luster and richness it once had. "This isn't what you agreed to. I mean . . ." He paused for a moment. "You deserve so much better, Clare Royce."

"Hush, you." She pressed her finger on his nose. "Now how was your day? Despite almost perishing in the blizzard."

His eyes widened and he wagged a finger. "Actually . . . there was some good cheer for us today. We got MacPherson back today. Signed a contract for a year."

"I thought that horrible Sean MacPherson said he wouldn't advertise in the *Daily* even if it was the last newspaper in the world."

"Did he say that?"

"He did, and worse."

Andrew cupped his hands and blew into them. "Well, apparently he now has a more favorable opinion of our fine publication. And he said it was because of you."

"Oh, that man is so fickle. He'll be cursing us in the morn."

"Your story about the Irish Regiments. The 63rd. The 69th. The 88th. What you said about them getting the worst of all assignments on the battlefields and how they should be admired for their bravery, but the generals ought to be . . . How did you say it?"

"That the generals ought to be cooked in oats for using the sons of Ireland as the battering ram of their imbecilic strategies." Clare shook her head. "But if MacPherson was astute, he would have complained how the *Daily*'s supposed war correspondent spends little of her time on the battlefields."

"Aww . . . you write those stories as if you're holding a smoking musket in your own hand. Besides, we'll be able to afford a full-time field reporter soon. That is, I hope." He started to stare into the fire, but then his face brightened again. "Anyway, apparently MacPherson has a nephew in the 69th and said truer words ne'er been spoken. Oh, and that wasn't the only news."

"Really . . . do tell."

"Your man stopped by for a visit."

"My dear Cyrus Fields. No doubt to pay his thanks for my article shouting down the naysayers of his Atlantic Cable. I hope you told him it was unnecessary to thank me and that I was merely doing my job."

Andrew smiled at Clare in the way that always made her feel loved. "He made his offer to us once again."

"For stock in his company, free of charge in gratitude for my continued belief in his dream. And, of course, you told him?"

"That my dear wife appreciates his kindly gesture, but it would conflict with her journalistic sensibilities, her integrity of *reportage*." Andrew let the last word roll off with his poor French accent.

She swatted his arm. "I have so much fondness for that man. He is a model of perseverance, especially in all of the opposition he is facing. To be a dreamer, you must always first be a fool."

"Well, I hope it didn't injure our integrity, but I did tell him he could thank us by giving us some grace on his paper invoice."

"Are we behind again?"

"I wish that was the only bill we were behind on." Andrew's shoulders drooped. "There are times when I just want to give it all up." He grabbed her hand. "But then I think of you and the children, and it's all I need to keep me going another day."

Clare leaned forward and kissed him.

"Hey," Ella shouted, startling them both. "You can't kiss the king!"

"Of course I can kiss the king." Clare stood. "As I am the queen."

"Give it to me." Garret reached for something Ella was hiding behind her back.

"Garret." Clare raised an eyebrow at her son.

Ella walked over to Andrew, pulled out the handmade crown she was hiding, and reached up to put it on her father's head, but she couldn't quite reach. Andrew bent down and she placed it with care.

"Now you can make me your knight." Garret grabbed a poker from the mantel and handed it to Andrew.

"That is covered with ashes." Clare clenched her jaw.

"What would an Irishwoman know about kings and knights?" Andrew held the poker like a sword before his son, who was already on one knee with his head down. "I now pronounce you Sir Garret Royce, Duke of New York."

Clare moved over to the fireplace and peered into the simmering stew. "I would only agree to my son becoming Duke of Roscommon. He most certainly would be an Irish lord." She dug into the boiling liquid with the long metal spatula and stirred it around, being careful not to splash the hot liquid on her. It had been some ten years since she had made pottage over a fire, and the scents of the potatoes, leaks, carrots, and broth brought her back to the old country.

"Where did you find that old kettle?" Andrew asked.

"In the back shed." Clare lifted the spatula, swiped her fingertip on it, and tasted the meal. "Ummm. Good. Yes. It's really a beautiful pot."

"Grandmother used to cook in that all of the time," Andrew said for the benefit of all.

Ella climbed up on the chair and curled up next to him, tucking her head against his shoulder. "You had a grandmama too?"

"Yes. Even me." Andrew rubbed Ella's back. "Such sweet times we had together in this house."

"Garret, hand me your father's bowl there from the table, will you dear?" She lifted the ladle resting against the hearth, then dunked it into the pottage and emptied it into the bowl her son held out to her. She filled it a bit too high and watched with concern as Garret carried it to his father with two nervous hands.

"Oh, Andrew, isn't this just marvelous?" Clare motioned to Garret to get her the rest of the bowls from the table.

Andrew brought his nose close to the pottage and closed his eyes. "Yes, this smells delightful."

"No. Not the stew. I mean that, you know, with Muriel and Caitlin leaving to serve the soldiers and Cassie so busy these days. I know it's made it difficult for us, with me having to write from home as much as possible. But it's been splendid for me to spend more time with these little ones. And for us to create sweet memories. It's just, I believe it's better we don't have a nanny. It's a blessing from God. That's what it is."

He laughed. "Well I should have gone broke a long time ago then."

"Please, Andrew. Don't talk about such in front of the children."

"I already know we're broke," Garret said. "That's why Ma had me ask Mr. Catton for some wood today. I brought it myself. Do you like the fire, Da?"

"I do. Very much, son." The defeat returned to Andrew's voice. "Let me pray over our meal. Father, we thank You for this day. Your ways are a mystery to us, but we trust You, and love You. Thank You for the many blessing You provide for my family, despite my . . . many inadequacies. Amen."

"Amen," Ella and Garret echoed.

Clare filled the other three bowls and handed one to each of her children and then sat next to her husband, who remained silent as he slurped his food.

Finally he spoke, his voice trailing. "And the stove?"

Her heart ached. Clare was hoping to make it through the night without explaining. She wanted his birthday to be the one day when Andrew wouldn't have to worry so much. She glanced up to see that her son and daughter were busying themselves with their meal.

She whispered, "Mr. Barnes said he wouldn't extend any more credit. It won't heat without coal, as you know."

"What's next?" His eyes watered. "For my children to march through the snow following the coal carts, hoping for something to fall?"

"If that's what we must do, we will. You are doing fine work, Andrew Royce, and we are behind you."

"Here I am trying to save the world when I can't even feed my own family." He sighed and shook his head. But then he smiled sweetly. "I love you, Clare. More than you'll ever know."

And that was it. He was finished being outwardly despondent about the coal bill. Andrew returned to playful conversation with the children.

After they finished their supper, Andrew threw some chestnuts in the coals of the fire. It took about five minutes, but they finally exploded, which were met with yelps, screams, and then laughter.

Then Clare shared stories of growing up in Ireland, and Ella asked to hear more about the grandmother she was named after.

The children fell asleep, leaving Clare to be cradled in her husband's arms as he ran his fingers through her hair. It had been a long time since she felt this content.

Chapter 19

THE FIELDS

TAYLORSVILLE, VIRGINIA
March 1862

 Ashlyn pressed the spade into the soil, and she lunged poorly and in turn felt the pain driving through her spine and up through her hands. She let out a deep moan.

"What is it, Ma?" Grace had a hoe in her hand and eyed Ashlyn with concern.

"Oh, still trying get accustomed to the spring work." Ashlyn rubbed her wrist and noticed a blister on her thumb had breached and was oozing.

"Or the winter work, or summer or fall." Grace wiped the sweat off of her forehead.

Ashlyn observed her daughter. At fifteen, she was sprouting into a beautiful young lady. She had noticed a big change in the girl since Seamus had preached that Sunday. And even more so when he left to join General Jackson's army. "You are a hard worker, Grace. I don't know how we would ever make it without your help around here. And I was so fearful you would hate living out here."

The girl shrugged. "I suppose we've all got to do our part."

"How are you doing?"

Grace shrugged and dug her hoe into the soil.

"With your father being gone."

"I try not to think of it too much. He did say it wasn't dangerous being a chaplain in the war."

"If your father said it, then it's true." Ashlyn tried to sound confident but she worried about him as well. How could anything be safe about being in a war? She tried to talk Seamus out of his decision, but he was right. They had few choices. If he hadn't enlisted as a chaplain, then he would have lost the opportunity to serve on his own terms. He didn't buy into the Southern ways, and how could she blame him? It was a difficult subject for her as well, and she had grown up around slavery all of her life. Yet she did love the land and she cared for her people, even if they did have it all wrong.

And with Union troops pressing down in the valley, even Seamus had changed his attitudes about the Confederacy. This war had become so much more complicated than merely the cause.

Most of all, she supported Seamus in his decision because he was convinced he was being called by God. It had been so long since he spoke in those terms, it was like having her husband returned to her. The man she so loved. Ashlyn was so encouraged to see the spark again in his spiritual fervor. She was willing to embrace any journey of his that would bring him closer to having those flames burn brightly again. At least, this was the belief she was using to try to comfort herself and bring peace to the worries that caused sleepless nights.

Seamus had blamed himself for abandoning their ministry of

La Cuna in San Francisco, but as she told him many times, she was ready to move on as well. They had help and resources and the orphanage probably was ready for fresh, new leadership.

Ashlyn's passion for the Shenandoah Valley and its imperfect people had never faded, and something inside her was uncomfortable with how she had left Taylorsville to avoid shame. Being back home again brought closure and healing for her. Now she prayed it would come to her husband too.

She knew it was unchristian for her to feel this way, but she couldn't see herself forgiving Davin for the hurt he caused Seamus. Although they were living without much financial margin in their lives, she was grateful they had weaned themselves from being dependent on Davin's support. In fact, they were far along in saving enough money to be able to pay him back for all they borrowed.

Ashlyn looked over to Tatum and Mavis who were off in the distance working on the farm. Where would they have been without those two? They had become more than friends. They were part of the Hanley family.

She surveyed the field. There was so much work to be done. Although Seamus didn't give himself much credit for being a farmer, his strong back and work ethic were greatly missed. Would they yield a proper harvest this year without him? They had no choice. They must. Just as many other women in the valley, she and Grace would need to labor harder.

Glancing toward the gateway leading onto their property, she saw dust rising from the road. Ashlyn squinted and saw a familiar cart heading their way. "Oh, dear, what now?"

"What is it?" Graced looked up from her work.

"It's that horrible man."

"Mr. Fletcher?"

"What could he want now? As if he isn't already squeezing as much out of us as we can bear."

"You're talking about Anders's father, Ma."

Ashlyn scowled at her daughter. "I would rather you run off with a pirate with a termite-riddled wooden leg than have anything to do with that family."

"Anders is so sweet and kind. He's not like them. Besides, Mr. Fletcher has been so much nicer since Da left."

This was something Ashlyn couldn't argue. Since his son had been conscripted, Fletch had been somewhat of a different man. Still, she didn't believe someone like him would be able to change enough to make him palatable to civilized society. Fletch had been Fletch since she was a little girl. Seeing him as anything else but a greedy, thieving bootlegger would take more faith than she had.

In a few minutes, Fletch was retracting the reins of the horse pulling his overloaded cart, and he came to a stop and climbed out of the wagon.

Ashlyn stabbed her shovel into the dirt, brushed her hands free of soil, and sauntered over to her visitor. "What brings you here today?"

He lifted his hat and then went to the back of the wagon and flapped down the rear tailgate. He tossed back the burlap cover revealing a rich bounty of cans, jars, and bulging sacks. "Let us see." He lifted out an empty fruit crate and began to fill it up with items he seemed to be carefully selecting.

"Mr. Fletcher, we haven't placed any orders." Ashlyn glanced over his shoulder. "Oh my, are those peaches?"

He grinned at her with yellowed teeth. "Peaches, pears, apricots, nectarines. Flour, barley. Got some shine in there . . . and some of the finest hard cider you've ever tasted." Fletch cupped his mouth with his big hand. "I won't tell the old man if you don't." His laugh was crusty but genuine.

Grace had made her way over and was craning her neck over the wooden sides of the wagon. "Is that—?"

"You bet it is, young lady. Peppermint. Licorice. Lemon drops. Let me know your preference."

She looked up to Ashlyn. "May I?"

Ashlyn sighed. "Mr. Fletcher. You know as well as anyone that we can't afford such frivolities."

He lifted up a jar of beets. "Look at this frivolity. These are pretties here."

"If . . . if we were to make a purchase, it would most certainly be that sack of flour."

Fletch held up a bag. "Not this? From the Caribbean." He unfastened the tie at the top of the sack and opened it for both Ashlyn and Grace to see.

"Is that . . . ?" Grace's mouth was agape.

"Only one right way to determine that." He held it out to Grace.

She reached in with her thumb and forefinger, pulled out a pinch of the brown crystals, then put it to her mouth and let out a squeal. "Sugar!"

"Where did you get all of this?" He hadn't folded back the cover entirely, but what was visible seemed to be an entire store of goods.

He squinted his one good eye and got close enough to her that Ashlyn could smell his foul breath. "There are two questions ne'er to be asked. One is a lady's age. And the other is where ol' Fletch gets his fineries."

"Well . . . I already told you. We have no means to purchase any of this, except for some necessities." Ashlyn gave Grace a purposeful glare and the girl reluctantly stepped back from the cart.

"Oh, you have the means, all righty." He cackled.

"Wh-what do you mean?" Ashlyn couldn't trust the old man.

"Your husband. Seamus. We made arrangements."

"What kind of arrangements?"

"He's keeping a good eye on my boy, and I'm keeping . . . well . . . the only good eye I have on you-all."

"Have you heard from Anders?" Grace clasped her hands together as if in prayer.

"Not much of a writer, that boy. Nah, just as long as I don't have no Confederate officer coming to our front door with bad reports, I'll consider myself good and lucky." He pointed a finger at Ashlyn. "Now, I'm a countin' on your husband good and proper. He promised me well. And Coralee too. In fact, she's the one said I needs come by and fatten you up, so as not to be short on our deal. We ain't want nothing missing on our side of the ledger." He lifted a jar of peaches and held it up to Ashlyn. "These here, from Georgia. Imagine you'd love a taste of these. Now girl, I best be going on my way soon, so time to take what you wants."

Grace shook her clasped hands and mouthed the word please to her mother.

"Well, all right I suppose. Wouldn't want to get in the way of any . . . arrangements you made with Seamus."

Fletch shook a fist. "Now, that's it. So let's fill this crate up nice and good and grab that sack of flour and a bag of sugar, and I'll be expectin' a slice of peach cobbler when I make my deliveries here next week."

"That, Mr. Fletcher, is a fair arrangement indeed."

They filled the wooden crate with all kinds of Southern delicacies, and it took two trips for her and Grace to tote it along with the other items. When she returned outside the second time around, Ashlyn was disappointed to see Fletch was already nearly out of sight down the road. She didn't have the chance to properly thank him.

Grace went to return to her tilling duties. She really had become such a hard worker.

"You put that hoe down, young lady. We are going to surprise Tatum and Mavis with something fresh baked this evening."

As Fletch's cart faded in the distance, a thought troubled her. Would Seamus be able to keep his end of the agreement?

How could she allow this thought to take root! She crossed her arms and rubbed her shoulders as if to chase the idea away.

But this wasn't the first time this concern pressed upon her. In fact, a question had been plaguing her since he left many months ago.

Had she given Seamus a proper good-bye?

Chapter 20

THE CHAPLAINS

Seamus tried to steady his hands from shaking.

Sitting on a tree stump in a clearing of the woods, he felt stiff and uncomfortable in his black chaplain's jacket, and the white collar around his neck made this even worse. But what he felt most uneasy about was that he was in the vicinity of tens of thousands of soldiers preparing for battle and he didn't have a gun. He looked over to see Chaplain Robert Scripps, arms crossed, watching him closely.

Seamus clenched his fingers into fists. "It's nothing. Just the Irish shakes. Runs in our family."

The chaplain, who was a short, bald man with a closed-cropped gray beard, pursed his lips then smiled. "Yes. I see it runs in a lot of families out here on the battlefield."

Seamus looked toward the woods before them, which earlier in the morning were gloriously decorated with the green leaves of spring. Now they were bent and disfigured, trampled by the boots of soldiers and the dragged artillery of a Confederate battalion that lumbered through in somber anticipation of their impending fate.

Left behind were the support teams breaking down mess tents, officers tracing maps with their fingers, medical personnel nervously preparing their supplies, and a few chaplains of varied denominations preparing themselves to do battle with men's souls.

A burst of ordnance was heard, followed by calls of bugles and rattling of gunfire.

"It's begun," said Scripps.

Seamus tapped his foot on the ground and clasped his hands together. "So we . . . just wait here?"

"We do." He looked up to Seamus with fatherly eyes. "Don't worry, my friend. You'll dip your beak in the action before too long."

"Can you tell me—?"

"Again?" Scripps exhaled. "All right. We wait until we're beckoned. Won't be long as one thing this war can be relied on is making wounded. We'll accompany the medical boys there, and the ones they ignore are the ones without hope. That's our handiwork then. To console the inconsolable."

"And how . . . are we consoling them?"

The man pulled his tin canteen from his belt. "This here is the water of life. With them screaming in your face and clawing at your coat with their bloody hands, you'll feel as useless as a headless tick. But at least you'll be able to give a dying man a drink. As they're bleeding out, that's what they'll be begging for."

Seamus pulled out his Bible from his coat. It was the pocket-sized one Asa had given him as a parting gift. "Do we read a passage or say a prayer?"

Scripps scratched behind his ear. "Oh yes, I like to give them a Sunday school lesson, perhaps blend in a bit of theology. You know, make sure they're knowledgeable about Trinitarianism."

Had this man been on the warfront for too long? "Surely, you're not suggesting . . . "

"Listen, son. I'm just trying to prepare you for what you're about to see."

"I've been in battles before."

"As a soldier?"

Seamus nodded.

"And as a chaplain?"

"Not . . . till now." Seamus didn't know what difference it made.

"Then you have no idea what you're about to encounter." Scripps twisted the cap on his canteen and took a sip. "When you're a soldier, you see your friend fall, you get to shoot back. When you're a surgeon and the kid's bleeding to death, you get to cut off a limb, pull out a bullet, wrap a wound. Us? We get to be the last one to lie to them. The last face they see on earth, and it's the face of a liar."

"Surely you don't . . ."

Scripps leaned forward. "The kid asks you, 'Mister, will you tell my mother I love her?' What do you say? 'Nah, son, I'd have to visit five thousand mothers after this bloody battle.' So you tell him, 'Sure, son.'"

Seamus squirmed on the stump, which was growing increasingly uncomfortable as was the conversation.

"I see you're looking at me strange. But really, I'm doing a good service. The kid looks at you and says, 'Am I going to heaven?' And you know he's the one that lanced some mother's son with point of his bayonet, and you say, 'Sure, kid, and save me a good seat for when I get there.'"

"You've been doing this too long, I think." Seamus turned away.

"Yeah, yeah, I know. You go running through those trees today, waving your Bible, and prepared to save a hundred souls." He raised the canteen. "Just don't forget your water of life, and when you're looking in their dying eyes and being the last liar they see on this blood-soaked earth, you remember what Scripps said."

Anxious shouts shot from the woods, followed by a loud rustling of the branches and leaves that drew Seamus to his feet, just in time to see a dozen or so baby-faced Confederate soldiers burst through, their eyes wide with terror.

"Are we being overrun?" Seamus looked around to find anything that would work as a weapon.

Scripps laughed and waved at the soldiers as they raced by them. "You are green at this. You've never been in the back lines, have you? That's what sifted out by the cannon fire."

The fleeing soldiers streaked past the camp and out of the clearing into another patch of trees, but right into the path of the rear sentry. There were shouts of "halt" and then shots rang out accompanied by screams.

Seamus winced. "Should we . . . go?"

"Nah. We can't console them all. We start with the officers, especially those with a chance to survive and give us a good report. Then the war heroes and the unremarkable. We leave the deserters for last." Scripps stood and brushed the dust off of his coat. "All right, young Chaplain Seamus Hanley. Time to make a name for yourself. The angels will be watching you closely."

A few of the medics had fastened on their backpacks and were working their way to the opening in the woods. One of them whistled and waved the two chaplains over. Scripps had removed an apple from his pocket and rubbed it on his sleeve.

Seamus's pulse spiked and his knees shook. Scripps was mad perhaps, but he was right about one thing. This was a more frightening assignment to Seamus than rushing an infantry line. He felt more inadequate than ever before. What could he offer these dying soldiers?

They didn't move far into the trees when the horrific screams of wounded and dying men reverberated through their souls. The medics ran forward with Seamus close behind. He glanced back and saw that Scripps was in no hurry.

As the hollering increased, he ran toward the desperate pleas. What foolishness his promise to Fletch seemed now. How could he protect Anders without bullets?

He looked down to his side and was relieved to see he hadn't forgotten the canteen.

At least he had the water of life.

Chapter 21

CAMPFIRE

 Seamus pulled off his cold, blood-soaked sock and cringed at the sight of his foot, blistered and bruised.

"You better not let the doctor see that." Scripps stoked their campfire with a long stick. "He's liable to put a saw to it while you're sleeping."

"I best be taking a look at that, Preacher." Dr. Taylor Fellowes, a Southern gentleman who seemed as misplaced in this rebel camp as any other, groaned his way up from the boulder he was sitting on and made his way over to Seamus.

Seamus was too tired to protest. The white-bearded man pulled a monocle from his pocket and leaned in close to his battered foot. He shook his head, drawing Seamus's attention to the feather rising above the man's hat. The doctor lifted the bottle of whiskey he had beside him, bit off the cork, then tilted it, allowing the alcohol to pour pain on the toes.

"Let's see now." The doctor tugged at his beard, his face highlighted by the flashing of the flames.

"I don't like the way you said that." Seamus leaned in to examine the foot himself.

"It's all right," Scripps said. "You've got two of them anyway."

"What is it, Doctor?" Seamus had learned to ignore most of what came out of Scripps's mouth. Although the only outward sign that he was a minister was the collar on his neck, Seamus had grown to realize the man's awkward attempts at humor was the grip that kept him from sliding down the slope of madness. Survival depended on finding some way to stay above the evil of war.

"You've earned your soldier's boots, all righty," the doctor said. "Welcome to Jackson's army, son."

"You've seen quite a few feet like these, eh?" Seamus's toes began to get cold so he put his socks and boots back on. He felt embarrassed to have even shown his injured feet to the doctor. What with all of the injuries the man had treated in the last few months.

"Much worse, I fear." The doctor moved back to his boulder and pulled out a hand-rolled cigarette. He lifted a stick from the ground and dipped it into the orange glowing coals of the fire, then used it to light his smoke. "I've told the general what these marches are doing to his boys."

"You got to speak with General Jackson? What did he say?" Seamus tucked his feet back into the boots, wincing as he did.

"Let me guess." Scripps worked at opening a rusted can. "He answered with a Bible verse. Perhaps comparing himself with David. And we all . . . we're his rough companions."

"Nope." The doctor threw the stick back into the fire. "In fact, never looked up from the letter he was writing, and I thought he hadn't heard a word I was saying. Then he said to me in a quiet voice, 'Dr. Fellowes, I pray every night I can soon send them back home to their mothers. And I pray every night there will be a home to send them to one day.'"

"Was that all?" Seamus tied the laces on his boots.

"No. Then he stopped writing his letter, looked up to me with those blue eyes, and added, 'I have not yet prayed for their feet, but rather that they be able to march faster.' And that was it."

"It's a rare thing to be able to speak to him at all." Scripps snapped his opener on the can and turned it slowly. "Few ever get to talk to that man."

"As it turns out, he is more open to advice about headaches than he is about tactics." The doctor looked past Seamus. "Well, I wonder what he wants."

"Speaking of headaches," Scripps scoffed.

Seamus turned in the direction they were looking and saw a man in an officer's uniform approaching. The gait and air of confidence was clearly recognizable. Percy Barlow. Or Colonel Barlow as he was known around here. What did he want? Seamus stood at attention with the others.

"Sit down, men," Percy said to the doctor and Scripps, but they remained standing. He walked over to Seamus and stood just a few feet before him, looking him over from eyes to boots. "I was told I would find you here, cowering in minister's clothing. But I thought I would see it for myself. How many know you're a deserter?"

The very words brought shame to Seamus. He felt his knees buckling, and it made him angry he was allowing Percy to have this effect on him. "That was a long time ago . . . and another war." He wished he could see the responses in the eyes of his friends, but he had to keep his attention focused on his superior officer.

Percy turned to the doctor and Scripps. "Did you know the company you are keeping? An embarrassment to President Davis's army? To the cause? I'd be interested in just what your cause is, Seamus Hanley." He spit out the name like bile.

"I haven't found him to be yellow at all, sir," Scripps said. "In fact, he's braver than most. Perhaps you're thinking of the man of his past."

Percy didn't peel his gaze from Seamus. "You just wait. When your back is turned, he'll show who he really is. Keep an eye on our horses. Did you know he was a horse thief?"

"Sir." It was difficult for Seamus to even use those words.

"Private . . . Hanley. I have every intention of exposing you as the fraud you are. When the general learns who you are, I shall draw great pleasure from hanging you myself."

"I was exonerated of that . . . sir." Seamus glanced to see the surprised faces of his friends.

Percy leaned in close enough for Seamus to smell the whiskey on his breath. "You . . . will never be exonerated of anything in my mind. I will never forgive you for what you have done. You've . . . stolen . . ."

Seamus wanted to say something. He wanted to defend himself. He didn't steal Ashlyn from Percy. He rescued her. When she was abandoned and unloved.

Percy turned to Scripps and the doctor. "I would suggest you keep a fair distance from this traitor, unless you would like to be dragged through the same mud." He glared at them until Scripps responded meekly.

"Yes . . . sir."

Percy spat on the ground and then he took a couple of steps and stopped. He turned around slowly, then walked back up to Seamus's face. "Another thing. I have some scouting duties to do. In Taylorsville. Might just have to check in on your . . . wife. See how she is doing. What she thinks about her decision."

Seamus's fists clenched and his teeth grinded.

This drew a sick smile from Percy, who like an animal must have sensed the emotional response and now was coming in for a kill. "And I'll be sure to check in as well . . . on your misbegotten daughter."

That was all he could take. Seamus thrust his fist in the air and it landed squarely on Percy's cheek. Then he sprang on the colonel and the two toppled onto the cold dirt and rolled toward the fire.

Seamus felt fingers probing toward his eyes and he moved his head. Then he felt a knee in his groin and buckled over just as he looked up to see Percy about to swing a rock toward him.

Seamus thrust his forearm up to Percy's wrist, and the pain seared as bone met bone, yet it dislodged the small boulder that fell harmlessly to the side. Seamus managed to get on top of his opponent and his knees pinned Percy's arms. And then in a flurry his fist was striking cheek, and then nose, and before he could hit again he found himself being yanked backward.

Trying to fling himself again, he was restrained by both Scripps and the doctor as Percy crawled to his feet. Once standing, he brought his hand to his nose, now pouring blood over his fingers.

"Let me look at that." The doctor stepped forward.

Percy held up his hand. "Stand back!"

Seamus panted, his chest heaving with anger, which was now giving way to the harsh reality of what he had just done. What was he thinking to have fallen prey to these taunts! What foolishness.

Percy pulled out a handkerchief from his pocket and covered his nose, and even in the dim light, it could be seen turning wet and red. "You both . . . you saw what this man did."

"Yes." The doctor glanced at Seamus with disappointment. "We saw everything."

Seamus put his hand to his lip, and it was already swelling and moist as well.

Percy dusted off his clothes with his free hand. "You men saw him jump me."

Seamus understood immediately the awkward position in which he had placed his friends. And how could he have done this to his family? What a horrible way to throw his life away.

"Did you hear me?" Percy's eyes boiled with rage. He turned to Seamus. "You'll be hung in the morning. I'll see to it. And with witnesses to prove it."

Scripps stepped forward. "Yes, sir. I did see it all." There was sadness in his voice.

Percy's shoulders lowered and a twisted smile came over his face. "Good man—"

"What I saw was you, a highly decorated soldier of war . . . getting a solid whooping by a man of the cloth. Ain't that how you saw it, Doctor?"

"I wouldn't have believed it so, had I not seen it with my own eyes." The doctor nodded at Scripps. "I would have thought all along the colonel would have taken the preacher."

"He jumped me." Percy stepped back.

The doctor spoke to Scripps as if only the two of them were there. "My thinking is the colonel would want us to keep this hushed."

"It's hard to lead men in war with a soured reputation," Scripps added, with a smile curling.

Percy's gaze darted from the doctor to Scripps and back again. Then he straightened. "So . . . this is how it's going to be?"

"Well now, Colonel," the doctor said, "the way I see it, it's all up to you."

"Very well." Percy lifted the handkerchief from his nose and looked down at it, then placed it back again. He pointed a finger at Seamus. "This isn't over, you know. Far from it."

With the crazed look of a caged animal, he turned and disappeared down the path he arrived from, toward the distant masses of campfires and tents.

All waited in silence until Percy had left entirely, then Seamus turned to his friends to see their faces bathed in anger. Before he could offer gratitude or repentance, Scripps poked him in the chest with his finger.

"You do that again, son, and I'll hang you myself." The chaplain circled back over to the fire and prodded it back to life.

"I'm . . . sorry."

The doctor stared into the darkness toward where Percy had disappeared. "I wouldn't worry about being sorry. I would be concerned about finding a way out of this battalion. Maybe out of this war."

The thought of bowing under the pressure of Percy's vengeance was foreign to Seamus. He had run his whole life. He was finished running. "I don't see that—"

"Men like that." The doctor appeared to have no interest in hearing what Seamus had to say. "They won't stop until they get what they desire."

"The doctor is right." Scripps sat down, lifted the can, and dug in a spoon. "I don't know what you did to that man . . . and I don't want to know. But he won't stop until you're dangling from a noose."

Seamus made his way over to the fire and sat. He had been reckless. He would be wiser from here on out. In an army of thirty thousand men, it was not impossible for him to keep his distance from Percy.

But what about Ashlyn? Grace? How could he protect them from Percy's unrelenting thirst for vengeance?

Maybe there was only one way.

Chapter 22

THE FORTUNATE ONES

MANHATTAN, NEW YORK
October 1862

 "My dear friend, there have been no greater days in this nation of opportunity." Tristan lifted a hand to the rim of his tall beaver-skin hat to keep it from falling off due to the bouncing of the carriage on the cobblestone road. He bore a smirk that boasted of both brilliance and prosperity. As always, he was impeccably dressed and groomed, which was a requirement when borrowing his father's buggy.

"Some would argue with that notion, I am afraid." Davin wore tailored clothes as well but could never keep up with his friend, who seemed to have something new each day. He glanced out the window to the street merchants and the many passing by, and it seemed as if it was a distant land outside.

"That's just it, my Irish laddie," Tristan said. "You see this world through the eyes of your poverty. It will never leave you. Once you've dug your fingers through the soil for sustenance, the stain of dirt never leaves your thinking."

"Who was it who told you arrogance was an attractive trait?"

"My arrogance is merely my being honest about my confidence. It would make a liar out of me to wear humility like some proud flag. But take comfort, my friend, as you can be both humble and truthful."

Tristan was so skilled at insults, Davin found it entertaining. Even when he was the target of his friend's cruel sport.

"You and your beloved heritage." Tristan pulled an apple from his pocket and brushed it against his royal blue vest before biting into it noisily. "Ease up, dear fellow. I just mean to educate you of the world." He wiped some of the apple juice from his lip. "You see, while you and your people are there planting roots and hoeing dirt and whatever it is that you do, you have no idea of how many other poor saps are doing precisely the same thing."

The carriage stopped and they waited for the driver to open the door before descending. Tristan stopped at a food stand and picked up a potato as the vendor eyed him warily. "But meanwhile, people like me are deciding what this is actually worth." He put the potato back on the pile of others and nodded to the disappointed merchant.

"Maybe I am happy at pulling potatoes . . . and gold . . . out of the ground." Davin hopped to avoid a mud puddle. "Perhaps that is who I am."

"Let's certainly hope this is not true," Tristan said. "I have much greater expectations for you."

They skirted across an intersection and dodged a wagon pulled by two large horses. "And who would ever want hard labor when soft labor is so much more pleasant and profitable?" Tristan snickered. "I wasn't going to share this with you, but now I must.

Do you know that it took you ten years in those gold mines of yours to build your small pile of wealth?"

"I remember every day of it."

"As I am sure you would, kind sir." Tristan paused and put his hand on Davin's shoulder. "Do you know in our partnership, my father and I made all you earned in ten years in less than ten hours? We accomplished more with our soft hands with a pen in it than you did with a shovel."

Davin tried not to show his disappointment, which would only feed Tristan's satisfaction. But Davin always suspected he got the worse of their dealings, and this, confirmed with his friend's own boastful lips, made his stomach turn.

Tristan grabbed Davin by his lapels. He straightened them out and then dusted his shoulder. "There you are. Fit to present to a king." He gave him a light slap on the cheek. "Are you frightened?"

"No."

"You should be." Tristan's eyes widened. "My father may seem like a decent enough chap at social gatherings, but when it comes to his business interests, he is not one to be trifled with. A very powerful man, my father. That he has requested a meeting with you is something that should not be taken lightly."

"How so?" Davin wasn't nervous before, but his friend's words were making his heart pace quicker.

"It means only one of two things. Either he wants to congratulate you."

"Or?"

"He wants to kill you."

Davin tried not to give his friend the pleasure of a reaction, but he must have failed.

"Oh, don't worry. He usually doesn't kill my friends."

Davin gave a nervous laugh in response, but how much truth was there to all of this? One of the things he had learned in the California mine country was a distinct distrust of everyone. Gold had a way of being poison in the veins of men. Davin knew first-hand what it could do to a man. It could cause him to steal from his own brother.

They headed toward the entranceway of the tall building, and the door was opened by a slender man in a bellman's uniform. After traveling through a lobby with marble floors and brass railings and up a well-lit, winding staircase, they came up to a room with large, smooth-polished oak doors. Tristan tapped on it with the back of his hand, stuck his head inside, then turned and waved Davin in to enter.

They walked inside a large office, and sitting behind a massive desk, with neatly piled papers on either side, was a man dipping into an inkwell and scribbling away at a scrolled document. From this angle, they could only see the top of the man's bald head, the broad ring of gray, bushy hair protruding from the sides.

Alton Lowery seemed to be more of a shadow patron in his son's life. Though Davin always knew Alton was the source behind Tristan's investing ventures, it was rare to see the two of them together.

Tristan began to speak, but his father held up a finger. Alton's beaked nose bobbed with concentration on his task.

A chill skittered down Davin's back when he realized they were not alone. He glanced back to see there was a large man with a face etched with scars who was tending to his fingernails with a knife. Although Davin couldn't recall the man's name, he knew he rarely left Alton's side.

They stood in front of Tristan's father in uncomfortable silence until he finally dipped the pen in the inkwell with a succinctness of completion. Then he lifted the scroll close to his eyes, blew on it, and admired his handiwork.

"I will need to get this to the alderman." Alton spoke with a voice both raspy and high in tone. "We'll need to keep our conversation brief." He stood, not gaining much height, and seemed as if he recognized Davin for the first time. "Come, boys. Sit in your chairs."

The two of them sat in the black leather seats and watched as Alton leaned back in his chair, which squeaked as he rocked. He clasped his hands together and narrowed his eyes in a way that pierced through Davin. Then he turned abruptly to Tristan. "This young man . . ."

"Davin," Tristan offered.

Alton's gaze sighted on Davin once again. "Yes, of course." He rocked a few more times. "Davin Royce, correct?"

"Um . . . no, sir. The surname is Hanley." Davin put his hand to his mouth and coughed, trying to clear his unexpected tenseness.

Alton put his hand to his forehead. "Yes. Your sister, she was Clare Hanley before marrying Mr. Royce, isn't that so?"

What did his sister have to do with any of this? Davin shifted in his seat.

"Tristan speaks quite favorably of you, young man. You know this, I'm sure."

Davin glanced to his friend expecting his familiar smirk, but Tristan sat with stiffness and was devoid of his typical élan.

"Well, it's true. Tristan believes the world of you. Has my son shared with you . . . our issue?"

Davin sought some explanation from Tristan's expression, but there were no clues on his friend's face. Tristan had been unusually vague about the purpose of this meeting. What had he gotten them into?

Alton pushed back from his chair and walked over to the window, his arms clasped behind his back. "Tristan says you are a shrewd investor."

"I've done well, yes." Davin couldn't help but notice the richness in decor of the office. "But perhaps not by your standards."

The man spun around. "Standards? Never judge yourself by another man. That's what the poor do. You make your own standards. You should never apologize for your success, for every part of it has been hard wrought." The sunlight came through the window in a way where half of his face was brightly illuminated. "Gold, right?"

"Yes . . . sir."

"I envy you, boy. You know that?"

"No, sir."

"Take my son here. Despite what he tells you, he doesn't know anything about innovation or a decent day's labor." Alton came over and patted Tristan on the shoulder.

Davin didn't like seeing his friend humiliated. It returned difficult memories of how Seamus was taunted by his father many years ago when they were growing up in Ireland. His first instinct was to defend Tristan, but strangely, he was enjoying his friend's vulnerability at this moment. It suddenly made him much more likeable.

Alton reached over to where a globe sat on the corner table and held it up to the light. "Work is what happens when the sword of failure is looming over your head. When you can sense the sharpness of the blade. When you know your mistakes could cost everything you have. My son here has lived under the umbrella of my patronage. His mother wishes it to be that way, and so it is. But you. You know what it's like to be under the sword. To be on the lowest rungs of society and then to rise above it all."

He gave the globe a spin. "Not even I have experienced where you've been, boy. My father gave me a start, much as I've given Tristan. And his father before him. So what's left for us? To sustain? To preserve the wealth for future generations to follow? For my son here?" Alton put the globe back in its place. "No. If we lose our taste of the hunt, we become consumed by the prey. Once the blade gets dull and the sword is no longer a threat, we become toothless, domesticated, unable to survive the wild."

Alton plopped back in his chair and sighed. "So how did it feel?"

"I'm sorry, sir?" Davin was still trying to figure out why Alton had mentioned his sister. He glanced back to see that the hulking man had put his knife away and was now eyeballing him with his arms crossed.

"To become wealthy after having nothing." Alton clenched his fist. "To pull the gold from the ground with your bare hands, like a carrot."

"I suppose . . . it was pleasurable."

Alton wagged his finger. "Uh-uh-uh. Try again. This time, really think of how it felt."

Davin swallowed. He thought back to the excitement he experienced when he first struck gold. And what the feeling was when he went to the next claim and found more. Then again when he met Tristan and they launched the hydraulic mine.

"You got it, boy!" Alton's eyes widened. "I saw it on your face. Go ahead and tell me. Put it to words."

"I was just thinking, of my times of discovering gold." Davin struggled to read this man. Should he answer plainly?

Alton leaned forward and the chair groaned. "Yes?"

"Well, sir. It seemed no sooner had I placed the gold in my hand that . . ."

"Yes?"

"That I began thinking of ways to get more."

Alton slapped his hand on the desk. "It's insatiable. And we need more and more."

Did he really believe this? Davin wondered if he was describing himself, or what he feared he would become? Was this what drove him away from Seamus? Was he being cruel because he wanted Seamus to leave him alone? His gaze met Alton's. "You mean, that drive, it never goes away?"

"It's how we know we're alive." Alton shook his head and laughed. "I like this boy. I really do."

"I told you that you would, Father." Tristan lowered his eyes.

"You were right, son. He is worth preserving. And investing in."

Davin moved stiffly. "Sir?"

"Oh. Didn't Tristan tell you?" He wrinkled his brow.

"Uh . . . no, Father. I thought it best if he heard it from you."

Alton leaned back in his chair. "I had expectations that . . . Well, you can tell him now."

Tristan turned to Davin. "You've been selected."

"What?"

"It's a terrible war, boy." Alton's eyes were upon him as talons once again. "The battlefield has been unkind to your Irish brethren. I'm certain you know that the casualties have mounted . . . and been so unfairly doled out."

"Selected?" Davin's head began to feel light.

"Your name," Tristan said. "You are set to be drafted."

"How would you . . . ?"

Alton laughed. "I own this town. The senators, the aldermen. I merely asked who was on the list. There is great power in that, you know. Have you any idea what people would do to have their names taken off the list?"

"I don't understand." Was it true? Was Davin going to war?

"Don't worry." Tristan looked to his father as if confirming it was all right to continue, which Alton answered with a nod. "We have a substitute in place for you."

"A . . . substitute?"

"Yes," Alton cackled. "That's how it works. There are those who die on the front line in the name of freedom . . . and those who live to prosper from it."

"It's been arranged," Tristan said. "You'll meet him tomorrow."

Davin didn't understand entirely what was being said but sensed he was indebted for it nonetheless. "Well . . . thank you, sir."

"Oh." Alton wagged his finger again. "We don't bother with gratitude. That's the currency of the impoverished."

"Then what—?"

Alton looked toward his son.

Tristan cleared his throat. "It's your brother. Well, not your brother, but your sister's husband."

"Andrew?" Davin gripped the arms of his chair. "What does he have to do with this?"

"It's all right, boy." Alton held up his hand. "We just want to share some information with you."

"What would that be?"

"Do you know the trouble they are facing?" Alton tapped his hand on the desk.

"At the *Daily*? Yes. I mean I know they are going through hard times."

"Hard times don't explain it sufficiently. They are about to fold. And it's a shame. Not a bad paper at all. And your sister is a fine journalist."

"I still don't know . . ."

"Andrew is a proud man." The words came out Alton's mouth with measure. "He needs a friend in times like these. Are you able to be that friend?"

Davin was growing more confused. First he learned he was scheduled to be drafted into Lincoln's army, and now he was discovering that Clare and Andrew were in a dire situation. But how could he assist them? They already refused his offers to help.

"I have a solution for them. One that will bring all of their advertisers back to them. For as easily as they left, they can return once again."

"And what would that solution be?"

Alton nodded and the large man walked over and opened the door. "You'll know when to speak up. You'll even know what to say. I'm confident of that as you are obviously a bright young man." Alton stood and reached across his desk and shook Davin's hand with a soft, fleshy one.

Then Alton looked to his son who stood along with Davin. "And the substitute?"

"Tomorrow." Tristan turned to Davin. "I'll let you know what you need to do."

Davin wanted to say something, to ask more questions, but he felt swept down the currents, drowning in his own indecision. So many thoughts swirled around his head, but one was paramount.

He didn't want to go to war.

"Thank you, sir." Davin left with Tristan. What dark contract had he just signed?

Chapter 23

THE SUBSTITUTE

The tapping on the door startled Davin, causing his pulse to pound.

He had been sitting in a chair reading *David Copperfield* under the lantern light of his studio. He should have been better prepared. "One moment."

Davin scurried around and picked up a few stray items of clothing and tucked them in his drawers. Living alone was a luxury few enjoyed in Manhattan, especially at his age. He was so far removed from those days when he and four of his siblings shared the same straw mattress in Ireland.

He walked over to the door, turned the brass handle, and opened it to the face of a frightened teenage boy. He was slender, with blue eyes and light red hair under a moth-worn wool cap. On the side of his cheek, difficult to see in the limited light, was a blotch of pink, a marking he most probably carried since birth.

Behind him stood a stocky, large-breasted woman, tightly wound in her black coat and scowl. She gave the boy a firm push, and the two entered the room with the woman appearing to discern as much as she could about Davin from his living arrangements, which made him feel somewhat exposed.

"I wasn't aware you were going to bring . . ." Davin spoke to the boy but watched the woman as one would a thief.

She spun and curled her face into a frown. "What? You aren't believing a mother would want to look in the eyes of the man sending her precious child off to war? Have you been reading what they've been doing to the Irish lads? Sending them in like fodder, they are. It's a plain horror, it is. Some Irish kings will be clawing their ways up out of their graves for what they've been seeing. No. Raised this one up since he was a sprout of green popping his head above the soil. A poor way to feed my family, it 'tis."

"Are you saying you don't want to go ahead with this?" Davin just wanted them both to leave.

"What? And let the rest of me little ones starve? Begging on the streets. No, William here is a hero. Taking his family's burden on his shoulders." She glanced toward the door where her son seemed to be cowering against the wall. "Well, William. Say something, child."

He lowered his eyes to ground and tucked his hands in his back pockets. "Name's Billy," he said in a whispery voice.

"Pleasure, Billy." Davin pointed to the couch, just large enough to fit two. "Did you want to sit down some?"

"We won't be long," the woman responded. "Just here to complete our affairs."

"Oh yes. Of course. It was a thousand dollars, yes? That was the agreed-upon price?" Davin wanted this all to be over as soon as possible.

"A thousand dollars for a child's life." The woman closed her eyes and shook her head. "Dear Lord, please forgive me for I know not what I do."

Davin looked over to Billy, who seemed barely sturdy enough to lift a musket over his shoulder, let alone use it as a weapon. "Is that right?"

Billy shrugged and glanced at his mother.

"A fine amount . . . if he was cattle being sold on the market." The woman blew a strand of hair hanging in her face. "A thousand dollars. Do you have it in cash?"

"Yes. Yes, I do." Davin went over to the mantelpiece and then paused a moment. He felt uncomfortable having this much money in the house. Tristan had brought it over earlier in the day. Davin gave the mother and son a questioning glance, and then he moved to the coatrack and pulled down his jacket, fumbling around to find the inside pocket. For a moment he thought the envelope was missing. But then with some relief, his fingers discovered it. "Would you like to count it?"

"Wouldn't you if it was your child? If it was in exchange for your boy's life?" She grabbed the envelope from his hand and pulled out the bills. Then she went to the corner table where Davin had a lantern and began the tedious process. She would lick her fingers, peel off a bill, move her lips in counting, and then stack it neatly in a pile, taking time to tuck the edges together. When she was finished, she nodded at her son. "It's all here, William."

"All right, Mother." He stepped forward to Davin and held out a hand.

Davin took it and shook it firmly. Was he truly sending this poor boy to his tomb? Then he remembered the instructions Tristan had given him earlier in the day. "Here, I'll need you to sign something for me." He pointed toward the envelope he had given the woman and she pulled out the letter and opened it, eyeing it suspiciously. "Neither of us can read."

"Oh, don't worry. It's the usual language. It just confirms our arrangements. I need to turn that into the draft officers." Davin went to his desk against the wall and lowered the flap, which folded down into a flat surface. He pulled out a pen and dabbed the silver tip into ink and held it out to Billy, who shifted uncomfortably.

"Well, go ahead, son." The woman gave him a nod. "It's not like we have any other choices."

Billy moved over and took the pen from Davin, then with a shaking hand signed an X at the bottom of the page.

Shame oozed from Davin's pores. What had become of him? As a boy he would have considered this all to be adventure. Now as a favored member of society, had he become a coward? Or was what Tristan had said true? That patriotism was best expressed when the greatest contributors to the well-being of the city continued on their path for prosperity. As he said, this was the only way to preserve this ailing country's wealth and standing among other nations.

Still, whatever explanation Tristan had fashioned, it wasn't settling well with Davin.

Billy handed him the pen and gave him a mournful nod. "Don't worry."

"I'm sorry?"

The boy smiled nervously. "I'll serve well . . . in your stead."

The woman glared at Davin and folded up the envelope, then jammed it down her cleavage. "Remember the name William Walsh. That's the brave young man who's risking his life for you. My boy. Let's go, son. He didn't pay us for a clear conscience."

The two of them strode out the door and Davin pressed it shut behind them. He leaned back against it and listened as the sound of their feet faded.

He suddenly felt warm and nauseated. Davin moved over to the marble water basin in front of the mirror. He cupped his hands in the bowl and then splashed the liquid against his face.

As the moisture dripped down, he stared for a long time, hoping to see the man he once was.

Chapter 24

BRIGHT FLASHES

FREDERICKSBURG, VIRGINIA
December 1862

 The explosions around Muriel were so loud and brilliant that Caitlin seemed to struggle breathing.

"You've got to keep it together." Muriel gripped her friend by the shoulders and peered deep into her eyes. But even she was getting rattled by the proximity of the blasts. She was supposed to be safe from all of this artillery fire, but it was not the rebels to blame. It was the incompetence of the Yankee commanders. Why wouldn't they cover their flank?

"What are you doing, girl?" Nurse Hollins, a woman with a slight hunch to her back but otherwise built of steel, glared down at Caitlin. She handed Caitlin towels that were red and soaked.

"Bring us some fresh ones and hurry. These boys are dying as you're standing there."

Muriel reached out and grabbed them. "She is having a hard time of it. I'll go with her."

"Then hurry along. You're needed with the doctors." Nurse Hollins gave Caitlin a dismissive shake of her head.

With her arm around Caitlin, Muriel escorted her to the boiling cauldrons. Arms stirred the wooden paddles in a frenzy. They were washing the clothing as fast as they could, but the pile of soiled linen was steeped high on the dirt. Muriel tossed the clothes in her hand onto the pile, then scurried Caitlin out of sight behind the supply tent.

Caitlin slid to the ground and cried openly, although her wails were muted against the background of artillery bursting around her as well as the screams of dying, desperate men.

"Caitlin?"

It was as if the world's madness was pounding in Muriel's head. And who wouldn't be affected by the visions of twisted, contorted men, breathing their last as blood spurted around them? The odor of death crawled through Muriel's consciousness like black, billowy smoke through her nostrils.

"Caitlin?"

"Muriel?"

"Yes. We need to go, dear." A bright light and a loud concussion erupted. Muriel flinched but then focused on Caitlin again, mustering strength and calm in the midst of their hellish environ.

"Muriel?"

"Yes. I'm right here. We need to go. The Confederate boys are breaking through. It's no longer safe here. They are evacuating the hospital tents."

"How?" Caitlin struggled to her feet, then staggered. She looked at Muriel. "How . . . how do you do it? Do this?"

Muriel guided her around the tent. "Come on, Caitlin. You've done what you can."

They entered into a flurry of men running in fear, horses limping with gashes in their loins, and gurneys being carried between jogging soldiers. And again the flashes and the screams. "Aren't we . . . winning?"

"No," Muriel shouted above the noise. "The Irish Battalion is being slaughtered. It's quite terrible."

Caitlin tried to pull free of Muriel's arm. "Then we should go . . . help them."

"Quiet, Cait. You are done for this battle."

Nurse Hollins scurried up to them. "Is she injured?"

"She is fine, ma'am." Muriel reshifted her arm around Caitlin.

"Then we'll need you back up front, Muriel." Nurse Hollins lifted Caitlin's chin. "Poor child. She isn't made for all of this. But then, who is?"

Suddenly a loud whirring was heard, and out of the corner of her vision Muriel saw something fly into the hospital tent beside them. And in a violent percussive burst of sound and light and hurling dirt, it vanished before her. Muriel pulled Caitlin into the tall weeds and they ran and tripped and rose again for several minutes.

A blur of screams and panic surrounded them, then a large shadow was upon them and she spun to see a Union cavalry officer with the stripes of a captain.

"What are you doing here?" His unshaven face was spattered with blood and, though handsome, was gnarled with the horror of war.

Muriel glanced around. In the madness of the moment, they had actually made their way closer to the battle's front lines. Now along with the sounds of the rebel yell and the anguish of the defeated and fallen, there was the whirring of musket balls flying around them.

Muriel pulled Caitlin to the ground and they tumbled into a thorny brush.

The captain's horse was anxious, and he fought to hold it steady with the reins. He reached a gloved hand out to them. "Come, I need to take you out of here."

Yet before he barely extended his arm, a horrible thud sounded. His eyes widened and he toppled over, his steed scurrying away.

Muriel crawled over to the soldier and lifted his head. A round hole dented his forehead and blood oozed out.

Caitlin collapsed to the ground. "I . . . can't . . . do this anymore."

Muriel crawled back. "I know, Caitlin. We need to get you away from this." She lifted her head and glanced around, gathering her bearings. Then she paused and her mouth opened. "I can't believe it."

"What?"

"It's the 69th. They are rushing the hill again. I swear it's the tenth time."

"The Irish boys?" Caitlin struggled to push herself up.

"See the green flag in the distance? They are making a run. Bless their dying hearts." Muriel shook her head. "What fools are these generals anyway?"

A soldier's voice rose above the brutal cacophony. "Please. Please somebody help me." It carried the familiar twangs of the South.

"Are we among the enemy?" Caitlin lay flat. "We'll be captured."

Muriel's muscles tightened. "Stay here."

Now Caitlin was grabbing her arm. "No! I won't let you go."

"Please. I beg you. I see you ladies."

"I won't let him die." Muriel yanked her arm free and crawled away, leaving Caitlin alone.

After flattening herself with each whistle of a musket ball, Muriel finally made it over to the rebel soldier, who looked no older than sixteen. His eyes were open, but she could tell by the gasping of his breaths he was almost gone.

"He doesn't look evil." It was Caitlin standing and peering down. "He just looks like a boy."

Muriel yanked her to the ground.

"He's a Confederate," Caitlin said.

"They bleed out all the same."

Caitlin lifted the canteen from the boy's side, unscrewed the cap, and then hoisted it to his lips. He smiled briefly, then his eyes closed and his body settled, the last gasps of life seeping from it.

Muriel folded the soldier's arms over his chest and nodded as if to say a prayer.

Then as the sounds of the battle rose fiercer around them, Muriel looked to Caitlin and spoke with firmness. "We need to get you back. Now."

"Yes," Caitlin whispered.

Muriel knew this would be Caitlin's last battle. She would see to it herself. It was time for her friend to go home.

The thought of being separated from the one person Muriel cared for and loved in the world was painful. But it was for the best.

From here on out, she would be friends to no one. There would be no more confusion. No more questioning her decisions.

It would be easier that way.

Chapter 25

EMANCIPATION

MANHATTAN, NEW YORK
January 1863

 "Oh, Andrew, what wondrous news have I!" Clare walked up to her husband standing next to a pair of legs protruding from under the eight-cylinder steam press, with a scattering of wrenches and bolts on the cold ground.

"Where are the children?" Andrew's face was splattered with ink and bore that look of exasperation that was increasingly becoming more of a standard part of his expression.

"Cassie is watching them. I just couldn't wait . . ." She saw the disappointment in his eyes. "What is it?"

Andrew cleaned his hands on a cloth and clenched his jaw. "Mr. Lincoln has issued his Emancipation Proclamation, and we will be the only newspaper in America that won't be able to proclaim it ourselves."

"He has? He went through with it? How did Abe ever get the votes?" Clare thought through the ramifications of what she just heard. This would change everything. It would alter the entire tone and purpose of the war. "How marvelous!"

"Yes. Just fantastic." Andrew slapped his hand on the machine, which ten years earlier had been the envy of most of the other newspapers in town. "Anything, Owen?"

This was met with a groan and the clanking of tools from below.

Clare's mind spun with urgency. "Well . . . then I should get my notes together for the story. I'll need to get a response from the mayor and—"

"Clare." Andrew even had ink spatter on his glasses. "You don't understand. There will be no story. We're finished."

Clare's initial excitement drained, and now all she could feel was empathy for him. How could anyone work harder and with such few rewards for his labor? "Oh, dear Andrew, I am so sorry." She put her hand on his cheek and her fingertips blackened with ink.

Suddenly there was a noise from the old press, and it struggled to grind forward. After a couple of false starts, it began to churn and then the cylinders spun steadily.

"Owen!" Andrew slapped the legs beside him. "You did it, my sweet boy. Come out here so I can kiss you on the lips."

The man rolled out from under the press and crawled up to his feet, adjusting his cap, his brown curls flowing from under it. He ignored the celebrations and attended to his patient with all of his focus, reaching down and adjusting levers and tightening bolts. Then he stood back up and rubbed his chin. "I wish she was doing better." Owen always spoke of the press as a captain would of his ship. "I may have earned us a few days. Maybe a week. If we don't get those parts changed, we'll be down for good."

Andrew let out a deep sigh. "Well, at least the papers will print for another day." He turned to Clare. "I suppose we'll be in need of that story after all. Should I assign it to someone else? It's going to be a late evening."

"You'll do so at your own peril." Clare gave the press a pat. "This is the story this old fellow was born to print."

Some muffled shouts sounded from the front of the building, and Clare looked up toward the front hallway to see a group of men making their way toward them in a huff.

"Just what we needed." Andrew wiped sweat from his fore-head, and it only managed to streak the ink further. "That's Tammany Hall folk. Boss Tweed must be sending his lackeys."

"Here to offer a few editorial suggestions, to be certain." Owen turned to Andrew. "Now before you swing back, I need to remind you how dearly we need those new parts. Try to tread softly, will you?"

The men marched up to Andrew looking like street thugs dressed in business attire.

"Mr. Sweeney," Andrew said with a forced flourish. "To what shall we owe this great pleasure?"

The man, his face peppered with black and gray stubble, had a pub-reddened nose. He gave a cursory nod and lifted his hat. "Just a courtesy visit, Mr. Royce. 'Tis all. Do we have somewheres to speak? Perhaps a wee bit more private."

"What you have to say can certainly be said before Clare and Owen." Andrew had the appearance of an Indian chieftain, with the ink streaked like war paint. He glared down at the other two men, who seemed less committed to this confrontation than their leader, whose green top hat matched the color of his jacket and vest. "Speak freely."

Mr. Sweeney curled a smile, more a weapon of confidence than an expression of joy. "Oh, Mr. Royce, I do intend to do that. I do." He tucked his hat under his arm. "And I pray you'll offer a more . . . tender ear to our words this time. We Irishmen take great issue with your man in Washington, as we were accustomed to oppression in our fair homeland but won't tolerate it none here. Now, I know we've had a fair disagreement here or there in the past. But as a courtesy to your dear father Charles, may he rest in peace, I must warn you of the great displeasure spreading through the Five Points."

He turned to Clare. "Now, dear lady, I am pleased you are hearing this as well. Because there is uncertainty about you among your people. Are you for us or against us? For now is the moment to choose your side and do so wisely as we intend to battle fiercely over this."

Clare clenched her teeth. "Thank you, sir. Yes. The *New York Daily* will always be a devoted friend of the Irish. As it will with all people who are being oppressed by the cruelties of these times."

He cringed. "Yes, and surely after the bloodletting of Fredericksburg, with our brave Irish lads thrown to body heaps like rubbish—"

"Yes, Mr. Sweeney, of which we reported with great earnest."

"Indeed, Mrs. Royce. Yet perhaps not with the zeal of one wishing an end to this godforsaken, purposeless war."

Clare knew arguing with people like Mr. Sweeney served little purpose but continued against her greater wisdom. "Well now, you have read enough of my words to know there is a cause that is worth both fighting and dying for."

"I don't see where this is leading to a proper resolution." Owen stepped forward and gave Clare a subtle nudge.

Mr. Sweeney pushed Owen aside and the men next to him stiffened. "And dying might be what happens if this . . . this newspaper continues to take the side of the Negroes against its own people." He glared at Owen. "You should be ashamed of yourself, a man of Derry like you, boy." He pointed to Andrew and spittle came from his mouth. "I can see this Englishman treating us like such, but you, sir, ought to be boiled in ink."

Andrew's eyes narrowed and his frame stiffened. Clare knew

he wasn't bothered at all by what the man said about him, but he would not stand by as she was being insulted. What had she started? The last thing the *Daily* needed was to be in yet another skirmish.

"Was that a threat I heard?" Andrew guided Owen back with his arm.

"You most certainly did." Mr. Sweeney dusted his hands together. "I came here with good intentions, but I leave in the foulest of tempers. I will report back to Tammany Hall that their recommendation of banning all merchants from tossing a penny at this . . . paper, should be taken fully to heart." He stepped forward. "I only came here in kindness to your old man, Andrew. You have disgraced him. We'll be dancing the day your doors are closed for good, and it will be soon I can tell you that. Good day."

With that he spun, the tails of his coat flying, and just as they entered, the entourage marched their way out of the office, the anticipated slam of the door not disappointing.

The three of them stood silent. Clare realized they weren't alone as a dozen or so of the newspaper's staff had made their way from their desks and were staring blankly at them.

"It's all right, everyone." Andrew spoke with a loud voice to those nearby and those leaning down over the upper balcony. "The press is back up and it will need to be fed with compelling stories. Today is a historic day for our country, and the *Daily* will tell it with a full and unfettered voice."

With some grumbling and shaking of heads, the employees retreated to their desks and Clare eyed Andrew with admiration. How did he remain so composed with the fires of dismay raging around him?

Owen was wiping his hands with a cloth, and then he tossed it to Andrew. "That was a fine speech, boss. But I suppose now that we've lost the last of our Irish merchants, you've got other plans for us to pay our people. That's not to mention ye ol' press there. It isn't going to heal itself."

Andrew sighed. "That's the good thing about this being God's newspaper. He'll be the one to fix it, because it's certainly beyond my doing."

"You believe that, don't you?" Owen scratched his chin. "You do know how much this paper means to me?"

"I do." Andrew patted Owen on the shoulder. "Some days I believe it matters more to you than me. Now. Go make sure that drum is going to spin. I'm going to share some encouraging words with my reporter here, and we're going to make some news."

Owen nodded and headed back to the press, leaving Andrew and Clare alone.

"What are we going to do?" Clare took the cloth from his hands, removed his glasses, and started to rub away the ink from his face.

"I'm a mess, aren't I?" He smiled at her.

"You have never appeared more handsome." She dabbed at his cheek. "Andrew?"

"Yes?"

"Have you thought about speaking to Davin?"

Andrew jerked his head back. "What about?"

Why wasn't this clear to him? They had spoken about this on several occasions. "You know. About my brother helping us out."

He relaxed his shoulders. "Oh. That again. Let me ask you a question. What about your Cyrus Fields and his grand scheme for his precious cable? How many times has he offered you, his most fervent supporter, a stake in his company?"

Clare poked the cloth on his nose. "That's hardly a comparison as Cyrus's stock isn't worth much as it is. And you know why I would never accept it anyway. But Davin is different. He has the means to help us and he is family as well. And it so happens he's been quite successful, which is no crime."

Something changed in Andrew's expression. Was it shame? Had she insulted her husband by talking about Davin's wealth?

"Why, Andrew, he could solve all of our problems and without causing himself much discomfort at all."

Clare wiped his forehead, which now seemed wrinkled with worry again. She was not comfortable questioning her husband's integrity, but was Andrew's pride getting in the way of doing what was best for their family? Maybe it was time for her to make a stand. Perhaps her brother could offer more than mere funding. Would Andrew be able to humble himself enough to get some counseling on how best to conduct his business?

"Clare?"

"Yes?"

"Remember when you first showed up today?"

"Uh . . . huh."

"You had good news."

She paused. Was he trying to change the topic of their discussion? "Oh yes! I did have good news."

He took the towel from her hand. "I could certainly use some of that right now."

"It's wonderful. I received a letter from Caitlin today. She's coming home."

Andrew's face tightened. "She's not hurt?"

"Oh no. Well, perhaps. She said Fredericksburg was all she could handle. Muriel supposedly is doing just fine. Caitlin described her as a war hero. But isn't it glorious? Caitlin is coming home."

He nodded, his gaze drifting.

"She can help us here. Have you read what she wrote on behalf of the Sanitary Commission? It's really quite strong. I believe with a bit of mentoring she could do well."

"That does please me." Andrew held her hands.

"It's just, I so need my family to be safe. To survive through all of this. If something would happen, I would never forgive myself for bringing them from Ireland . . . to . . . well, all of this."

She looked to Andrew for affirmation, but all Clare could see was sadness. There was something he wasn't telling her.

"Andrew. What is it?"

He gripped her hands. "We better let Cassie know you'll be late tonight. Bless her for all of the help she provides."

Andrew made his way to the staircase and sauntered up slowly, deep in thought.

Clare mourned this moment. Because it was the first time she ever sensed he was keeping a secret from her.

Chapter 26

THE FUNERAL

The pipes bellowed through the vast chamber darkened with grief.

They stood off at the back of the crowded St. Patrick's Cathedral as the somber notes of Mozart's Requiem rose from the symphony at the front of the majestic building. Davin, who had never ventured into this sanctuary before, was awed by the architecture, with its vaulted domed ceilings. As he thought about it, he couldn't remember the last time he was in any church.

In the midst of the thousand or so who wore black and veils and cried openly was General Meagher himself, the leader of the 69th Irish battalion. Despite the sad purpose of their gathering, Davin felt strangely drawn to his fellow countrymen, and it reminded him of the wakes of his youth.

It was difficult to see from their distant vantage point, but the archbishop of New York was presiding over what appeared to be a large coffin, meant to represent the many Irish soldiers who had fallen in the Civil War. The last battle in Fredericksburg had nearly wiped out the Irish Battalions, and this requiem was as much a political statement as a chance to mourn.

Although they were being hailed as the bravest of the soldiers fighting for the North, the presiding sentiment was that the Irish were merely the most expendable.

Davin leaned into Andrew and whispered, "Should we be finding a place to sit?"

Andrew raised his eyebrows. "If they knew the publisher of the *New York Daily* was here, they might be tempted to put me in that coffin up there."

"Are you going to tell me why you wanted to meet here?" Davin already knew but hoped that Andrew would just get on with it. He didn't see why there was any need for pretense. Everyone knew the *Daily* was on the cusp of collapsing.

"Do you know what a Requiem is?" Andrew's tone wasn't patronizing, but it also wasn't that of one who was about to ask for a favor.

"I have a notion." Davin would play along.

"There were seven hundred Irishmen who climbed to their deaths at Malvern Hill. With the green flag of their battalion hosted with pride."

He knew this. Why would an Englishman be giving him this lesson in history?

"They stepped over bodies. Slipped in the pools of the blood of their friends as they pressed forward."

Unease grew in Davin's stomach. Was it the dark mood of this room? Or was it the way Andrew was speaking? Maybe he shouldn't help the man at all.

"What do you think drives a man to do something like that?" Andrew's head nodded to the sway of the music. "To sacrifice everything."

"I don't know." Was there anything he believed in that profoundly? Was there anything he would die for?

"Here." Andrew reached into his jacket and pulled out what

seemed to be a few pages from the *Daily*. "We printed these today. Have you seen these?" He handed them to Davin.

"What are they?"

"Go ahead and read them yourself."

Davin unfolded the paper. What he saw was a list of names in fine print. "I don't understand."

"See if you recognize any of them. Those are the fallen of the Irish Battalions. Each of those names there represent the hopes of a mother for her son. A father for his boy. A generation lost." He reached out to take it back, but Davin withdrew it.

There was something Davin wanted to see. Yes, the names were alphabetical. He ran his finger down through the list toward the bottom. Then he saw it. The name William Walsh. His shoulders sank. His substitute was dead!

"I . . . so admire them." Andrew's eyes watched as a procession of officers made their way up to the front of the church. "I've been told by so many, that the work we've done at the newspaper is our battle, our participation in the war, but sometimes I wonder."

So this was what this was all about. The *New York Daily*. Andrew's newspaper. When was he going to just ask for the money?

But Davin found himself struggling to be angry at Andrew. Instead he was moved by the solemnity of the moment. He had a sense of belonging, a sense of purpose in this room. Was this the destiny of his people? This suffering? This dedication to causes that were hopeless? What had he done while others were risking their lives? Enjoyed the life of a prince?

And as much as he disliked the boy's mother, he grieved heavily for William Walsh. It was as if Davin had killed the boy himself.

There was indeed a profound sadness in the room, but there was something else as well. A passion. A sense of purpose. Although those gathered here could barely afford to put a bowl of soup on their family's table, they had a communion among each other. A connection. A vibrancy of life.

In contrast, Davin had emptiness. Vain pursuits. He didn't know why, but he was fighting back the urge to cry.

"Do you remember when you left us to find Seamus when you were a boy?" Andrew's voice could be heard, but now it was merely a distraction.

"I do," Andrew continued. "Your sister cried for days. Weeks. She thought she let you down."

"I should have written." Davin wanted him to just stop talking.

"Do you know what Clare's battle in life is? The one she would lay her life down for? For any of you?"

The officers had made their way to the front and they were encircling the coffin.

"What?" Davin grinded his teeth.

"Do you know?"

"Listen." Davin reached into his coat pocket and pulled out his checkbook. "I know what this is about. How much do you need? Just tell me. Any amount will do. What do you need?"

Andrew's face blanched. "What are you . . . ?"

"I know all about you, Andrew. The paper. It's failing and everyone knows this. You're right. I owe this to my sister. To your family. Just please . . . quiet yourself and tell me the amount."

Andrew's brows collapsed behind his glasses, and his confusion turned to anger. He grabbed Davin by his arm and dragged him out of view of the others, in a small alcove lit with dozens of burning candles.

"You don't know what this is about, do you?"

Davin had been startled by Andrew's abrupt actions, but there was something in his tone that was fatherly in nature. "I don't know what you're talking about."

"I don't want your money. Any of it. In fact, we couldn't accept a dime although I've been offered thousands."

There were voices in the background as the music had stopped, and echoing loudly was the beckoning of the archbishop and the sounds of the assembly rising together.

"What do you mean?" Andrew's accusatory tone was bringing Davin to a stark realization. Did he know? No. He knew nothing of his world. It was dark but hidden.

"Your Mr. Lowery."

Davin's knees began to wobble. How could he have known?

"Mr. Alton Lowery. His son, your good friend Tristan, offered thousands of dollars. More than we would ever need to mend our finances."

"What . . . what for?" Would he sink even deeper in the lie? It seemed the only way out.

"And when that didn't work, he threatened to blackmail us. Or should I say you. If we went ahead with our story, they would have you ruined and taken Clare down with you."

The music started again, a dirge deep and foreboding, and it was the perfect accompaniment to the sickness growing throughout Davin. They had said it would be impossible to get caught.

"Yes. They set you up, Davin. They listed you as the primary in their transactions. It's the only reason we haven't run the story yet. I needed to clear your name."

"What does Clare think?" Davin's childhood flashed before him. Who else was left for him to betray? He ruined his brother's ministry, laughing and mocking as the water washed him down the slope of the Sierra. But Clare? She was untouchable. Everything in his life suddenly was toppling.

"She doesn't know. Clare doesn't know any of this. Which has been nearly impossible to keep from her. But it would destroy her to learn of what you've done. Her brother, involved in the smuggling of cotton from the enemy. The very ones who are responsible for all of this." Andrew nodded toward the gathering. "Your people. You've turned on them. And your family as well."

Davin began to cry. And as he did, he expected the eyes before him to claw deeper, but instead, Andrew's expression melted to one of deep compassion, and in a moment, Davin was in his arms.

"I know who you are," Andrew whispered in his ear. "I know who you can be."

These words were even more painful to Davin because he was shaken by Andrew's grace.

"What am I to do now?" Davin stepped back and wiped his eyes, pleased to see they were still unnoticed.

"The story will run in a few days. We're going to be taking them down. As it turned out, they had the secret blessing of the United States government who needed the cotton for uniforms as well as keeping the economy healthy. But that will all be denied and there will be a great uneasiness for anyone involved here in New York."

"So you are saying I should leave town."

"Tonight if you can. I don't think it's safe for you with the Lowerys anymore. They'll think you gave them up."

"What about Clare?"

"You'll have to leave that for me to explain."

Davin reached into his pocket and pulled out his checkbook. "Then you must allow me to make this right."

Andrew held on to Davin's wrist and nudged it back. "We can't take any of your money now, Davin. We have to keep our distance. That's to protect Clare."

The words sunk in deeply. First he had disgraced Seamus and now he was about to do the same with his sister. He was ready to run. To get away from all of this. But where would he go? Back out West?

He put his hand on Andrew's shoulder. "Thank you."

"There is a better way to thank me." Andrew smiled. "Come back, Davin. To the boy you were. The man you could be. That's what your sister would give her life up for. What she's dedicated every day of her life for. Her family. If not for yourself. Do it for Clare."

Davin put his hands in his pockets. "Are you leaving? I should be going."

"I might as well cover the requiem for the paper." Andrew grabbed Davin by the arm. "This time. Make sure you write."

"I will." Davin slid away and down the hall, then opened the great doors to the light outside, which was bright enough he had to cover his hand over his eyes. What would Clare think of him when this all came out?

He moved down the steps and felt a strange bounce. There was shame he experienced. But something else as well. Relief. As if he was free of the burden he was carrying, the one he didn't even realize existed.

Tristan had been right. There was nothing illegal about what they were doing. His father had made sure they had clearance with the authorities. But in his heart and deep in his soul, Davin knew it was unethical. It wasn't who he wanted to be.

He would miss Clare. And he would even miss the city. But it would be good to get a new start. Here he was following in the steps of his older brother. It had been more than fifteen years ago when Seamus had to leave town in a hurry.

And what did his brother do? He joined the United States Army.

Davin walked past an office and was ten steps beyond when he returned and glanced at the poster in the window. It made a plead for healthy men to enlist in the 69th Irish Battalion. There was an ink drawing of a harp framed with clovers.

He laughed. It was perfect. Redemption would come swiftly, be it by glory or bullet.

Another thought came to him as well. One that surprised him. Someone else was serving the Irish boys in that regiment.

Someone who had captured Davin's imagination. But why would he be thinking of Muriel at a time like this? Was it because she was Irish and reminded him of being back home? Was it because she was a unique woman who was unflappable in this world dominated by men?

Or was there a vulnerability in her, a mysterious yearning, a search for purpose and acceptance they both shared?

Whatever the reason, her face gave him hope. She had something genuine to offer in his life that had become such a fraud. In some strange way, she offered a cleansing of his conscience.

But there was much to do before he left.

Chapter 27

RUMORS OF WAR

TAYLORSVILLE, VIRGINIA
March 1863

 The Seed Festival was one of Taylorsville's most fancied occasions. For more than thirty years, farmers from all over the neighboring valley would come to celebrate the planting season. To Ashlyn, this was always one of the highlighted events of her youth.

As she observed Grace knitting with several of the town's women, Ashlyn worried of how her daughter's childhood memories would be tarred with the fear and anxiety of war. What terrible stress this young generation had been subjected to in these difficult times!

Ashlyn walked over and admired Grace's handiwork. She had learned so much in her short time in the Shenandoah Valley and was growing up to be a fine young woman.

"That's lovely, dear." Ashlyn touched Grace's shoulder.

Grace looked to the work of the other women and grimaced. "I am so desperately slow at this. Look what they have all done in the same amount of time."

"You're well ahead of where I was at your age," Coralee said, who was sitting beside Grace.

Ashlyn grabbed a chair and sat with them, so the three were in their own small circle. "You shouldn't be so critical of yourself, Grace. You are so talented."

"It's true." Coralee winked. "It's one of the many things Anders says he appreciates about you."

"Dear Coralee." Ashlyn reached over to a small table where there was a pitcher of lemonade and poured herself a glass. "You know I don't approve of you stoking those fires."

Coralee laughed. "I am afraid the flames are burning well enough on their own. Isn't that right, young Grace?"

Her cheeks burned bright red and she held back a smile. "Have you heard from him?"

"Who?" Coralee lifted a spool of yarn from the table. "Who would that be? I am not allowed to even discuss the issue."

"Oh, Coralee, you are beyond hope." Ashlyn took a sip of the lemonade. "Ooh." She put her hand to her lips.

"Those will pucker you well." Coralee lifted her glass and took a sip herself. "Ooh wee is right. Fletch brought those in last night."

"Well?" Grace put her needles down.

Coralee took another sip. "Well . . . if I was allowed to discuss it, I would inform you that my son, the handsome Anders Fletcher, did mention you in his last letter. But since I haven't been . . ." She made a motion of zipping her lips.

Ashlyn laughed. She had fashioned a warm friendship with her meddling friend. Since Seamus had left, both Coralee and Fletch had become their caretakers. "Really, Mrs. Fletcher. Now that you have tortured my poor daughter so needlessly, you might as well complete the task."

The woman leaned forward, as if she was about to share some scandal. "Yes, then this being the case, I will tell all. Young Anders asked about the beautiful Grace several times throughout his letter."

"He did?" Grace's green eyes sparkled. "What did he ask? Please, Mrs. Fletcher, tell me everything."

Coralee put a finger to her chin. "Well now, let me recall it. Yes, he inquired as to whether you got your horse yet."

"Is that so? What else."

"And . . . he asked if we would bring some wildflowers to you on his behalf."

Ashlyn reached over and took Grace's knitting from her lap. "Let me repair a few of those loops for you. Go ahead, Mrs. Fletcher, as the banks of the river are well overflowing now."

"Then he also wondered as to why you were not writing him."

"What?" Grace's jaw dropped. She looked to her mother with accusatory brows.

Ashlyn cleared her throat. "Well, it's not unusual for letters to get delayed or lost. Mail delivery in times of war is quite suspect."

"Ma!"

She was caught. Ashlyn sighed. "I am sorry. It was terrible of me. I promise, we'll get them posted this week. All twenty of them."

"There weren't twenty." Grace lowered her head. "And that's horrible of you."

"What would your father do? That's the question I always ask of myself."

Grace shrugged. "I suppose . . . he wouldn't approve."

"Then maybe," Mrs. Fletcher interjected brightly, "we'll just let Anders correspond to you through our letters. What about Seamus? What has he written?"

The question drew pain for Ashlyn. Her husband wasn't much of a letter writer, and the couple she had received read more like a newspaper. "He seems to be doing well enough, I suppose. As well as one would expect in these circumstances."

Music started, and they looked over to see a fiddler standing on a crate jabbing his bow as a few people started to gather around him. This was about the time the wind shifted and the smell of the pig roasting filled the air.

"Do you suppose it's proper for all of us to be celebrating like this, you know with what all is going on?" Grace squinted from the sun which was shining in her direction.

"I think it's a fine thing for us to take our thoughts away from war, if only for a day." But as these words came out of her mouth, Ashlyn looked over to Callie Fernsley, who had already lost two sons in the war.

"Celebrate we must." Coralee picked up the pitcher of lemonade and refilled all of their glasses. "And soon, I believe we will have much more to cheer about."

"Oh, Coralee." Ashlyn swatted at a fly buzzing around her ear. "I wish I shared some of your optimism for the progress of this war."

"Don't believe me then. Believe Fletch, who is the worst of all pragmatists. He's heard from some dependable sources."

"You mean the smugglers and moonshiners?" Ashlyn interjected.

"Indeed. You would be surprised what a soldier will share for a nip of hooch." Coralee lowered her voice. "I hear word our General Lee is now pushing up north. With all of his victories, he's got the gumption now to give the Yanks a bit of their own measure. See how they feel with enemy boots marching on their own fields. Why if they make it up to New York, you can consider this whole conflict settled."

"I certainly wish that would be so. Anything that would bring our boys back home." Ashlyn knew better than to mention this out loud, but if the rebel army made it up to New York, it would put Seamus in a precarious situation. He would not participate in anything that might put Clare at risk. He would draw that line. As it was, it grieved him not being able to correspond with his family up north. This war was tearing apart much more than just a nation.

A banjo player and a man with spoons joined the fiddler, and now a few of the women and old men were beginning to move to the music.

A voice came from behind them. A familiar one. "May I have a dance?"

Colonel Percy Barlow, in full uniform with polished brass buttons, stood with his hand extended to Grace. She looked to Ashlyn for rescue.

Ashlyn stood to her feet and the knitting dropped onto the dirt. How had she ever been so enamored with this man? The mere sight of him now made her ill. Was he different in his youth? Had the rigors of the army turned him into a much different man? Or was it she herself who had changed?

Coralee stood as well and gripped his hand in both of hers. "Why Colonel Barlow, our own dear Percy. What brings you here? What news do you have from the front?"

He retracted his hand and fixed his gaze on Ashlyn, his eyes probing deep, as if looking for some trace of the feelings she once had for him. Then after an uncomfortable pause, he turned to Coralee. "I have just returned from Richmond and was in the company of President Davis himself."

"Ooohh my, have you really, Percy?" Coralee fluttered her hand before her face.

"There is a great mood of hope among our leadership." He returned his gaze to Ashlyn, which she avoided.

"What with all of the whipping you boys have put on them Yanks, it is no wonder the president is well pleased." Coralee clasped his hand again. "But tell me, Percy, have you truly spoke with the president? And to think I scolded you when you were knee high. Perhaps you will forgive me for this."

"As a matter of truth, I am here on behalf of President Davis. He requested I visit the people of the valley to share the president's deep gratitude."

"Well . . . well . . . Percy, I mean Colonel Barlow." Coralee's voice dripped with even more twang. "Why don't you go about spreading some of those compliments with us?"

"I will." Percy glanced around the gathering and he took advantage of the pause in the music and stood on a chair. "I am here to share encouragement with all of the farmers who are doing their part to feed our brave soldiers. President Davis wants you to know that the Shenandoah Valley, with its rich harvests provided by your labors, is one of our greatest assets in this conflict."

This was met with applause and some hoots, and then the musicians began their next song.

"Isn't that wonderful?" Coralee smiled at Grace. "Did you hear that, child? You are a war heroine."

Percy straightened and faced Grace again. "Now, would the young lady favor a dance with the colonel?"

"Oh yes, please do." Coralee stopped herself once she caught Ashlyn's glare.

Ashlyn did all she could to gather herself. "Colonel Barlow, it is most kind of you to offer my daughter a dance; however, her heart is already given to a young man in the war."

"I see." He lifted his chin. "And does your daughter know who I am? If she did, maybe she would answer the officer's request more favorably."

It wasn't just the words he was saying but the smugness in his face. All of Ashlyn's maternal instincts were about to overcome her Southern sensibility. Still, she struggled to restrain herself. Would Grace be able to recognize herself in this man's features? It would be confusing for her to know the truth. For all she could remember, Seamus was her father.

She must have understood Ashlyn's discomfort, because Coralee became an ally. "Well, Colonel Barlow, you are one of the most impressive bachelors from Taylorsville. I am quite certain you will not struggle in finding a lady over there to dance."

"Have you not yet told her?" Percy put his hand on the hilt of his sword. "Does she not have a right to know?"

"Know what?" Grace wrinkled her nose.

Ashlyn drew Grace in close to her. How would she ever be able to protect her daughter from her past? Was this a mistake to bring her back to Taylorsville? Surely, Ashlyn knew this would always be the great risk of their return.

"Has Seamus told her about me? Well?" Percy's tone began to frighten Ashlyn.

"What about my father?" Grace's body tensed.

"Why, my good Percy." Pastor Asa made his way over. "What brings you back here to Taylorsville? Have the Federals surrendered already?"

Ashlyn's shoulders relaxed as she had never confided to the pastor about Percy, but she always felt he somehow knew. She saw disappointment in Percy's eyes, as his attempts to confront her were now thwarted.

"Good afternoon, Reverend. I am afraid it is too early to declare that kind of news, but progress does seem to be leading us in that much-desired direction."

Pastor Asa put his arm around Percy's broad shoulder. "Well, son, we must have you share your good graces with the rest of the townspeople. They will be so encouraged to hear more of your exploits."

They started to walk away, and Percy looked back over his shoulder. "I will look forward to continuing my conversation soon, ladies. A fine day to you."

Realizing her daughter's gaze was upon her, Ashlyn forced a smile.

"What did he mean by all of that?" Grace was too smart and sensitive to let Percy's intentions go unnoticed.

Ashlyn squared Grace's shoulders to her and then brushed back her daughter's light brown hair. "There are some people you must avoid. That man is one of them."

"What was he saying about Father?"

Coralee leaned in and whispered, "I never liked that man, even when he was a boy." She glanced with apology at Ashlyn. "No offense to you, dear. We all dallied with foolishness in our youth."

This brought another curious glance from Grace. Poor Coralee couldn't keep from tripping over her own tongue, but she meant well. "Just pay the man no heed, Gracie," Ashlyn said. "Do you understand?"

She nodded, but Ashlyn could see her curiosity was still simmering.

Pastor Asa's ruse had worked well. Percy was surrounded by many well-wishers and seemed to be enjoying all of the attention.

"We should go home now." Ashlyn lifted her daughter's knitting from the ground and dusted it off.

"Yes, Ma."

"Good day, Mrs. Fletcher. Please give your husband our regards, and thank him for the turnips."

Then the two of them scurried away, able to depart without much notice. After they had walked down the pathway, Ashlyn ventured a glance back. Percy had freed himself from his admirers and was watching the two of them make their way home.

She pressed Grace on the back. "Let's hurry a bit."

Clare looked back again and he was gone, and a terrible thought came to Ashlyn that brought her shame.

She hoped Percy would not make it back from the war.

Chapter 28

ST. PATRICK'S DAY

STAFFORD COUNTY, VIRGINIA
March 17, 1863

The screams and shouts saturated the camp of the Army of the Potomac.

Davin stepped on a table to try to get himself a better view of the surreal revelry. It was hard to believe he was in a war at all. After two months of enlistment, this was the closest he had come to battle and never had he imagined such quantities of champagne and whiskey punch would be distributed so freely to the soldiers.

Thousands of men, many of them boys, formed a wall around the makeshift steeplechase course, fists raised with wagers, and arms and voices urging along their favorites. Davin could barely venture a view above the flailing of the crowd, but in the distance he saw horses and riders from the cavalry toeing up to a starting line.

This crude competition participated by the finest of the Union's cavalry was ordered by new commanding officer General Joseph Hooker. This, along with heavy libations, a grand feast, and several other planned activities was all part of a St. Patrick's Day celebration aimed at lifting the tilting morale of the troops.

The North had strung together a few demoralizing losses and the Irish Battalions, although credited with exceptional bravery, had been hard hit with casualties during recent battles. So it seemed a slice of unorthodox brilliance to host an event that could salve so many wounds. Certainly, none of the soldiers were complaining, least among them the lads from Dublin and Cork.

Except perhaps for Davin, who wanted to get started with his penance. He figured he could start relieving his guilt in the throes of battle and was anxious to hear the sounds of angry gunfire.

But on a day like this one, even someone with a burden as heavy as Davin's could forget his problems. That and a cheerful friend like Private Barry Magee, who worked his way up beside Davin on the table.

"Can you believe all of this, Davey boy?" Barry always spoke with a melody. "Why if this isn't Bobby Lee's most brilliant plan, getting all of these boys liquored up and dumb. I imagine the rebs will be popping out of the trees soon enough."

"I believe you may be right, my friend." Davin stepped on his toes to try to get a better view. "Ol' General Hooker has done lost his senses."

"Well, if he has, don't help him find them none because I haven't eaten this proper since my great-aunt's wake."

A gun sounded and a dozen or so horses surged down the nearly oval track, their hooves pounding against the turf in a fury.

"Which one is yours?" Barry asked.

"Huh?" Davin's gaze was tracing through the crowd.

"Which of them mares? Who'd you wager on? Goodness, Davey, it beats betting on bedbugs for a change."

Davin glanced at the horses that were taking turns clearing the first hurdle. "Uh . . . the brown one."

"What? That's no use. They're all brown." He patted Davin on the chest. "It's that girl of yours again, isn't it?"

The last of the horses and its rider barely managed to clear the log it was jumping and stumbled awkwardly, which resulted in gasps, shouts, and drunken mockery.

"What?" Davin resumed his search.

"The Irish girl. The one in the infirmary. You think we don't all know about this nurse?"

"You mean Muriel? Ah . . . she's just a friend I knew from back in the city. She used to watch my sister's kids. A nanny."

"Oh, is that so? Well then, you wouldn't mind me giving her some affection then, will you?"

Davin shot a glare at his friend but realized he had been trapped into revealing himself. "All right, then. I like her some. But don't breathe a word of it because those Sanitary Commission ladies will send her on her way."

"Yes, yes, Davey Boy. And what does the little nursie say about her brave soldier, the one who hasn't even caught a whiff of gunpowder?"

"She's trying to keep her distance, it seems. Doesn't want to risk getting sent home for flirting. But there's only so much you can do to resist this much charm."

"Hey, speaking of the girls, here they come again." Barry pointed to the horses approaching their second turn around the course. He cupped his hands and shouted, "Ah, that's me boy Collins, race 'til she drops."

Even with the roaring of the crowds, the pounding hooves rose above the clamor, and the ground itself seemed to rumble.

They all prepared their jump, many of them jostling against one another and even throwing fists, for these riders were not trained to be jockeys but warriors, and they ran the race as such. As the first horse arrived at the steeple, its front hooves reached out to clear the obstacle but its hoof caught, and in a moment that seemed to stretch time, it landed hard and suddenly the horse was tumbling on the ground, its desperate rider being rolled over before curling tightly to avoid being trampling by the rest of the competitors.

In normal circumstances this horrific spectacle would have hushed the crowd. Instead there were only jeers and taunts, as these soldiers were men hardened by the tyranny of war.

In a few moments, bystanders attended to the fallen rider, and a gurney emerged from the crowd, bobbing between two hefty soldiers. Right behind them, out into the grassy clearing, came Muriel in nurse clothing she seemed to always wear.

Davin lunged, as his first thought was that Muriel would be in danger from running across the course in the middle of the race. But he kept standing on the table so he could watch closely as she knelt beside the fallen jockey. Her entrance was greeted with vile taunts, hoots, and jeers from the female-deprived audience.

How difficult it must be for Muriel, and for the rest of the few women at camp, to be working in such conditions. What bravery it was on their part to serve their nation in this way! The horses had circled another lap and were approaching again.

"Hurry yourself," he shouted, although she was much too far away to hear. Then the lead horse cleared the steeple, and it landed only a few yards away from Muriel and her patient. Then another. And now a group of three.

Still, Muriel never flinched. She attended to the injured man as calmly as if it was in a quiet hospital room. Then she rose and directed the two men to roll the injured rider onto the litter. They lifted it and crossed through the field and into the crowd, which opened up to make room for them to pass.

What was it about her? Why had she so captured his fancy? And did she even know who he was? Sure, she was cordial and polite to him. But out here, he was no longer a Manhattan dandy, a well-dressed, handsome, and wealthy suitor. He was just another blur in a thousand faces. The battlefield was a great leveler between the poor and rich. If you weren't an officer, you were just another grouse.

"Where you going, young man?" Barry gave him a poke in his ribs.

Davin hopped down from the table and ran over toward where the gurney was emerging from the other side of the crowd. He shoved a few soldiers out of the way, which resulted in more than a few curses and glares before he was alongside the patient. The cavalryman's nose was bloodied and bent, but he seemed mostly unscathed beyond muddying his clothes.

"Here lads, let me give you a hand here." Davin went to grab one of the handles.

Muriel, whose focus was on her patient, glanced up twice, the second time she appeared startled when recognizing him. "I think we're fine." She gave him a sharp look of dissuasion. Then she nodded over to the medical tent where they were heading, and there standing with her arms crossed was Nurse Hilda Meldrickson scowling at him.

Davin peeled away, covering his face by pulling down the brow of his cap. Nurse Meldrickson, or "Horrible Hilda" as the men referred to her, had already pulled Davin aside a few weeks ago and chided him for spending what she termed an inordinate amount of time around the medical tents. She had figured him out, even if perhaps Muriel had not.

"Come, brother." Barry had come up to him and grabbed Davin by the elbow.

"What are you doing?"

"I am going to bring you fame and wealth."

Davin ventured a glance up and saw Muriel and her patient had disappeared into the tent, and he grieved that she was out of his sight. "What is this now?"

"We're going to get rich."

"I already am rich." Davin squared his hat on his head.

"Your gold is meaningless out here. We're going to seek real treasure."

"Is that so?" Davin followed his friend. He glanced back again. Was that why he had joined the army? To be closer to Muriel? Had he become this pathetic?

"There. They are just greasing her up now. Come, Davey boy. Time for you to distinguish yourself at last."

Davin let out a groan once he saw where he was being guided. There was a large pole buried in the ground, and a couple of men standing on ladders were using brushes to lather on some gooey substance.

"This kind of fame doesn't interest me." Davin started to dig in his heels, which only caused Barry to pull harder.

"Come now, Davey. Can you see what's at the top of the pole?"

They had managed to be among the first to arrive, but a quick look behind revealed that the steeplechase had ended and the throng was making their way back to the food and over to this location.

"It looks like currency," Davin said in an unimpressed tone.

"Yes. Fifty dollars. Which for those of us without silk breeches is a fine wage, but keep looking, there is something else as well."

The men greasing the pole had come down from their ladders and were now admiring their handiwork, adding a dollop here and there. One of the men, who was large and with stringy black hair, beckoned to them. "You lads ready to give her a shake?"

Barry stepped forward and rubbed his hands together. "You know I am." He turned to Davin. "There's fifty dollars up there . . . and fifteen days of leave."

Davin shrugged. Fifty dollars? He already had more money than he could think of spending. And fifteen days of leave? The whole purpose of enlisting was so he could be here. But the thought of his friend embarrassing himself on the greased pole was enough to make Davin watch.

Around them a circle of soldiers was forming, most of them heavily touched by drink.

Barry walked around the pole, rubbing his chin, apparently formulating a strategy. Then he touched it with his hand, pulled it back, and held his greasy palm toward Davin.

"Get on with it, you fool," came a shout from the crowd, which was met with similar jeers.

After shaking a fist at the crowd, Barry squared up to his foe, and after a few moments of contemplation, he leapt as high as he could and grasped the pole. Almost instantly, he began to slide and his boots jabbed at the pole in a desperate attempt to gain traction.

At first Barry appeared to have some success, but after getting some initial footing, he made little progress before panicking and shortly slid back down to the ground. The crowd pummeled him with boos and catcalls.

The burly man pointed toward Davin. "You're up, laddie."

Davin looked around hoping the man was pointing to someone else standing beside him. But then confirmed it by pointing to himself.

"Yes, Private. Now's your chance for freedom and fortune."

Barry was shaking the grease from his hands onto the soil. "Go ahead, Davey. I stripped her clean for you. And you're the only sober man in the entire regiment."

"Let's go, boy," the pole tender hollered. "There's plenty a waitin'."

There was a large gathering now, the faces blended together in twisted frivolity. He tried to determine if they would be most hostile if he failed miserably or didn't bother to try. They might not even let him out of the ring without lathering himself up with grease.

He gave Barry an angry elbow and then made his way to the post, which now suddenly seemed to tower far above him.

At the top of pole flapping in the wind were the dollars. For some reason, he remembered back to his time in Ireland as a boy, where he and his sister nearly starved for lack of a bowl of soup. What good Irishman wouldn't take on a herd of jealous bulls for a chance to pick a dollar from the ground? The gold definitely had spoiled him.

It was time for good sport. Time for him to be a lad again.

He raised his arms and bowed to the crowd, just as some of the boxers had done in earlier matches today. Then he focused on the pole as his greatest enemy, and the task grew in significance far beyond the dollars. What if these men cheering him actually knew what he had been doing? Importing cotton from the South? They would probably tear off his limbs. He had to start proving himself. Earn their respect.

Fortunately for Davin, he had climbed quite a few trees in California during his mining days. Barry's pathetic performance notwithstanding, surely this couldn't be that hard of a task.

He grasped the pole, began to pull himself up, and immediately understood the difficulty of this endeavor. For every three pulls upward, he would slide down two. Even if he managed to make progress, it would only be a matter of time before the fatigue of his strenuous efforts would wear him down to submission.

There would be no success. It was impossible. It was just a matter now of reducing the level of shame. He would hold on as long as he could.

But Davin became suddenly resolute and he pressed on, gaining some distance but ever so slowly. Then a slip and he was down several feet. He closed his eyes, clenched his jaw, and moved upward, despite the pain and the general discouragement of the soldiers, who no doubt feared his success would eliminate their opportunity.

"Aren't you getting tired?"

"Just let go."

"Give it up, Private."

When he had made it to within two feet of the prize, which fluttered tantalizingly in the breeze, he had tapped all of his strength and stamina. And then he made the mistake of looking down. How did he get so high? How would he ever get down?

"That's all he has, boys!"

"Pay up, friends."

Glancing down over his shoulder, he could see the drunken and shouting soldiers pointing angry fingers and colluding with bellicose laughter. Why had he fallen for the ruse of his own pride? What a foolish cage he had locked himself into.

The pain in his arms was winning the battle, and it was clearly evident there was only one way out of this predicament. He would have to let go and absorb the brutality of taunts from his fellow jeering Irishmen. But then he saw someone working her way to the front of the line. Muriel!

Why did it matter what she thought? Would she think any less of him if he failed?

Yet something other than logic prevailed, and suddenly he was rejuvenated with energy only a woman could infuse in a man's prideful spirit. He glanced upward with one last desperate hope. And before the pain or the jeers or the failure of his muscles could force him to quit, he gave a jarring lunge and his hand barely missed its target, but not the edge of the pole that cut his palm.

Once again and with all remaining fortitude, he reached up, this time clasping both the currency and the note in his fist. There was a brief moment of exaltation, buoyed by the crowd's urging, and then the realization of his folly became evident. For the very same momentum that allowed him to fill his triumphant talons caused him to lose his balance. With arms flailing and his mouth shouting, he tried to preserve his grip without success.

He changed his tact and now started to slide down the pole, but it was too late. And quite similar to the helplessness he felt when once bucked out of the saddle by an angry bronco, he headed for the cruel, hard ground.

He managed to plant one foot, but it immediately gave way and the pain streaked from his ankle to his head. He crumpled into the dirt and rolled, his face buried in the dust.

"It doesn't count if he's cryin', does it?"

"Nah, he has to give it all back."

A battle raged between the flames in his ankle and the embarrassment of the fall, and his immodesty had him struggling to his feet, just as Muriel and Barry arrived.

Barry picked up Davin's fallen hat and dusted it off, then patted his shoulder.

"Can you stand?" Muriel said, with more than just the concern of a medic.

"I should be fine enough." Davin waved to the belligerent onlookers and was shocked to see the crumbled bills and the leave notice still in his grasp. He went to plant his foot, but the agony was too great and he curled it up just like a limping dog.

"Here's a shoulder, Davey boy, give her a good lean." Barry tucked his arm around him and Muriel came along the other side, and they moved him through a pathway reluctantly surrendered by the audience.

Once they had cleared through the masses, Davin pointed to a table. "Put me down there."

"Ah, I will, my friend. But they'll be a wee charge for transport. Say, about fifty of those beauties ought to cover it. Or better, how about that fifteen-day leave? You haven't had the first bullet whistling by your ear, and you're already getting time away."

Davin sat on the edge of the table and then scooted back so his feet were up as well. Muriel rolled up the cuff of his pants and untied his boot. "I can take care of that." When was the last time he washed his feet?

Muriel slid her red, wavy hair to the side of her face out of her way. "You keep quiet, Private Hanley. You think I haven't untied a boot before?"

Barry whistled. "Now that's a fine boot there. None of these Union issue." He kicked his foot up on the table, and it looked as if the sole of the cheap leather was about to free itself from the seams.

"Why don't you get those replaced?" Davin couldn't believe they managed to stay on Barry's feet.

"Replace those?" Muriel continued to untie Davin's boots as she looked at Barry's. "Those are the good ones. Many of the boys out here are better off walking bare than trying to march with the boots they have. You should see the condition of the feet I see."

"Is it broke?" Davin winced as she pulled off his boot and then removed his sock.

She gripped his heel with one hand and slid her fingers across the swollen ankle with the other. Although the pain was present, Davin's pulse rose at the feel of her gentle touch. Just before she gave it a firm twist.

"What's that, dear woman!"

"That's it, give it a good bend, let's hear him squeal." Barry gave Davin a pound on the shoulder.

"It appears to be sound. Just a sprain, but a bad one at that." Muriel slipped the sock back on and then went to the boot. "We're better to keep this tight. That will keep the swelling from getting too big on you."

"Well, seeing as he's going to live, I'd like to give her another try on the pole there." Barry swiped off grease from his shirt and flung it to the ground. "I got to get me own leave from this place."

Davin thought of asking his friend to get a towel for him, but he was actually relieved that he would be left alone with Muriel. Was that Barry's intention? Maybe he was a better pal than he imagined. His friend made his way back to the cheering throng and then got swallowed into the mass of bodies.

"If I knew this would be what it took to get alone with you, I would have broken it a long time ago." Davin worried if this was being too forward. Something he used to not concern himself with.

She gave the boot lace a firm tie. "It's not broken. And we are not alone. In fact, we are with 40,569 other men."

"So precise."

Muriel gave his foot a gentle twist, but it was enough to get his attention.

"What was that for?"

She patted him on the nose with her finger. "That, was for being stupid enough to climb a greased pole in order to fetch a mere twenty dollars."

"It was fifty dollars. And a fifteen-day leave."

Muriel pulled out a handkerchief and began to wipe the grease from his face. As she did, he could tell she was doing it with a tenderness and affection beyond her duties.

"You are a kind nurse, dear Muriel."

"I am Dr. Muriel to you," she said smugly. "You of all these brutes should know this, Private Hanley."

"All right, Doc." He propped himself up by his elbow. "I won't slight you again."

"Why did you sign up for the 69th Battalion?"

"I'm Irish, I suppose."

"You suppose you are Irish?"

"What's with the interrogation?" Davin sat up and spun his legs around, careful not to cause pain in his ankle.

Muriel glanced around, and apparently convinced they were out of the line of sight, she sat beside him. She narrowed her eyes, watching him for a moment and then slightly curled her lips in a smile. "This isn't the only Irish regiment. Are you stalking me, Private Hanley?"

Davin was startled by her question. But then again he found himself surprised by most of what she said. "No. I am not stalking you." Something in her expression demanded honesty. "Well, perhaps my knowing you were here helped me decide between the 69th and the 88th. You know, on account of Clare and all."

She raised her brows, which were light and hard to see now that the dusk was descending upon them. "On account of Clare? I see."

Why was she making him nervous? "All right. On account of myself . . . as well. I suppose I find you interesting."

"Is that so?" She nodded. "What if I was to say I do not find you all that interesting?"

The words jabbed at Davin, but he refused to step back. "I would not believe that."

Muriel slapped him on the forearm. "So certain of yourself. And there are women who see this as charming?"

"I would say most ladies are charmed by someone who is young, handsome, and of considerable means. Isn't that attractive to you?"

"Certainly. There is value in finding a man who can pay for all of your whims and fancy." She winced and then looked toward the gathering of soldiers off in the distance. "It's just that there are 40,569 others here in camp for me to choose from. Some younger than you. Some handsomer. And many who are wealthier. So if that is all you have to offer a lady, it wouldn't seem to be enough."

He laughed. "Is that so? And what else would you be looking for in a man?"

Muriel crossed her legs and leaned back on her palms, looking up to the sky, which was beginning to reveal stars. "Well . . . let's see. So far you've described a man who only believes in himself. That would get tedious after a while, don't you think? But a man with a cause. A belief in God. A care for others around him. Now tell me, Private Hanley, does that describe you?"

It most certainly did not. Davin felt as if he had been skinned like a fish and left bare on a hot rock. "It sounds . . . as if you should have met me when I was a boy."

"You keep talking about that boy. Where did he go?"

"I don't know, but if you find him, let me know, will you?"

She tilted her head and her smile grew. "Do you think you'll find him out here on the battlefields? Is this your plan? What did he believe in? The boy."

Was she taunting him? With Muriel it was difficult to know. "That's a hard question. I suppose God as you say. And my brother, Seamus."

"And now?"

He chuckled. "The boy needs to make peace with both."

In the background, the soldiers were on the move again, some dispersing back to their tents, while others began to gather around the many large bonfires being started. Davin grieved that their time was short. He could see she was beginning to look around, probably worrying that she would get spotted by one of the older nurses.

"What about you, Muriel? What do you believe in?"

"What?" She stood and straightened her dress. "What do I believe? I believe you should buy your friend a new pair of boots."

"Boots? You can't just leave me here, wounded as I am. Don't you want to escort me back to the camp?"

"You'll be fine, soldier. It's only a sprain."

Davin stepped down gingerly. She was right. It was painful, but he would be able to walk fine. "Wait. When can I spend time with you again?"

"I am afraid that is not permitted," she said coyly. "Besides. If I was going to risk everything, the chance of getting sent home, I would do so with a man. Not a boy."

"Right." Davin stared blankly as she made her way toward the medical tents, and soon Muriel was gone, leaving him alone in the growing darkness. Davin suddenly felt chilled by the night air, especially with his clothes moist with grease.

All around him, the events of the day were winding down. Many of the soldiers were making their way back to their tents, some having to be propped up by their friends. Davin thought about going to one of the fires to warm up, but most of all he wanted to get some sleep.

He straightened out the money and the letter and tucked them neatly into his pocket, then limped on his way while trying to recall every word of their conversation.

A cause? Doesn't she realize what my cause is by now?

Chapter 29

THE OTHERS

Davin woke slowly from his deep slumbers and realized a commotion was brewing outside. The seam of his tent was breached and the reddened face and black straight-haired head of his friend Barry poked inside. "Move your lazy carcass. You better get yours quick, before they are all gone."

"What is it?" Davin rubbed his eyes.

"And I won't be waiting for you none. Not with the condition of mine being as they are." Barry shut the tent, taking the morning light with him, and his steps could be heard fading away amid the shouts and cheers of men.

Davin tossed aside his green wool blanket. Barry was right in that he didn't want to miss any of the excitement. After grabbing his trousers and holding them up, he stepped into them slowly, careful not to reinjure his left foot. Only three weeks had passed since he fell from the greased pole, yet his ankle was healing nicely. This would be a terrible time to injure it again.

209

With rumors of a battle approaching, his life depended on being healthy and strong.

In just a few moments, he was dressed and out of the tent, squinting in the sun and feeling the cool air over his body.

Men ran to and fro, many of them half dressed, and hundreds of them gathered together, encircling something that captivated their attention.

Davin made his way over to the crowd and nudged in between others until he could see what was the cause of all of this ruckus. As it became clear what it was, he started to laugh.

There as a large prey surrounded by hundreds of ravenous lions were two wagons filled and overflowing with boots, each tied together by their laces.

Standing on the end of one of the wagons was a sergeant, who had an early morning cigar in one hand and a long wooden pole in the other. He was shouting out commands and he, along with a few other soldiers assisting him with the task, seemed to be the only reason they hadn't turned into an unrestrained mob. "No fighting, boys. No elbows. There is enough for everyone and we'll be keeping this all civil, taking turns."

A young private stepped forward and then felt the brunt of the stick in his side, which caused him to clasp it with both hands.

"Not you," barked the sergeant.

The boy's face turned red. "You just said it was for everyone."

"Only if you're in the 69th." The crowd responded with loud affirmations.

"Who says I'm not Irish?" The boy raised his arm to fend off the hands jabbing at him.

"Both your mother and your father!" a voice shouted, and it was echoed with more poignant derision.

Davin felt a tug at his arm and turned to see Barry beside him, grinning to the point it seemed painful. "Can you believe all of this?" He pointed to his ragged shoes. "We've been marching in these, with a thin thread holding our shoes to our toes, and suddenly the army decides to fancy us up. I might just have to reenlist."

"And those just aren't any boots, my friend," Davin said. "Those are Angell Finches." He straightened Barry's hat for him and then turned and headed out of the crowd.

"Aren't you going to get a pair of your own, Davey boy?"

Davin lifted his foot. "I already have my own pair." After working his way through the soldiers, pressing in tighter against the sergeant's orders, he was relieved to make it out to a clearing.

Something drew his gaze over to a group of tents to his right, and then he looked a second time, now locking gazes with a startled face.

"Well . . . I'll be," he muttered to himself. How could this be? Was this some apparition? He stomped over in the direction of the young private he spotted, but the boy took off into a village of tents.

"Hold up!" Davin shouted, but to no avail. He started to run over in that direction, desperate not to lose track of his target.

There. The boy had made a turn and the chase ensued.

Davin pushed past angry men just emerging from their tents, still in long underwear and stretching their arms.

Then he nearly collided with a clothing line, with shirts flapping in the wind.

Where did he go? There! The redheaded boy glanced back with fear and was running again. And then into the mess area, where oatmeal was being served from large black cauldrons raised over wood fires.

Not wanting to lose him at this point, Davin ran as fast as he could, paying no concern for his ankle.

He bumped into a man, perhaps an officer, and coffee splattered on them both.

"Hey!" he heard echoing behind him.

Then past a row of men waiting in line. Where did he go?

There up ahead. He was heading toward the horses. And Davin could now tell, the boy had a limp, which was probably the only reason he was able to keep up with him. But that didn't stop the boy from jumping over the corral and into the herd of cavalry steed.

At this point Davin was determined. He hurdled the split-rail fence but regretted it the moment he landed when his foot buckled under him. Now he was limping heavily as well. He pressed through the horses and slapped them on their hindquarters, nearly getting kicked.

Finally he was past the last of the horses, and he climbed over the other end of the fence. Now before him was a small patch of trees. Could he be in there?

Davin took a bearing of where he was. In the scramble of the chase, he had managed to take himself to the outreaches of camp and they were alone. Had he strayed too far? Would he risk getting shot by one of his own sentries? Or those of the enemy?

Just when he was considering heading back, he decided to step into the grove of trees. He needed answers. There was a cracking of twigs. He stopped and listened.

Nothing. Silence.

It wasn't wise to press farther, and he turned around, only to see the boy who had light red hair and an off-colored birthmark on his face, glaring at him, breathing heavy with a bayonet in his hand.

"Why are you following me?"

Davin looked down at the blade and gently guided it away. "You know why."

"What do you want? You aren't going to cause no trouble, are you mister?"

"What was your name? William, right? William Walsh."

The boy shrugged. "Billy."

"William. Billy. You are supposed to be dead! You died in Fredericksburg. Your name, I read it in the newspaper."

He seemed to be measuring up Davin. His eyes narrowed, but then his cheeks relaxed and he lowered his weapon. "William Walsh did die in Fredericksburg."

"What? I don't—"

"James O'Brien survived with a leg wound. I'm Jimmy."

"You're not making sense of any of this."

"Are you going turn me in?"

"What, for being a ghost?"

The boy shook his head. "Listen, mister. I've died five times now. And my mother has made a new thousand dollars each time."

It was starting to become clear to Davin, and he was embarrassed it had taken him so long to solve the mystery. "So . . . you fake your death so you can sell yourself as a substitute again?"

"You gonna tell?"

Davin rubbed his hand through his hair. "No. I'm not going to tell. I'm going to . . ." Suddenly a great weight lifted off of his shoulders. "You have no way . . . of knowing . . . how happy I am. I thought I had killed you."

"Killed me?" The boy spat on the ground.

"Yes. When I thought you died in battle, I blamed myself."

Billy shouldered his rifle. "So you aren't going to say anything?"

"Yes . . . yes. I'm going to say, 'Thank You, God.'" He looked heavenward. "Thank you!"

"Sir?"

"Yes." Davin suddenly realized the pain in his ankle. That was foolish. But who cared? The boy was alive.

"Well . . . then, if it's fine with you, sir . . . I'm . . ." He pointed back to the camp.

"Yes, Billy. Jimmy. With my blessings. Go be alive."

The boy gave him a strange look and then turned and walked away, glancing back a couple of times.

Now satisfied he was alone, Davin put his hands over his face and he began to cry first and then sob. It was as if some great poison was draining from his body, making him feel alive again. He didn't know exactly how long he was there, but he heard a noise and quickly wiped his face dry of tears, coughing a couple of times in order to disguise his moment of emotion.

Yet walking toward him was not another soldier, but Muriel, who was not dressed in her white nursing outfit, but simple olive pants and shirt.

"Davin? Is that you?"

How could she have found him here?

"It is you." She stepped toward him, looking around briefly. He must have seemed surprised to see her because she started to offer an explanation. "I saw you running away back there at camp. Which, of course, with the condition of your ankle was not wise." She pointed behind her. "Who was that soldier?"

"Won't you get yourself in trouble being out here with me?" That was odd. If she had been following him, Muriel was coming from the wrong direction. Did she see him crying? He wiped his eyes again.

"I am allowed to take walks. In truth, I usually take them at night when I can be alone and stray outside of camp without being noticed. Accompanied only by fireflies. You know, sometimes I just need to get away from all of this." She pointed to his foot. "How is it?"

"You mean before or after I decided to leap the fence?" Davin reached down and felt his ankle. "Not my most brilliant decision."

She flipped the red hair back that had fallen down her forehead. "Well . . . we should get you back and I'll take a look at it more closely. But first, I did have a question for you."

"Oh?"

"Yes." She eyed him with curiosity. "I was wondering, how many boots can you buy for fifty dollars?"

He smiled, nodded, and they started to walk back. "I suppose quite a few."

"And . . . I wonder how much it would cost someone to purchase boots for, say, an entire regiment?"

Davin learned there was no sense being coy around Muriel. She was too smart. The only way to speak to her was plainly. "Probably all a person had."

"All?"

"Everyone needs to have a cause, right?"

"Davin?" Muriel wrinkled her lip.

What now? Was she going to get deep and mysterious again? Couldn't she just celebrate the boots for a day? "Yes?"

"I like you."

He started breathing again. "Is that so?"

"Very much." She lowered her head and spoke in a whisper. "And I know you like me as well."

Who was being presumptuous now? But she was right.

She stopped and faced him. "But I can't do this. I don't want to do this."

"We can be careful, so no one will know. For that matter, we shouldn't walk back to camp together."

"Davin. Davin. You're not hearing me. I don't want to like you." She raised her arms. "I don't want to like anyone. It's difficult to explain. And I can't explain it. But let's just say I have a serious responsibility out here, in this war, and I can't let anything or anyone allow me to be distracted. Even a charming young man."

"Don't say that." He started to reach a hand toward her face, but she pulled back.

"You don't know me. Trust me on that." She glanced around. "I don't want you to get hurt. You should find someone who . . . who can love you."

"Why must things be so difficult with you?"

"I can't risk this. Any of this. My work here is too important. Nurse Meldrickson is quite clever. In fact, it's foolish for me to tarry."

"So what if she catches you? What if you get sent home?"

"You don't understand." She kicked her foot in the dirt. "What I do here. It matters. I don't want to go home. And there isn't anyone, yourself included, who is worth the chance of this happening."

The muscles in his face tightened. Was her cause this important? Important enough to live her life alone? "I understand." Davin glanced up, unable to look directly in her eyes. "I won't bother you anymore."

"You don't need to say it that way, Davin."

He closed his eyes and shook his head. "You're right. I am sorry. These soldiers need you. It's selfish of me . . . of both of us, to let our feelings for each other get in the way."

"Then you'll understand when I tell you that we should not speak again."

"Yes."

Muriel surprised him by leaning in and kissing him on the cheek. Then she turned and scampered back toward the camp.

What was that? What did it mean? Did she speak and act in code? What a strange woman. Maybe she was right. He needed to leave her alone to her cause and he could be alone on his own journey of redemption.

The war was no place for love.

A shout rang out in the distance, and he sought to find its source somewhere in the woods. Probably just some sentries.

Then he thought of Seamus. Where was his brother? Would they face each other soon, at the point of a musket?

The banks of the Rappahannock were not far away from where he was standing. And on the other side were rebel forces. Probably tens of thousands. A breeze stirred up and he shuddered.

For some reason he knew it.

Seamus was on the other side of the river.

Chapter 30

THE PASSAGE

CHANCELLORSVILLE, VIRGINIA
CONFEDERATE CAMP
April 1863

 "How do you do it, Seamus?" Chaplain Scripps was sitting in a chair outside the hospital tent, a metal flask in his hands.

His tired and unshaven friend startled Seamus who was on his patient visitation rounds and had his head down and his hands in his black wool coat pockets to protect against the chill.

"I tried going in there. A few times." Scripps lifted the container to his lips and tilted it all of the way up, then wiped his gray whiskered chin with the back of his hand.

At first Seamus was irritated by the interruption. It was already dark and he had many more of the injured to visit. But he took a deep breath, exhaled, and then sat in the empty chair beside his friend. He had learned in his service as chaplain that his most important responsibility was availability. God did the most amazing things through him when he allowed himself to be interrupted.

"And look at you, my friend." Scripps voice drawled with both the South and the booze. "The master comes to the student for advice." He looked down at the tin in his hand. "And look at me."

"Have you seen about getting some leave?" For several months, Seamus had noted a deterioration in Scripps's ability to serve as minister, and now he was of little use to any of the men. In fact, he was becoming a detriment to the faith of those who listened to his rambling.

"Leave this? How could I ever leave any of this? This paradise?"

Seamus refrained from responding. He had learned not to fill in the silence of conversations he had with men, as it got in the way of his most important assignment, which was listening.

Scripps crossed his arms and leaned back. "I mean, you see it all. The gore. The piles of limbs. The desperate gaggle of breath fighting through pools of blood in the lungs. Looking into the faces of these boys . . . telling them everything is going to be all right when we know none of it will be. None of it." He shook his head and flung his flask onto the ground.

They sat quietly for a while, though from where they were sitting, they could hear the groans from inside the tent. Scripps covered his ears with his hands. "Can't get away, from any of this. So . . . hopeless."

"There is always hope."

"Where? Where Seamus?"

"General Lee has been—"

"What? We lose five thousand; they lose five thousand. We

step onto new blood-moistened grass and we declare victory. What for?"

Seamus wished an answer would come to mind, but he couldn't find the proper words to respond. He had long given up on determining who was right and who was wrong in this war. Seamus had seen enough atrocities on both sides to know that few would survive this war without deep scarring on their consciences. The mission had long since been buried by the pride and ambition of men.

He also knew he was fighting for the wrong side. So why was he here? These questions were too painful to ask. But again, he had a strong sense of purpose, one that was beyond explanation. In all of the horror, he had seen the hand of God at work.

"Robert."

"What?" Scripps spat on the ground.

"You asked how I do it."

"Yes. Please. Tell me why you've endeared yourself to all of the soldiers. The officers. The horses. If they are going to die, they all want to meet with the great Reverend Seamus Hanley. When they see me coming. I see the disappointment in their eyes."

"That's not true at all," Seamus said, though the words stunk as lies as soon as they left his mouth. He scurried to come up with something to defuse the obvious. "Perhaps, I carry with me a spirit of forgiveness . . . only because I'm in such desperate need of it myself."

"Forgiveness? Ha! What is possible to forgive with all of this? Don't you know what this is all about? We're getting to experience hell, right here on earth. To escape it? Or to prepare us for it?"

The statement was so dark and onerous, Seamus didn't know how to defuse it. Was there some truth in it as well? "It is all so difficult. Confusing." He thought of something. "I do have a secret. One I use. Maybe it will help you. I think of all of these boys as my own sons."

Scripps's brow wrinkled. "You have your own family." He leaned forward. "What about that, Seamus? Your wife. Your daughter. When is the last time you've seen them? Wrote to them?"

This caught him off of his flank. Seamus was used to asking the questions. He went to protest but paused. "Yes. You're right." He looked around and saw the flickering of many fires in the campground. "I don't know why. Why I haven't corresponded."

Scripps wagged his finger. "I tell you, son. It's because they wouldn't understand. You can either tell them the truth about all of this, and frighten them. Or you can mislead them. So what you do instead is you make a new family. Your brothers. And all of you preparing the way for the furnaces that lie ahead. There is no good in any of this, Seamus. Is there anything clearer than this?"

Was this true? Had Seamus been fooling himself all of the while? That he was serving some type of divine purpose? Perhaps he was lost again, just drifting in a new wilderness of his own making. Why had he stopped writing to Ashlyn? Had he abandoned his own family while on some new quest of his own imagination?

He wanted to help his friend, but Seamus didn't have the right words to say, and others were expecting to see him. He patted Scripps on the shoulder. "I best be going . . ."

"Yes. Nice talking to you, Preacher."

Seamus stood. "We'll talk. Later." He entered the hospital tent, almost relieved to escape the darkness of his friend's demeanor, but this brief reprieve was instantly met with the foulness of the odor. Eight beds were in the lantern-lit tent, and each was filled with soldiers who had been injured in a skirmish today at the outskirts of camp.

A doctor sitting at the side of one of the patients waved him over and stood to offer his chair. His face was grim and exhausted, but he seemed to try to infuse some fervency in his voice. "Chaplain Hanley. The private here has been expecting you."

"Is he here? Is the pastor here?" The weak sound came from the patient's mouth, whose eyes were wrapped in cloth stained with spatters of blood.

Out of sight of the boy, the doctor shook his head. Seamus had witnessed this silent language so many times before. It meant the young man would not be alive much longer. Probably wouldn't make it through the night.

Seamus put his hand on the exhausted doctor's shoulder and the man moved on to care for other patients.

"It's me, son." Seamus sat on the stool and clasped the soldier's hand. "What do they call you?"

The boy's lips curled into a smile. "Ah, I am so glad you came."

"Of course I came. What's your name, son?"

"Dawson. My name is Dawson, Reverend Hanley."

"Well, I'm here now. What shall we talk about?" Was he really here? The words shared by Scripps were boring wormholes into his faith. *Am I a fraud in wearing this collar?*

"I ain't never done it before." There was a wheezing in the boy's voice, the familiar rattle of encroaching death.

"What, son?"

"Pray. I mean. Sure I say words while others listen and watch me. But it wasn't even as if I was speaking to no one. Just words, you know."

Seamus did know. "What would you like to pray about? I'll pray with you."

The boy adjusted in his bed and winced. "That's what they say."

"Who? What do they say?"

"That you talk to God."

The boy's hand grew weaker in his grasp. "I do speak with God, it's true enough. That's all prayer is, son. I talk with Him all of the time. It's the listening I have a stumble with. That's the other part of prayer I'm still working on."

"What does He say?"

"God?" Seamus began to wonder who was ministering to whom. He tried to hide back the laugh the boy might not understand. "Well. Just a little while ago, He told me I need to write my wife."

"He did?" Dawson coughed, and it sounded like gurgling. "My mama. I ain't write Mama none neither. Why is that?"

Was he wrestling with God himself? "I don't know. I suppose it's our way of trying to protect them from all of this. Maybe it's because we don't know how to explain this war. These battles. Even to ourselves."

"Reverend Hanley?" The tone was now soft and fading.

"Son. Let's pray. Now." He was losing the boy.

"Mama?"

"What should I tell her, Dawson?" He squeezed the boy's hand.

"Tell her." He smiled dimly. "Tell Mama you learned me how to talk to God."

"Doctor." Seamus nodded the man toward the bed. He crossed Dawson's hands on his chest.

The doctor reached over and pressed his finger on Dawson's neck. It won't be long, he mouthed the words. Seamus held the boy's hand as he fell to sleep.

"Seamus."

Turning around, Seamus saw Scripps leaning inside, curling a finger at him. Was he drunk?

In a moment, Seamus was outside again in the crisp air, and the smell of wood burning filled his nostrils. "What is it? I've still got more boys to visit."

"You've been summoned . . . by . . . the general."

"What general?"

"*The* general."

"General Lee?"

"Not that general. You aren't that important. No. It's Stonewall."

Seamus's heart jumped. "General Jackson?"

"Yes." Scripps seemed agitated. "That one."

"What could he want with the likes of me?" Seamus had spent time with many of the officers of the camp, but General Jackson had an inner circle of which Seamus had never been included.

Scripps gripped him by the arm and walked him away from the tent. He still had alcohol on his breath, but this news seemed to have sobered him up. "Captain Ross was the one who brought the news. When I pressed him on it, he said he didn't know but noticed that the request came right after he was visited by Colonel . . . what's his name?"

Seamus's shoulders sunk. "Colonel Percy Barlow."

"Yes. Isn't he the one—?"

"It is. The one I got in a scuffle with."

"But that was so long ago. If he was going to say something about that, it would have been many months back. Besides, I'll tell them myself he had it coming."

Could it have been about that? No. Seamus knew this day was coming. When his past would catch up with him. He knew his role as a defector in the Mexican War would haunt him. Up to now, no one had ever called him on it. No one even seemed to care. But Percy had this on him all along. "When am I required to show?"

"The captain said in an hour. General Jackson was meeting with General Lee and wanted to see you next."

"Which means I have about forty minutes or so left."

"What are you going to do? Do you need a map?"

Seamus laughed. "I am not going to run away. Not this time."

"They'll hang you. Or shoot you. Or just to save bullets, they may just run you through."

"They aren't going to be hanging me." As he said this, Seamus was trying to convince himself of this as well. Percy had tried before to see him hung. Seamus was convinced now that the man would never stop until he was successful in tightening the rope around Seamus's neck.

"Well then, if you aren't going to run, you better start preparing what you're going to say. You got to think through all of it. We've got to think through all of it. I mean, you're all I have left to remind me of why I'm here. I can't lose you."

"You're right."

"I am?"

"Yes," Seamus said. "I need time to think. Alone, my friend."

"Oh." Scripps nodded. Then for a moment, he became the mentor again. "You're a fine man, Seamus. A fine man of God. It will be all right. I know it will. And I'll be praying."

"That would most welcome." He held out a hand to shake, but Scripps pulled him in with both arms and hugged him tightly. Would this be the last time Seamus saw the man?

They parted and Seamus hurried to his tent. There was little more than a half hour remaining, and he was desperate to seek counsel through prayer. With his pulse rising, he hurried over to the edge of camp, beside a boulder on the banks of the Rappahannock. While they had been camped here, this was the place he had chosen for early morning visits.

He sat for a few moments and listened to the music of the river's currents, which blended with the night chorus of crickets.

Seamus gazed off in the distance, and there were flickering lights as well on the other side of the river. The evening dalliances of the enemy. But to him, they were not to be feared or hated. They were just men in different uniforms.

He pulled out his Bible from his inner coat pocket and gripped it between his fingers. Even with the moon at full light, it was too dark for him to read, but Seamus sought out words of consolation nonetheless.

"For I will give you a mouth and wisdom, which all your adversaries shall not be able to gainsay nor resist."

Yes. The words will come. But that wasn't it. There was something else. What passage could he share? Stonewall Jackson was a man of God, a passionate reader of the Bible. What better language could he use to defend himself?

Seamus felt pressed. Surely he needed to get going. He certainly couldn't be late for a meeting with one of the most powerful men of the South.

He thought back to his time on the mountain with Pastor Asa. Yes. There was something the man had spoken while they were high above. From Joshua. He had read it many times. Seamus smiled and a sense of peace came over him.

Then he saw Ashlyn's face. He fumbled for his pocket and pulled out the photograph, the one that had long since faded. He couldn't see it well in full daylight, and he certainly couldn't see much now. But it didn't matter. She was with him.

He brought her picture to his lips. In all of his ministry to others, all of his good works on the battlefield, he had neglected his most important assignment. He was reminded of how desperate he was to find Ashlyn when he first saw her face in this photo, which he discovered in a letter among the wreckage of a stagecoach crash. He traveled more than a thousand miles across impossible terrain to meet her for the first time.

He dreamed of calling her his wife. And now what? Had he taken the gift she was from God for granted? What was holding him back now? Why hadn't he written but a few times? Why hadn't he insisted on taking a leave as others had?

There was an answer to this question. But he just didn't know what it was.

And now he was out of time. Would he see her again? Would this be his last day?

Seamus was unable to walk through the camp without getting a wave or handshake and tonight was not an exception. But he was worried others would see the grimness of his expression.

He had endured dodging artillery fire, exploding ordnance, and whistling musket balls and bullets.

Yet he hadn't been this uneasy since the beginning of his service. What was he so afraid of? Maybe it was because he respected the man with whom he was about to speak. This was a man he didn't want to let down.

But now what would happen once he visited General Jackson? After all Seamus had gone through in surviving disasters, what a way for it all to end. Maybe this was the proper response to decisions he made long ago. Maybe it was merely what he deserved.

As he approached the officers' tents, which were peppered with guards and much more serious-minded soldiers, there was a palpable sense of anxiety in the air. Seamus had recognized this before. It was the smell of the air just before the rain. He knew what this meant.

They were about to go to battle.

"Who goes there?" A cavalry officer tending to his horse looked up with alarm. But before Seamus could answer, his demeanor shifted. "The general was asking for you, Chaplain. He just returned from his meeting and he'll be pleased you showed up early."

It was unnerving for Seamus to be noticed. He was used to it with the noncommissioned soldiers, and even the younger officers, but he didn't know many of the senior leaders personally. Had they all been talking about him? Did they all know of his past?

The captain tied his horse to a post and then motioned with a gloved hand for Seamus to follow. They wove their way past several of the administrative tents and exchanged salutes with several officers until they came to what Seamus recognized as General Jackson's tent.

"Wait here." The captain turned. "General?" There was a sound from inside, and then he entered and Seamus heard muffled voices.

Did he even want to hear what was being said? He took off his hat and rocked on heels to try to reduce some of the wobbling in his knees. He glanced around and noticed a scurrying of activity even though it was getting late in the evening.

Orders were being delivered. No doubt even the soldiers in the camp would know of their impending plans by the time Seamus had returned. If he was returning.

Don't think that way. He started to pray but stopped when he sensed someone staring at him. He tried to glance around without appearing startled, but it was difficult to see too much with only the light offered by lanterns.

Then he saw him. Just a hint of the man. But then as a shadow, the officer turned and disappeared in the darkness between two of the tents.

"Percy," Seamus whispered.

"The general will see you now."

The captain's voice returned him to his present danger. He was holding the flap of the door open.

"Oh. Yes. Thank you, Captain." Seamus gave him a nod, then straightened his hair with a brush of his hand.

He went inside, prepared to accept his fate.

Chapter 31

STONEWALL

If it was under any other circumstance, this would have been an opportunity Seamus would have cherished.

The inside of the general's tent was stark but well kept. Just a small bed, a table with two chairs, a trunk, and a desk where he was sitting reading under candlelight.

"General." Seamus breathed out slowly.

The general pulled back a ribbon to mark his page and then closed the book, on which were inscribed the letters *Holy Bible.* He stood and was still dressed in his uniform, although his sword and hilt were resting against the wall. The top buttons of his jacket were unfastened, and his long beard nearly reached down to his shirt.

Seamus didn't know what the protocol was between a chaplain and a general of such high rank, but he clicked his heels and gave a firm salute nonetheless.

The general tucked his hands behind his back and examined Seamus with eyes that were both intense and kind. He turned, lifted his candle, and set it on the edge of the table. The general rolled up a map, tied a leather cord around it, and held it up to Seamus.

"I pray over each and every one of these." He pointed for Seamus to have a seat. "I must beg your forgiveness because I will need to keep this meeting quite brief. Not even time to offer you something to drink."

"That's fine. I don't drink."

The general smiled at him. "Well, I drink water on occasion." He picked up his Bible from the desk and plopped it on the table in between them. With a groan, he slid into the chair opposite Seamus. Then again, he peered at him with his steely eyes.

Seamus shifted in his chair.

"Do you know why you are here, Chaplain Hanley?"

"I have an idea."

"You do? And what would that be?"

What was he thinking? Should he try to be surprised by Percy's allegations? What if that wasn't what the general wanted to discuss? But then, of course it was.

"For I will give you a mouth and wisdom, which all your adversaries shall not be able to gainsay nor resist."

Seamus leaned in. "I am here to face the consequences of my past, General Jackson."

The general pulled the black leather Bible toward him and ran his fingers over the cover. He pointed to Seamus's face. "Is that?"

Seamus lifted his hand to his cheek and his fingers traced over the scar, where the branding iron once seared.

"How did it feel? When it was pressed into your face?"

The question alarmed Seamus. "The worst pain I have ever experienced."

"And . . . how many lashes?"

"Forty-nine. Or so they told me. I didn't stay conscious for all of them."

"Would you not consider those consequences?" The general turned his head.

Seamus didn't know where this was leading. "Quite so, sir."

"Do you not believe in forgiveness, Chaplain Hanley?"

"I suppose I would not be much of a pastor if I didn't."

The general's shoulders lifted and there was a slight bend in his lips as if he didn't know how to fully smile. "Do you know General Lee remembers you?"

"What? I mean, sir?"

"You served with General Lee?"

Seamus recalled his missions in the Mexican War and having served under the leadership of a military engineer, who was Captain Lee at that time. "I was with him when I . . ."

"Deserted?"

This word always irked Seamus. He did not desert; he did not run away from the battlefield. What he did was change sides and fight for the other army. "Yes."

"A genuine member of the San Patricios Battalion. Don't see those too often."

"Most were hung. I was one of the fortunate ones."

The general flipped through the pages of the Bible. "When I mentioned your . . . situation to General Lee, he said you showed bravery. He had the same question I had."

"Why did I fight for the Mexicans?"

The general nodded, his eyes probing for more than words.

"Never understood that much myself. I was lost in those days. Didn't have much to cling to."

"And now? Are you committed to our cause?"

That was the question Seamus was terrified of, the one he hoped he wouldn't hear. Would it be selfish for him to answer this honestly? Should he lie for the sake of Ashlyn and Grace?

"For I will give you a mouth and wisdom, which all your adversaries shall not be able to gainsay nor resist."

Seamus tapped on the Bible. "There is a verse. It was given to me by another pastor. When I told him . . ." He paused and swallowed. "When I told him I didn't believe in the Southern cause."

He looked for a response in the general's face. Even the slightest of twitches, but the general was as unmoving as he was in a spray of bullets.

"He shared with me a passage in Joshua."

General Jackson held up a hand. Then he flipped through pages, and after some crackling of paper, he drew the candle in close. "'And it came to pass, when Joshua was by Jericho, that he lifted up his eyes and looked, and, behold, there stood a man over against him with his sword drawn in his hand: and Joshua went unto him, and said unto him, "Art thou for us, or for our adversaries?"'"

The general raised his head. "Is this the one, Chaplain Hanley?"

Seamus was amazed. "It is, General Jackson."

Then the general nodded and continued. "'And he said, Nay; but as captain of the host of the LORD am I now come. And Joshua fell on his face to the earth, and did worship, and said unto him, What saith my lord unto his servant?'"

He paused and turned the Bible toward Seamus. "Here, Chaplain, you read the rest."

Seamus drew the candle closer. "'And the captain of the LORD's host said unto Joshua, Loose thy shoe from off thy foot; for the place whereon thou standest is holy. And Joshua did so.'" He closed the book slowly and then pushed it back.

"Is that you, Chaplain Hanley? You find yourself on God's side?"

"Is there any other side to be?" Seamus's hands clenched the sides of his chair. He realized he might sound arrogant. "I am a very flawed man, General Jackson. I am only here to provide some comfort to the hearts and souls of these men."

The general tugged on his beard. "Let me ask you this. Not as your superior officer, but as a man seeking a deeper understanding of God."

How possible was this? Here this man would decide life or death for Seamus. "Sir?"

"Tomorrow, we go to battle again. And again, as it has been in each of these conflicts, I will order young men, boys, to their deaths. And on the other side of the river, there are good officers. Good men, I know, because many I have served with before. They will read their Scripture as I do. They will pray. Each of us convinced that we are in God's will.

"And when our boys, our soldiers, learn tonight of our plans, they too will speak to their Maker, petitioning for His caring hand. For their protection. And to be in His will. On both sides of the river. How is this, Chaplain Hanley? Who will God choose?"

This was something Seamus had pondered many times himself. Because as disinterested as he was in the institution of slavery, he had met fine soldiers, true men of God, in the Confederate army. "I suppose, General, that this is the wrong question."

The general raised his brow.

"Or at least the wrong observation."

"How is that?" The lines etched in the general's face made him look weary.

"If there are soldiers, men, women, thousands and hundreds of thousands praying on either side, desperate for their Father, then maybe the victory is already won."

General Jackson smiled broadly and then tapped his hand on the table. "Well . . . that is certainly a fine way to end our conversation." He stood and Seamus rose as well.

Would he be getting out of this alive?

The general gripped Seamus by the hand, wrapped his other around it, and tugged on it firmly. "I have a message from General Lee, and it's one I share as well. He would like to thank you for your service to our men."

Seamus feared meeting the general's eyes, for it might cause him to get emotional. Only earlier this evening he was wondering if all of his efforts were futile.

"But, Chaplain. There is one thing."

"General?"

"Your accuser. Colonel Barlow."

"Yes, sir."

"He is not a man who knows forgiveness."

Seamus nodded. Then he turned and left the general and his tent. Once outside, Seamus buttoned his coat and pulled in his arms to try to warm himself up.

Because there was a strange chill in the air.

Chapter 32

CHANCELLORSVILLE

CHANCELLORSVILLE
April 1863

 Davin nearly fell asleep to the muted sounds of distant artillery as he sat in his Union blue uniform, which appeared distinctively newer than those of his fellow soldiers.

So when the loud explosion discharged, it caused him to flinch. He blinked and glanced over to see if the others noticed he had jumped.

Barry was sitting nearby, cleaning his rifle, and he spoke without looking up. "It's all right, Davey boy. We all remember our first day of battle. Don't we, boys?"

About a dozen soldiers were within speaking distance. Davin's full regiment as well as others were scattered across a grassy field peppered with cow excrement and located not more than a hundred yards away from a rather impressive farmhouse.

Off to the left was where the fighting was heavy. A conflation of flashes of ordnance bursts, dirt flung in the air, the echoing of trumpets, the shouts of men, and the neighing of horses. But it was far enough away from Davin to cause grumbling among his fellow Irish soldiers who weren't pleased they were being left out of this confrontation with the Confederates.

Off to the right, a thick forest of trees served as a barrier of protection, making their assignment comfortable and uneventful. The Irish Battalion had received a rare reprieve from its typical position on the front lines, perhaps another nod to the political outcry to the disproportionate number of casualties they had suffered in this ill-fought war.

Yet there was a bustle of activity near the farmhouse with officers coming and going because it was where General Joseph Hooker and his aides were commanding the Union's efforts. Certainly they were inside monitoring progress through maps and reports from sentries who raced up in sweat-soaked horses.

Private Maloney lifted his rifle and pointed it at Davin. "You're as skittish as a mosquito on a frog's tongue, and that's with all of the good sport being more than a mile away. What will you do when the lead starts clipping those pretty ears of yours?"

Despite the discomfort of having the barrel of a weapon pointing in his direction, Davin kept his nerves so as not to feed the brute's pleasure. Private Maloney, with his farmer's shoulders and bulldog face, held the title of corporal a few months ago before he was caught sneaking out on an unauthorized soiree in one of the neighboring towns.

Davin reached out calmly and gripped the barrel and pushed it aside.

"Back off, Maloney," said Barry. "You're a fine one to be provoking anyone, seeing as no one in the battalion has proved faster at fleeing from musket balls than you, dear friend."

"Is that so? And I suppose you've had a musket ball planted in your head as I have?"

"Ah, indeed." Barry laughed. "And I will remind you it was in the back of your hard skull, which only further proves my point."

"I told you. It was in the back of my skull because I was behind rebel lines. They snuck up on me, barefoot cowards. General Burnside came up to me hisself afterward and tells me I was his bravest Yank that day."

"And that did him good and well. Ol' Abe has Burnside washing dishes for Mary Lincoln now."

"What do you think about General Hooker anyways?" Davin fumbled through his haversack for something to eat. He pulled out some hardtack and then bit into it, nearly cracking a tooth.

"I dread today," Barry said.

"Why's that?" Maloney pointed his rifle toward the trees. "Pow. Pow. Pow."

Barry took out a handkerchief and shined up his bayonet. "Well, Mr. Robert E. Lee has whipped every one of Abe's generals, and I'm sure we're just another battle away from Hooker being hooked."

"And why would that be bad?" Davin kept his eye on Maloney as it wasn't beyond him to accidentally shoot one of his own. He noticed the new shoes the pudgy private was wearing and smiled. Only Muriel was able to discover him to be the boots benefactor and she swore not to tell anyone.

"Why he's fed us better than the rest," Barry said. "If we can't never taste victory, we can at least say we tasted good food."

"Will you look at that cheeky fellow?" Maloney pointed to the sky beyond the trees.

A brown hot-air balloon rose swiftly while being tethered by a long rope.

"Is she one of ours?" Maloney shielded the sun with his hand.

Barry scoffed. "If it was ours, it would be behind us."

"I know that." He lifted his rifle. "Maybe I should empty it of its hot air."

"Save your bullets," Barry said. "You might need one for the back of your head. You couldn't hit that balloon even if you were standing atop one of them trees."

"I know that. You don't have to tell me that. I ain't no fool. Hey, I have just what we need." Maloney hurried over to his pack, unlatched it, and dug around inside. "Tell Mr. Hot Air to hang in there for me. Just a minute."

"You've got your own balloon in there?" asked Davin.

Maloney's eyes widened and he held up a telescope, which was tarnished and had some dents but was of officer-grade quality. "Picked her up on patrol a few weeks back. Probably belonged to a rebel general."

"Let me see that." Barry put his rifle down.

"Mind your patience." Maloney unfolded it and then put it to his eye.

"What do you see?" Davin squinted at the balloon. It must have been five miles or so away.

"Well. It appears like they are hanging down something." Maloney pulled the telescope all of the way out and turned it slightly. "Some kind of flags with markings."

Barry went to grab it from him. "Are you even using the proper end? You're probably seeing the inside of your head." He glanced back toward the farmhouse. "What's that? Davin. It looks like your little wifey is coming."

Davin spun around, and there was Muriel walking toward them at a good pace. She was wearing her Sanitary Commission-issued black dress, with a white apron and hat. What was she doing out here? The hospital tents were set up not too far behind the farmhouse, but still it was a stretch for her to explain to Nurse Meldrickson why she was out here.

"Yes indeed." Maloney whistled as now he had the telescope

pointing in Muriel's direction. "Red hair. Blue eyes. Is that a small mole on the side of her cheek?"

"Give that to me." Davin snatched the scope out of his hands.

As she came up upon them, Muriel looked skyward in the direction of the balloon and slowed down for a moment and then with her head down marched directly to Davin. "I need to speak with you."

"Can't you share a few words with all of us?" Maloney asked. "We're all a bit scared and could use a lady's soft voice for our nerves."

Muriel didn't take her eyes off of Davin. "Alone. Now."

"All right then." He couldn't help but be agitated. She had been avoiding him for days and now she was going to issue demands? He held an arm out and they headed to a clearing about thirty yards away from everyone. This would be all the privacy they would be able to muster.

"What do you have there?" A small shock of her hair flapped from under Muriel's cotton hat.

"This?" Davin held the scope out and balanced it in his hands. It was of a good weight and well constructed.

"May I?" She held out a soft white palm.

Davin shrugged and gave it to her.

She examined it. "This is an officer's scope. A Confederate's." She lifted it to her eye and pointed it toward the balloon.

"That's Maloney's. The squat fellow." Davin's gaze traced to the balloon. "What do you see? Maloney said there were some type of—"

"Those are signal flags."

What didn't this woman know? "Can you read what they are signaling?"

Muriel lowered it and folded it up. She handed it to him. "That's a rebel balloon. Their signals are different. Besides, I am a woman. I was only seeing if his scarf matched his coat."

"I thought you told me you weren't going to talk to me anymore." Davin tried to be nonchalant.

"I wasn't. But . . . for the sake of your sister . . . I thought I would warn you."

"Warn me of what?"

"Davin, do you know how few soldiers survive their first battle?"

He was surprised and pleased by her concern. "That will do well for my confidence."

"It is not your confidence I am concerned with. Soldiers don't die because they lack confidence. They perish because they lack common sense."

"What would you know about any of this? Are you a war general now?"

"Who would know more about the dangers of battle, the general who sends the soldier out to the battlefield or the doctor who needs to mend them when they return?"

Her pondered her point, which he had to admit had merit.

"I know everything about this war. About these soldiers." She spoke with a tinge of anger. "When boys are dying, they tell me everything. I am their doctor. Their mother. And if they are fortunate, their savior."

At first he was taken aback. Was she boasting? He never thought Muriel would be one to suffer from arrogance. No. It was something else. A different emotion.

"You care about me, don't you?"

"What?"

He smiled. "Why can't you just say it? What if you were right? What if I was to die in my first battle? And you had a chance to tell me you cared about me, but instead you stood out here on this field and refused to acknowledge your feelings? No. Instead you've only told me I am no different than forty thousand other soldiers. How long would it take you to forgive yourself?

When you realize maybe I was more important than . . . whatever it is that is so important to you now?"

"Are you two doing all right there? Should we call in some artillery support?" Barry was beaming a smile, and Davin realized they were providing entertainment for many of the soldiers.

Muriel's cheeks flushed and she covered her eyes with her hand. "This was a dreadful mistake. Please forgive me, Davin. Truly. But I can't do this anymore. Someday you'll understand."

She turned and pounded her legs away, raising the hem of her dress to clear the tall grass.

Davin stared as she walked away with his mouth agape. He lowered his head and returned to the others, preparing himself for the snickers and berating. What a fool he had made of himself.

When he looked up again, it was much worse than he imagined. His friends were staring at him with pity.

Why would he ever fall for such a strange woman? He had entertained so many ladies in his lifetime, most who never caused him any grief. None of them behaved in this manner. None of them made him feel so incomplete.

And none of them were Muriel.

Only a few hours had passed, and from their vantage point it was difficult to tell which side had an advantage in the battle. Davin mostly sat with his gaze on the horizon while Barry and Maloney passed the time with a game of cards.

But Davin felt uneasy. The words Muriel had shared resonated. Was he prepared? He looked at his uniform and his weapon lying beside him, and they all looked like toys in some schoolboy's game. What was he doing here? What did he know about war? Had it been a mistake for him to come here?

A shout of surprise sounded from his right, and several soldiers pointed in the direction of the forest. Davin strained his eyes and could see nothing unordinary, but then there was a rustling of the branches and bushes and he stood and grabbed his rifle. His two friends tossed their cards and stood as well.

Suddenly a large buck burst out of the tree and ran across the field.

"Ah, she's a beauty." Maloney aimed his rifle. "A ten-pointer."

"Get him, Maloney. We'll be eating well tonight." Barry patted his stomach.

Another doe followed and then several others, as well as a couple of foxes, and it was as if the forest emptied of its animals, all surging forward in panic.

Barry raised his rifle as well. "What . . . ?"

Which was right about the time the rebel yell was heard in unison, and what must have been a major division of the Confederate army burst through the woods in a maddened frenzy.

Chapter 33

TIMES SUCH AS THESE

"Did you want milk for your tea?" Clare just finished pouring hot water into the china teacup and placed it back on the round table between them.

Cassie let out one of her big laughs. "All these years and you still askin' me how I like my tea? Black like me, with a sugar like you."

"How terrible of me to forget. Of course, my dear, if you remember well, for most of those years you were serving the tea to me."

Cassie shook her head. "Well, it's a good thing we got that ship landed in the right harbor."

Clare poured some milk in her own teacup and Cassie stirred hers with a silver spoon while looking outside through the porch window. Despite Cassie's carefree laugh, the bags under her eyes told a different tale.

"My friend." Clare reached over and held Cassie's hand. "How are you? Really? I've . . . we . . . Andrew and I have been concerned about you."

The woman reached her time-etched fingers around the cup and drew it to her lips. Then she peered outside again, where a hummingbird hovered around a primrose bush. "It's this whole tired city." She sighed and then shook her head. "Just when we think things might be changing for what's right, all of the wrong comes back again, worse than before. Makes you wonder whether any of it's worth trying for."

She squeezed Clare's hand. "Oh dear, I truly worry about my husband. It's this draft. Mr. Lincoln's draft. Why I's afraid there's much too much hate around it. People blames us for everything. Ain't just words no more neither. People's gonna get hurt. And still my fool husband pratting about like a rooster, thinking he too loved by God to be hit by a bullet."

"Have you been threatened?" Clare sometimes struggled with the line between being a newspaper reporter and a good listener for her friends. Was this her journalistic curiosity, or was she just trying to be helpful? She supposed it was just a casualty of the profession.

"When have there not been?" Cassie rested her cup in the saucer. "Except, these ones now. Filled with such anger. You can see it in their eyes. My people have all but done cleared out of the Five Points. Ain't safe to be there with dark skin. But even when we leave, the trouble follows us."

"What about the church? What does Zachary plan to do?"

"Ol' Reverend Bridger? He's just thick as thick can be. His people have moved from the neighborhood, but they still come on Sundays. Many miles. Whole families. He says, 'We ain't going nowhere.' And all the whiles, we's thinking Mr. Lincoln gonna change things."

Ella skipped into the room with her blue dress. "Cassie!" She hugged the woman around her wide waist. "Should I get my doll?"

Clare loved how the children adored the woman. It made

it easier for Clare to be away from home when she needed to. "Cassie is not here to tend to you. It's just a visit."

Cassie squeezed the girl's cheeks. "But I am gonna be here soon enough. And more times too."

"Oh Cassie, we certainly couldn't impose on you any further. Andrew and I have been ever so grateful for what you are already doing to help us."

"That's all nonsense." Cassie retied the bow on Ella's dress, which barely fit her anymore. "Zachary tells me he wants you out of the house. He wants you writing them stories. You and Andrew doing the good work, you is. It ain't easy writing against your kind."

"I am not writing against my own people. Not all of the Irish have such poor manners." Clare lifted the teapot and poured more into Cassie's cup. "I hope you don't judge us all by the few."

"Just as long as you ain't judging us none by our rotten types."

They both watched as Ella made her way back out of the room and they heard her heavy steps on the stairs.

"How's Miss Caitlin faring?"

Clare was grateful to change the subject to her sister. "It has been so wonderful having her back. And do you know, she can write stories and we can't keep her away from the newspaper."

Cassie stared at her for a few moments. "You acting like you don't know why."

"What?" Clare knew Cassie and Caitlin had developed a strong friendship from their time working together at the Underground Railroad. In many ways, Cassie had become their third sister. "Tell me."

"You really don't know about this?" She held up her hands and shook them. "All right then. You ain't hearing this from me none, but she's takin' to dote on a young man who is making her heart fly like that there hummingbird."

"At the *Daily*?" Clare tried to think of who it might be. But at the newspaper there were only boys and old men. The rest had left to fight in the war. The only available one she could think of was . . . "Owen?"

Cassie's brown eyes widened. "That sounds 'bout right."

"Owen?" He spent every minute of his life obsessing about the newspaper. It was as if he loved the *Daily* more than anyone. "That's impossible. My sister only falls for corrupt officials, drunken rebels, or unfaithful barristers. Owen is much too sensible."

"Maybe the little girl, she be growing up some."

"Owen, he is a fine man." Clare continued to imagine what kind of husband he would be to her sister. "I don't know where Andrew would be without his help. Oh, my poor dear man."

"And what is all of this about poor Andrew?"

Clare jumped and turned to see him standing in the doorway with his mischievous grin. "What a horrible person you are to sneak up on two ladies while they are trying to gossip."

Andrew came over and kissed Clare on the top of her head. "It's not called sneaking if I'm entering my own home. Although I suppose it's mostly the bank's home now."

Heat rose in her face. "Andrew, please don't burden Cassie here with our financial concerns."

Cassie raised her hand. "I alreadys know you be on hard times. That's another reason Zachary wants me to help with your children."

Andrew took off his jacket and rested it on the arm of the chair, and he also put a brown paper-wrapped package there as well. "The better question would be, who doesn't know we're bankrupt? We might as well print it on the front page of the paper for the two or three people in Manhattan who still don't know." He motioned his hands. "Here's our headline: Hapless Son Single-handedly Sinks Royce Empire."

"No, there ain't no truth in that, Mr. Royce." Cassie's tone always changed around Andrew, as she chided him with the authority of a woman who once changed his diapers as his nanny. "Your pappy be proud about his boy, what you does with his newspaper. I tell you this. The *Daily* does its speaking for God. And He ain't worrying none about whethers you have money or you don't. Why if Mr. Moses still be around, he come to my boy Andrew and he say, 'I got ten things I want you to print and I ain't gonna print it nowheres else. Because you's the only one darin' to speak the truth.'"

Andrew cocked his head. "Now, Cassie. I may have to have you preach that at my office for all to hear. Maybe we would stop losing good people to those other newspapers."

"Oh no, we didn't lose anyone else, did we?" Clare hated the thought of her husband facing yet another obstacle.

"No." He pointed two fingers at them. "Quite the contrary. As it turns out, we just earned ourselves the largest advertising customer we've had in five years. Just today, they committed to ads in our paper for a full year."

Both Clare and Cassie clapped. It was refreshing to hear good news.

"Who is it, Andrew?" Clare loved seeing her husband shine with hope.

"It's a firm named . . . Angus . . . umm . . . Angell Finch, that's right. A boot company of all things."

"Maybe our prayers are being answered after all," Clare said. "Is that why you came home early? To share this news?"

"Oh!" He went over to his jacket and pulled out an envelope and held it up.

Clare stood and clasped her hands. "Is it?"

"It is."

"From which one of my never-writes-to-me brothers?"

"Private Davin Hanley."

Clare snatched it out of his hand and retreated back to her chair. "Should I get you some tea?"

He waved her off with a smile.

Her hands started to shake as she looked on the table for a knife. Not finding one she lifted her spoon and dragged the handle end under the envelope flap. After slicing it open, she pulled out the letter slowly. Then she fanned her face with her hand.

"If he's writing, that means he is alive, Clare." Andrew's words were calming, but she couldn't push away the thought it might be Davin's last letter to her or written from some battlefield hospital bed.

"Oh thank You, Jesus, he is alive." Cassie held her hands up.

Clare remembered how little Cassie followed the war. "Do you know about Chancellorsville?" The blank look she received answered her question. "It was Davin's first battle, and it so happened to be the most humiliating defeat of all for the Union. And again, it was our Irish boys, the 69th and the 88th regiments, wouldn't you know, that held the lines while the rest of the army retreated."

"It was a defeat, yes, but there at least was the news about General Stonewall Jackson." Andrew leaned against the wall with his arms crossed.

"Oh Andrew," Clare said, "I don't cheer any man's death."

Andrew addressed Cassie. "He was shot in the arm by his own men. Died a few days later as a result of the wound."

"That's horrible." Cassie always got emotional when they spoke about such things. "Just terrible. People goin' about shooting one another. And this Stonewall man. You say he's a friend of Davin's?"

He cleared his throat and pointed to the letter. "Maybe you should read that."

Clare waved it in her hand and shuddered. Then she handed it to Andrew and he unfolded it as he walked back over to where he had been standing.

She watched his every facial expression looking for the smallest of clues that would reveal what was written. Even as a journalist it was difficult to get information about deaths and casualties.

Especially with the toll being so high at Chancellorsville, they were still sorting through the bodies and injuries.

What would she do if Davin had received some terrible wound? If he had lost a leg or an arm? When she had pulled him and Caitlin from their shanty in Branlow and sailed with them to America, she did so with the full expectation that she was bringing them to a better life.

Had she made a terrible mistake? Would they have been much better to rough it out on the Hanley farm, just as her family had done so many generations before?

Was the reason she brought them here to pursue her own ambitions as a journalist? Was it the fame she had received as a woman in a man's industry? She had always believed her decision to bring them back to Manhattan to be for their own good. And to support Andrew's ministries and roles here. But all along, had it been about her?

"What does it say, Andrew?" Clare didn't like the seriousness of his expression. "Is he injured?"

"That little boy should have never left us," Cassie said. "How many times have I said this. Should have never gone."

Andrew held up his hand and then flipped the piece of paper and continued reading. Then he released a slow exhale. "He's fine. Davin is fine."

Cassie pounded the table. "Sweet Jesus. Why didn't you just say that all the while? You had me and Miss Clare in a knot. You always was a misbehaver. Since you was wee high. I ought to have spanked you a few more times when I had a chance, and I got a mind to do it now."

"The only one who ever cried when you chose not to spare the rod was you, Miss Cassie. You never did have a heart for punishment."

"And look at you now, all full of mouth on account of my weak heart." She shook her head.

"What does it say?" Clare held out her hand.

Andrew looked down at it again. "Let's see. The Irish Battalion was not supposed to be in the battle at all, but they were ambushed by Jackson's army.

"Many of the men in his regiment did not make it out alive. But they held firm, and he was one of those who had been able to hold off the advance and they were able to just barely retreat to safety."

Clare put her hand to her chest. "Thank You, Lord. Was that all?"

"Well no. He writes quite some about Muriel. Rambling really."

"Muriel? Are you sure?" He had seemed so indifferent to their nanny when she was in New York.

Cassie's face brightened. "The redheaded girl? We seen her all of the time at our Underground meetings. Always full of questions."

"She was quite useful around the newspaper as well," Andrew said. "We certainly missed her when she left."

"Not to mention how much our children loved her." Clare waved her hand at Andrew again. She wanted to read every word for herself. "Who would have thought Davin would show interest in a woman who was . . . well so spirited and brilliant? Most men find themselves intimidated by this, don't you know?"

"I know how precisely . . . disconcerting that can be." Andrew handed Clare the letter.

"Maybe our boy Davin, he's just like Caitlin," said Cassie.

Clare didn't look up from the letter. "Oh, how so?"

"Maybe he's just grown up some."

"Maybe out of the ashes of this war there will be some good after all." Clare halted. "Andrew, you didn't say anything about this. It says he is very concerned that we are in danger. They believe Lee's army may have its sights on New York." She set down the letter. "Then the rumors may be true."

"And that isn't the kind of thing he should be writing in his letters."

"If them Southern boys makes it to New York, we'll be finished for sure." Cassie rubbed her wrists. "We'll all be in chains again."

"Which brings me to my next surprise." Andrew grabbed the wrapped package on the chair and left the room.

Clare glanced up. "Where is he going now?"

"Yes. That one there always has his surprises."

"Why, Cassie, I think you may be right about Davin."

"Of course I is. Now what is I right about?"

"These are the words of a young man in love." Clare put her hand over her mouth and laughed. "Listen to this. 'I only wish my eyes were open to Muriel when we were both in the city, when we could have freely walked on the banks of the Hudson and could have enjoyed the trees blossoming in Central Park.'" She giggled. "Oh dear boy! He's quite smitten."

"You sure that's him writing?"

"There's more. Oh, this is not as cheery." Clare held the letter up to the light of the window. "He says, 'Instead we are surrounded by the screams of dying men and injuries and horrors beyond description, yet Muriel is a remarkably calm spirit in the tempest.'"

Cassie gasped.

Clare looked to Cassie and then followed her gaze to see Andrew standing in the doorway, dressed in a military uniform. She dropped the letter and stood, nearly knocking her chair to the ground.

"Well? What do you think?" Andrew spun around with his hands raised to his side.

"I think you should remove it immediately." Clare's voice began to waver.

The front door slammed and they all looked to the entranceway to see Garret entering, chewing on an apple. He gave a double nod when he saw his father. "Da's going to war?"

"He most certainly is not." Clare propped her arms on her waist. "Andrew . . . what?"

"Now that's one boy who shouldn't be about bullets," Cassie said.

"All right, you two, that is enough of your fussing." Andrew seemed disappointed in their response. "I am afraid to say you are both correct. I am not going to war, and I should not be around gunplay. If you paid any attention you would know this is not Union blue. This is merely a state militia uniform."

"But they are drafting state militia." Clare went over to him, not wanting to share with him how handsome he looked.

Andrew gave her a hug. "These are the times we are facing. The rebels are moving up toward Pennsylvania. Manhattan has been stripped of most of its Union officers. Clare, there is genuine concern that the Confederates could come to New York. Why, if we are defeated here it would be over for our cause. There is pressure on Lincoln from our own people to end this war. They asked for us to post a call for recruits for the militia in the *Daily*, and I thought . . ."

"You thought what, Andrew?"

"That it's time for me to do my part. Not to sit idly by."

"Idly by? Don't you know how important the *Daily* is to the war effort?"

"If the rebels come to Manhattan, Clare, there will be no *Daily*. There will be no North. And if they don't come here, then I'll be able to return this uniform unused."

"I think you look brave, Da." Garret reached out and felt the material. "Can I tell my friends?"

Clare walked over to the bay window and peered outside. Was her whole world shattering? And what could she do about it by cowering in her own house? Maybe Andrew was right. Perhaps it was time for them to get more involved. For her to take her position at the *Daily* with a greater level of seriousness.

She couldn't bear a weapon, but she could influence others

through her pen. Could she use it to protect the men in her life? Andrew? Seamus? Davin? And her children?

Turning, she saw her husband pulling Garret into his arms. "Andrew?"

"What? What now, Clare?"

"I understand why you feel you need to wear that uniform. It's this sense that we can do more. That we *should* do more. So . . . I must share with you what has been on my mind. It's been bothering me for several weeks now."

Andrew didn't say anything, but she could tell he knew.

"If the rebels are coming. If this could be the end of the war. If my brothers could be fighting it on either side. Then I need to cover that story. And I need to cover it from the battlefield."

Chapter 34

THE CORRESPONDENTS

GETTYSBURG, PENNSYLVANIA
UNION CAMP
July 3, 1863

 "What brings you here, Clare?" Ben Jones flashed his familiar smirk, but it was filtered with the weariness of covering a long war. "Doing a story on Pennsylvania's summer squash harvest and stumbled into this little scuffle? I haven't seen you out in the field since that . . . picnic at Bull Run."

Clare tried to think of some clever retort, but her soul was winded. Besides, Ben was right. She had only been to a few actual battle sites and this would be her last.

The two of them had peeled away from their vantage point above the battleground in order to take a respite from the unfolding drama below. But it didn't keep them away from the sound of the explosions and the distant screams of war in the background.

He took a draw on his hand-rolled cigarette, and for a moment she understood why one would take on such a vice.

"Why am I here?" Clare sat on a boulder. "I suppose we couldn't bear to be the only newspaper without a field correspondent anymore."

"No, my dear. You should know you can't lie to a trained reporter." He tapped off a cigarette ash.

Long before she arrived from New York days ago, and even as she watched the Pennsylvania farm countryside from train and carriage windows, she admitted to herself why she was here. Certainly part of it was to be able to confront the enemy face-to-face, with her pen if not the sword.

But her real desire was to see her brothers, perhaps for the last time. Clare had a bad feeling about this battle and was inexplicably drawn to being here.

Yet by the time she had arrived at Gettysburg, it was too late and perhaps all of this was a waste. The conflict had already begun, the troops were entrenched, and it was impossible for her to get close enough to see Davin, let alone even know where to find him amid the madness.

War appeared organized and simple when it was traced on a general's map, but she had learned that once the first shots were fired, chaos prevailed and the survivors and winners of the conflict were those who could rise above the panic.

And if her brother Seamus was out there fighting for the other side, he was only one of tens of thousands of faceless specks crawling up green hills in gray uniforms, through flashes of light and rising smoke to be hacked down and rendered lifeless. She could only hope and pray that Seamus was back home dragging a hoe on some farm in Virginia.

"How have you survived?" Clare asked.

"That would depend on your definition of survival." He glanced upward. "I had thought the despair, the darkness, that it was all about the losses we've suffered. But here today, the generals are telling us this is the Union's greatest victory and all I can see are thousands of dead soldiers on both sides. And still, the shadows remain. Even in victory."

Ben flicked his glowing cigarette on the soil, then pulled a watch out of his chest pocket. "I suppose I should get my story wired in. There is a telegraph booth for us, but a line is forming already. What about you?"

Clare flapped open her leather satchel and pulled out a folded piece of paper. "The northern front earns a rare Robert E. Lee defeat. But at what cost is victory? The quiet fields of harvest give way to a calamitous portrait of twisted bodies and ephemeral dreams."

"Well stated. Shall I send it in for you?" He held out his hand.

She always liked Ben, but journalism was war as well. Her trip to Gettysburg came at a great cost and inconvenience to Andrew and the *Daily*, not to mention her children. So Clare felt obligated to write powerful and protected articles while she was here. "I should telegraph it in myself."

He grinned, not as if he got caught, but as if he admired her professionalism. "I'll always have a heart for the *Daily*, you know. I don't believe in regrets in life, but . . . I wish I had stayed and fought it out with you and Andrew. What you are doing there is important."

"Thank you, Ben. Your words will bring great encouragement to my husband."

He made his way up the hill and then down the dirt road that led to the makeshift telegraph station the reporters collaborated on setting up as their link to New York.

Imagine if Cyrus had succeeded with his cable across the Atlantic? She would have been able to share news of this battle with Europe. Poor Cyrus. The continued failures of his efforts were under investigation by a committee, and the report was due out any day. Clare had already heard the news would be damning. Still, she believed he would somehow persevere.

Clare made her way back up to the hill, where other correspondents and artists seemed to be breaking down for the day, most certainly to jockey for telegraph time and to send their drawings off with couriers. The sun was descending, and the three-day battle seemed to be winding down as well.

The clouds had been darkening, and the first flashes of lightning filled the sky, although blending in with the occasional flashes of ordnance.

Suddenly a strange feeling overwhelmed her as she looked down on the smoldering and cadaverous rolling hills. An impending danger. Something terrible was about to happen.

She could sense it in every core of her being.

Chapter 35

THE RETREAT

These were to be Confederate skies—bold, bright, and destined to secure victory against the impossible odds.

But instead, the impending darkness crept over fields piled with bodies of so many sons of misfortune, their last movement, brief spasms, hands raised in flailing desperation and groans and wails to be unanswered, except for the thunder that played in harmony with the smattering of artillery rounds.

All was lost. And all that was left for the once-brilliant maneuvers of Southern generals was a retreat of haste.

The lightning cast illuminations on the land of the dying, and before him Seamus grieved with the agony in the face of Anders, who wrestled to free himself.

"Please, Chaplain Hanley. I ain't meaning no disrespect, but he's out there." Anders pointed up the hill, to someone he believed was alive among the hideous and contorted pile of bodies. The rest of the Southern battalion had begun their hasty retreat. Amid orders and shouts, they limped off in pain and defeat.

Which left Seamus and Anders eerily alone.

Seamus glanced up at the peak of the hill. Inexplicably, the Union soldiers had not followed to finish the task of decimating Lee's army. At any moment, he expected the shadows to rise and the fury of the North to sweep down the hillside.

"I won't let you go out there, Anders. Your father, your mother, my daughter—they would never forgive me." He looked at the boy's eyes, hardened by what they had seen. There was no longer any mission left for Seamus in this battle at Gettysburg. All that remained was to see to the promise he had made Fletch back home.

"It ain't a right thing. Leavin' my friend to die. I'm tellin' you, sir, he's just up a ways."

"And so are snipers, all around us, my son. You are a brave lad, but the fight is done in us now. Come, let us go together."

Another brilliant flash and the ghosts rose again, twisted bodies and faces, framed in a mist that was either fog or smoke. Seamus sensed the danger was impending. Step-by-step, rifles pointed, hundreds of Union soldiers would emerge over the hill.

The boy's body relaxed and he nodded at Seamus. One glance back up the hill, and then defeated he began to turn and they were walking side by side.

But it was only a feint, and in an instant Anders was racing through the open field stepping over bodies and slipping, then rising again and approaching the crest of the hill.

He moved with alacrity. "Anders!" It was all Seamus could do. The boy slipped from his grip.

Then just as the boy rose above the peak of the hill, a shot sounded, then another, and Seamus watched in horror as the boy's body jerked and fell backward, tumbling down.

"No!" Seamus closed his eyes. What was he to do now? He couldn't save them all. The battle was lost. He would fight another day.

He turned and his shoulders slumped. There was a voice in

his head. It was Pastor Asa. *"What if all of our lives are spent with the purpose of saving one? Would it be worth it then?"*

Seamus lowered his chin to his chest and turned back. Now the distance seemed so far, so impossible to survive a run. What about Ashlyn? His daughter, Grace? Should he not retreat for their benefit?

Then he heard Anders pleading, rife with pain. "Seamus!"

Surely the boy was dying and there was not much he could do. If he made his way up the hill after him, Seamus would only serve as an escort to gates out of this world. Was he ready to die? To leave his wife and daughter?

He glanced down to his side where his canteen hung. The water of life, as Chaplain Scripps once referred to it. If he could give the boy his last sip and hear his final petition to God, it was the least he could do for Fletch and Coralee. He suddenly knew his promise to Fletch was much deeper than the old moonshiner understood. There was no better way to care for the boy than to be there for him to make his peace with the Father.

Seamus prayed for protection and started his way forward, but he had only taken a few steps before he heard the pounding of hooves and the rattling of a bridle, followed by a neigh.

"Have you not heard the orders?"

Seamus spun, and in the foggy twilight was the confident figure of a man mounted on a horse, its front legs rising.

"The order was to retreat, soldier!"

The lighting flashed again. And though it only briefly illuminated, he clearly saw who was before him.

"Seamus Hanley!" The words came out with deliberation and vileness.

Seamus was speaking to a shadow again. "Colonel Percy Barlow."

The thunder rocked through the valley, and it added to the tension of the moment. And if not for movement of the horse struggling against its reins, there wouldn't be any motion at all.

"And now I am just as David." Percy shifted in his saddle, glancing around as if to see if they were alone.

"I am afraid, sir, I do not understand."

"You are a preacher, are you not . . . Chaplain Hanley?"

Again, another burst of light flared, and now Seamus could see a revolver pointed at him.

"When God had delivered his enemy Saul to him in the cave," Percy laughed, "David didn't have the courage to fulfill his destiny. But I do, Chaplain."

"There is a man up there," Seamus said. "He is dying. It is Fletch's boy. You know him as well."

"Always hated that old coot."

"I promised his parents I would care for the lad. And it is a promise I will be keeping."

"The order was to retreat, Chaplain Hanley."

"I don't believe you intend to allow me to retreat."

"This is true. What's one more fallen soldier? Especially a traitor?"

Seamus turned. Then he heard the sound of the hammer being cocked and paused. "You going to shoot a man of the cloth in the back, Percy? Is that who you've become?"

With his life hanging from the thinnest of twine, taut and fraying, Seamus stepped forward. Then again. "Please, Father. I pray for Your protection."

Then another. Should he run? No. If he moved quickly, it might startle Percy.

Now Seamus lumbered over bodies and his ankles buckled. And he soon would be in the sights of Union soldiers. His body tensed with each meticulous advance. The fear screamed through the pores of his skin but he continued. The drive to reach Anders prevailed.

Then he saw Ashlyn's face. Just as in her picture he had carried with him all of these years. "Oh, Lord, please let me see her again."

In that very moment, he sensed his ministry of the tents was finished. As if God had just relieved him of his duty. It was time for him to go home. To be with Ashlyn and Grace. He stepped again. He just needed to reach Anders.

The clouds lit up again, revealing the tormented faces of death all around him. A loud clap rang out and Seamus felt a pressure against his back. He fell forward and landed into a pile of bodies. A pain ripped in his side and he lay still, terrified to let it be known he was still alive.

He heard the sound of reins, a whistle, and then the pounding of the ground. He was alone. Terribly, terribly alone. Accompanied only by the thunder and the groans of men.

Soon he would not need to feign death because it was coming upon him, and he cried at the thought of never seeing his wife and daughter again.

Then the agony grew. Until he succumbed to the darkness.

Chapter 36

THE VISITOR

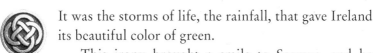

It was the storms of life, the rainfall, that gave Ireland its beautiful color of green.

This irony brought a smile to Seamus, and he looked up to the grayness of the sky and opened his mouth as the sweet rain poured in his mouth. He was sitting on the bank of a small stream, only a few hundred yards from his house.

It was here he would come to escape, to be all alone in his own thoughts.

But he wasn't alone, for a man sat beside him, dressed in white, yet he wasn't getting wet or muddy.

"Am I dead?" Seamus was surprised at how the question didn't disturb him.

"Do you want to be?" The man's eyes were strong yet soft, full of laughter and of grace.

"I don't believe I do. But, this place is so pleasant and peaceful." He watched the flow of water in the stream. "Isn't this where . . . ?"

"You know that it is, son."

Seamus liked being called son. But he thought of that day, how many years back, when he found his brother Kevan floating in the water, blue and lifeless. And as he pulled the three-year-old out of the currents, Seamus knew his own life had extinguished, the coals doused with the water of that river. He was worthless to this world. For he was the one supposed to be watching his little brother.

"Why don't I feel—?"

"The shame? The burden?"

"It's gone."

"That's forgiveness. Grace. It's what heals us. It's what sets us apart."

"But why? Why must we go through this at all?"

"The suffering. The pain. Without it there can be no forgiveness."

Seamus heard voices in the background, and he wanted them to go away, but they came closer and grew louder.

"And Kevan?"

The man smiled at him. "He's fine."

"Isn't there another way? Without all of the . . . misery?"

"Let me ask you, son, how would you know not to choose pain, suffering, and death if you never experienced it yourself?"

This seemed such a strange response, but it made sense to Seamus.

"Wouldn't it be crueler if the existence of darkness was kept from you? Then there would only be the lies of the enemy to mislead you."

The voices became clearer. "Look here. There's a priest?"

Seamus wanted to remain here forever on the bank of the river, but the man sitting next to him began to fade.

"Can you believe it?" said one of the men's voices. "The bullet went clear through his canteen. Probably saved his life."

"Let's turn him. This rain, when will it ever let up? It's going to wash us all away."

"Oh no. Will you look at that. He landed on a bayonet, sliced through his coat. Poor sap. That's an ugly wound."

"Is he one of ours?"

"I don't know. These priests all look the same to me."

"Here's a Bible in his pocket. Yep, there it is up front. His name is written. Seamus Hanley. Do we have any priests by that name?"

"I don't know; we should find out."

"He's dead anyway. What's the matter?"

"We're supposed to find the living out here. Let's get moving. Take the Bible with you and we'll see if anyone knows him."

"This cursed downpour. When will it ever stop?"

Chapter 37

THE WOUND

 The rain pounded on the roof of Davin's tent, which glowed with the flicker of candlelight. "You shouldn't be here, you know."

"Hush and hold that candle closer to the wound."

Through the tenderness of her hands, Davin felt little pain beyond what the morphine had taken away. "There are others who need you."

"You were shot, Davin." Muriel reached into her bag and pulled out some tweezers, then slowly moved them toward the wound in his shoulder. He winced as the metal hit flesh. "Good. I am glad that it hurts. What were you thinking not going to get someone to tend to this? If it wasn't for your friend Barry telling me about you, why you would be in here bleeding out."

"Come on, Muriel. You should know as well as any how I feel. To be there and watch my friends hacked down, without limbs, and spattered across the fields." He pointed to his arms. "This isn't anything."

"Most of them can't be saved." She pulled out the instrument and then held it up to the candlelight. "You are fortunate. It's just a fragment. After I clean this out and sew it up, you should be fine."

"I told you it was nothing."

"I didn't say it was nothing. You have a high chance of this swelling up on you, and it will be days before we will know if it turns foul."

Muriel pulled out a bottle of alcohol and poured it on the wound. Then she reached into her bag and pulled out a needle and some surgical thread.

As she tugged in and out of the stitches, he gazed at her with admiration. There was something so attractive to him about her focus, her talent, her ability to heal.

After a few minutes she looked up at him. "You know, I've never done this before with someone smiling so foolishly at me."

"You are a very beautiful woman, you know."

"That is the morphine lying to you. Now hold still."

"Muriel." He grasped her chin. "I am terribly sorry if it is shallow of me to consider you my cause, but when I was out there today, thinking I was going to die, all I could do was fight, not for freedom, or to make a name for myself. It was so I could survive, so I could see you again."

Even in the dim light, he could tell she was blushing. She lowered her head. "You still don't know me, Davin."

"Then start teaching me. I want to be your best student. Your only student. I want to learn everything about you."

She bit her lip and started to cry.

"What is it? What did I say? What made it so difficult for you to open up, to share who you are?"

Muriel wiped the moisture from her eyes. "Let me finish what I was doing."

They were silent as she completed her task, and he was comforted by the soothing music of the raindrops tapping on the canvas roof. Davin knew what was outside—the weather, the horror, the bloodshed. He also knew that in a few moments she would need to leave and he wouldn't see her again for days.

But right now, away from the explosions and inside the safety and warmth of this tent alongside Muriel, this was where he wanted to be.

This moment of calm ended abruptly when the flap of their tent opened.

A head stuck in. Davin was relieved to see it was only Barry.

"How is your patient?" Barry had a bandage wrapped around his forehead.

"Ornery," Muriel said. "Come in before you get soaked."

Barry stepped inside and closed the flap behind him. "I just came for a quick question for Davey here."

"What do you want?" Davin wasn't pleased that his moment alone was being disturbed, especially since he knew she was about to leave.

"You're right about this one. He is ornery." Barry held up a book in his hand. "I'll be quick about it." His expression grew serious. "You said you had a brother, right?"

"Yes." Davin's gut started to jolt.

"What was his name?"

"Seamus. What is this about?"

Barry looked down to the floor. "There were some fellows asking about a priest they found out there by the name of Hanley."

"What are you saying?" Davin nudged Muriel away.

"This is his Bible."

Davin grabbed it from his hand, and although it was soaked and muddy, he recognized it. He opened it to where he knew Seamus had signed his name and then he shut it. "Where is he?"

Barry shook his head. "They said he's dead. With this rain, you're best to wait until morning to pay your respects."

Muriel went to put her arm around Davin, but he crawled to his feet. He held up the Bible. "I need to see who gave this to you, Barry. Now."

Chapter 38

THE FIREFLIES

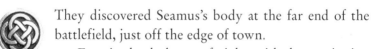 They discovered Seamus's body at the far end of the battlefield, just off the edge of town.

Even in the darkness of night, with the continuing showering of rain, the fields were still scattered with soldiers, medics, and undertakers who carried lanterns as they peered down into torn and empty faces. But they were so far off, they appeared like fireflies fluttering above the cold, wet fields.

"He's still alive." The rain splattered on Muriel's face, and her hair was matted against her cheeks as she looked up to Davin and Barry.

"That's . . . not . . . possible." The soldier who had escorted them to this location took a step back.

"You just left him here to die!" Davin clasped the soldier by his jacket, and pain seared in his injured shoulder.

"There is no time for blaming." Muriel's voice demanded attention. She looked at the young boy. "You can go now. Help the others."

"I swear. He wasn't alive." The soldier turned away and scurried over the hill and out of their view.

Muriel turned to Barry. "See if you can find a wheelbarrow or gurney. Anything we can use to get him back to camp."

"Right." Barry gave Davin a consoling nod. Then he ran off, soon blending in with the blackness.

"Hold this." Muriel handed the lantern to Davin and he held it over his brother's face, which looked tranquil despite the surroundings and the pelting rain.

"Are you certain he's alive?"

"He has a pulse," Muriel said. "It's weak, but he is still with us . . . for now." She unbuttoned Seamus's jacket and peeled back his shirt, then she pointed to the wound in his stomach.

"Is it bad?" But Davin could see the severity for himself.

"We need to get him someplace warm. He's lost blood and he's been out here for so long in the cold. What's left of him will be gone soon."

Seamus's eyes opened.

Davin leaned down beside him. "Seamus."

"Ashlyn?"

"No. This is Davin."

"Be still." Muriel squeezed Seamus's hand.

Seamus turned his head toward her. "Ashlyn?"

"You are going to be fine," Davin said. "I'm going to make sure of that." He leaned down and kissed his brother on his forehead, which was cold to the touch.

Then Seamus's eyes closed again and they were alone.

"There is nothing I can do out here in the dark. At least the bleeding has stopped." She buttoned his shirt and closed the coat. Then she put the back of her hand against his cheek. "We have to get him some warmth."

Davin took off his jacket and winced at the pain in his shoulder. What an insignificant wound it was now considering his brother's condition. He laid his wool coat over Seamus. As the water beat on his brother's face, Davin was reminded of his cruel prank back at the gold mine, spraying Seamus's tent with the hydraulic hose. Just like then, Seamus was drenched, but everything seemed so different to Davin.

What kind of person was he anyway? How could he have ever been so calloused to behave so cruelly? Now, as he looked at Seamus's face, Davin realized he would do anything for his brother. But now he may never get a proper chance to seek forgiveness. He would carry this burden for the remainder of his life.

He looked over to Muriel, whose once-white apron was now muddied, bloodied, and wet. This was taking her away from the medical tents where she could be attending to dozens of fallen soldiers. Was it wrong for him to take her away from her work? If she minded, she wasn't giving any indication.

There was a noise and a small covered wagon, pulled by a single horse, approached with a lantern bouncing. It came to a stop and two figures stepped down.

"You ain't say nothing about it being Johnny Reb." The man who spoke pulled the lantern from its hook and stepped forward, his face framed with a tight-cropped silver beard.

"He's a preacher, friend." Barry walked beside him.

"I suppose that makes a difference." The man put a hand on his waist. "Don't look much lively."

Barry stepped forward. "I went to that house over there and saw a wheelbarrow in the yard. When I knocked on the door, Mr   "

"Mr. Miller. But before I offered, I didn't know it was Johnny Reb."

"Do you have a fireplace, Mr. Miller?" Muriel didn't seem to be interested in the side banter.

"Why, yes."

"Can we take him to your house?"

"You don't want to take him to the hospital tents?" Davin whispered.

"They have no heat, and they are overrun, and if they learn that your brother is . . . Well, he'll die before they get to him." Muriel turned her attention to the old-timer. "Mr. Miller?"

"He isn't gonna, you know, pass on in my house, is he?"

Davin stood and started to move toward the man when Barry stepped between them.

"Mr. Miller," Barry said with a sweet intonation, "how often in our lifetime does one get a chance to save a man of God?"

"Well . . . I suppose."

"And to save such a man whose brother happens to be a famous gold miner?" Barry pointed at Davin.

"Is that so? Well . . . that's interesting enough. You know what I say. Anything I can do for you boys. We all have to do our part, right?"

Chapter 39

THE CARRIAGE

"So what's it like, son?" Mr. Miller handed Davin a bowl of pea soup.

"Pardon? Oh, thank you." Despite the crackling wood fire in the hearth, Davin's hands were still cold, and it felt good to wrap his hands around the clay bowl. While he dipped the spoon into the green liquid, he kept his gaze on the rising and falling of Seamus's chest, fearing at any moment it would cease moving. "What was that?"

"To find gold? I've always wanted to do that. Even thought about making a trip out to California myself."

Davin took a deep sip of the soup, which was salty and flavorful, and it felt warm and soothing as it went down his throat. What was with this man? He was sitting next to a preacher lying on a mattress in front of his fire and he was asking about gold. "It's exciting, I suppose."

"How come you don't do it anymore?" He pulled up a chair and started eating a bowl of his own soup, making loud slurping noises. "You know, the gold mining."

Davin wished he could be alone. It had been several hours since Muriel finished cleaning and stitching up Seamus. Muriel stayed longer than she should have, but Davin hated to see her go. Not only because of her medical expertise, but he didn't want to be without her companionship during this time.

Barry as well had again demonstrated his friendship by making a trip back to camp in the rain to retrieve all of Davin's belongings. But when he left an hour ago, Davin just wanted time alone with his brother. Yet the old man certainly deserved companionship in exchange for his hospitality, which was much more generous than they initially thought it would be.

"I spent a lot of time trying to dig riches from places that were probably better left alone." Davin looked up at the ceiling. "It's odd to think how much that all meant to me at one time."

"Yes," Mr. Miller said. "This war has a way of shifting perspectives."

Davin glanced around the interior of the house, which was simple but tidy. "Did you stay here?"

"What? During the battle?" He took another sip, and part of it dripped on his beard. "No. I'm not that big of a fool. I own a carriage shop in town. I stayed there until the artillery stopped railing. Why I hadn't been back here long at all before your friend . . . what's his name? Barry? Yes before Barry came by. Really startled me some."

Davin pointed to his face.

"What? Oh . . . thank you." Mr. Miller lifted a napkin and dabbed it on his beard.

There was a melancholy about the man that Davin could relate to. "You have a wife?"

"Me. No. Well, I used to." He winced. "She died a few years back."

"I'm sorry."

"Oh, don't be. We had many good years." He stared into the

fire. "Many good years." Mr. Miller waved his spoon at Davin. "You like that girl. That nurse. Don't you?"

It made no sense to lie to this man. "Yes. I like her quite well."

"She fancies you as well." He started to scrape the spoon along the inside of the bowl.

"I know she does."

"What about your brother?" He nodded toward Seamus, who continued to sleep. "Is he going to . . . make it through?"

"No." Davin had a hard time uttering these words. "Muriel says that she's done all she can, but he'll die in a few days." He looked at his brother, who was wearing his chaplain's uniform again, which they had cleaned and dried by the fire. "Might have been better if he had died right away . . . as opposed to lingering on."

"No sense speaking for God. He makes up His own mind when people come and go."

"You believe all of that?" Davin scraped the last of his soup into a full spoonful.

"About God? Yes." Mr. Miller reached out for Davin's bowl. "More?"

"If it's not an inconvenience."

"Not at all." He got up, left the room, and came back carrying a full bowl while watching it carefully in his hands. "Got a bit ambitious."

"Not a drop will be wasted." Davin cheerfully accepted it.

"Now, my wife." Mr. Miller sat back in the chair, this time with a groan.

"She was a good cook?"

"No. I mean, yes she was a good cook. But you were asking me about my belief in God. Now, my wife." He stepped around Seamus and reached up to the mantelpiece and pulled down a frame. Then he wiped the dust off with his sleeve and handed it to Davin.

It was an old daguerreotype and it appeared to about fifteen years old. "She's a lovely woman." He handed it back.

Mr. Miller looked at the face smiling back at him. "Mildred was a very faithful woman." He looked up. "You'd have to be to put up with a man like myself. When she died, I am afraid she took some of my faith with her."

The picture reminded Davin of something. He set his bowl down on the table beside him and reached down into Seamus's front shirt pocket, and sure enough, there was the faded photo of Ashlyn. Or what was left of it.

"What's that?" Mr. Miller went to the fire and added a couple of logs.

"This," Davin glanced at the fading image, "is the photo that drove my brother to travel more than a thousand miles in search of a woman."

Mr. Miller stepped up and clapped his hands together. "Ashlyn?"

"Yes . . . how did you know?"

"That's the name I keep hearing him mutter."

"Yes, of course."

"Was he always a man of faith? Your brother?"

"No. That came later. I suppose right around the time he found Ashlyn."

"Women have a way of doing that for us, don't they?"

This struck Davin. Was his pursuit of Muriel causing him to rekindle his faith? The old man was right. He realized why it was referred to as falling in love. It was like falling off a cliff and hoping there was water below. This type of risk took more than a man could do on his own.

"Hey," Davin said. "Would you want to see some?"

"See what?"

Davin reached down into his pack and poked around a bit and then pulled out a small glass with a cork sealing the top. He held it to his eye, pleased to see the two large gold nuggets were still in there. He handed it to Mr. Miller.

"Is it real?" They were now in the hands of a wide-eyed child.

"They better be. It's all I have left of my possessions."

There was a knock on the door, and then it cracked open. "May I come in?" Muriel didn't wait for an answer. She was carrying her medical case, and she went over to Seamus and examined him. "How has he been doing?"

"He's woken a few times," Davin said. "What are you doing here?" He couldn't imagine how exhausted she must be having worked in the medical tents for a day and a half without rest.

"What?" She turned to Davin and seemed agitated. "Well I've been worried about him."

"Keeps asking for his Ashlyn," Mr. Miller said. "Poor soul." He stood. "What manners. May I get you a bowl of soup?"

"That would be delightful," Muriel said without turning from her patient.

Davin was thinking of something Mr. Miller had just said. "Muriel?"

"Yes?"

"Are you sure there is . . . no hope for him?"

She broke from her work, turned toward Davin, and her face softened. "There is always hope. But," her eyebrows lowered, "the cut is deep. I have sewed it up as best I can. And I have given him morphine to help with the pain. You need to prepare yourself. There is nothing we can amputate here. I've seen these wounds so many times before. He has two, three, maybe four days left."

Davin touched her arm. "I don't want to just stand around and watch him die."

Muriel shook her head as if she didn't understand. "Are you just going to leave him?"

"No. I want to take him home."

"Home?"

"Where is home, young man?" Mr. Miller returned with another bowl of soup. He directed Muriel to the chair, and she sat and began to eat the soup.

"A town called Taylorsville. It's in the Shenandoah Valley."

"Well, that's a fair distance." Mr. Miller walked over to the other side of the room and fumbled with papers on his desk.

"I know it is madness," Davin said, as Muriel sipped her soup. "But if he has a chance to see his wife again, and if I have any way of granting him that last wish, then it would at least be something I can do for him. And myself."

"The travel would hasten his death," Muriel said, in between quick ladles of her soup. "He needs constant care."

"I know it's not safe for him, Muriel. But if he is going to die anyway, then there isn't much to risk."

"No. You don't understand. Your brother needs continued care, and he'll get that."

Davin shook his head. "I don't know what you're saying."

She put the empty bowl on the table and stood, wiping her chin with the back of her hand. "He will get constant care because I am accompanying you."

Her words lifted his spirits. She would come with him? It provided a sudden confirmation to his plan. But then his enthusiasm melted as quickly as it had arrived. "No. You can't leave here. The commission needs you. This is what you've always done. This . . . this is your cause."

Muriel took both of his hands. "Causes change."

Davin tried to comprehend the depth of her sacrifice. He was grateful to have her expertise, her fellowship. But something was disturbing him about all of this. Was there something more to her explanation? There had to be. It was so unlike her to leave her station.

"Here. I found it. Come here." Mr. Miller flung open the map by the hearth so they could see it in the light. "This may be a little old, but most of the roads should hold true. You may want some civilian clothes so as not to stick out so much. We're not exactly the same size young man, but I can see what I have."

Davin glanced over at his brother and realized there was a major flaw with this plan. They had no way of moving his brother. "Will he be able to ride a horse?"

"That won't be a problem. You are going to take my wagon."

This was all surreal to Davin. How could this all be coming together? There was something wrong. Or odd. Or supernatural. Davin leaned back against the hearth. "This is all rubbish. I couldn't ask you to let us use your wagon. And even if we did, there's no hope of us getting past roadblocks without getting stopped. None of this will work."

Mr. Miller took over the proponent's role. "You can't give up on your brother. It would be a great gesture. A wonderful story. Some joy in this miserable war. Besides, I would not be giving you the wagon. I would be selling it to you."

Davin raised his hands. "I used to have money."

"You've got something better." Mr. Miller pulled out the vial of the two gold nuggets. He uncorked it and pulled out one. He resealed it and handed it back to Davin. He held the nugget up to the light of the fire. Then he held out his hand to Davin. "Fair price?"

In his head, Davin tried to calculate the value of the nugget and it didn't take long to figure it wasn't near worth the value of a horse, let alone the wagon. But the fact he had something to exchange gave him some peace about the transaction. He shook hands with Mr. Miller, whose smile glowed through his beard.

Still, there were too many impossibilities left for them to solve. "Now, how are we going to make it past the sentries without getting stopped?"

Muriel was already packing her medical bag. "I've got a plan for that. But it begins with us leaving now. In the cover of dark."

Chapter 40

BACK HOME

Clare had lingered in Gettysburg for two days after the battle had ended, and she had yet to get any answers.

With more than twenty thousand casualties, it was understandable that the soldiers would be busy and the doctors would have no time for a reporter's questions, but she found it excruciatingly frustrating that she couldn't find out anything about Davin. Not from his superior officers. Not from the men in his battalion. They could only say that he was missing, and although they couldn't confirm he was a casualty, they hadn't seen him for several days.

Was he out there lying in some field? One among the many bodies being stacked and waiting for the embalming surgeon? The mere thought made her stomach churn, but until his death was confirmed, she clung to the fading hope that he was still alive.

Equally frustrating was her inability to locate Muriel. In the last day, Clare had gone from hospital tent to hospital tent, past the carts stacked with body parts, and peered in to see some of the worst horrors mankind had ever witnessed. But still no Muriel.

Clare was determined to get the answers she was seeking. Finally she hunted down a lead. Clare was told that Nurse Hilda Meldrickson was the type of woman who put her nose into all things, and if anyone knew where Muriel was, it would be this Sanitary Commission officer.

But to pursue this lead meant Clare would have to endure the screams and the moans as the surgeons performed their awful craft.

In little more than a day, the doctors and nurses and their teams had set up what appeared to be a city of tents, each over-filled with the diseased and dying. It took Clare most of the day to track Nurse Meldrickson down, and when she did, she found the lady to be in the foulest of moods. Which under the circumstances, certainly was understandable.

Clare skipped exchanging pleasantries with the woman glaring down at her and got to the point. "I am seeking a woman by the name of Muriel McMahon. My understanding is that she reports to you."

The mention of Muriel's name seemed to crack the brittleness of the woman's expression. But only momentarily. "There are many people who report to me. May I ask who you are and what business you have in the matter?"

"I am Clare Royce, a correspondent for the *New York Daily*, and I have some questions for her."

Nurse Meldrickson leaned back on her heels and crossed her arms. "In that case, Miss Royce, I have no comment on the matter." She turned to go into a tent.

Clare grabbed her by the arm, perhaps a bit too brusquely, and this was met with a glare of daggers.

"I am very sorry, Nurse Meldrickson. Please forgive me as I am quite exhausted."

"As we all are." She freed her arm from Clare's grasp.

"Wait. I am not here in the capacity of a reporter. I am here as Muriel's friend. She was our nanny and I'm quite concerned about her."

The nurse flared her nostrils and looked at Clare from shoes to forehead, her lips curled. But then she seemed to soften. "I have not seen Muriel for several days now."

"Several days? Hasn't she been helping out with the wounded?"

"She hasn't been here to help a single soul. Before the first shot was fired, I was approached by some officers and they were quite insistent that they needed to speak with Muriel. I shared this news with her, and she seemed . . . affected by it, frankly. I had not seen her since."

Clare lowered her head.

"I'm sorry," the nurse said. "I wish I had more to share with you. I do. Muriel was a fine nurse for us, with the skill of a doctor. She will be missed. Now, I must . . ." She pointed to the door of the tent.

"Yes, of course. Thank you."

What was that all about? What could the officers had wanted to discuss with Muriel?

"Clare!"

She looked up to see Ben Jones jogging toward her. He stopped and put his hands on his knees to catch his breath. "Here, this telegram came in for you from the *Daily*."

Clare took it from him and noticed that it wasn't in an envelope.

"The army opens everything coming in," he said for explanation.

"I suppose then, you can tell me what it says."

He shrugged. "I can't help my curiosity. I am a journalist."

She read the words slowly:

THE MILITIA HAS BEEN CALLED TO SERVICE. THE *DAILY* HAS BEEN THREATENED. PLEASE COME HOME. ANDREW.

"What does this mean?" Clare looked up to Ben's concerned eyes.

"The news is just coming in on this, but it appears it's about Lincoln's draft. They are giving a three-hundred-dollar exemption, which means the wealthy can buy safety for their sons. The poor, and the Irish in particular, have had it. And they are blaming the blacks for the war in the first place. It looks quite serious. Many of us in the press corps are making plans to head back as soon as we can, but finding transportation will be difficult."

How could this be? Here she was desperately trying to find out if her brother was alive, and now she had to worry about her family back home. What should she do?

"It's worse," Ben said. "The word we're hearing is that the newspapers are going to suffer retaliation. Well, at least those who have been supportive of what they are calling 'The Negro Cause.'"

"The *Daily*," she whispered.

But was she too late?

Chapter 41

CROSSROADS

"You know, if you sat next me to up here, I wouldn't have to shout." Davin turned back and saw Muriel peering out of the shadow of the covered wagon, seeming to enjoy the sprawling farm countryside.

"And how would that look? A Union soldier with a civilian beside him? That would only stir curiosity."

Muriel was right. So far he had only drawn friendly waves from those who passed by or observed him from the fields. To their eyes, he simply appeared to be a supply driver. "But if you were beside me, it would mean my neck wouldn't hurt so much from turning to admire your pretty face."

She strained to speak above the rattling of the wooden wheels on the gravely roads. "If I felt you meant that, I would certainly be flattered."

That was it. Davin pulled on the reins and then pulled up hard on the brake. "Why must you do that?"

"What?"

"Not believe me. When I tell you how lovely you are?"

Her light red eyebrows bent in and she stared at him for a moment before speaking. "We are out of camp now. No longer am I the only woman under fifty years of age. So you can enjoy these beautiful farm girls. And without any discomfort in your neck."

"Who did this to you?"

"Did what?"

"Made you so unlovable."

"Unlovable?" Hurt shone in her blue eyes.

"Not that you are unlovable, but that you won't allow yourself to be loved."

"Davin, you must keep this wagon moving. It will appear suspicious for us to be stopped for no reason."

"I am not starting this wagon again until you answer my question."

Muriel crossed her arms. "Then your brother will never make it home."

He should have known better than to square up against Muriel. She would always have the advantage. Davin released the brake, tugged on the reins, and then they were grinding away on the dirt road once again.

What was indisputably beautiful was the farm country they were traveling through. Muriel had been navigating them through remote country roads, and in this part of Maryland, it was hard to know a war was raging.

This was their second full day of travel and it had been surprisingly uneventful. Whether the Union army was busy recovering from its wounds or chasing retreating Confederates, they were nowhere to be seen so far. Yet Davin was well aware that all it would take was one scout team, soldiers coming from the other direction, or even a curious farmer and they could risk being arrested and even hung for deserting their posts.

"My uncle."

"What?" Davin didn't intend to have so much anger laced in his response.

"My uncle," Muriel shouted. "He told me when I was young that I wasn't going to earn a good husband with my appearance. He said I would have to try harder than other women."

What kind of man would say something like that to his niece?

"He wasn't being mean," Muriel added. "He was a practical man and I appreciated his honesty."

"What about your parents? Didn't they treat you with more kindness?"

"They died."

"What?" They were almost shouting at one another now, making it an awkward conversation.

"When we came to America, I was only a baby. They died of yellow fever aboard the ship."

What would he say now? What Davin originally intended as a compliment was now becoming a discussion not designed for hollering. "Well, your uncle was mistaken."

Muriel didn't say anything for a few moments, and he glanced back to see if she was finished speaking. Had he pushed her too far? "Thank you, Davin, but there are traits more significant than a person's appearance, are there not? That's all my uncle was trying to teach me."

It was clear. She wasn't going to take praise without a fight. Davin decided to talk about something else. Anything else.

"How is he doing?"

"My uncle?"

"No."

"Oh, your brother?" she said with relief in her voice. "He is still coming in and out. Part of that is the morphine we've given him. This road isn't doing him any favors for his pain."

"Imagine how much more difficult this would be without Mr. Miller's generosity." The carriage builder had given them a strong horse and his finest wagon, which because of the craftsmanship of its springs, absorbed much of the bouncing.

And Mr. Miller joined them as outlaws. Despite their pleadings, he insisted on helping them flee past the Union army. Under the evening sky and through muddy roads, he drove them down the first mile of their voyage, while they hid in the back just in case they were halted. Peculiarly, they encountered neither Yanks guarding the back roads nor signs of the rebels who had drifted away as elusive apparitions in the night. It was as if the great battle was merely some unruly dream.

"Your brother should be dead already," Muriel said flatly. "For us to have the good fortune of encountering Mr. Miller, and even now to have these roads clear for us, maybe God does protect His soldiers."

He enjoyed the idea of Seamus being a soldier for God. "You know, I used to revere my brother because he was able to rise against the cruelty of our father, and the difficulties of his life. He was an outcast, one who would shake his fist at the skies. But when he became a . . . man of God . . ."

"You lost your hero," Muriel said.

"I thought he was a coward. A man should find happiness and respect on his own, right?" Davin rued the words, but they were true to how he thought back in California.

Was this why he had cheated Seamus? Why he misled his brother about the mine of Ashlyn's late father? Everyone believed the claim was finished and drained of its gold. But years later when Davin returned to the mine, he made a discovery. An untapped vein. The mother lode.

"I thought I earned it. Why should anybody else know?"

"What are you talking about, Davin?"

He didn't feel comfortable enough to share this inner conflict of his soul. Was what he did truly wrong? Why did Seamus deserve to know? If his brother didn't care about the gold, and even preached against it, then why include him in the riches of the stake?

Looking back to that time, Davin could clearly see now this

decision was the fork in the road with his relationship with his brother. Somewhere in those mountain trails of the Sierra, Davin chose the gold over everything else.

"Hello. Are you there?"

Davin cleared his throat. "I'm sorry. I was thinking of somebody I used to know."

It wasn't the wealth. It never was about the money for Davin. It was the independence that had seduced him. The spirit of the West, the chance to be his own man. This was the Golden Calf that had swept him away. And now, the romance had lost its luster. This independence he once cherished only led to loneliness, a place Davin no longer wanted to reside.

He reached into his pocket and shook the vial of gold, then held it up for Muriel to see. "My last nugget. All of those years under the cracking sun with picks, shovels, and pans, and this is all that remains."

"Well I say it's good to get rid of what's ill begotten."

Her statement gave him pause, but then she didn't approve of the hydraulic mining. She wasn't aware of half of it! But she was right. He couldn't wait to dispose of the last of it. To cleanse it from his blood.

"You know," Davin said. "I figured out why I am doing this."

"Doing what? Rescuing your brother?"

"Yes. Except I am not rescuing my brother." Davin thought of throwing the vial into one of the fields, but he gave it one more shake and returned it to his pocket. "Seamus is rescuing me."

His comment was cryptic. Muriel wouldn't understand how desperate it was for him to return Seamus back to Ashlyn. To give Davin a measure of peace by paying them back in some small way. But it all depended on Seamus making it there alive.

"How is my brother? Is he speaking at all?"

"When he wakes. And when I change his bandages. Mostly all I hear is him repeating Ashlyn's name over and over again. That, and sometimes he speaks of someone named Anders."

He listened to the rumbling of the road and the lowing of a few cattle. "Is Seamus going to make it back home?"

She paused. "How would you like me to respond?"

"Honestly. Tell me what is true, Doctor."

"This wagon will surely become a hearse before we are done."

He rounded the bend of the road, prepared to speed up the pace, but suddenly pulled hard on the reins. Up ahead, about a half mile down the straightway, were a group of men. "Muriel," he said in a hushed voice.

"That's a Union roadblock." Muriel stepped out from the back and leapt on the ground, and then she moved up to the front of the wagon. She grabbed the bridle of the black horse and guided it around in a tight circle as Davin watched closely to see if there was any movement out of the figures in the distance.

"Have they seen us?"

"No. I don't think . . ." Davin turned his gaze from the soldiers in front of them and noticed for the first time a young shirtless boy of about twelve years or so, holding on to the handles of a plow and staring at them with curiosity. All Davin could think to do was to wave. But, it was not responded in kind. Instead the boy turned and ran in the direction of a barn, brightly painted red.

"Get in, Muriel!"

She didn't hesitate, and in a moment and with some dexterity Muriel was in the back of the wagon again as he brought the horse to a full gallop. He glanced back to see if the boy had made it to the barn yet and noticed the large plume of dust rising from his wheels, which surely could be spotted from a distance. They had to get off of this road.

"What are we going to do?" Davin looked to Muriel who had provided all of the directions up to this point. If they had to circle back there would be no hope of Seamus making it alive to Taylorsville. "Tell me what to do."

"Yes. I am thinking." She climbed her way to the front and sat on the padded leather bench beside him.

"What about bringing attention with the two of us up here?"

"Stop."

"What?"

"Stop the wagon."

He saw the intensity in her eyes, whistled, and slowed the wagon to a halt. "What are we doing?" Davin looked behind them. They had traveled far out of the view of any soldiers or farmers and were being watched only by a large bull. But there was no time for them to delay.

"You need to get out."

"What?"

"Listen closely, Davin. We are about to enter Virginia territory. As soon as we do, that uniform you are wearing will either get you shot or put under military arrest."

"I can change out of this. Mr. Miller gave me some clothes."

"Do you know what happens as soon as you take that uniform off and then cross that border?"

He shook his head.

"If you are caught, you will be considered a Northern spy. Do you know what they do to spies? They hang them. That's after they torture them for information." She put her hand on his knee. "Davin. I don't need you anymore. I can do this by myself. I can bring your brother home."

"What about you? When they find out you are a nurse for the North?"

A lock of Muriel's hair fluttered in the breeze. "They don't kill nurses. There are too many dying soldiers. Just as they don't kill preachers. Your brother and I will be safe. You need to let me do this."

Davin's eyes started to water, and he didn't know if it was from emotion or the dust. "Why? Why would you do this?"

Muriel started to speak, but then she paused and squinted up at the sun. "It's not . . . some grand benevolence . . . in me. My motives are my own. And I don't want to disappoint you. More than I already will."

He held his hand to her face, and she flinched. "Why are you so difficult on yourself?"

"Trust me," Muriel said. "It is better if we are able to recall each other in this light. In this moment. From this point forward, there can only be regret."

Davin let out a deep sigh. This was no time for her spoken puzzles. But she was right about one thing. Once they crossed into enemy territory, a woman driving a wagon with a dying pastor would have a better chance of making it through the South. It was Seamus's best card to play.

But this was Davin's mission. Not hers. "I am not leaving my brother's side until he is returned to his family. Alive. It's you, Muriel. You're the one who must get off and go back to camp."

"I can't . . . go back, Davin." Her brows lifted and she smiled, now appearing sweet and vulnerable for the first time.

Of course. She had her fill of the violence, of the horror. And why wouldn't she? The sights those in the hospital tents were forced to endure were worse than anyone else in the war. Even for the hardened eyes of a trained doctor.

This was an honorable way for her to escape it all. They were both on the run. Different motives, but a shared purpose. All of this time he thought she was unable to be broken. She was the strong one.

But now he saw something else in her eyes. Something he knew and understood well. Loneliness. He could see she was beaten down by it as he was. They were fighting the same enemy. And they saw hope in freedom from it in each other.

Without any other words, they leaned into one another and embraced, Muriel cried, and it was a sweet sound in his ear.

Then she snapped up and pulled the red strands of her hair

behind her ears. "Then Private Hanley, if you are going to come with me, you will follow my orders . . . and closely. Go into the back and get changed. I will be driving now."

"Fine. But where are we going? We can't go back."

"There is a side road just up the ways. There is a . . . place I know about. I hadn't wanted us to go there. But it is now our only choice. Our only way to get your brother home alive."

Chapter 42

THE UNDERGROUND

"Davin? Is that you?"

Having been nodding off to sleep, Davin thought he was hearing Seamus's voice in a dream. But a jolt of the wagon snapped him awake and he found himself sitting beside his brother, his face just a couple of feet away.

"Davin?"

"Seamus. Yes. It's me." Davin was pleased to be recognized for the first time, but his brother now appeared at the grave's edge. His face was pale and puffy, and coated with beads of sweat. Davin put his hand to Seamus's forehead and it was hot to the touch.

"Where are we?" The wheels bounced again and Seamus clenched his jaw.

"Muriel, the morphine is wearing off!"

"Davin?"

"We're going home, Seamus. We're taking you home."

"Ashlyn?"

"Yes." Davin dipped the towel in the wooden bucket of water and squeezed it until it stopped dripping. Then he wiped down his brother's face. Would this be the last chance he had to speak to him? Should he take this moment to apologize? For everything?

Sadness swept across Seamus's face. "Anders?"

"Who is Anders?"

"I tried to . . . tried to help him." He began to get agitated.

"It's all right, big brother. Keep still. We need to get you well." This was no time for a confession. No time for him to relieve the pressure of his guilt. That was Davin being selfish again. No. He would only think of Seamus's well-being. Until he was able to return his brother into Ashlyn's arms, there would be no further focus on his own personal redemption. Perhaps that was the lesson of this all.

The wagon began to slow. Good. Muriel would be coming to give Seamus more medicine. Davin looked down again just to see the lids closing on his brother's Hanley blue eyes.

There were voices outside and Davin strained to listen.

"What danger we have now because of you." It was an older man.

"There was nothing else for us to do," Muriel said.

They were far enough away from the wagon for the conversation to be difficult to hear. Davin crawled to the front opening of the wagon, but the evening was upon them, and only after straining could he see they had arrived at a large farm. He could hear sheep bleating and dogs barking.

Muriel climbed back on the seat and without explanation she drove them toward a large barn. There, a woman holding a lantern opened the door and with a snap of the reins, Muriel directed the horse to pull them slowly inside.

Once the wagon glided to a stop, Muriel pulled on the brake and climbed down. Should he come out? In a moment, the back hatch of the wagon opened and Davin turned to see Muriel and two elderly faces peering inside.

"Is that one dead?" The man's face was elongated and stoic, his lips drooping down in a permanent scowl.

"He just spoke to me a few moments ago," Davin said.

"Who is that?" The woman's face was round with kindness and wrinkled, like an apple left in the sun.

"This doesn't feel proper," the man said.

"Oh, Pieter, there's nothing can be done about it now." The woman summoned Davin with her slender arms. "Come on out, young man. Let's get you fed and warmed."

For a summer day, it did feel particularly cool and Davin was in no mood to refuse hospitality. With his head crouched, he crawled his way around Seamus and stepped out onto the ground matted with hay. His knees buckled and he hadn't realized how stiff he had been from the long ride and how refreshing it felt to be able to stretch.

Pieter extended a reluctant hand of greeting.

"And I am Anika." She nodded at Davin and then stuck her lantern inside the back of the wagon. "What about this poor fellow?"

"Yes," Muriel said. "We should get him to a fire. Do you have something we could use to carry him?"

"A wheelbarrow will needs do." Pieter spat out a black puddle of tobacco and then walked off.

"All right then." Anika handed the lantern to Muriel. "I'll need to add more meat to the kettle. This is most unexpected."

"Does he . . . know?" Anika nodded toward Davin who was devouring his meal, disappointed to have to even look up to acknowledge them.

"Oh yes, I should have told you this before." Muriel sat cross-legged on the floor, close to Seamus who she was trying to feed as he lay on blankets by the fireplace. "Davin is Caitlin Hanley's younger brother. This pastor, Seamus, is her older brother. I don't know if you know their oldest sister, Clare."

Pieter sat in a rocking chair, glaring down at them as it creaked back and forth. Leaning up against the wall next to him was an old musket.

"Clare? Clare?" Anika scooped out another ladle of the steaming porridge into Davin's bowl.

"She writes for the *New York Daily*." Muriel wiped the side of Seamus's mouth with a cloth.

Anika shook her head. "We certainly know beautiful Caitlin. And, of course, Cassie as well. How is she?"

Davin deduced the connection. Caitlin and Cassie had been working together for the Underground Railroad for years. And he heard that Muriel had volunteered also while she was in New York. He noticed a strange expression come over Muriel's face and it appeared to be shame. What happened between Caitlin and her that would draw this response? Or was this about her relationship with Clare?

"Is this a safe house, then?" His gaze now traced Muriel, seeking out clues in every word they exchanged. If she wouldn't tell him what lay deep within, he would discover it himself.

Pieter cleared his throat and stopped rocking. He looked to Anika. "That's how we want it to remain."

"I must apologize for my husband." Anika walked over and put her hand on his shoulder.

"I need no apology."

"Yes." Anika looked down. "I am afraid we discussed it and we won't be of any assistance to you. Besides the meal, of course, and you can stay the night."

"The morning you leave." Pieter lifted the weapon and placed it across his lap.

"I understand," Muriel said. Davin could sense she had regretted bringing them here. Perhaps it was the knowledge of the risk they might have brought if they had been followed. Maybe this was what was bringing her such unease.

Yet the more he observed Muriel, the more he became fascinated with the posture she took, the subtle bending of her lip, the shifting away of her blue eyes, the lifting of her light red brows. Something about this journey was shifting her countenance, was lowering her pretenses. The tough, and at times surly woman, was yielding to inner fragility—a gentle rose, someone more vulnerable, more conflicted. This made him even more drawn to her because though she was speaking with their hosts, he knew she was communicating with him, welcoming Davin to the inner reaches of her soul.

"It's just . . ." Anika struggled to get the words out. "It's just that all of this is a bit odd to us. We help people come up north. There isn't anything we can do about assisting you to go south."

"We only need guidance in how we can evade the soldiers." Muriel stood. "I don't know this area, but there must be a way to get around them."

"Most unusual," Pieter droned.

Anika sighed. "I wish there was something we could do." She looked at Seamus with eyes of compassion. "Do you think it wise to take this minister any farther on this journey?"

Davin put his bowl down. They were getting nowhere. He had no energy to explain what they were doing, and it was obvious the old man wanted no part of this. They would have to find a way on their own.

"I help the preacher man."

The voice, deep and weathered, startled Davin who rose to his feet. There, blending in the shadows of the doorway leading to another room in the house, was a tall black man, whose white cotton shirt was unbuttoned and hanging loosely on his muscular frame.

"I take these folks."

"Jacob." Anika didn't seem surprised, and her tone retained her tenderness. "But you only just arrived."

"Dat means the path still in my head the ways I see it."

"Where did you just come from?" Davin asked.

Jacob stepped into the light of the room, revealing gray, tight curls and scars on his face and chest, ones that had long since healed. "I just comes up from 'Lanta."

"You mustn't allow Jacob to do this." Anika stepped toward Muriel. "They'll kill him. He barely made it in and he's still healing from the bites from the hounds he shook."

Davin saw an unfamiliar emotion rising in Muriel. Was she losing herself in all of this? She was biting her lip as if to fight back tears. The gesture of this man had affected her in some strange manner.

Jacob walked over to Seamus, bent down, and put a large hand on his chest. "He dyin', the preacher is."

"Yes." Davin went over and grabbed his brother's hand. "We know. We're just trying to bring him to his family before he . . . passes."

"Then we don't wait." Jacob's eyes were soft and tender, seemingly so misplaced in this man's body, which Davin assumed was chiseled from many years on the plantations he had heard so much about.

How could he ask this man to risk everything, when his brother had little chance of making it home? Unless this, like Muriel and Mr. Miller, was another angel sent to protect the soldier of God.

Davin began to choke with emotion on the thought of this notion. Even on the brink of death, Seamus was teaching him about faith.

"Come," Jacob said, this time with authority. "We need it dark. We go now. Or the preacher, he die."

Chapter 43

THE PATRIOTS

 "Ma'am. You seriously want to go there?" The ferryman pointed at the Manhattan skyline, which was blackened with smoke.

Clare got shoved backward, as refugee passengers disembarked on the Staten Island port and blended into the large, frantic crowds along the shore. The July heat and heaviness of the air only added to the foul disposition of the people. She waved an arm up to the man with the bushy beard and tired face, who was leaning down over the railing of the ship, and he merely shook his head.

"My family is there. I must go."

"Listen, ma'am, even if I wanted to, I couldn't haul you back."

She wasn't finished. After what she had gone through to get from Gettysburg to this point, Clare was determined to swim across the Hudson if she must. What should have amounted to a three- or four-day trip ended up taking her an excruciating week, with all of the delays in available transportation, checkpoints, and carriage breakdowns. And through it all, she wrestled with sleepless nights, anxious about what might be happening back home.

Clare went to shout up at the ferryman one more time, but he turned and disappeared out of sight. She lifted her luggage and forced her way through crowd, moving upstream against the flow of angry currents.

After being battered with elbows and insults, Clare made it to the gangway and climbed up, trying to make progress while avoiding being seen. By the time she made it to the top, she had a moment of relief, only to bump into the ferryman who grabbed her arm with force.

"Our orders were quite clear, ma'am. We can take passengers out of the city, but no one goes inside. Can't you tell? Manhattan is under siege. It's not a place for a woman. Or for anyone."

"You don't understand. I am with the *New York Daily*. A reporter."

"You could be Mary Lincoln herself and I ain't taking you across. Those are United States Navy ships out there with young eager lads looking for an excuse to fire those cannons."

A short, stocky man came up to the two of them. "What is the problem, Emmet?"

Clare recognized the uniform. She held out her hand. "Captain. I am Clare Royce."

He gave her a cold stare.

"Of the *New York Daily*."

"I know who you are."

"Captain, sir. I am seeking passage back. I'll pay anything you want. I need to get back. It is most urgent."

It was almost as if he took satisfaction in her pleading tone. But finally he turned to the ferryman. "Send her to the lower deck with the others. Should make for some interesting . . . conversation."

"But, Captain."

"Do as I say. Then let's push off."

"Yes, sir." The ferryman went to lift up Clare's luggage, but she grabbed it herself and followed him. She wasn't sure what lay ahead for her, but at least she was on board. "Thank you, Captain."

"You may want to wait on thanking me."

The ferryman winded around the few remaining passengers and took her to the other side of the ship. Then he opened a wooden door that was lit below with lanterns. From the noise rising up, it appeared to be the engine room. He waved her in with mock formality.

Clare went down the wooden steps and after just a few, she saw there were about a half dozen brutish-looking men sitting around the large iron steam furnace, their faces blanched and their clothes damp with sweat.

One of the taller men, who had a green plug hat and bushy sideburns, had been leaning against the wall but he straightened. "What do we have here?" He lifted his hat and gave a bow. "Welcome to the revolution."

She didn't respond but sought out a place where she could keep to herself. But as the door closed on them above, the only available choice was for her to sit on the steps. Clare set her suitcase down and noticed that each of the men were without any belongings other than brickbats and other crude weapons.

What had she gotten herself into?

"The name is Fergus." The man leaned back against the wall. He looked her over as if he was trying to read her intentions. The boat lurched and the other men grabbed on to whatever they could to keep their balance. "And this would be the time where you would tell me yours."

"Clare. Clare Royce."

"Where you from, Clare Royce?"

What did he mean? "The city. Manhattan."

Fergus smiled. "No. Before you came across the pond." His brogue was heavy.

"Oh. Roscommon."

"Donegal." He nodded to the others, who seemed less interested in conversation. "Same as these lads. Although, not Donegal. Let's see. Two from Cork. A Dubliner. Then let's see . . . Connall from Mayo, right boy?"

One of the oldest of the men nodded and shifted his stick into his other hand.

"And then Jimmy there, he says he's from Waterford, but we can't believe anything he says." He raised his arms. "Why we've got the makings of a right, proper Fenian party, don't you think?"

Every grain of wisdom in Clare told her to keep quiet, but her anger and disappointment in herself won the battle. "What are you doing, Fergus?"

There must have been something in the way she said it that caused them to exchange glances of surprise.

"Why, pretty lady, whatsoever could you mean?"

"A fine thing you're doing, making a shame of our people. You're going to go over there, smack a few heads, break some glass, and burn some buildings, all in the name of our oppressed people?"

This brought a mixture of laughter and angry faces. But she didn't relent.

"Who are you? Brian Boru? Hugh O'Neill? Rory O'Donnell? You one of the lost earls?" She tried to think of other Irish heroes of the past.

He crossed his legs and arms. "And suppose I was? Suppose I didn't want to stand by and continue to be bloodied and bludgeoned by everyone else in the world? Maybe we are tired of having boots pressing against our necks. Maybe this is our time. To be heard."

"Do you know how many of our people have been slaughtered in this war?" The man named Connall spoke now, but without any attempt at charm. "They get old General Tommy Meagher, tell him to gather his countrymen like the fools that they be. Give him a green flag with a harp, name it the Irish Battalion and put them all on the front line. Call them heroes while their mothers are left childless. And now the wealthy and privileged want to take more of our babies while they stay home in their city mansions, peering out their windows from above?"

"So you fight back?" Clare spit out.

"You're right we do," Connall said.

"You brave patriots. All of you." Clare stood. "You get bullied, and what do you do? You become the bully yourself. You repay cruelty . . . with cowardice."

"Wait," Fergus said. "Now I recall you. You're that Negro-loving reporter from the *Daily*, aren't you, lassie?"

"That is the only true thing you've said." Clare reached down for her suitcase.

Fergus pounded his brickbat on his palm. "And you are fine with us Irish dying so your Negroes can step over our bodies to take our jobs?"

Clare's moment of bravery was wavering, and she could sense violence roiled in the air. If they saw her shaking knees, it would betray all she had said to them. So she lifted her shoulders and spoke as firmly as possible.

"Let me be clear in saying this, and I mean this with every part of my heart. You, sirs, are not my Ireland. You are some foul creatures who crawled aboard ships or up through the sewers of these streets.

"Do what you want, as you will. But don't tarnish the name of our fair land. You, sirs, are not my Ireland. When you do your foul, disgusting deeds, lay down your banner and do it as the thieves you are. Don't you dare call yourself Irish."

Clare stomped up the steps, drew her breath, and prayed that the door handle wasn't locked.

Chapter 44
ENEMY LINES

 The shattered glass crunched under the weight of Clare's boots, and she stared at the ragged hole where the front window of the *New York Daily* used to be.

All around her were the sounds of scattered, throbbing crowds, an eerie blending of terror and glee. Shouts of anger. Cries of babies. Cheers. Laughter.

Down the road which was lined with tall buildings, smoke flared from windows and roofs. Much of what she saw now was similar to every street she passed on her way from the harbor. There were no pushcarts or carriages, just people running on foot, and at the turn of every corner, she risked the chance of running into a frenzied mob.

Clare walked to the front door of the newspaper Andrew's father had built, which was now in tatters. The splinters and shards of wood showed signs of having been mauled by an ax, surely wielded by some madman brought to a froth by the wild encouragements of his cohorts.

This was the kind of damage she would expect from a battle fought in a city. It would make sense if it was the workings of the Confederate army. But no. It was an attack by an enemy within. They had turned on their own people.

Her heart pounded as she stepped inside. What would she find in the debris? Bodies? Blood? She would never forgive herself if Andrew was gone. What a regrettable choice it was of hers to cover the story of Gettysburg. She thought the purpose was to catch a glimpse of her brothers, but was it merely about her own ambition? Away from her family chasing down her next great story?

Clare started to cry but then strengthened herself on the sharpening stone of fear, her senses heightened once again.

The devastation was instantly apparent. Glass lay like shimmering diamonds, papers fluttered with the wind coming through the broken window, and desks were shattered, their contents sprawled across the floors. Even the walls and staircase railing fell prey to the blade of the ax and whatever other cruel instruments were used.

What about the press? Clare stepped forward. "Hello?"

"Who is that?" The voice was familiar and defeated.

"Owen?" Clare hurried into the pressroom and only briefly noticed that the great machinery had been battered and covered with black ooze. There sitting on the floor in the middle of the violent debris was Andrew's editor, his curly brown hair disheveled and his face splattered with blood.

Clare fell to her knees beside him. "Oh my goodness, Owen. Are you all right, dear?"

He nodded over to the press with profound sadness. "I . . . I tried Clare. There were too many of them. There was nothing I could do. They just kept coming at me." Owen winced and then put both of his hands around his leg.

"What is it?" Clare looked down and saw it was bent.

"They . . . broke it. I tried, Clare. You need to believe that I did."

"I am going to take care of you. Don't you worry." She looked around to see what there was she could use.

"No!" He reached over and grabbed her hand. "You must go."

"I am not leaving you. I don't care if they come back."

"No. Your sister Caitlin left just before . . . the mob arrived here."

"Why? Why would she leave you?" As she asked the question, the horror of the answer crept into her mind. "Where are they?"

"No one thought they would attack our neighborhoods."

"Where are the children?"

"They are home. With Cassie. That's why Caitlin left."

The words were difficult to come from her trembling lips. "Where is Andrew?"

"He's been fighting with the militia since this had started. But . . . we haven't seen him."

As Clare stood, the instincts of a mother took over and there was no fear, no time for contemplation, just the rush of horror at the prospect of any danger coming to Garret and Ella. How could she have ever left them!

She paused for a moment, now conflicted at the thought of leaving Owen lying there alone in pain.

"If I could stand, I would go as well," Owen said.

Clare nodded and then she turned and ran.

The smoke was everywhere, and buildings that normally would be surrounded by firemen passing pails of water were left alone to become ash. She ran past mothers carrying babies in their arms, young boys throwing rocks, and old women casting bricks from windows.

Some policemen tried frantically and heroically to stay the madness, but many others stood by idly or even contributed to the bedlam, joining in the perverse sport of tearing down anything that symbolized civility.

There was no escaping the target of this unfettered aggression—the immigrants and their families from Africa. For as rabbits being chased by rabid hounds, it seemed as if every terror-filled black person was being hunted in the streets.

Clare wished she could do something. To stop the evil. But all she could do was run, tripping and falling over the flotsam of rebellion flung across the smoldering paved roads.

Yet despite her singular focus on making it back home to her babies, something brought her to a halt. A horrific sight that caused her pain to the depths of her soul. As she came across a crowd, she noticed them gathered around a lamppost.

Their faces were contorted, open mouths of anger, fists and sticks raised, and they celebrated the result of their sick labors. With eyes wide and white with fear, a black man had been stripped naked and strapped by his neck to the top of the post.

Clare screamed. It was almost inaudible among their revelry. The man was grasping the wire around his neck to loosen it, and then he kicked, another one, and then he was limp.

She leaned over out of breath and started to choke on her vomit. Then Clare spat the acid out and glared at the gathering as they hit the body with sticks.

Then she ran.

The last mile of her journey was a blur as she tried to block out all of the hate around her. Clare only wished she could run with her eyes closed and erase the terrible visions from her mind. Could she not just wake from all of this? A nightmare, the worst she ever dreamt?

But there would be no reprieve.

Finally Clare came to her block, and as she rounded the corner on the curve, there was another crowd gathered at the end of the street.

Please, God! Don't be my home.

She knew it was terrible to pray as such, but all she could think about now were the faces of her children. If anything happened to them!

As she drew closer, it was apparent the mob was farther down the road, and they were not attacking any house but were huddled around something in the center of the street. Clare was grateful they were distracted so she could slip into her home unnoticed.

She leapt over the short, black iron fence and landed in her garden, her boots crushing several of the tulips she had so meticulously planted. Then she ran up the brick walkway and leapt up the stairs.

She froze. The front window had been smashed and the door was ajar.

Clare picked up a large stone and gripped it tightly. She was prepared to crush the skull of anyone she encountered. Anyone who would do harm to her children. Her teeth clenched and her body began to quiver with rage.

Then she was inside. "Garret! Ella!"

She moved toward the kitchen, passing through the dining room where glass was scattered across the wooden floors.

"Caitlin! Where are you?"

"Clare?"

Before Clare could enter the kitchen, she saw the barrel of a shotgun poking out at her, and then the terrified face of her sister holding on with trembling hands to the weapon.

"The children? Caitlin, where are the children?"

"What?" Her sister's lips were trembling.

"Garret. Ella." Clare pointed to the shotgun.

"Oh. Yes." Caitlin lowered it and set it against the wall.

"Where are they?"

Caitlin moved back into the kitchen and Clare trailed her. Her sister opened the pantry door, and there sitting on the floor, cuddled tightly with fear, were Garret and Ella.

When they saw their mother, they sprung up and were instantly entwined in her affection. She gripped them tightly, and the tears flowed, serenaded by the high squeaks of their sobbing.

She glanced up to her sister, and then held a hand out her face. "Thank you, Caitlin. Bless you. Bless you."

But then a dark thought came upon her. "Where is Cassie? I thought she was with you."

"She was," Caitlin said, breathlessly. "When they came, she handed me the . . . the gun and said the crowd meant the children no harm. She said she would draw them away."

Clare stiffened. "Stay with the children!" The strength of her command caused Garret and Ella to step back, and Caitlin bent down and pulled them close to her.

In the living room, Clare grabbed the shotgun, which she had never before fired and probably had no idea how to shoot. But it didn't matter. There was no time to think. With only a few angry steps, she was running out the door over the lawn and fence into the street. Then she pointed the shotgun at the center of the crowd.

"Get away!"

A few remained from the large group she had initially seen. They must have already moved on to their next place of violence. To target their next victims. The expressions on the faces of those remaining were more of shock and remorse than hate. They stepped back and through their parting, Clare saw a figure lying on the ground.

"Back away!" She flared the weapon and several of them turned and fled.

"Is she dead?" asked a young man.

Clare flopped to the ground and put her arms around Cassie, who lay motionless, her eyes swollen, and a thin stream of blood dripped from her nose.

Clare looked up to the sky, of which both the murky haze and dark clouds obscured the sunlight, and she screamed.

Chapter 45

THE WOODS

"Remember, friends. It's not the soldiers you need to fear." These parting words from Anika's lips echoed disturbingly in Davin's thoughts.

They were about to cross the most dangerous geography in America, and neither the soft rain or the early morning darkness would provide much protection. Lawlessness reigned and thieves and murderers preyed without impunity on hapless sojourners in these constantly shifting border regions between the South and North.

"How much farther?" Davin tightened his grip on the handles of the makeshift litter they had made to carry Seamus through the wooded areas of the lower mountains.

"Some." Jacob had provided the same response each of the many times it was inquired in the last few hours. The man who led this haggard footrace through the moist foliage carried the front end of the gurney as if it was weightless. And for most of the distance he had been pulling Davin forward over toppled trees and bushes and through low-lying branches and spiderwebs that struck their faces often.

Davin didn't like the plan at all.

After leaving the safe house and using many unmapped side roads, they had come to a point in their travels when they encountered a huge dilemma. All of the paths narrowed into a low mountain pass and through a small town that had a high risk of being congested with bandits or soldiers or both. Yet any attempt to circle around this point using roads would extend their journey by as much as a day.

With Muriel fearing that Seamus might not survive the detour, they decided to risk going through the dangerous town. But only after emptying the wagon of Davin, Seamus, and Jacob.

This was Muriel's idea. She argued with success that she would have the best chance of passing through safely if she didn't have to explain why she was transporting a deserting Union soldier, an injured rebel pastor, and a runaway slave.

So Jacob and Davin were tasked with carrying Seamus by foot, through the woods surrounding the mountain village. Once past the town, they would meet up with Muriel at a rendezvous point where they would continue their journey by wagon.

But now Davin regretted agreeing to this strategy. Why would he have allowed Muriel to travel alone in darkness through a land of villains? He was relieved at the thought the sun would soon rise, but perhaps that would put her in even more danger.

More and more he was questioning why he had allowed her to come along at all. Was he so blinded with his drive for restitution with Seamus that he had risked the life of this woman? Forget that he was falling in love with her. What right did he have to put anyone else at risk in this desperate pursuit? And what about Jacob?

If they made it safely to the other side of town, Davin would send both of his companions on their way.

This decision was what pushed him through the pain in his lungs and the weariness in his arms and legs as he tried to keep up with Jacob. Soon. It would only be him in danger.

Suddenly he felt the litter being yanked from his hands, and it was all he could do to keep it from sliding through his grip. He then stepped awkwardly on one leg and the momentum began to pull him to the ground.

All he cared about was keeping Seamus from tumbling as it would rip out the stitches. If his brother started bleeding again, he would surely die. All of this was going through Davin's mind in the instant he guided the body toward the ground.

Jacob must have shared his commitment because between the two of them, they managed to lower Seamus's gurney to the moist ground without dumping their fragile patient.

"What happened?" Davin noticed Jacob limping over to a fallen tree. Then the large man reached down to his ankle.

"I sorry for this." Jacob snapped off a branch and tossed it.

Davin knew the grave situation they were now facing. He would have no way of carrying Seamus by himself, and if he flung his brother over his shoulder, it would rip open his wounds. Which was why he was relieved to see the runaway limp back over and reach down and clasp the handles.

They were off again, but with each step, Davin could almost experience the searing pain in Jacob's injured ankle. At first, the man was able to hop along at a good pace, but with each step he slowed further, until it was apparent he could barely hold himself upright.

Wishing there was some way to relieve Jacob of the burden, all Davin could do was urge the man on. Because the longer this took, the more dangerous it would be for Muriel.

Finally they started heading down a slope, and to his great relief, Davin saw the road below.

Please, God, let Muriel be all right. Please let Jacob make it to the road.

Now with Seamus's weight bearing downhill, Jacob could continue forward with short hops on his good foot, and they made it quickly to the bottom.

Muriel must have heard them coming through the bushes because she ran up and, seeing Jacob's struggles, relieved him of the handles. "We must hurry!"

"What is it?" Davin didn't even get the opportunity to celebrate seeing her again.

"I made it through town, but there was an old lady who was eying me suspiciously as I passed through. She could have been there to scout, which means we could be followed at any moment."

They scurried to the wagon and loaded in Seamus, who was now awake and moaning.

"Jacob," Muriel said. "I know the way from here. You should go."

"We can't send him off with his ankle injured," Davin said. "He can barely walk. If we leave him here, he'll either starve or be captured." As he spoke these words he realized his intentions to set both Muriel and Jacob free were dashed. Their present circumstances had sealed them in this together for good. At this point, there was only one choice but to press forward, all together. They weren't all that far from Taylorsville, and if they could somehow make it there, they would all have refuge.

Muriel bent down and ran her hands over Jacob's ankles. "Davin is right. It's terribly swollen already. It will be two weeks before you'll be able to walk freely. Get in the back of the wagon." She nodded at Davin. "You as well."

He didn't like the idea of leaving Muriel alone up front, but she said this with such force he followed her directions, and soon the three men were packed in tightly.

Muriel climbed up to the wagon seat, and almost instantly they were moving again with speed. Davin remembered they had tied his rifle to the bottom of the wagon. It would be useless to them down there, but there hadn't been time to retrieve it either.

It was difficult for him to move in the cramped space, but he worked his way to the front where he could see Muriel urging all she could from the tired horse. By now, the sun was emerging, which made the road easier to see as it winded down through the trees to the farming valley below.

They had only traveled a mile or so when Muriel looked back and her shoulders slumped, and she began to slow the wagon.

"What's going on?"

"Lie down. Both of you."

"No," Davin said.

"Let me take care of this." Her expression held both concern and calm. "You must trust me."

Jacob lay prostrate as directed, but Davin remained perched where he could peek out the opening.

In a moment, they could hear and feel the sound of horses approaching, then three men came up to Muriel standing in the road, waiting to greet them.

He was only able to see the men's faces briefly before they stepped out of view, but two of them were young and bore enough of a resemblance to be the sons of the oldest, a portly man with a wide-brimmed black hat.

"Why, gentlemen, is there some reason you would come upon us with such great haste?" Muriel spoke with the soft accent of a well-bred Southern woman.

At first Davin thought there must be another lady speaking, but he was shocked to see these words coming from Muriel's own lips.

"The fact is, Mama told us you passed through Garson in a bit of haste yourself, little lady." It must have been the older man. "We reckon when somebody comes through without the courtesy of a salutation, it means they're holding. Holding something of value. Figured we ought to check for ourselves."

"Well now, gentlemen, I surely can understand your curiosity. But I'm supposing you don't recognize me. Otherwise you wouldn't be messing with me on account of my uncle. He always was rather protective of me."

"And why should I care who your uncle is?"

Davin pressed his ear against the canvas of the wagon to try to hear, but their voices became muffled. Then the men started to laugh. Then he heard the sound of steps as they were approaching. Davin turned just in time to see the pudgy face of the older man appear at the back of the wagon. A grin emerged and then a cackle before he pulled his head out again.

"Looky there. She ain't lying none."

The two younger men took their turns at peering in and glanced at each other in amazement, then they withdrew in laughter as well.

"Well, if she ain't just like her uncle."

"I'll say."

After some more cordial, filtered conversation, Davin heard the horses leaving and he watched out the back as the three men galloped away.

He climbed out the front of the wagon opening and stumbled onto the bench beside Muriel just as she was pulling away, and the jolt nearly unseated him.

Once he righted himself, he looked over to Muriel as his stomach knotted. "What was that? What did you tell those men?"

Muriel didn't answer for few minutes, and then she turned to him with sadness in her eyes and spoke with a slow drawl. "I merely told those men the plain truth."

"Really? And what was that?"

"That I am the niece of the most notorious slave catcher in the South. And a Confederate spy."

Chapter 46

THE WRECKAGE

Clare had never seen Andrew so despondent.

Perhaps it was the bandage wrapped around his head. Or that the presses of the *New York Daily* continued to be silent. Then again, it most probably was the devastation of the building's interior, which other than a board being placed on the shattered front window remained in the same condition it was following the riots a week ago.

At least the family was safe. The children were doing fine, all things considered. Andrew's condition was much improved after taking a brick to his head while serving for the militia and sitting out most of the uprising in the hospital. The news on Cassie was also encouraging. Although she endured a brutal beating, she was healing well and already insisting on doing her chores again.

But the mortal blow appeared to be the newspaper that Charles Royce had founded and which his son, Andrew, had toiled so gallantly to keep its doors open.

"After all we've been through, we can't just give in." Owen readjusted the cap on his head.

Andrew leaned back in his office chair with his hands clasped. "Tell me honestly. What is your assessment of the press?"

"Well, there were quite a few blows with a sledge, I'll admit to you." Owen shifted in his chair. "But the old lady, she's built like a canon. I can fix her. She'll be singing again, I promise you that."

"Oh, Owen, those are sweet words to the ear," Clare said. "Where would the *Daily* ever be without your talents?"

"And what about the ink?" Andrew crossed his arms and raised an eyebrow.

"The ink?" Owen went to blurt out a response but then stammered and lowered his eyes. "That's the real hurt there. Those brutes poured it all over the equipment. It will take a barrel of patience to get it done, but I'll get her cleaned up, even if I don't sleep until I do."

"How long, Owen?" Andrew pressed.

Owen looked up to the ceiling and his lips moved as if he was counting. "Let's see, if I was doing it myself . . . maybe . . . three, four weeks."

Andrew's chin sunk to his chest. "Four weeks! Even three weeks with the press down and no revenues coming in will sink us to the bottom of the Hudson." He placed his hands on the back of his head. After a moment he threw his hands up. "We're done. There is nothing else we can do."

He stood up and walked over to the gold-framed painting of Charles Royce, whose pudgy cheeks, glistening eyes, and stern demeanor resonated with strength. Andrew removed it from the wall and admired it. "Father, I did all I could. You certainly deserved a more capable son."

"Oh, Andrew." Clare's heart ached for her husband. "Owen is right. Surely we will find a way to persevere as we always do. After all, who has more experience with hopeless than we do?"

"Yes. We've dealt with hopeless. And impossible. And impassible. And . . . and . . . all of those wonderful expressions of despondency. But it appears hopeless has finally had its way with the once-glorious Royce dynasty." With his bandage, Andrew looked as if he had just limped off a battlefield, which in many ways he had.

A tap sounded on the door to their office. The handle turned and Caitlin stuck her head inside. "Umm . . . you might want to come out and see this."

"Is everything all right?" Clare's pulse triggered. Could they bear any more hardship?

They exited the office, and she saw Cyrus Field sitting outside holding a package with a bow. Clare instantly knew why he was here and she wasn't in the mind-set to engage with the man. In the midst of Gettysburg and the draft riots, the report on his failed attempt at launching the Transatlantic Cable had come out and it was highly unfavorable. He certainly would be desperate for a supportive story from Clare.

He started to stand and extend a hand but Caitlin intervened. "Mr. Field," she said, "could you give us just a few moments?"

Cyrus nodded, his face turning red, and he retreated back to the chair.

It was then Clare noticed the chatter below. Caitlin led them to the balcony looking over the first floor, and there with brooms in their hands, picking papers off of the ground and carrying in what appeared to be a new window, was what seemed to be half of the congregation of their recently adopted church.

Directing the traffic and barking commands was the Reverend Zachary Bridger.

"What is this?" Andrew's mouth opened wide.

The reverend waved at them and then worked his way through the crowd of joyfully working dark faces and met them halfway up the staircase.

"I hope you don't mind us coming by without a proper invitation." Zachary let out his deep, loud laugh.

"How is Cassie?" Clare clasped his hand with both of hers.

"Oh, that woman is fine, fine, fine. The fact is, all of this was her idea, but I wish I would have claimed it myself. This newspaper has been the only voice our people have had. And this is no time for my people to be silenced, wouldn't you agree, Mr. Andrew?"

"That is a lot of hands down there," Owen said. "I think I'm going to put some of them to work on that press." He hustled down the stairs.

"Reverend Bridger." Andrew took off his glasses and wiped his eyes. "This might be the greatest act of kindness I have been granted. But I am afraid even if we clean things up, we just won't have the wherewithal to continue."

"Yes, right." The reverend, who always was impeccably dressed, reached into his black jacket and pulled out an envelope. "Now there isn't too much in here as my folk ain't the kind to be hiding diamonds in their mattresses, but we passed the hat and it seemed as if everyone was willing to do their part, share a little. Can't think of one who didn't, although that old codger Evans probably pulled a coin or two out if I know him well enough, and I surely do."

Andrew held out his palm as if to say he couldn't accept it, but Clare snatched the envelope gratefully from the pastor's hand and thumbed through the contents. "Why, Reverend Bridger, this is so very generous."

The reverend patted his forehead with a handkerchief and looked down lovingly on the people who were laboring below. "Indeed, we are poor in pocket, but God has us rich in spirit, now don't He?"

Clare laughed. "Indeed He does." She put her arm around Andrew, who was still dumbfounded, and she rested her head against his shoulder. As she did, Clare saw her other guest waiting patiently in his chair.

"Oh dear. I have forgotten about poor Cyrus."

She walked over to the man whose face showed some irritability but cheered up instantly when Clare arrived. He shook her hand with enthusiasm. Clare pointed toward the office door, and once he entered she followed in after him.

"Go ahead and have a seat, Mr. Field. I do apologize for keeping you as I know how busy you are."

She circled around and scavenged through Andrew's desk for a piece of paper and a pen to take notes. Surely Cyrus would want to defend himself against the scathing report, and she would do her best to hear and tell his side of the story.

Clare dipped the pen in the inkwell, put the tip to the paper, and waited for him to speak. But there was only an awkward silence. "Don't you have something to discuss with me?"

"About?"

"The report."

He waved a dismissive hand. "Oh that! Don't trouble yourself about that ludicrous report one dollop. There is much truth to it, I must admit, as there was many ways we can improve our processes, but then you take what's true, get some tired old politicians and greedy bankers involved, and then they feel the need to seek mortal punishment. All this will pass, my dear Clare." He looked down at the box in his lap, startled as if he had forgotten it. "And now look at me ramble. No, this is why I am here, and I can assure you for no other reason." He held it out to Clare.

She smiled. For a relentless, hard-pressed, wild-eyed dreamer, he was certainly a kind and sweet man. "Now, Mr. Field, you know we can't accept any gifts." She thought of the destruction below and paused. "Even in our present condition, it would be most improper, and this is not our first discussion on the matter."

Cyrus cleared his throat and lifted his shoulders. "Now you listen, Mrs. Royce. I have tried to express my utmost gratitude and respect for you and your husband and this newspaper for many years now. We are indebted to your steadfastness in understanding the full vision of my cable. And now I arrived today, to find the *Daily* . . . in ruins . . . and I am planting my feet here and will not retreat until you at least open what I have brought for you. A very small token of my appreciation."

Clare laid the pen down on the desk. Then she reached across and drew the gift toward her. "You are most fortunate, Mr. Field, to discover me in this time of fragility, with the moats of my castle dried up and the knights in deep slumber. I am simply much too exhausted to protest."

She unfastened the blue bow carefully so as to preserve it to be used again, then she peeled back the paper. It revealed a jewelry box made of fine polished wood.

"It's teak." He beamed at her with childlike delight. "Fashioned with the finest craftsmanship, of course. I had it made especially for you."

"Delightful." Clare rubbed her hands on top of the smooth finish, and her fingertips glided over the flawless surface. "It's just lovely."

"Go ahead and lift the top, dear Clare."

She raised the lid and the inside was lined with padded purple velvet embroidered with their name "Royce" in delicate, swooping lettering. Then music began to play as the cylinder began to turn.

"Do you recognize it?"

Clare nodded with joy.

"'The Faithful Shall Hear His Voice.' It's my favorite hymn."

It was an emotional day. An emotional week, for that matter. And something about the song playing caused her to weep.

"Don't you like it, Clare?" He frowned.

"No, no. I mean yes. I love it. We will cherish it forever. You have lifted my spirits so. This makes me so happy."

Clare circled from behind the desk and embraced him.

He stepped back and put on his jacket. "And that smile, dear Clare, has made me happy." Cyrus started to turn but glanced around the room. "What about all of this? The paper? Will you continue?"

Clare lifted the music box off of the desk and lifted it to her ear. The song made her smile. "Yes, Mr. Cyrus. I believe today, we have heard His voice."

Chapter 47

THE SPY

They rode side by side in silence for many miles, although the pain was screaming inside Davin's troubled heart. His fists clenched on the reins and the horse trotted its way down the country roads leading them to Taylorsville.

He was drifting, lost in his own dark imagination, betrayal pecking at him like vultures on his innards. How could he have been so daft? Now as he thought back, there were so many signs of Muriel's deception that seemed so obvious to him now.

It made sense why Muriel had chosen the Royces as the target of her grand beguilement. Andrew and Clare felt blessed by Muriel's offer to help at the *Daily*, but unwittingly they were providing her with access to highly placed officials and timely information, the kind that would be of great value to the Confederates.

And her so-called friendship with Caitlin and Cassie? Undoubtedly it was for the opportunity to get inside the Underground Railroad and to learn their networks and ways. Even as they were benefiting from the assistance of Anika and

Pieter, Muriel must have been plotting of how she would betray their whereabouts to her Southern allies.

How brilliant it was of her to earn a position as a nurse with the Sanitary Commission! There she would be able to report on the size of the army, its movement, and whatever sensitive details she could pry from dying and injured officers under her care.

How could he have missed all of this? How she was able to read the signal flags in the rebel balloon, and how she was so concerned about his safety at his first fight at Chancellorsville. She must have known Davin's battalion was about to be ambushed by General Stonewall Jackson.

But then why *did* she warn Davin?

And how could he discount all she had risked to bring his brother back to Taylorsville?

He glanced over to Muriel, who was brooding beside him and seeming to be sunk in her own pools of sadness.

But was this display of emotion just another part of her ruse? Was this all part of her next plan, and would he once again be the fly, helplessly flapping it wings while imprisoned in her web of lies?

How could he love someone he could never again trust?

Summer was at its peak across the Shenandoah Valley, and on either side of the road, many of the farms were already making early preparations for harvest. Some farms were small and others expansive with hundreds of laborers in fields bursting with their impressive yield. As they passed by, their wagon was largely ignored, nothing more than an occasional, unassuming stare from a field worker or a wagon coming the other way.

There was a gentle peace in the pastoral elegance around him, which served in dire contrast with the anguish and resentment he was experiencing.

Finally Muriel turned to Davin. "I don't want to lie to you ever again. Ask me anything and you'll get the truth. I promise."

He was so disgusted he wanted her to be gone. But there were questions remaining. "The way you speak now?"

"I was raised in the South. My family is from Ireland originally, but I learned the brogue to disguise my accent."

"But that telegram you received, or should I say, you plucked from my hand when I was at my sister's house. You said it was from your aunt in Canada."

Muriel nodded. "That was one way my contact was able to communicate with me. And only when there was something urgent, which is why I reacted so brusquely. I didn't have an aunt in Canada. My uncle here in America was unmarried."

"And all of this, about your parents dying on a ship?"

"That was all true."

"And your uncle is a slave catcher?"

"He was a slave catcher. One of the most notorious, people would say. He was not a good man. I understand this now. But I knew him as the only person who treated me with kindness." She looked away.

"Now you are going to turn in Jacob to your uncle? Collect your reward?"

"My uncle is dead."

Davin was disappointed to hear this. Not because he felt compassion for Muriel, but he didn't want to express pity for her in any way. "When?"

"Last year. He was making a run up north. Very dangerous work with the war going on. He was one of the few still making runs. He was taking three slaves he had captured, and one of them managed to get free. My uncle was found hanging from a tree with his throat slashed."

How could he believe any of what she was saying? But when he looked at her now, she was different. There was gentleness in her face with her eyes reddened with tears. It was as if the burden of her deceit was lifted and she was pleading for a chance to begin anew. A request he was desperate to grant.

"Why did you tell me all of this? Why now?"

Muriel met his gaze and tried to smile through her melancholy. She spoke in a subdued voice. "Davin. Don't you know by now?"

He wanted to draw Muriel into his arms and tell her how much he loved her as well. How she was the only woman who could challenge him deeply. To be stronger, to be a man of true depth and character. That he had never met a more fascinating, brilliant, talented, and—yes—attractive lady.

He wished none of this had ever happened, that all she had said wasn't true.

But it was true. She had betrayed him and his family.

With his mind tormented, his emotions piercing his sensibility, it was all he could do to shift his attention back to his initial mission. To bring Seamus back home safely to Ashlyn. And for this, he still needed Muriel.

"Why don't you look in on my brother?" He kept his gaze before him on the road.

"But we are here."

"What?"

"This is Taylorsville."

"Would you see . . . ?" He didn't want to even utter the words. If they had come this far only to lose Seamus, it would destroy Davin. Especially now that his hopes for a life with Muriel were certainly dashed.

"Yes." Muriel nodded. "Of course." She stepped over the bench, crawled through the wagon's opening, and disappeared in the back.

Several minutes passed and he heard nothing. He shouted back, "Well?"

There was no response from inside.

"Muriel!" He was angry at her. Angry at his life.

"Your brother is . . ." Muriel poked her head out. "He is growing weak. We are almost out of time."

Davin slapped hard on the reins and the horse jumped. As hard as it had been driven these past couple of days, he was grateful the mare didn't just lie down. He raced onward until he came up to an elderly couple walking in the road. He stopped only long enough to ask for directions to Seamus's farm. Then they were off again, the wheels of the wagon spitting up pebbles and dust.

Please, Lord. Get my brother there alive. Even if it's his last dying breath.

He was willing to try anything, even if it required leaning on Seamus's faith. Davin didn't feel worthy of a respite from God, but his brother had earned it.

It was more of a command than a prayer because Davin was consumed with anger and frustration.

Until he came to a sign at the front of a gatepost that read, "Whittington Farms." Suddenly all of his anxiety was replaced with gratitude, and overwhelmed by it, he began to cry.

Thank You.

But was this premature? Was he too late? Davin guided his spent horse to turn down the pathway leading to a country house, and he resumed his prayers. This time with humility and a softness to his pleas.

He looked back with the renewed discomfort he had experienced off and on for the past couple of days. There. He saw it, indisputable now for the first time. The shadow of a rider.

They had been followed.

Chapter 48

THE HOMECOMING

Ashlyn laid down the handles of her wheelbarrow and approached the wagon with apprehension.

Davin waved, already wanting to cushion the emotional hardship she was about to face. "It's just me. Seamus's brother." He climbed down from his seat and his cramped legs buckled when his boots reached the soil, and he nearly lost his balance. It had been many hours since they last stopped, and it had been days since he slept much at all. The rattle of the road still vibrated through his numb joints, and he had to fight back sudden dizziness.

"Davin?" Even in her work clothes, Ashlyn remained as rustically elegant as she had been when he first saw her at the Whittington mine back in California many years ago. Her long wavy auburn hair, her slender build, those deep brown eyes—it was clear her return to the Shenandoah Valley had indeed been kind to her.

Muriel made her way out of the back of the wagon, and Jacob followed shortly behind, hopping awkwardly as he landed.

"What is this all—?" Ashlyn turned and shouted back toward rows of tall cornfields. "Grace!"

"You may not remember me," Muriel said in a voice that matched Ashlyn's intonations of the South. "But I lived with your sister Clare. I cared for her children."

"Yes." Ashlyn looked to Davin for some explanation as Grace emerged from the husk-tipped corn stalks. Mavis and Tatum with alarm expressed on their dark faces followed behind.

"We brought your husband home." Muriel put her hand on Ashlyn's shoulder.

"Where is he?" Ashlyn moved toward the wagon. "Is he? Oh dear God, please tell me he is not." She put her hand over her mouth and moaned.

"My father?" Grace put her arm around her mother, and it surprised Davin to see how much she had grown up. She was a young woman now.

"No. He is still alive. But he might not have long." Muriel spoke with both firmness and compassion. "We must get him inside."

Davin lunged toward Ashlyn as he saw her beginning to buckle.

But then she regained her footing and sprung free as Muriel, Jacob, Mavis, and Tatum pulled Seamus out of the back and loaded him onto the gurney.

"Oh, my dear sweet husband!" Ashlyn leaned over and stroked Seamus's pale, clammy face. Grace circled around to the other side.

Muriel gave orders to anyone who would listen, and Davin took hold of one end of the litter. In short order they had Seamus lying on his bed inside the house, and there was a scurrying as food was being prepared and water was being boiled.

Ashlyn came to Seamus's side and clasped his hand. "How long has he been like this? What happened?"

On the other side of the bed, Muriel seemed to be taking

advantage of finally having room to work on Seamus. She removed his clothes and checked his wound, which had a red glow to it. Davin couldn't help but be grateful he had Muriel here with him.

"There was a battle in Pennsylvania." Davin spoke with tenderness. "He was injured when he was ministering to his fallen soldiers. Seamus is a hero."

Ashlyn sobbed. "I don't want a hero. I just want my husband." She turned to Muriel. "Should we fetch him a doctor?"

"She is a doctor," Davin said, which drew an appreciative smile from Muriel and then she went back about her work.

"Mother," Grace said. "There are no doctors in town or anywhere near us." She turned to Davin. "They are all on the battlefields."

Ashlyn took out a handkerchief. "Will he be all right? Please tell me you can make him better." She clasped her hands and leaned over Seamus's face. "Speak to me, my love."

"He hasn't said much." Davin adjusted a pillow under his brother's head. "But when he does speak, it's to ask for you."

Mavis came in the room with a basket full of steaming towels. Muriel pulled one out and cleaned Seamus's face.

This must have startled him because his eyes opened. "Ashlyn?"

"Seamus!"

"Da!"

Muriel and Davin stepped back in amazement as the man who was on the precipice of death reached his hand up to Ashlyn's cheek and she cried.

"Da." Grace had made her way to the other side of the bed and was now resting her head against his bare chest. Soon both she and Ashlyn were on their knees at Seamus's side and the three of them were in a sobbing embrace.

Davin became overwhelmed himself and lifted his hand to his face. He had never really believed this would be possible. And now that this euphoric scene was unfolding before him, tremendous relief came upon him, followed by a dizzying swoon. He fell back against the wall, and the room started to spin.

Muriel was lifting him under his arms, her concerned eyes just inches from his. "You need rest, Davin . . . and something to eat."

The large bowl of corn-and-bacon soup and the drinks of water had rejuvenated Davin. And almost as soon as he regained his senses, he remembered the present danger and was a soldier once again.

He was alone outside, peering into the darkness beyond the front porch railing, with his rifle tucked under his arm. A summer breeze rose up every so often among the corn husks, causing them to bend and appear as dark shifting figures under the star-filled sky.

His military training taught him to appreciate the loud boasts of the katydids and crickets and those other creeping evening dwellers. It was a sudden turn to dead quiet he was listening for, because it would be the harbinger of approaching boots.

A noise behind him snared his attention and he saw through the window that Jacob was getting his ankle tended to by Muriel, who unlike him never seemed to have tired from the journey. He turned back, but after a few minutes the front door opened behind him.

Davin wanted to be bitter. He wanted to hate her. But he couldn't muster the emotion. Maybe he was too exhausted to care. Perhaps he was distracted by the greater danger lurking somewhere out there.

Muriel came alongside him while she wrapped a scarf around her neck and then crossed her arms as if to squeeze off the evening chill. They stood silently together, looking out into the same darkness.

She spoke with a quiet voice that sounded almost like an apology. "I can't explain it in any other way than a miracle, but it seems like your brother is going make it through this. It was as if seeing Ashlyn's face brought him back to life."

"That is . . . good to hear." He didn't feel comfortable cheering on any news she had to share, but what else could he say? Was this all part of her skill? To bewitch him once again?

"Do you believe that two people can be that much in love?" Muriel looked heavenward. "So much so that their very lives depended on one another?"

Davin turned and glared. "If they trusted one another."

She dropped her head. "I deserve that . . . and more." Muriel put her hand on his arm, but he shook it off. "Oh please, Davin, Let us not end things this way. We have so little time left together."

"Are you leaving?" This thought disturbed him. He meant to punish her with his words, but he wasn't ready to see her go.

"Me? No. I am in no danger. It is you who are leaving."

He was surprised at this for a moment, but then understood by looking into her deep, mysterious eyes. "You saw we were being followed."

"Yes." She put her hand on his shoulder, and this time he surrendered to her touch. "There was nothing we could do to shake them. At least that wouldn't have endangered our chances of getting your brother back in time."

"I thought they had let us be out of respect for your uncle, the legendary slave catcher." The words were more accusatory than he intended.

"They knew my uncle was dead. But he had many friends, and a few even more feared than him. I am sure they followed to see if I was working with anyone else. No. The bounty on a runaway slave and a Union spy will attract more vultures than these."

"Now I am the spy?"

"So strange how it all depends on the ground we stand on, the flag we wave. Isn't that so, Davin? We cross a border, an invisible line, and all of the deeds we committed, the murders, the lies, the betrayals—they are forgotten and forgiven because once again we are patriots."

"I will never forgive you. No matter where these feet stand." What was he saying? He didn't mean it, but there was a reaction he was seeking. What was it?

Something came over Muriel's face. Her resolve returned and a sudden distance came between them. He regretted what he said, his tone, but he couldn't get himself to say it.

"You may hate me, Davin, and for this I cannot blame you." Muriel stepped back. "But the facts are that I am home, on friendly ground now. It is you who are in great danger."

"I just can't leave Seamus." But it was Muriel he didn't want to leave. Did he despise her or love her? What was happening to him?

"Davin. You must listen. If you can't protect yourself for the sake of your family and those who care for you and love you, then at least think of Jacob, who has risked so much on your behalf. Both of you need to return to northern soil."

He squinted. A light was approaching in the distance, and before long he saw it was lantern dangling on the front of a wagon. Muriel wasn't alarmed. "You know about this?" he asked.

"I told Ashlyn we were being followed. And that you and Jacob needed to leave right away. She sent one of her servants to fetch someone. Someone she said would be able to help you."

"What about you?"

"I won't leave your brother's side. He will either get better . . . or . . . I already promised Ashlyn. This is my gift to you. Whether you're willing to accept it or not. It is all . . . all I have left to give."

This was all happening so fast. But Muriel was right. Not only was it dangerous for Jacob and him to be here, but the longer he tarried, the more risk Davin brought to everyone in the house. He needed to leave immediately.

But what about his brother? Davin had so much to tell him, and now he wouldn't get the chance.

And what about Muriel? Was this how it would all end between them? Yes. Because he felt it deeply and it was confirmed in her eyes.

He would never see her again.

Chapter 49

THE OUTPOST

 The burlap sack tied over Davin's head made him want to scratch, something he couldn't do with his hands tied with heavy twine.

He could see obscurely through the pores of the sack and knew it was dark outside, that they had traveled far, and the last stretch of the journey had climbed to a higher elevation based on the angle of the wagon.

With his vision limited, his other senses were enhanced and he could hear the playful taunts and laughter of men, and someone playing, or more accurately tinkering, with an out-of-tune banjo. He could smell pine resin, a campfire burning, and venison being roasted.

He felt a tug and then was guided out the back of the wagon. "Is this really necessary?"

"They kill men for knowing the whereabouts of this place, son," Fletch said. "This is me doing you a favor, and not even for you, but your brother. So give thanks and shut your yapper."

Davin stood for a few moments, taking in the chill air, and then he felt the presence of another beside him and he knew it was Jacob. They were being tied together.

"What is this place?" Davin asked, hoping Fletch was close enough to hear him.

"This is a place that don't exist."

He was pulled forward and tried to slow the pace since Jacob's ankle would be throbbing with pain. "Are you all right, friend?" He received no answer.

"What do you have there, Fletch?" The unfamiliar voice was gruff and raspy. "That don't look like no shine and that is depressin' me some."

Through the filtered vision of his sack, Davin saw the flickering light of what seemed to be more than a dozen fires, and he could see better than surely his caretaker would have wanted. Shadowy shapes of men gathered around tables, some eating and others playing cards. A few others gathered around the pits, with their hands reaching over the flames and passing bottles among themselves. Their entrance into the campsite drew the attention of most of them.

"You dealin' Negroes now, Fletch?" shouted a voice in the distance.

"Or bawdry women?" Heckling laughter and whistles broke out. "I'll give you two bales for 'em."

"Judson," shouted Fletch. "A word with you."

Catcalls and hisses came next. "Jud ain't got nothin' for you."

Davin felt the tug on his elbow and they were being led away from the fires. Then they were joined by another man who sounded young.

"What you got thar, Fletch?"

"I got a Yankee and a fugitive here."

"That right? They ain't puttin' up much of a fight, knowing they's about to be hung."

"There won't be no hanging."

"Whatcha gonna do, then?" Judson spat out something.

"I ain't doing nothing. You gonna take them."

"That so? And whereabouts I takin' 'em. I'm gonna claim bounty?"

"No. You're gonna run them."

"Wha? I ain't dumpin' them up north. Why that's just good fish back in the river."

"You do this and I'm clearin' your debt."

"You ain't lyin' are you, Fletch? All of it? Why? What's these fellers to you anyway? What ain't you tellin'?"

"Two favors paid. One to a man who risked his life to save my son. And the other to Roy Perkins's niece."

"Nah? That redhead girl? With her knowin' it was some Negro boy who slit her uncle's throat? Now I knows you lying."

Fletch lunged and there was a grunt. "You gonna call me a liar? Or you gonna clear your owings with me?"

Jud coughed and bent over and spit. "Now come on, Fletch. Why you go and choke me? Made me swallow this tobacky. All right. I take 'em first at dawn."

"No," Fletch said. "With all of these runaway soldiers here, I don't think it would be safe for our boys here to stay overnight. Either of them die, and you still owe me full and proper."

"All right then." Jud reached over and grabbed the rope that bound Davin to Jacob. "I'll load them up while you fetch me one of those Shenandoah Shines. I know you ain't come here without things to swap and I've got the need for courage. 'Cause I got me a long, dangerous run ahead."

Still covered with hoods and bound with twine, Davin and Jacob were placed under bales of cotton, which Davin could tell by the smell and the fibers brushing against his face. Then they were covered with some type of tarp, because it became completely dark, and he worried whether he and Jacob would suffocate under all of this.

They lay on the cold, splintered wood of the wagon, and despite the discomfort and the bounce of the trail, it didn't take long for Davin to drift to sleep, catching up for being nearly a week's short.

When he awoke, he worried about Seamus and his family. Should he have warned them about Muriel? That she couldn't be trusted?

Or could she? Maybe they were all rebels now. Seamus. Ashlyn. All of them. And he was the outsider. The one who was the enemy. The drunkenness of his lack of sleep made him queasy and his mind strayed to dark thoughts. Had this all been for naught? Hopelessness swamped him.

But then he fell asleep again. At some point, he remembered waking and hearing the sound of a deep voice singing softly. It was a spiritual hymn, one he didn't recognize, but Davin could tell it was full of reverence and joy.

He listened to Jacob's voice and found it soothing, soaking it in for a long time before speaking. "Jacob?"

"Yessum?"

"How can you sing? When we lie here in bondage?"

The man laughed. "My chains? They was cut long ago and for all times. I ain't get my freedom from no man. And no man can take it from me."

Then Jacob sang again, accompanied by the rattle of the wagon wheels and the chorus of the night.

Chapter 50

THE RETREAT

 "Woah!" The horses protested the abrupt halt. "Will y'all take a look at dat there? Ne'er seen so many with tails between their legs."

How was Davin expected to see anything having been crammed in the back of this wagon with his head covered for more than a day? They had only stopped once to get drinks of water and to relieve themselves, but that was about ten minutes of the entire journey.

So when he felt the weight of the cotton bales being lifted around him, it was as if he were being released from a dark prison cell.

"Wait there and just so there's no foolin', the both of yous should know this is a shotgun." Davin felt his forehead being jabbed with an object, which definitely could be the barrel of a gun, and he closed his eyes for fear they would be gouged.

He lay still as he heard grunts coming from Judson, who seemed to be wrestling with Jacob. Then there was a thud and a groan.

"All right, Yankee boy. You climb yerself out now. You get yer wings back." Davin felt another poke at his head. He sat up and wiggled his way toward the end of the wagon where he was grasped by a strong hand that flung him to the ground.

"Get up, boy." Davin was lifted again and now was being led. "Right here now. That'll give you a proper view of Dixie's finest. I best be gettin' on myself. Those Johnny Rebs will be in a foul mood."

Davin's hood was swept off his head and he blinked to defend against the bright sun. His hands were still bound, and a rope tethered him to a tall oak.

He was surprised to see the face of his captor—blond scraggly hair, with rounded cheeks and a paunch belly. The kind of man he could easily lick and would love to have the opportunity.

"Those be eyes of hatred. You best be savin' that for those fellers." He pointed down to the valley far below, where there was blurring movement. Davin blinked again and could see it was a great army, tens of thousands perhaps, making their way up the slope.

"I's give you maybe twenty minutes or so, 'for the wholes of General Lee's army passes by here. After gettin' whooped by y'all, I s'pose they'll find pleasure in takin' their grief out on you, boy."

He tossed a knife on the ground, which Davin recognized as his own. "There's your good fortune. That get me time to be gone and you to be on your way. But you best be gettin' to it or you'll be Yankee stew."

The man returned to the wagon with the cotton lying beside it. Sitting upright, with his neck tied by a rope, was Jacob who sat there with vacant eyes.

"What are doing with him?" Davin shouted, as Judson loaded up the bales again. "He was supposed to be freed with me."

Judson continued his work, shut the back gate, clamped the

bolt, and then dusted his hands. "Ain't lettin' no Negro free. I got me some honor."

He climbed on the driver's seat and lifted the reins. "Now don't kill any of our rebel boys, or I ne'er sleep sound again." Judson tipped his hat, and with a jolt the two horses lifted dust in the air and disappeared around the bend.

"Jacob!" Davin shook his head. How could he betray the man who saved his brother's life?

He glanced in the other direction, down the valley, and although it didn't look as if Lee's retreating army had moved much, there would be scouts all over the area. He was probably already out of time. How terrible it would be to go through all of this, only to get captured and hung by the army he helped defeat ten days earlier?

Davin shimmied down, picked up the knife, and then propped it between his ankles. It didn't take too long for him to cut his hands free, and then shortly thereafter he severed the rope holding him to the tree.

But there was little chance of catching up with the wagon taking Jacob away.

Still, he tried. He ran along the trail until it broke into three directions. He had no way of knowing which path to choose or of catching them on foot.

Then he heard the sound of horses coming behind him, and he scuttled into a thick grove of trees. Davin watched as two of Lee's cavalrymen passed by, and then in sadness and anger, Davin headed north.

"So, Private Hanley, you want to explain to me why I shouldn't have you court-martialed for desertion?" The captain had a jigger of whiskey on the table next to him as he sized up Davin.

"Oh yes." Davin reached into his pant pocket and unfolded a soiled and worn piece of paper. "It's right here."

The captain eyed him suspiciously as he unfolded it. Then he read it out loud. "A fifteen-day leave. Signed by . . . General Joseph Hooker himself. How about that." He lifted the glass, gave Davin a curt nod, and emptied it in one swig. "According to this, son, you've got a few days left to spare."

"Yes, sir. But I am ready to serve."

The captain smiled and twisted the waxed tip of his black mustache. "I believe you might serve us best by cleaning yourself up, son. You are a mess."

Davin nodded and started to walk away but then turned. "Sir?"

"Yes, Private."

"I would like to report . . ." He paused for a moment. Did he really want to do this? This would certainly be the end. But for the past couple of days as he traveled by foot, his rage about what happened to Jacob had been festering in his every thought. Yes. He had a cause now. And there was an enemy.

The captain leaned forward. "What is it, son?"

Davin straightened. "I would like to report the whereabouts of a Confederate spy."

Chapter 51

Healing

"And what kind of patient has the young man been?" Pastor Asa entered the house with his usual cheer and bluster.

"Are you here to visit the invalid?" Seamus sat in front of the fireplace. He placed his Bible down on the table beside him.

"May I take your coat?" Muriel closed the door behind the pastor.

"No, thank you." He lifted his hat and held it in front of him. "I am just coming by for a brief moment."

Ashlyn, who was in a rocking chair alongside Seamus, looked up from her knitting. "To answer your question, Pastor Asa, my husband is restless and unruly."

"A clear sign of improving health, to be certain." Asa plopped down on the couch next to Seamus and let out a deep sigh.

"Yes. And his doctor would agree." Muriel bent down by the fireplace and put in another log. "Two months have passed, and I can say my work here is almost complete."

"Oh, Muriel dear, please go sit down." Ashlyn lifted a spool of blue yarn. "She makes us dizzy trying to keep up with her."

"I have heard this sweet lady has been a real blessing." Pastor Asa appeared exhausted. "What about your brother? What was his name?"

"Davin." Seamus glanced over to Muriel and then back to Asa. "We . . . haven't heard from him."

"Oh. I am sorry to hear this. Such strange times." Pastor Asa looked around the room. "And where is my dear Grace? No doubt she's heard the news?"

"She is riding her new horse." Ashlyn rolled her eyes. "Her father here has decided to spoil her, even if it means we'll be eating hay as well." She paused from her craft. "It is getting dark. I do hope she'll be home soon."

"And yes," Seamus said. "Grace, of course, was thrilled upon hearing her young Anders had survived Gettysburg and that the North had agreed to send him home as part of a prisoner exchange."

"So sad." Ashlyn tilted her chin down. "It's a hard life for a farmer to only have one arm. I must say, Coralee has been taking all of this well."

"Well?" Asa chuckled and this brought on a hoarse cough. "She is planning the grandest celebration Taylorsville has ever seen." He turned to Seamus. "And they are mighty grateful to you, I must say. Never seen Fletch cry before, even when they tried to hang him years ago. But he read me Anders's letter and couldn't make it through when it got to your part."

"Me?" Seamus lifted his cane from the side of his chair. "What did I have to do with any of it?"

Asa gave him an inquiring glance. "Is that you being modest? Or are you milking out the story from me?"

"What? What is it?" Ashlyn set her knitting aside.

"He never told you?" Asa rubbed a gray eyebrow. "Your

husband put his life at stake in trying to rescue Anders. Apparently the boy saw everything, including when Seamus was shot."

"He did?" Seamus was surprised to hear this himself. He looked over to Ashlyn, who he thought until now was the only other person who knew about what Percy had done. They had decided that without witnesses, there would be no proof to convict him, and the story would only bring shame on Grace.

"Well, it should take care of itself," Asa said. "Apparently the colonel hasn't been seen since . . . his encounter with you, and we shouldn't expect to be bothered by him in Taylorsville ever again."

They sat uncomfortably for a few moments until Asa coughed a couple more times.

Muriel walked over to him and placed her hand on his shoulder. "That doesn't sound good. Can I get you a glass of water?" She left the room without allowing him a response.

Asa shifted in his seat and spoke with what seemed an effort to imbue some cheer back into the room. "Which brings us to the real reason for my visit."

"Oh?" Seamus planted his cane on the floor. "That wasn't enough news?"

Muriel returned with a glass and he took a long sip. "No need for concern. It is merely the hacking of an old preacher. A very old, tired preacher I am afraid. Thank you, my dear." He drank again and then placed the glass on the table beside him. "I have something for you to pray about, Seamus."

"Yes?" Seamus replied cautiously, knowing when it came to Pastor Asa, that statement was usually followed by a request that was expected to be accepted.

"I would like for you to consider pastoring the church. When you're ready, of course."

Seamus laughed. "Oh, is that all? Well, yes. We spoke about this before and I have prayed about it. In a few years when you—"

"No, Seamus. Not in a few years. I am ready now. In fact, I have never been more ready. This . . . this war has taken about everything out of me."

There was an odd silence. Seamus clasped his chin. "Now?"

"And I suppose I have no voice on any of this?" Ashlyn said.

Seamus reached for her hand. "Of course. You have as much say in this as anyone." He was relieved she would rescue him. It was difficult for him to say no to the kindly minister.

Ashlyn's beaming smile widened, and he knew he was in trouble. "Well . . . I am quite in favor of it. And Grace will be so proud of her da."

"Then it's settled." Pastor Asa stood up.

What had just happened? Was he ready? Was this God's timing? "It's settled," Seamus said, "that I will pray about it."

"Yes, of course, son. Pray all about it." Pastor Asa looked up to the ceiling. "But I should let you know I've already cleared it with the highest of authority."

He laughed and Seamus wanted to rise as well, but it was still too much of a strain for him to get up too abruptly. "Before you leave. I never did thank you properly."

Asa put his hat on his head. "For?"

"That time you brought me up to the mountain."

"Oh, that."

"No. I want you to know that ever since that moment, when you had me listen to the songs of the Shenandoah—that changed everything for me. I've been listening to them ever since."

The old preacher smiled, adding wrinkles to his weary face. "Then I suppose my forty years of ministry hasn't been squandered after all. You know. I've always wished I could bring the whole congregation up there. Complaining. Bickering. Grumbling. All the way to that mountain." He appeared to be envisioning this for a moment, but they turned to them abruptly. "Well, I must be on my way."

The door flung open and Grace bounced in, and she gave Asa

a hug before he left. When the door closed she turned and her eyes lit up with joy. She came over to Seamus and kissed him on his forehead. "Oh, Da, I love, love, love Sierra."

Seamus gave Ashlyn a shrug. "The child loves her horse. And her da. Did you hear that, Mother?"

"I did." Ashlyn gave him an exaggerated grin.

A firm knock rapped on the door, loud enough to startle them.

"Pastor Asa must have forgotten something." Grace went over and opened the door, then took a quick step back.

Seamus planted his cane on the floor and pressed himself up, but the pain kept him from rising. How would he pastor a church if he couldn't stand?

"Please." A man's voice bellowed from outside. "My friend's foot got rolled over. He's in a bad fit with it. We were told there is a doctor in your home."

Muriel made her way tentatively to the door, now opened wide by a man in a long black jacket wearing a tall otter-skin hat. "Where is he?"

She had barely made it to the entrance when she was grabbed violently. And suddenly two other men stepped in with guns pointed while Muriel screamed.

Seamus wrestled himself to his feet, and planting the cane on the ground, he moved toward the door but then stumbled, and Ashlyn caught him before he fell.

One of the men with a gun laughed at Seamus's efforts, and then with a smirk, he slammed the door shut behind him.

"No." Ashlyn tried to restrain Seamus. "I'll go."

But Seamus broke free and lurched for the door, which he swung open. In the lingering light he could see they already had loaded Muriel into a carriage, and the two horses darted down their pathway.

Helpless, he hobbled out on his cane. Where was Tatum? "Tate!"

After the carriage had traveled about thirty yards, the door of the carriage swung open and Muriel leapt out and ran toward the field, lifting her dress as she did.

Almost instantly a loud boom sounded accompanied by a flash of light, and Muriel crumpled to the ground. One of the men looked back to Seamus and pointed a gun in his direction while another dragged Muriel's rag-doll body by the ankles toward the carriage where she was thrown in roughly.

Then the horses reared their legs, and with Seamus hopelessly limping after them, they were gone.

Chapter 52

THE SOLDIER

MANHATTAN, NEW YORK
July 1864

 Clare ran her hand along the mantelpiece and looked at her fingertips, now blackened with dust.

She closed her eyes and laughed. There just never seemed to be enough time. Clare ran the cotton cloth along the wooden shelf and took some pleasure in seeing it remain white where she wiped.

More and more, it was these simple pleasures, these quiet moments she revered the most. Then she came upon the teak music box. What a precious gift from Cyrus! She flipped the cloth and dusted it tenderly.

Then she lifted the top, twisted the small crank, and swayed as the music played. When the song ended she played it again.

She heard a noise behind her. The children must have come home.

Clare turned and then gasped.

"Should I have knocked?"

"Davin!"

She started to tear up at the sight of her youngest brother, once a freckled child, now standing before her with a brown tight-cropped beard and dressed in his Union blues. Clare reached out to him and they embraced. She stepped back and clasped her hands. "Oh, my dear, sweet Davin."

He removed his hat and his curly hair was wet with sweat. "I am sorry, Clare. I have such a short time to visit. Is this an inconvenience? I should have given you notice."

"Well since you don't write, I wouldn't expect anything else but for you to just . . . drop in." Clare straightened out his collar. "But you can drop in anytime. Oh, Davin. I used to worry and pray mostly about your brother." She laughed when she thought of all the trouble Seamus had navigated through in his life. "But now? Almost all of my prayers go to you."

He stared down at his hands. "I suppose those are well needed."

"We are all in need of prayer. Believe me." Clare had seen with her own eyes the horrors of war, and the thought of her little brother being subjected to them made her shudder. "I can only imagine what you've seen, what you've gone through."

"Clare." He shifted his feet. "You mentioned Seamus. That is why I'm here."

"What? What is it? Is he all right?"

"Oh no. Well I am not certain. You know how difficult it is to get any news from the South. But it's not that. I've been reassigned to General Sheridan's regiment. I'm cavalry now."

"You? On a horse?"

He wrinkled his brow. "I rode them all the time out West. I am considered to be quite skilled." Davin's cheeks reddened.

"Of course. You are capable of great things. And now with General Sheridan?" The general had earned the attention of General Grant. He was rising through the ranks. She tried to remember what she had heard about Sheridan recently through her sources. "He's been ordered to . . ." Clare halted.

"Yes." Davin met her gaze. "We're going to the Shenandoah."

"You can't." Clare spoke forcefully. "You simply mustn't."

"Clare. There is nothing that is simple anymore."

She drifted over to the front window and stared outside for a few moments. "Davin. I don't know why, but this makes me very uneasy. Was there no other assignment available?"

"I requested it."

Clare spun. "You what?"

"Look." Davin stepped toward her and put his hand on her arm. "I don't even know if . . . Seamus is alive. Without letters getting through, there is no way of knowing other than just showing up at his doorstep."

"With a gun? A cannon?"

"I know it seems odd." Davin's sad brown eyes glazed. "A strange way to arrange a visit."

Clare didn't want their discussion to be tainted with gloom. It had been so long since she saw her little brother, so she managed a smile. "I understand. I suppose I would dress up in a uniform and go down there myself, if they would let me. Oh, what I would do for us to all be together again. Safe from all of this." She paused, sensing something hiding in his thoughts. "But that's not all, is it?"

"What?"

"That's not the only reason you are going to the Shenandoah Valley." Despite how impressive he was in his uniform, broad shoulders and beard, she spoke with the authority and concern of an older sister.

He laid his hand over his heart. "You always were impossible to fool."

"Do you think she'll be there as well? With Seamus?"

"The traitor?" The word blurted from his lips.

There was so much she had to share, but should she? When she heard the news, she felt betrayed as well. "Andrew and I, we have already forgiven Muriel. You must try as well. Until you do, you will carry this wound with you, and it will be much deeper than any you could receive in battle."

Davin's composure cracked and he spoke softly. "It's too late for all of that."

"What do you mean it's too late?"

"Clare. I've done a terrible thing. One for which there is no forgiveness."

"Tell me." Clare saw before her the ten-year-old boy she had helped to raise.

"I reported Muriel to my command . . . as a spy. And I don't know what . . . they've done, but I fear something awful."

Clare tried to meet his gaze with tenderness. "You really loved her. Didn't you?"

Davin nodded. "Very much."

"Which is why I wasn't going to tell you this, but I think now I must." Even as she was saying this, Clare questioned the wisdom. Would her words only prove more hurtful?

"What do you know?"

"After you had told me about Muriel in your letter, Andrew and I became quite concerned. As you can imagine, it was disconcerting to know we had been so foolish as to allow a Confederate spy into our home." She waved her arms around the room. "To have her tending to Ella and Garret!

"So . . . through the newspaper, we had a contact who we had befriended. General Blaine. He is at the highest levels of leadership, coordinates efforts with the Pinkerton Agency, and even reports directly to President Lincoln. We sought his counsel regarding Muriel and he agreed to investigate for us."

"What did he have to say?" Davin tightened his shoulders.

How much should she share? "We were told quite plainly that our own Muriel has caused devastating and irreparable damage to the Union. Not to mention the harm caused to the Underground Railroad. Imagine that! Attending meetings alongside Caitlin and poor dear Cassie . . . and all along acquiring information to pass on. Not only this, but she was communicating to the Confederates through the classified section of the *Daily*."

Even as she spoke these words, Clare found it difficult to think poorly of Muriel. She seemed genuinely kind natured and certainly was talented. The children still asked about her often. "I just wanted you to know. You did the right thing in reporting her. It was a very brave act, and a most difficult one as well."

He narrowed his eyes. "But why? Why would she do this? I thought she cared for us."

"Oh, Davin. Why do we do anything? The South believes in their cause as much as we do ours. And even here, our own people acting with such cruelty and barbarism. It's so difficult to know what to believe in these days." She sighed. "I think she did care for us. And I like to believe we made her job all the more difficult. And you did say she helped you rescue Seamus. Oh, dear Davin, I am afraid I haven't made any of this easier for you. I've made a right mess of it, in fact."

"No. It's good to know I wasn't the only one who was confused." He put his hat back on.

"You know," Clare said. "I believe confused is a good place for us to be with all of this. Anyone who has clarity during times such as these is someone we should fear."

"I suppose you're right. Well. I must be going. I have a train I need to catch, and I have a ways to travel just to get to the station."

Clare hugged him, gripping him tightly. "How terrible it is that you must leave already. And for me to spend all our time in such difficult conversation. What wicked days we live in!"

He nodded, having to gently pry himself away from her embrace.

"Davin. Please do be careful."

"I will. I promise."

"And write as soon as you learn about Seamus. Don't forget that this war will be over soon enough, yet we will still be family."

He moved sullenly toward the door, seeming to be distracted by his own thoughts. She watched him leave down the front walkway, turn, and then disappear from her sight.

Clare shuddered. Should she have told Davin the rest of the news about Muriel shared confidentially by General Blaine?

Or was it better that Davin never knew?

Chapter 53

THE SOLDIER

WINCHESTER, VIRGINIA
September 1864

 The streets of this charming village at the tip of the Shenandoah Valley swarmed with blue uniforms, military wagons, and cavalry horses, which surely wouldn't be a welcome sight for the exhausted local residents. Already they had seen their small town change hands between the South and North dozens of times.

Now once again, Winchester was under the authority of the Union army.

Davin wished his fellow soldiers would handle their victories with more humility, but no ranking officer would be able to squelch the unbridled giddiness of the conquerors. Especially now that under General Philip Sheridan's leadership, the North had wrestled control of most of the strategically significant Shenandoah.

For his part, Davin had no desire to celebrate as this part of the country brought back poignant memories of his voyage to return Seamus back home. Especially now upon learning of a rumor that was causing him great distress. Could it possibly be true? Has the war come to this? And at what price victory?

He veered off Main Street and hurried up the wooden stairs to an office building with the words "Gordon Chafee, Attorney-at-Law" painted in gold on the glass window. He went to the bright red door guarded by a private.

"Lieutenant Hanley, sir." The man saluted.

"I am here to see the colonel."

"Yes, of course. Let me see if he is available." The private opened the door and Davin entered without awaiting a welcome.

"Colonel Jenkins." Davin stepped in to see the gray-haired officer attending to paperwork at the desk of a finely appointed office.

The colonel looked up and must have noticed the distress in the private's face. "It's all right, son. You can leave us alone. Come in, Lieutenant Hanley."

The private left and closed the door behind him. The colonel waved Davin to a chair across from him at the desk.

Having sat in the creaking leather chair, Davin realized how sweaty he was in his warm uniform. His anxiousness to see the colonel had caused him to ride his horse hard in order to get answers from his superior officer.

Colonel Jenkins opened the bottom drawer, pulled out a bottle of gin, and set two glasses on the desk, but Davin waved him off. "Are you sure? The barrister was kind enough to have left me a bottle. True Southern hospitality I would call it."

"No thank you on the drink, sir."

"Well, Lieutenant, you seem preoccupied." The colonel poured himself a glass of the clear liquid. "Speak plainly."

"Colonel, sir, I heard something that . . . I found troubling."

The colonel's hair, although gray, was full and well brushed, and this combined with his thick, black eyebrows and cleft on his chin gave him a distinctive appearance. "You've heard of 'The Burning,' I suppose?"

"Yes, sir, I did. So it's true?"

"It seems philistine, doesn't it? Here in the peak of harvest, to have orders to burn every field in the valley, and to slaughter every cow, pig, and sheep?"

Davin always respected the colonel, as he was a competent, well-liked military officer who didn't seem as infatuated with the trappings of war as were most of his colleagues. "That is what I heard. Is this solely on General Sheridan's orders?"

"All the way to General Grant on this one. I am afraid this isn't an order that will get countermanded by conscience. This is one of those we do and try our hardest to forget we did. That's the war, Lieutenant."

"But, sir. How will these people feed themselves? They will starve."

"The point is to starve out General Lee. The Shenandoah Valley has served as his personal kitchen for the Army of Northern Virginia. I suppose General Sheridan is only trying to smoke the bees out of the hive."

Davin now questioned the wisdom of his visit. He should have known it would be futile to protest, and now it would be more difficult to operate surreptitiously. "Will there be any exemptions? To the burnings?"

Colonel Jenkins placed the cork on the bottle and set it back in the bottom drawer. "You mean for a certain pastor in the town of Taylorsville?"

"Yes." Davin worried as to whether he should have confided in the colonel in regards to his brother. But how else would he find out about Muriel?

"It will be a clean strip. Not another loaf of bread or ear of corn will be served from this valley until hell comes to claim all of us. No exceptions."

Davin felt the sudden urge to leave. "How soon will they be in Taylorsville?"

Colonel Jenkins gave him a worrisome look, like that of a father to a son. "They are moving up from Staunton and should make their way up within a couple of days. But, Lieutenant Hanley."

"Yes, sir."

"You're a fine officer. Many, including myself, have taken notice of you. It would be a shame to see you throw it all away in some hopeless effort to try to stop what is inevitable."

Davin stiffened. "I understand your concern, sir, and it is noted."

The colonel stared at him for a few moments and laughed. Then he emptied the contents of his shot glass. "I would expect as much from you." He leaned back in his chair. "Now about that other matter."

"You were able to follow up on that, sir?" With all of the attention given to the recent battle, Davin wasn't expecting any progress on his request.

"Yes. You wanted me to inquire about that woman . . . the Confederate spy."

"Muriel McMahon." His heart pounded.

"Well, it turns out her real name is Muriel Perkins, and I don't have many details to share." He leaned over and lifted a folder on his desk and opened it up. "It does indicate here that you reported her as a Confederate spy. But according to this, Muriel Perkins had already turned herself in several weeks earlier with a letter of confession left at . . . let's see . . . the residence of Anika and Pieter Vandenbroek. Do you recognize those names?"

"Yes sir, I do." Davin couldn't share this was the couple who gave them shelter on his unauthorized journey to bring his brother home. But a letter of confession? What could this mean? Why would she sign her own death certificate? "I appreciate you took time to look into it for me, sir. I am much obliged."

All Davin wanted to do was to leave the office. His time was short if he was going to make it to his brother's farm in time. And now there was another possibility, one he had not given much hope for until this moment.

Perhaps Muriel had evaded capture. Maybe she was still at his brother's home and was merely in hiding. After all she had done for Seamus, his brother would do just about anything to protect her.

"Lieutenant Hanley?"

The mention of his name jarred him from his thoughts. "Yes, sir?"

"Be careful, son."

Davin stiffened his legs, squared his shoulders, and gave the colonel a firm salute.

He turned and walked out the door, thanking the private on his way past. When he arrived at his chestnut mare, he gave a quick inventory of all he had. Yes, he had all he needed to travel for a few days.

He untied the horse and began to trot his way down the dirt road. Davin would have to restrain himself until he passed all of the main sentries. With his rank he would have few obstacles making it out of town. Once there, he would ride at full pace.

He glanced to the side for a moment and saw he was being saluted by a black soldier, who was tall, strong, and impressive looking in his uniform.

"Jacob?"

The man paused, then seemed to recognize him as well. "Sir?"

Davin stood before the very slave who had risked all to help him deliver Seamus to safety. "Jacob!" He leaned down and grasped the man's hand and shook it firmly. "What happened? How did you . . . ?"

"The man with dat crooked neck. He done freed me few days after I seen you gone. Drove me cross the border hisself."

Davin tried to remember the man's name who had delivered both Jacob and him to the trader's camp but couldn't recall it. None of that mattered. Jacob was free and serving with the Union army.

"It's mighty well to see you, Jacob. You are a good man, and I'm sure you are a fine soldier as well."

"I don't know nothin' about bein' no good man or good soldier, sir. But I knows God ain't finished with Jacob yet."

"No. I suppose He is not." Davin saluted the runaway slave and continued out of the beleaguered town of Winchester.

He was anxious to make haste and it took all of his discipline and patience to wait until he could open to a full gallop.

In the meantime he pondered Jacob's words. Davin knew God wasn't finished with himself either. But what about Muriel? Would he see her again? Was there any chance she remained at Whittington Farms? If so, she was in terrible risk of being captured and hung.

Up in the distance, it seemed the skies were already darkening with smoke. Or were those merely storm clouds?

Finally Davin passed the last outpost, and the hooves of his horse thundered against the fertile land as he was heading south now, deep into the Shenandoah Valley.

Chapter 54

THE MESSAGE

"Do you not think it wise to consider changing your sermon this morning?" Ashlyn whispered to Seamus during a brief lull in their duties of greeting congregants at the door.

"It is, I am afraid, too late for that my dear bride." Seamus adjusted his collar constricting his neck. "But it is not too late for you to take my lovely daughter home so she can avoid the embarrassment of seeing her father stoned."

"Speaking of your lovely daughter." Ashlyn, who was wearing her long, blue dress, pointed with a finger of her white gloved hand. "I find it so dear how she continues to dote on young Anders, even with his condition being as it is. I believe it is a fine testimony to her character."

Seamus observed his daughter approaching on the walkway leading up to the old wooden church, her arm under the elbow of Anders's remaining good arm. His left sleeve was folded up to nearly his elbow. Ashlyn was right. When the young man

369

returned to Taylorsville with his injury, Grace never wavered in her affection for him. If anything, it grew stronger.

Ashlyn gave Grace a hug as she came up, while Seamus tapped Anders on his shoulder.

"You're getting along better each day," Seamus said.

"He's an inspiration." Grace beamed at Anders.

"I don't know what all the fussin' is for," Anders said. "I still got one good arm left."

They entered the doors of the church and behind them trailed Anders's parents.

"Good morning, Coralee." Ashyn held her hand out to the woman, who wore black from her hat to her shoes with Fletch accompanying her in his usual overalls.

"There is nothing good about today. Nothing at all." Coralee pulled out a fan from her purse and flapped it open. "This is the darkest of all Sundays I fear."

"Fletch." Seamus held out a hand to the smuggler who shook it and offered a disconsolate nod.

More entered into the small church sanctuary, and it was clear the mood was more akin to a funeral procession. As the parade of grief filtered by him, Seamus reconsidered Ashlyn's advice. So many widows and parents had lost husbands and sons. They had sacrificed so much and would no doubt be unwelcoming to today's sermon.

It had been months since Pastor Asa had died rather suddenly. When Seamus assumed leadership of the tiny Taylorsville church congregation, the transition had not been easy as Asa was beloved and had baptized and married most of them. But for the most part, they no longer saw Seamus as a Northerner. Whether he was comfortable with it or not, they believed he was now one of them.

Much of this could be credited to Ashlyn's deep roots in the community and her heart for caring for others. Although Seamus was the pastor, it was her love of Taylorsville's people and history that allowed them to forgive any of his reservations about their traditions.

But it also was his service in the war. Even though he was in the position of chaplain, the South treated all of their Confederate veterans with a high degree of honor, and Seamus was no exception.

Most of all, it was Seamus's growing love and acceptance for his congregation. They were flawed and difficult at times, but they were the people God had trusted to him to shepherd. And who was he to complain of the shortcomings of others?

So with all this being considered, and with his hands shaking at the prospect of what he was about to say, was it worth risking this hard-fought rapport with the people?

Seamus already knew the answer, because it was a message God had not only shared with him, but insisted that he deliver to others. It was as if all of his life was leading up to the words he was about to preach.

"I think that's all of them, Pastor Hanley." Ashlyn gave him her usual smile of assurance, the one that brought dimples to her cheeks.

Now that the last of the stragglers had arrived, he escorted Ashlyn inside to her seat next to Grace, who ever since Anders had returned sat in the front row with the Fletcher family.

When Seamus made his way to the lectern, there was a hush among them in anticipation of what he might have to say. He could see in their faces an anxiousness, a craving for some word of encouragement. They were all desperate for something to ameliorate their pain. To soften the hurt of defeat. As he panned the faces, he saw mostly women, children, and the elderly. Each of them now locked gazes with him, thirsty for the waters of restitution.

He closed his eyes briefly, then exhaled. "As I am sure you are all aware, our precious valley has been lost. Our own brave General Jubal Early has been defeated. Having nobly defended this territory on our behalf, he and his army have been driven south, leaving us at the mercy of the soldiers of the opposition.

"Many of you have suffered both personally and dearly for the sake of this war. Sons. Husbands. Brothers. Lost. Generations impacted by this tragedy. As you all know, I am not here to judge the merits of this conflict, and many of my opinions are not shared by most here."

There was an uneasy shifting in their seats at this reminder.

He glanced to Ashlyn and drew strength from her lifted chin and steady gaze. No stumbling of speech on his part would erode her support as she understood the intentions of his heart.

"It is not my aim today to instill any sense of hope in the plans and intentions of our generals in striving for victory, nor to dissuade you of that possibility. Neither do I claim a stake in those outcomes for my interests lie solely in the strength of your faith and your proper expression of this faith."

Seamus looked out among them for some sense of affirmation, but there was only numbness and some emerging hints of discomfort.

His throat felt dry and he coughed in his hand. "We all see the danger rising on the horizon, a terror approaching, and we know these well to be the orders of the Union's General Philip Sheridan. It is by his command that the fields of the Shenandoah have been put to the torch, and our livestock scattered or slaughtered."

There were groans and gasps from the assembly.

"The reports are they will be here tomorrow. For those who remain behind, we will be helpless to stop them."

"We are not helpless!"

Seamus held up his hand. "It is beyond our strength to protest because we are overrun. Our boys have fought bravely. Many have laid their lives down to protect us. But it is over now."

"It will never be over!"

"We'll fight to our last breath!"

"We will be stripped of all we possess." Seamus raised his voice to speak above the clamor. "So what can we do?" He lifted his Bible and opened it to where a red ribbon was holding its place.

"Hear this from the book of Proverbs: 'If thine enemy be hungry, give him bread to eat; and if he be thirsty, give him water to drink: For thou shalt heap coals of fire upon his head, and the LORD shall reward thee.'"

"How can he speak this way!"

"Shall we bake them bread as they burn our fields?"

"We will spit in their faces."

"They may believe us to be captives," Seamus said. "There is one word in which we have great power. One that is capable of breaking all chains. It is not bitterness. It is not anger."

The doors at the back of the church flung open and light filtered into the room. It was a Confederate soldier, but sun behind him was shadowing his face.

"Come in, friend," Seamus said. "You are not too late."

"I am here on the general's orders. The Yankees are approaching and will be here within a few hours."

The congregation rose to its feet as one, and panic beset them all.

"You have all be ordered to leave Taylorsville," shouted the soldier, who now could be seen as young and his face bright with terror. "Up northeast you will find sanctuary. But you mustn't delay." These last words were unnecessary as the flock had already begun emptying out of the church to sounds of nervous chatter and shouts.

Seamus's shoulders slumped for a moment. But then he shifted to concern for his family, and he walked over to Ashlyn who was in discussion with the Fletchers.

"Fletch has offered to take us to his cabin," she said. "They have provisions."

"That's very kind." Seamus rested his arm on the man's broad shoulder. "You are a good friend to us."

"We should git on with it." Fletch pointed them toward the door of what already was an empty room.

"What about Sierra?" Grace's eyes glazed with concern. "The Yankees are killing all of the animals."

Seamus pulled his daughter into him and kissed her head. "I'll go back and take care of your horse, Gracie."

"Oh, Seamus, do you think it wise?" Ashlyn asked, her forehead wrinkling.

He pulled her in as well and the three of them embraced. "I'll be fine." They held each other for a while, and then he stepped back and nodded down to his pastor's clothing. "I'll be wearing this. They won't cause me any harm."

Seamus turned to Anders. "You will take care of my ladies?"

"Yes, sir. I will do that." The young man corralled them toward the door, and they reluctantly made their way out, leaving only Fletch standing behind.

"So?"

What was the old trader asking about? Did he want to get paid for the supplies in the cabin? He shrugged his arms.

"The word? What was it?"

"The word?" Seamus laughed. "You mean the word in my sermon? At least one person was listening, I suppose." He thought back to where he left off when he had been so abruptly interrupted. "It's the one word that gives us the power for freedom in all circumstances."

"Yeah. What is it?"

"Forgiveness, Fletch. The word is forgiveness."

The man glared at him with his one good eye while the other wandered as he seemed to be pondering the meaning. Then he put his hat on his head. "I believe that soldier did you a fine favor 'cause that word woulda had you lynched." Fletch turned and waddled his way outside, leaving Seamus alone.

"Forgiveness," Seamus whispered to himself.

Suddenly aware of the danger that lay ahead and the shortness of time he had remaining, Seamus blew out the candles in the church. He went outside where the road in front of the church was a scramble of wagons and carriages.

Seamus looked to the darkening sky. He could already smell the smoke.

Chapter 55

SIERRA

 "Do you know the trouble I got into the last time I spoke to a horse?" Seamus ran his fingers across the coarse chocolate-colored mane of the animal his daughter considered one of her best friends.

It seemed so long ago when he was alone in his rustic cabin in the Rocky Mountains, wildly bearded, freezing, and on the brink of starvation. Had it really been fifteen years since he rescued the army horse in the stagecoach crash, the same event where he discovered Ashlyn's letter that led him to her?

More than time passing, it was the man in his past who seemed so distant. Back then he was grizzled, alone, and desperately seeking his sense of purpose in the world. How empty his life was without Ashlyn and Grace.

And without forgiveness.

Was Fletch right? Was it better his sermon was never completed? Or should he have insisted they all sit down so he could finish? He chuckled. That wasn't going to happen.

"What am I going to do with you, pretty lady?" He gave Sierra a carrot, and her lips extended and then her large teeth grabbed it from his hand and began to chomp.

Looking around the inside of the barn, which Grace had done a good job of keeping clean, he considered his options. The Union cavalry had descended quickly around Taylorsville, and in the short time it took him to get back to Whittington Farms, they were already close by, burning farms in the perimeter around him.

He could saddle up Sierra and make a run for it, but only at the risk of appearing to be a fleeing soldier or spy, and this choice could easily lead to him getting shot or arrested. And they would certainly confiscate or destroy Grace's beloved horse then.

Seamus couldn't bear letting his daughter down.

Sierra paused eating her carrot, and her ears perked to alertness.

"What is it, girl? Do you hear something?"

Seamus's nerves tensed and his senses heightened. He had been in many battles. Why was he reacting this way now? He looked down at the cane in his hand. Was his injury causing him to feel insecure and vulnerable? Or was it that it had been more than a year since he was in the thick of a battle?

Suddenly the latch snapped and the barn door creaked open. Seamus positioned himself between the entranceway and Sierra, as a father would in protecting his child.

The stench of burning crops entered with the breeze, and standing before him was a soldier adorned in full battle regalia.

Yet the uniform was not blue. It was gray. Seamus stepped back, planting his cane in the hay on the floor.

The man gazing at him was Colonel Percy Barlow.

"Seamus. I was so hoping I would find you here." Percy's uniform seemed to be without wrinkle or blemish, his hat bore the full flourish of a feather, and his broadsword hilt shone with luster.

But the face of the man in the impeccable outfit was worn, defeated, and there was sadness in the blond-haired officer's eyes Seamus had never before seen.

"Percy?" Seamus surprised himself. His nervousness was now replaced with an overwhelming compassion.

"I believe you are the only man who can help me now. Who can relieve me of my burden." Percy stepped inside, his polished boots contrasting with the matted straw on the floor.

"Where have you been?" Seamus could almost feel the pain in his healed wounds at the sight of this man. "No one has seen you since—"

"Since Gettysburg?" Percy passed by Seamus and patted Sierra on her broadside with his white gloved hands. "A fine mare, this one." Squinting with the pain of something buried inside, Percy looked up to Seamus. "Where have I been? Since I . . . since I shot you in the back?"

"Yes. Since then."

"On the run. After I watched your body crumple to the ground, imagine my grief in seeing there were several faces looking back at me from among the wounded on that hill. We weren't as alone as I had believed. And . . . I expected you to die."

Seamus jolted. Was Percy here to finish the job? He clenched the handle of his cane. "I cannot say I regret your expectations falling short."

Percy tucked his hands behind his back and circled around the interior of the barn. "If one was to be killed in here . . . shot . . . left to bleed to death . . . no one would know who to blame. The body would be discovered in a day, maybe two, and all would surely believe it was just another unpardonable crime by our northern invaders. And the Yanks?" He turned to Seamus. "They wouldn't waste any time investigating it either. Truly, it seems so perfect, does it not?"

"I suppose you may be right." Seamus glanced around for a shovel, a crowbar, some tool he would be able to grab.

The colonel pulled out a revolver from his holster. He popped out the cylinder and eyeballed the chambers and then gave it a spin, which clicked cleanly as it turned. "Have you seen one like this? I don't believe so. At least if I am to believe what I was told. That this was one of Samuel Colt's own custom models. That was what General Breckinridge told me when he gave it to me. Said I would have a brilliant career. Ha! My career." Percy pulled back the hammer. "You know what I used this very weapon for? Do you?"

Seamus's knees began to quiver.

"I thought one bullet would solve all of my problems." Percy pointed the weapon at Seamus. "One shot. Then I would have Ashlyn back. My daughter. I would get to make that choice again. And this time . . . I would choose rightly."

The mention of his wife and Grace stiffened Seamus's nerves.

"But you know what I learned when I shot you? Hmmm? I knew even as the flint was firing. Before you hit the ground." He glared at the gun. "There was only one way for the bullet to save me. To take away my pain. And I didn't even have the courage for that.

"And now . . . I am hoping you do." He spun the weapon, and with the handle out, he offered it to Seamus.

Seamus took the weapon from Percy's hands.

"Yes." Percy eyes watered. "You have every reason to do this. For all I've done. To protect your wife. Your precious daughter. I will be out of your life forever. It will be as if I never existed. Do this now and no one will know."

The craftsmanship of the revolver was unlike any Seamus had ever seen. He ran his fingers over the cold metal, and it brought back memories of his days in the Mexican War, the whistles of musket balls, explosions all around him. How long had it been since he shot at a man? How would it have felt for Percy to fire this at his back on that rainy evening on that bloody field in Gettysburg?

Seamus's fingers moved to the hammer, and he carefully pulled it back and guided it slowly until it rested safely on the pin. He leaned down and slid the gun back into Percy's leather holster.

"Do you have any idea of how many soldiers I talked out of putting barrels in their mouths?" Seamus's voice was stern. "So many of them I came upon . . . strewn across muddy fields, their arms or legs blown off and scattered away from their bodies. Their faces disfigured and them begging me to take them out of this world. To end their pain."

Percy squeezed his eyelids shut, but Seamus continued. "And these were good men. Fine soldiers. With wives waiting for them at home. Children missing their fathers. So if I had not been willing to compromise my beliefs for those men, why . . . why would you ever think I would do this for you?"

The colonel stumbled backward. "Don't you want . . . revenge?"

"I do. I am planning on revenge of the worse kind for you."

"What? I don't understand."

Seamus gripped the man's shoulder. "You, sir. You are going to be the only one in all of Taylorsville required to listen to the entirety of my sermon."

"Your sermon?"

"Yes. It's one I've been preparing for all of my life."

Chapter 56

WHEN TREES WHISPER

 Davin didn't know how much his beloved Strider could endure. And yet after nearly two days of riding, he continued to press even though he was quite fond of his horse.

All around him were the signs of the devastation he feared. The skies were blackened with rising billows, fields were ablaze, and everywhere he looked, the carcasses of livestock lay scattered, their throats slashed and left either to burn in the flames or to be scavenged by buzzards and coyotes.

Yet as he galloped through the smoldering countryside, he clung to whatever hope remained. If he could get to Whittington Farms before his fellow cavalrymen, he would use his rank to every advantage, even if it resulted in him getting court-marshaled.

As he drew closer to Taylorsville, Davin tried to recall the location of the farm by referencing it against the background of the Massanutten Mountain range, which was draped with autumnal colors. He halted and allowed his horse to walk him over to a stream by a patch of trees. Then he opened his side leather pouch, extracted a map, and unfolded it.

One thing was for certain, he could spare no time getting lost. But these farms appeared so similar to one another, especially with most of them burned. Was he already too late?

And with everything appearing abandoned, he couldn't count on finding a local, let alone trusting one to give Davin proper directions. He felt a twinge on his neck and smacked his palm against it, then looked at the crushed mosquito and splash of his own blood on his hand.

It was unusually quiet. So much so that Davin could hear the loud lapping of his horse as it quenched what must have been a bitter thirst. He stroked Strider's long, sweat-soaked neck, then turned his attention back to the map. He pinpointed his current position and glanced up at the mountains and then again at the paper in his hands.

He was much closer than he thought. Perhaps just a couple of miles. Davin folded his map and tucked it back into the pouch.

A shot rang out, and in a panic he looked up to see a mounted soldier leaping from the woods across the stream with a revolver firing. Davin's horse reared and whinnied and suddenly it began to topple back.

Davin struggled to keep his balance, but he was lurched backward and was now helpless as the great beast fell to the ground, the full force of its weight coming down upon him. Pain seared through Davin's leg, and rather than his horse continuing to struggle, it collapsed motionless, trapping its rider beneath it.

Panic came over Davin. He was unable to move much at all. His legs and hips were pinned, and his weapons were out of arms' reach.

"Easy, easy, soldier." The man standing over him was dressed in Confederate gray, with a long officer's broadsword in his scabbard and blond sideburns reaching down from either side of a plumed hat. He pointed a revolver at Davin.

So this was how it was to end? How could he have allowed himself to be ambushed? It was foolish enough for him to be traveling alone in enemy territory. But to take his eyes off of his surroundings for even a minute was inexcusable for a soldier of his experience. The rebels were defeated, but they certainly wouldn't give up this territory without seizing any opportunity for retaliation.

He extended his arms in surrender and closed his eyes, waiting for the sound of the explosion at any moment. Then he heard boots scraping across the dirt. Davin opened his eyes to see the man sitting on a fence post nearby.

"Doesn't look like you're going anywhere." The soldier holstered his handgun and pulled out a hand-rolled cigarette from his pocket, put it in his mouth, and then struck a match. He cupped his hands, lit the end, and then waved his wrist to extinguish the flame. "Beautiful time of the year for the Shenandoah Valley, wouldn't you say?"

Davin had come so close to seeing Seamus again. Perhaps even Muriel. To fall just a couple of miles short, and now to die here on the road . . . Was there a way out of this? Did he have a knife in reach?

"What's your name?" The man blew smoke into the air.

What should he tell him? His name and his rank? What difference would it make? With all of the destruction caused by his own people, Davin could hardly expect this soldier would follow any protocol. "Lieutenant Hanley."

The words startled the man. "You don't say? Why, I know a man named Hanley."

Of course he would. "That's my brother. Seamus."

The man tilted his head back and laughed. "It would seem Seamus's God has a strange sense of humor." He hopped down from the fence, walked over to Davin, and crouched down. "You do look like him." He held out a hand and Davin shook it cautiously. "I am Percy Barlow. Colonel Percy Barlow. How are you enjoying your visit to our fine land?"

Davin remained silent. This man had all power over him. One misstep and it would be over.

"Let me answer that for you. Not . . . too . . . well." Percy laughed heartily. He threw his cigarette on the ground and pulled his revolver out again. He pointed it at Davin's head, his hands beginning to shake.

This time, Davin didn't close his eyes. He watched the man's face twist with conflict and turmoil.

Suddenly Percy stood. "Why this isn't proper. Two officers. Gentlemen." He set the gun tantalizingly close to Davin, bent down, and lifted on the horse's hindquarters, grunting, and gave it a shove.

In one motion Davin freed himself, grabbed the weapon, and then stumbled to his feet.

Percy stepped back and dusted his hands. "Is that any way to return my generosity?"

Davin looked down at the exceptionally crafted weapon in his hands. "You wanted me to have this."

"A duel. How about that, Lieutenant Hanley? I win and all of you Yankees go home. You kill me and we'll set all of the captives free." He pulled his sword from his hilt and held the point vertically in front of his face.

"You're mad." Davin pointed the gun at him. "Put that blade down."

"Tell your brother." Percy lowered the sword slowly. "Tell him he may forgive me, but I will never forgive him. Never." Percy's teeth clenched. "For a man's pride, his dignity, respect— that is all he has. Nothing else matters."

Davin stepped back. "Put down that weapon. I won't tell you again."

Percy smiled and relaxed his shoulders, then with eyes bulging with hate he lunged toward Davin.

The shot seemed to echo for a long time, and Percy crumpled to the ground and his horse darted back toward the woods.

Davin flipped the body over, and there was a tear in the chest pocket of Percy's jacket where blood was oozing out. Then Davin placed his fingers on the colonel's neck. No pulse.

He went over to Strider, relieved to see the horse was gone. He wasn't suffering. Davin stood, dropped the colonel's gun on the ground, and limped southward as the world burned around him.

Chapter 57

THE BURNING

 Thirty minutes ago the Yankees had left Whittington Farms with their torches, taunts, and yelps of glee. The fields still glowed with small fires, flying embers, and the air was rank with the smell of burning corn.

Seamus slumped on the wooden stairs of his front porch, watching all of his labors of the past few years turn to ash. He had thought his preacher's collar would earn him some mercy, and as he looked over at his blackened barn and his smoldering crops, he realized how futile this hope had been.

At least they didn't burn down the house. There was this to celebrate.

But his heart grieved for the people of his town, of his congregation, who had farmed here for generations. How would they ever be able to rebuild their lives once again? Although the fertile Shenandoah Valley had been generous in its yields, the war needs of Jefferson Davis had stripped clean most of the harvest, and even before the torching, those who lived here were barely able to survive. The fires would prove to be the last indignity.

Seamus glanced up toward the dirt road leading into his farm. Something approached in the distance. He squinted. After a few moments, he discerned a figure emerging through the smoky haze. A Union soldier.

Hadn't they done enough damage? Were they coming to take more pounds of flesh?

Something was wrong. The soldier lumbered forward with a heavy limp. A few more steps and Seamus recognized the face of the bearded man. Seamus reached for his cane and pushed himself up to his feet.

"Davin?"

"Seamus!" Davin loped his way forward, almost dragging his foot along the way.

The two brothers met in a strenuous embrace, both hobbling to keep their balance and sobbing with joy.

"Oh, Seamus, you must forgive me." Davin put his hands on his head and surveyed the devastation. "I tried . . . so hard to get here. I could have stopped them."

Seamus no longer cared about the damage, the smoke; he was joyous. He grabbed a handful of Davin's hair. "Is this really you, little brudder? Can this be?"

Davin laughed and loosened himself from the grip, then he winced.

"What happened to you?" Seamus pointed to Davin's leg. "Come let us broken warriors have our rest."

They carried each other, arm in arm, Seamus leaning on his cane, and they used the porch railing up the stairs to settle next to each other in a sitting position. They both let out a groan as they sank in place.

Davin put his hands around his lower leg. "It may be broken."

"I should get something for that." Seamus went to rise but Davin tugged him back down by his shirt.

"No, Seamus. I am too tired. And too happy to see you. Let us . . . just rest." Davin pulled out his canteen, unscrewed the top, and offered it to Seamus, who took a drink before returning it. Davin lifted it to his lips and swallowed several times before clearing off the moisture from his lips with the back of his hand. "When?" He pointed to the scorched earth.

"You just missed the show."

"If only I could've pushed harder. Rode faster." Davin pulled up his pant leg.

"Well, little brudder. You always did run a wee bit late."

Davin raised an eyebrow. "Shouldn't you be more bitter about all of this? I mean, you ought to shoot me. Or something."

"That would make you the second person making that request today." Seamus clasped his hands around his knee. "I don't know. I suppose it would have been hard to explain to my congregants why the pastor's farm was the only one spared."

"So you're back in the pulpit again?"

Seamus smiled. "You aren't going to hose me down again, are you?"

"Ah, Seamus, that's something I ain't proud about. That's one of the greatest regrets of my life."

"It shouldn't be." Seamus put his arm on Davin's shoulder. "Do you know, that's what brought me out here? Looking back at it now, I see it was all part of God's tapestry. Every stitch. And here I am, with a wife I love, a beautiful daughter, and I live in this place."

Davin glanced around at the scorched fields, then back at Seamus.

"Isn't as impressive as it was yesterday. But maybe this is what it will take for these folks to actually listen to my sermons." Seamus nodded to Davin's leg. "How did you get that?"

"This." He pulled up the pant leg, revealing a large purple discoloration. "I got it while . . . killing the last man I hope I ever have to."

Seamus's demeanor changed. There was a weariness in his eyes, a shadow in his soul. "I am sorry." Then he was Chaplain Hanley again. "Would you like to talk about it?"

"Not much." Davin leaned back on his palms and peered at something unseen in the distance. "It's just. It was strange."

"Go ahead."

"It was as if I shot the man I almost became."

Seamus closed his eyes at the beauty and depth of what his brother just shared. It was hard to imagine this grown man once had been the freckle-faced boy he chased in the grassy fields of their Irish farm.

He pulled Davin in close to him and his brother rested his head on his shoulder and wept. They remained quiet for a few moments before Seamus spoke again. "I, for one, am proud of the man you've become."

Davin sat up, wiped his eyes, and laughed with embarrassment.

"You know, we should find a doctor for that leg."

His brother leaned down and rubbed his leg again before he turned to Seamus and spoke with some difficulty. "What about the doctor I left behind?"

Seamus's heart filled with sorrow. If the letters hadn't reached Clare, then Davin would have no way of knowing himself. "Muriel was a precious gift to us, Davin. She nurtured me night and day. She saved my life."

In Davin's brown eyes a deep yearning emanated, a lingering hope that he would see Muriel again. Now he needed to know. Seamus had performed this role of telling mothers and fathers and wives that their loved ones were gone. But it was even more painful to tell this to his own brother. "I am afraid I fell short when it came to saving her life."

"What do you mean?"

"After she had been here for a couple of months, some men came to get her one night. I don't know why. It all happened so quickly. She tried to free herself, a shot was fired. Then they dragged her body into their carriage, and she was gone."

Davin drew his hand to his face and he was still for several minutes.

Seamus could see his brother's spirit emptying. "You loved her, didn't you?"

"A fine way I showed it."

"It's not you, Davin. It's this war." Seamus thought of saying more, but sometimes just sharing in the silence was the best way to ease the pain.

After a few minutes he suddenly remembered something. He tapped Davin on the shoulder. "I'll be right back. I have something for you."

He grabbed his cane, rose, and hobbled into the house. Seamus entered the kitchen, pleased to see that other than knocking a few dishes on the floor, Grace's horse hadn't caused too much damage. It still wouldn't be safe to bring her outside yet.

He rubbed her head. "My brother is here, Sierra. And don't worry about his blue coat, he's one of the good ones."

Seamus went to the room he used as his office, and in the oak desk he opened the bottom drawer and shuffled through papers until he had found the sealed envelope. Then he went back outside and handed it to Davin who had gathered himself.

"What is it?" On the front of the envelope was written in large letters: "Confidential. For Davin Only."

"We found it in Muriel's room when she left. Believe me. We were tempted to open it but considered it her last request. We would have mailed it but feared it would only be lost."

"I am glad you didn't." Davin traced his fingers over his name. Then he flipped it over. After pulling out his knife, he opened it carefully. He pulled out a document, which he unfolded.

Seamus anxiously awaited to see what it was, but his brother appeared confused. Then Davin's eyes widened and he laughed.

"Well?" Seamus leaned in.

Davin smiled and held up the piece of paper. "She bought Jacob's freedom. This is the deed of ownership."

"Jacob?"

"That runaway slave." Davin extracted another piece of paper from the envelope.

"A letter?" Seamus was prying now, but the suspense overran his manners.

"Just a note." He shook his head as if trying to decipher something.

"What does it say?"

Davin handed it to him.

Seamus read the line a few times, but now understood his brother's confusion. "Whence again ye shall find the gold in your heart."

"Is that from the Bible?"

"Not the one I read."

Davin glanced down, then looked out to the fields. "What are you going to do now? Now that this is all gone?"

"You mean after I find a doctor to treat that leg?"

"Yes. After that. Are you going to keep farming?"

Seamus smiled at the question as he never considered quitting. "Yes. I will continue to be . . . a farmer of men."

Davin started to fold the papers and put them back in the envelope. "Listen, Seamus. While you're busy, you know, doing your farming of men, what would you think about me lending a hand here on the farm?"

"What about . . . ?" Seamus pointed to his brother's uniform.

"My term is up. They wanted me to reenlist, but I'm through." He grinned through his pain. "My whole goal, after all, was to conquer Taylorsville. What's left to fight for?"

They both laughed. Seamus looked at his brother. "Are you serious? Would you like to stay? Because, we would love to have you. I mean, I would need to talk to Ashlyn, but ever since you saved my life, she's been rather partial to you. But there is one . . . problem."

"What would that be?"

"We put all we had into this harvest. I don't know how we'll even be able to afford seed."

Davin tapped at his shirt pocket and then unbuttoned it. He pulled out a small glass vial and displayed it to Seamus. At the bottom was a gold nugget.

"That's right, you probably have plenty of those."

"No. This would be the last." Davin rattled it.

"That's all? What happened to all of your gold?" Seamus held up his hand. "No. Don't bother telling me. I like you much better when you're broke like me. Besides, it's like we're back in Ireland again, you know, the two of us."

Seamus enjoyed seeing the joy trickle back into his brother's eyes. "Davin?"

"Yes?"

"Do you think now that you and your brave lads have vanquished Taylorsville, we might get better mail service? Maybe you could get one of my letters to actually make it to Clare."

"I suppose a soldier of my rank and importance might be able to arrange for that."

"Good." Seamus looked out to the fields and beyond where the smoke cloaked the sun, making night arrive early across the Southern skies. "'Cause I need to let her know we're all right. That we're all going to get through this.

"And that our little brudder has grown into a fine young man."

Chapter 58

THE CABLE

TRINITY BAY, NEWFOUNDLAND
July 1866

 "Why is it that I could sit here and rest in your arms forever?" Clare kept her eyes on the horizon as the sun tucked under the water's edge in a burst of orange.

Seagulls dipped overhead and seals bickered on craggy rocks along the shore, which was dotted with anchored and moored ships and boats. She nestled against Andrew, enjoying his warmth in the cool air as both of them rested on a sea-worn wooden bench perched on a hill overlooking the coast.

"How did you know those same words were about to spill from my lips?" Andrew stroked her long, black hair.

"Because we are getting old, and that's what old couples do. They share each other's thoughts 'cause it's cheaper that way."

They were lulled by the crashing of the waves, and Clare couldn't remember when she last felt so comfortable, so relaxed. It had been a year since the war ended and the *Daily*'s unwavering antislavery positions and support of Abraham Lincoln had won it favor once peace was settled. The worst days of their financial struggles seemed to be behind them at last.

"Shouldn't we be joining the others?" Andrew spoke with regret.

Clare lifted her head to look back to the telegraph station up on the hill. The past few days had been filled with many exhausting emotions. First there was the nervous expectation as they and many other reporters were there to witness the *Great Eastern* emerging triumphantly through the fog hovering over Trinity Bay. The mighty ship arrived as part of Cyrus Field's latest attempt of laying cable across the Atlantic Ocean.

There was the waving of flags, the raucous cheers, the tiny boats filling the harbor; all part of the exuberant greeting by the residents of this tiny fishing hamlet joined by many distinguished visitors from around the world. Then was the jubilant celebration by those privileged to be in the small, humid telegraph building to experience the miracle of this version of the Great Atlantic Cable first coming to life.

Through this all, there had been little sleep.

Which is why Clare sunk back into Andrew's arms. "Let's just enjoy this a little while longer."

"All right. But remember. It was your Mr. Field who insisted we remain inside the telegraph station this afternoon. Something about a surprise."

"I am so thrilled for dear Cyrus." Clare observed the gentle swaying of the *Great Eastern* resting far offshore. She marveled at the thought of this remarkably engineered ship spooling out cable all the way from Ireland to here in Trinity Bay. "Hopefully, the line doesn't fail after a few weeks as it did . . . what was that?

Eight years ago? I am afraid if it does Cyrus will surely hurl himself from this cliff."

"Or more likely, be hurled by his investors." Andrew reached for her hand and pressed his lips against it.

"And those scoundrels will be the same ones parading him on their shoulders should this all work, telling him they believed in him all the time." Clare looked up to Andrew and even in the fading light could see how much he had aged since their last visit here.

"Andrew?

"Yes?"

"That terrible war . . . our difficulties with the newspaper . . . how do you think all of this has affected our children?"

"Hmmm. Maybe it would make them stronger. More reliant on their faith."

Clare could hear the doubt in his voice and she shared his fears. She glanced as far as she could and imagined she could see her beloved Ireland in the distance.

"We should join the others."

"Yes." Clare felt her eyes closing. "But let's first say a prayer for Cyrus."

"Mrs. Royce. Mrs. Royce." Clare felt a tug on her arm and opened her eyes. A full moon illuminated the otherwise dark sky. How long had they been sleeping on the bench?

"What is it?" Andrew was groggy.

One of the telegraph operators stood in front of them, a stocky man with thin, pointed eyebrows.

Clare sat up abruptly. "Oh no. Did we miss Cyrus's surprise?"

"I believe it is right here, Mrs. Royce." The man beamed as a father holding a newborn. "We have received many messages already through the wire. Including this one, with your name on it."

"What?" Clare reached out for the handwritten note.

"It came from Valentia. That's Ireland, of course. I recorded it myself as it arrived. It's quite official. Now you have something to pass down to your grandchildren and theirs as well someday."

"Thank you so much, sir." Clare rubbed her shoulders, numbed by the cold, and she waited until the man had left them to make his way back up to the station. Then Clare queried Andrew with her eyes, who in return only offered a shrug. She angled the piece of paper so it would catch as much of the moon's radiance.

Clare. My Great Encourager. My Success Is Yours. Listen Closely To The Music. Cyrus.

Despite her well-seasoned journalist skills, Clare was unable to pry a single additional clue out of Cyrus in Newfoundland. All she learned was that he had made arrangements for the cable to be among the first of those wired from Ireland.

The peculiar message provided entertainment as Andrew and Clare tried to unravel its cryptic meaning on their long trip back to Manhattan.

Since it was nighttime, with everyone slumbering when they returned home, they tiptoed their way to the mantelpiece. Clare pulled down the music box and carried it to the couch, and they sat, setting it between them.

Andrew struck a match and lit the oil lamp on the table beside them, which revealed once again the exquisite craftsmanship of Cyrus's gift. Clare opened the smooth teak lid, reached inside, and winded the tiny metal crank. The music sounded and the two of them listened as one would to a symphony performance. When it winded down, slurring the final notes, Clare cranked it up again and they tried to discern clues within the melody.

"Maybe he just wanted us to listen to the music together." Clare closed the top and ran her fingers over the smooth surface. "It is romantic, wouldn't you say?"

"I have a thought." Andrew reached into his pocket and pulled out a small knife.

"Andrew, what are you doing? You'll scratch it."

"Here, hold the lantern close."

He flipped the box upside down and examined it closely. Then he lowered the blade. "There!" Something snapped.

"Don't break it, Andrew."

"No. Look. There's a panel. Bring that candle closer."

"Oh, Andrew, does this remind you of anything?" She grabbed on to his arm.

"You mean when we were in the graveyard, uncovering your Uncle Tomas's hidden ledger book? Or should I say Patrick Feagles?"

Clare slapped his arm. "You should say neither." She shook her head. "Poor . . . miserable Uncle Tomas."

Andrew slid the knife under the interior panel and lifted it. Beneath this was a small chamber in the box, and inside this was a folded document. He pulled it out as Clare brought the lantern closer.

"Is that . . . ?" Clare put her hand to her chest.

"It appears to be . . . original issue stock of the Atlantic Telegraph Company. No. No. Can that be true?" Andrew adjusted his glasses. "My dear lady, we are suddenly very, very rich."

Clare squealed, and then remembering the children were asleep upstairs, she covered her mouth. Then she froze. "Andrew. We can't accept this."

"And why would we not?"

"For the same reason we wouldn't take it before. And the time before that. And the time before that. Oh, Andrew. We write newspaper articles on Cyrus's project. It's as good as taking a bribe."

"Ahh." Andrew held up a finger. "But that, my dear sweet Clare, is the beauty of the music box. You never knew this stock existed. Therefore, it never compromised your writing. Mr. Cyrus Fields is a veritable genius."

Clare tried to object but couldn't argue with his logic. It was beginning to be more about her pride and stubbornness than anything to do with integrity. At this point, it would be unfair to her family to continue to refuse this blessing. "I will just write one last story about the music box. We'll let everyone know about Mr. Cyrus's persistent generosity.

"Why, Andrew, do you know what this means? We can finally purchase the new press for the newspaper. We can hire more people so everyone won't have to work as many hours. All that we had hoped to do." She expected this to bring a smile to him, but instead he sunk back in the couch and looked away. "What is it? What did I say?"

He ran his fingers through his blond hair. "Oh, it's just there's something I've been wanting to share with you for quite some time."

Clare placed the lantern on the table beside them and took both of his hands. "Tell me, Andrew. What's on your heart?"

He gazed at her for a few moments with nurturing in his eyes. "I never liked the newspaper. Not the ink on every part of my body. The stress of the finances. The customers clawing out my eyes, and the community kicking my ankles."

"What?"

"That was my father's newspaper. The great Charles Royce. And I kept it going for him. But then, it was you. You are such a talented writer, and I know how important—"

She put a finger to his mouth. "Say no more, Andrew. I am tired. Very, very tired."

"You as well? I am so glad to hear this. I mean, not that you're tired. But that, you know what I mean." He put his hand to her face and smiled.

"Yes." Clare melted at his touch. "And now, my love, I have a secret I have been keeping from you. A deep yearning. One I have ignored because it has been impractical. Impossible. Not even worth mentioning."

She took the Atlantic Telegraph Company stock from his hand and held it up. "Until now."

Chapter 59

THE WEDDING GIFT

"Should we have spent so lavishly?" Clare shifted in her green glass-beaded gown, feeling both uncomfortable and awkward in her dress shoes.

Andrew took a sip from his glass of cider. Then he spoke above the playing of the string quartet, whose music was encouraging the merry feet of dozens of ballroom-dressed dancers, exchanging partners with laughter and cheers. "You told Caitlin she could have the wedding of an Irish princess."

"Yes, and she must have thought I said English queen."

He curled a finger around his glass and pointed toward Caitlin dressed in a long, slender white dress. Standing beside her was Owen, graciously accepting handshakes and congratulations. "How could you deny such joy to your sister and the *Daily*'s most valuable employee?"

Clare nudged Andrew with her elbow. "I thought I had that honor?"

"You used to be the most valuable until, of course, you retired to begin writing your novel. And I suppose Owen won't be an employee much longer either."

"Oh, I suppose I shouldn't be concerned about money on a day like this. With Cyrus's generosity, this is hardly a strain. And Caitlin does look so happy." Her sister glanced over to them and smiled broadly.

"And there is . . . much to celebrate." Andrew gave her a knowing nod.

She tapped him on the chest of his long-tailed black suit. "Now don't you go giving away our little surprise before its time."

"I cannot preserve the secret anymore. Could I at least confide with the holy man?" Seamus was across the room, still wearing the black suit and white collar he wore to perform the nuptials. He had his arm locked with Ashlyn, who flowed with elegance in her navy dress, and they both were in cheerful conversation with Grace and Anders, who seemed to be enjoying his first visit to New York.

"You best be kind to Seamus," Clare said, "as he is now much better connected than either you or I. Who would have believed that?"

Andrew pointed and Clare followed the direction of his finger to the edge of the dance floor, where Garret was patiently teaching his sister, Ella, how to dance. "He's become a real gentleman," she said. "So much so that I am afraid he won't share with us his true feelings. Do you think he will be fine with our decision?"

"He seemed genuinely excited, I must say." Andrew set his empty glass on the tray of a server passing by. "If not, at least Garret will have many years to get over his deep regret."

"Which means only one family member remains for me to fret about." Clare waved to try to catch Davin's attention, who leaned with his back against the wall, his arms crossed. Finally he noticed Clare, and with some reluctance he ventured his way toward them.

Clare straightened out his tie and dusted off his shoulder.

"Look how handsome you are without that scruffy beard you've been wearing. There now. I can see around this room at least a handful of delightfully eligible young ladies, each no doubt grieving your sour disposition."

"I am terribly sorry. Is it that obvious?"

Clare gave an "I am afraid so" nod.

"All right then, I will do better. It's the least I can do for Cait." He held out a hand to Andrew and they shook. "This is truly a wonderful wedding you're hosting."

"It is all Caitlin's doing. She had been planning her wedding for more than a year. It's just . . . with Andrew and my recent good fortune, we were able to sweeten her arrangements a tad. And she's never been pampered before. Never in her whole life." Then Clare sighed and straightened the rose pinned to his coat. "But we were discussing you, dear brother. How are you?"

"Me? I am doing well enough. The farm is coming back nicely and I enjoy the labor. Seamus and Ashlyn have been so generous with their hospitality."

Clare could see there was something else. "But?"

He hesitated. "I haven't shared this with them yet, but I'm feeling as if I should be . . . going somewhere. There is a stirring in my spirit I can't explain."

"Clare, Andrew, what a magnificent celebration this is." They all turned to see they were joined by a gray-bearded man outfitted in a Union officer's dress uniform.

"And we are so pleased you made the trip out here." Andrew put his hand on the man's shoulder. "You've been a dear friend to us."

"General Blaine," Clare said. "This is my brother Davin. He served in the Irish Battalion and then Sheridan's regiment."

"Is that so?" The general's eyes were glazed with drink, which he must have smuggled in with a flask.

"Lieutenant Hanley, sir." Davin shook his hand. "Or should I salute?"

"Careful, son." The general leaned in and swayed. "I detect a few rebels in our midst."

Davin turned to Clare. "The general's name sounds familiar. What am I remembering?"

Clare cleared her throat and looked to Andrew. "General Blaine is our friend who worked as the army's liaison with the Pinkerton Agency." She feared where this was heading.

"Is he the one you spoke about in regards to Muriel?" Davin looked at the general with renewed interest.

"Muriel?" The general faced Clare.

"Yes. Remember the young lady who had been in our house?"

"Oh. The reb spy."

Clare put her hand on Davin's shoulder. "Yes, but I suppose this isn't a good—"

"Ah yes." The general's eyes lit up. "This reminds me, I need to fess up on a little lie." He turned to Davin. "National secrets and all."

"Really, General." Clare pleaded with Andrew for assistance.

"I told you she was killed. But that wasn't the truth. I couldn't tell you then, but I can now."

"What?" Davin asked. "What was the truth?"

The general gave Davin a dismissive look and continued to speak to Clare. "She turned, the little lady. Arranged to fake her own death and the Pinkerton boys helped her with that. Then she worked for us. Old General Sherman has her to thank for Atlanta."

"So she's alive?" Clare asked.

"I don't know about that. Can't be too loved by either the North or the South. More than a few people would string her on a tree if they recognized her."

"Then why would she do it?" Andrew reached for Clare's hand.

"Turn?" The general laughed, loud enough to draw attention. "That's the humorous part of it all. She told them the reason was she fell hard for a Union soldier." He looked at Davin. "Now that's a fella I'd like to salute."

Clare could see the emotion churning in her brother's gaze and she needed to rescue the day for Caitlin. "Andrew, do you think now would be a good time . . . for our announcement?"

"Already?" He met her stern eyes. "Yes. Of course. I'll gather the others."

It was not a simple task to sweep the bride and groom away from their admirers off into a private adjoining room, but Andrew could be resolute when given an assignment. Clare's sudden nerves as she stood before her brothers and sister underscored the levity of what she was about to share. She signaled to her husband.

Andrew reached into his pocket, pulled out an envelope, and handed it to Owen. "This . . . is our wedding gift. We pray it is received with the joy of our intentions." Then he shuffled over to Clare and held her hand as they watched with anticipation.

"What could it be?" Caitlin leaned over Owen's shoulder as he tore carefully at the envelope. Once opened, he slid out a long document, and the two of them read through it with confusion forming on their faces.

"I don't understand." Owen held up the papers.

"It's the deed to the *New York Daily*." Andrew squeezed Clare's hand. "The newspaper is yours."

Clare worried she saw disappointment in their eyes. "Of course, unless you don't want it."

"Of course, we do." Owen burst into a beaming smile. "I've dreamed all of my life of owning my own newspaper. And the *Daily* is the best of them all."

"Well," Andrew said, "maybe not the best, but it's been with the family and we'd like to keep it that way." He put his arm on

Owen's shoulder. "But that's after we put in the new press, and we'll have an account to help you keep operations going. We don't want the two of you to get old as quickly as we have."

"That's wonderful. Amazing." Caitlin held back her tears. "But what about you? What will you do?"

"That?" Clare glanced toward Andrew. "That's something else we need to discuss with all of you."

Chapter 60

THE SEA AIR

MONTEREY, CALIFORNIA
October 1866

Davin felt alive again with California flowing through his veins.

The voyage from the East began with many reflective hours spent gazing out the windows of whistling, smoke-spewing trains. The great, shining engines blazed across newly laid tracks, and he reveled in the landscape of a healing nation unfurling in all of its youthful promise.

Then he chose horseback to savor his return to the soil where he once harvested prosperity. He traveled through the High Sierra, with its majestic mountains lofted with granite spires and alpine forests dusted with early season snow. In the hills of gold country, Davin passed burro trains and wiry, bearded, sun-reddened prospectors, their shovels and picks slung on their shoulders as loosely as their dreams. Then he traversed alongside undulating hills and winding rivers, past verdant farmland and ranches spattered generously with grazing cattle.

To the burgeoning metropolis of San Francisco, the still-untamed Barbary Coast. With its harbors awash with tall-masted ships and billowing steamships bearing eager-eyed passengers. They arrived from the farthest reaches, of many tongues and nations, yet shared the same hopes for riches and a better life.

Much was different since he left this rustic territory six years ago, as California was mostly isolated from the bugle calls, the cannon shot, and the winds of devastation. But the greatest change was deep within his soul. Because of this, he was seeing all of this country as a new man and for the first time again.

It grieved him to think of how much of his journey in years past he had squandered, distracted by the inner callings of his desires. Sending him on long, thorny trails leading only to emptiness and unfulfilled expectations.

He yearned to do as Seamus had taught him, to hear those sweet melodies that had so ably guided and ministered to his brother. Was that not what brought Davin here? Across this distant land? Or was this another wild pursuit?

Davin rode his gray stallion across the sprawling green field, which he shared with meandering sheep who watched him with curiosity as they chewed tall grass. He continued until arriving at the edge of a dark, rocky sea cliff. Carefully, he leaned over his saddle causing the leather to squeak, and he peered along the sweeping coastline, where deep shades of blue waters arrived at the sandy shore with white, frothy waves.

He breathed in the crisp sea air and enjoyed the sky dances of seagulls.

This was it. It was time.

Davin turned the reins and they were trotting southward

toward a group of buildings sprawled along a broad plateau. Once close he saw a small country house, a barn, and a shed; each built with wood that had grayed over time by the ocean's burnishing winds and salt air.

Davin worked his way around a slatted fence to the gate. There hung a sign that creaked in the wind. The words painted on it read: "The Cliffs Veterinary." He dismounted, feeling the wear of a long ride in his thighs. He opened the wobbly gate and entered, leading his horse behind him.

In the field, he discovered the purpose of the fence, as animals wandered about, including a cow that was limping and a sheep that appeared injured by shears. He passed by wooden tables covered with rusted wire cages occupied by rabbits, raccoons, birds, and other creatures.

Davin heard a muted conversation ahead and noticed a wagon in front of the barn, its horse standing patiently.

"Make sure you feed her twice a day. The milk should be warm but not too hot." The voice he recognized.

The barn door opened and a boy holding a foal in his hands emerged with a man similar enough in appearance to be his father. The man seemed startled to see Davin lurking but recovered and gave him a tip of his wide-brimmed black hat.

With his heartbeat ascending, Davin observed as the boy gingerly placed the baby horse on straw in the back of the wagon before climbing in with it. And in a few moments they were moving, then out the gate and heading away.

"May I help you, sir? Is something troubling your horse?"

Davin took off his hat, combed back his hair, and turned slowly, praying he would be well received. He couldn't think of the proper words, so he just stood there with his head bowed.

"Davin?" The bucket of milk the woman had in her hands dropped to the ground with a thump, causing white rivulets to form on the soil. She wore working clothes, a long leather apron, and tall black boots. But with her curly red hair tousling in the breeze, fair complexion, and soft blue eyes, she appeared more beautiful than Davin remembered.

Muriel put her hands to her mouth and started to cry. "I am so sorry. Look at what a mess I am. What are you doing here?"

"Muriel." Davin said her name with a full expression of the joy and relief he was experiencing to his core. He had dreamed of this moment so many times when he had fallen asleep on the train and on those nights on the cold ground staring up at the stars. But this was beyond what could be imagined. It was a feeling of completeness, a profound affirmation that this wild vision of his destiny was one the two of them shared. "Do you know just how difficult it is to find a spy when she doesn't want to be found?"

"Apparently not difficult enough." Muriel grinned. "Besides, I did give you quite a clue."

Davin reached into his pocket and pulled out the note she had left for him, which was now soiled and torn. "Let us see. 'Whence again ye shall find the gold in your heart.'" He raised his eyebrows at her.

"What? I'm a doctor not a poet. It seems clear enough to me. Go back to the place where you found the gold the first time."

"This is Monterey, not Sutterville."

"I got you to California. Besides, I needed to be convinced the gentleman would make significant effort to prove his true affection to the lady."

"It was a general who got me to California. He said you wouldn't be welcome in the North or the South, which along with this note led me here. To this . . . rather large territory."

Muriel put her hands on her waist. "There aren't that many women doctors."

"Which brings up another difficulty in my search." He waved his arms around them.

"Oh, yes. Well, a woman doctor to animals. I suppose the gentleman has proved his merit."

"What is this?" Davin asked with a smile.

"The Cliffs Veterinary. It appears the world is not ready for a female physician, but they seem willing to let me tend to their animals."

"It's all the same, no?"

"Not so, I am afraid. If you haven't noticed, you have neither hoof, beak, nor tail." She cupped her hand by her mouth as if to shield the conversation from those in the cages. "Don't tell my patients, but I've had to all but start over in my education. Reading books and fortunately finding an old, dear, retired veterinarian who has nearly adopted me. I even call him Doctor Dad."

She smiled sweetly and Davin held his hands out to hers, which she awkwardly clasped with moist palms. "Muriel. I am so . . . terribly sorry."

She squeezed his hands and tilted her head. "For what?"

"I . . . betrayed you."

"Betrayed me?"

"I reported you. After I left Seamus's house, I was confused. And angry. And worried about my brother and his family."

"Davin." She shook her head.

"What?"

"The war ended, am I correct?"

"Well. Yes."

"Then let's not bring it here. Not today." Muriel covered her eyes with her hand and looked into the sun. She turned with a whimsical grin. "There's something I want to show you. Something I want to share with you."

The mystery had never evaded this woman. Davin nodded.

"Good." She started to unfasten the tie on her apron and walk toward the house. She pointed to a large bucket of water. "You seem a little road worn. Why don't you use that?"

Then she skipped up the stairs of her house, and the door rattled behind her, leaving Davin to himself and many peering eyeballs.

He moved over to the bucket and was about to splash water on his face, but he paused to look at his wavering reflection. Davin hardly recognized the man smiling back at him. How long had it been since he felt . . . this happy?

"Hurry." Muriel took off her sandals and was now in bare feet. She lifted the hem of her dress as the waves crashed around her.

Davin stood on the shoreline and watched as she moved her way out to a large rock, dodging waves and giggling as they splashed against her.

She spun and beckoned him to follow. "Come quickly, Davin." Then she vanished behind a large island of craggy rocks.

He bent down and removed his boots and his socks, then set them in the cool sand. He followed the path she took in the rough waters and discovered the ocean bottom to be lined with jagged coral and boulders covered with sea moss. It was only with a clownish wave of his arms that kept him from tumbling in on a couple of occasions.

After taking the broadside of a few chilling waves, he finally turned the corner and climbed up the shell- and-barnacle-covered rock to where she was sitting on a perch, perfectly aligned to face out to the ocean. Muriel reached her hand down to him and tugged, and soon they were sitting beside one another, nestling to keep warm.

"This is . . . marvelous." He rested his back against rock and extended his legs, with his toes curling in open air.

"I try to never miss the sunset." Muriel took his hand and covered it with both of hers. "See, we have arrived just in time."

The yolk of the sun burst in hues of red and orange and gold and filtered through the low-lying clouds, spread far on either side of the horizon.

"Look." Muriel pointed out to where the silhouette of a great ship could be seen in the foreground. "I would come here every night and listen to the gossip of the sea lions and the laughter of the gulls and wait for the ships, hoping that one would be bringing you to me."

"I came by train," Davin said.

"I believe a ship would have been so much more romantic."

"I could try again."

"Oh no. You mustn't leave now."

"Muriel?"

"Yes."

"How did you know I was coming?"

Muriel reached down and pulled a starfish from the moist rock and held it in her hand. "Your brother told me."

"My brother?"

She handed the orange starfish to him, and he accepted it without disguising his discomfort. "When I was caring for Seamus, I pried him for details about you all of the time. I am sure he knew of my feelings for you. He told me the story of how he had journeyed across the West, through desert and mountain snow, all in pursuit of a woman in a photograph. A woman he had never before met.

"And then he told me of how you had stowed away on a ship and traveled by sea a thousand miles, just to be with your brother again. And your sister Clare, travelling twice across the ocean, all to care for her family. So I knew. Such foolishness was in your blood."

Davin handed the starfish back to her, all too happy to return it, and he watched her lovingly place it back down in a small pool of brackish water. "I suppose that is somewhat of a Hanley tradition."

"Besides, I knew you would return to California to find your gold."

He took her hand again and pressed his lips against it, and they listened quietly for a few moments to the soothing rhythms of the ocean's ebb and flow.

"Muriel?"

"Yes, Davin?"

"What do you suppose it would be like . . . you know . . . being married to a spy?"

She laughed loudly, as it could barely be heard above the waves and Muriel didn't seem to care if someone else heard anyway. "Well. There will be no secrets between us. Because I will know them all."

"Then, you must know what I am thinking now."

"Yes." Muriel's eyes lowered and her dimples showed, her red hair blowing gently against her cheek.

Davin lifted her chin to face him, they leaned into one another, and their lips met. They kissed tenderly as the sun tucked under the horizon, the stars appeared, and the two were misted by the cool, evening splashes of the sea.

Chapter 61

SHENANDOAH MOUNTAINS

 The colors of autumn were splattered across the magnificent landscape of Shenandoah Valley. As they made their way up through the trail he once shared with Pastor Asa, Seamus believed he could not have chosen a finer day.

He put his arm around Ashlyn. "You know, I never thanked you properly."

"Thanked me for what?" Her brown eyes sparkled with mischief.

"If it wasn't for you wanting to return home, I would have never come out to this beautiful country. These beautiful people."

"Perhaps I did not choose the best of times for us to return to Whittington Farms."

The trees opened in the trail, allowing a partial view of the valley far and wide below. "I don't believe that. Not at all." Seamus pointed. "See how the land has healed so nicely already?"

"I was surprised at how well it recovered. It's almost as if there never were fires."

He nudged her and they started along again, this time beginning a gradual climb on the dirt path. "I believe the timing of our arrival was exactly what was intended. How could we minister to these families, these people of ours, if we hadn't shared in the darkness of their experiences? And what if we had never met Asa? What a right shame that would have been. No. It was you, Ashlyn. It was your doing."

She paused for a moment and bent over to breathe. "How much farther is it, Seamus? This place that Pastor Asa shared with you."

"Not far at all." He embraced her and swayed with her gently. "But we should wait a bit for the others. The sermon I have today is for all to enjoy."

They turned, and now they could see far along the trail behind them, a bobbing of heads, as people made their way up the mountainside behind them. Entire families—children, parents and grandparents, widows and bachelors. There was Grace and Anders, and Fletch and Coralee. The entire congregation save for but a couple of the oldest members.

Ashlyn kissed Seamus on the cheek, then adjusted his white collar and dusted off his shoulder. "What do you think Asa would say about all of this?"

"That I can't be sure." Seamus looked across the valley and listened closely as the wind winnowed the brown leaves from the trees. "I suppose, as long as we don't lose any of his faithful on the climb, then he'd be thankful for seeing his dream come to life."

They turned and continued up the hill, with their hands clasped.

"Do you think Clare will follow through with all of her grand plans?" Ashlyn asked, her voice laced with tenderness.

"Clare?" He laughed. "When my sister shares her intentions, you can consider it as good as done. Besides, she's already accomplished all she set out to do."

"And what would that be?"

"To tend to her brothers and sister. Didn't matter any if we were ten or fifty, she wasn't going to give up on any of us. But her job is well done now. She's rested her siblings in God's hands. The only reason she ever came here was to take care of all of us. That's Clare. And now it's her time and I couldn't be any happier for her."

They rounded a corner and arrived at the vantage point. They walked to the edge and watched an eagle glide with the wind.

"What about you, Seamus? Do you believe you will ever go back?"

"That's why we're coming up here. To seek our answers."

Ashlyn squeezed his arm. "Yes I know, Pastor Hanley. That is the sermon you intend to share with the congregation. But I was requesting to hear *your* thoughts."

Seamus glanced over the valley. "This is my home now as much as anywhere else. I am fond of it here. With you, Gracie, and all of these folks I have been trusted to care for. If it's all right with Him, and you, I might intend to stay awhile."

"Ha! You planting your feet somewhere."

"Well. At least I don't see myself leaving soon. But Ireland? Now that's a land you never do leave. Those of us who have lived there and even those who merely carry the thought of that place in their hearts, we are all heirs of Ireland."

They both watched the eagle fluttering gracefully, allowing itself to surrender to the patterns of the wind.

"Oh, Seamus. I have something for you." Ashlyn reached into her pocket and pulled out a small photograph and handed it to him. "There was a photographer who came through town a few weeks back, and I thought it was time. To replace that old, tired picture of me you carry everywhere."

What? Get rid of one of his most valued possessions? His chest tightened. "This new one of you is very beautiful, Ashlyn." He withdrew his faded photograph of his wife from his shirt, the one he had found in a letter among the stagecoach wreckage so many years prior. He held the two pictures side by side.

"Now, my dear Seamus, you appear as if you are going to cry."

He stared at both for several moments before tucking them together neatly and placing them in his pocket. "I will keep both." Seamus placed his hand on her cheek. "One of a young lady who rescued a lonely, desperate mountain man. And the other of a most-precious woman who so faithfully climbed the mountain with the man."

He put his arms around her and they swayed together, together and inseparable, even as the others began to gather around them.

Chapter 62

HANLEY FARMS

BRANLOW, COUNTY ROSCOMMON, IRELAND
Spring 1867

"Where are the buildings?" Garret had his head out of the flap of the carriage window.

As Clare listened to her son, she marveled at how quickly his voice had lowered, at how he had grown and matured into a proper gentleman. "We left those in New York. They will be there when you return."

"And how long are we here for?" He sat on the bench near Ella, who was sleeping with her head resting against a blanket.

Clare turned to Andrew, who was dozing in and out himself. "Your father and I haven't decided. It could be for the summer. It might be forever."

"Forever?" Garret's voice droned. "That is a long time. Forever."

"Not you. We already told you we wouldn't commit you to a life of being a potato farmer until you are gray and withered. There are fine colleges in England, and we can always return to America if you become too terribly bored."

"We'll make certain you won't be bored." Andrew stretched his arms. "Are we close?"

Clare glanced outside and a rush of emotions swept over her. She bit her lip as she didn't want to cry in front of them all. "What your father is saying is there will be much to do. We haven't been to the Hanley Farm since . . . oh . . . nearly twenty years ago. Why it will be all in tangles and brambles. We may have to use this summer just clearing it all out. It's very possible we won't even be able to plant until next year."

"Next year?" Garret rolled his eyes. "I thought we weren't staying that long."

"This will be good for you, son." Andrew put his arm around Clare. "There is much to savor in the simplicity of life. It will do well for all of us to slow things down and to spend more time with one another. You and I will work the fields while your mother will be composing her novel."

Clare chuckled. "Well, we'll see how that goes."

Garret ran his hand through his black curls. "I don't understand. We get rich all of the sudden, and then you want to go live on a farm. In Ireland."

"Not just any farm," Clare said. "This is the Hanley Farm. The farm of your family for many generations."

The wheels of the carriage jarred and then they bounced steadily.

Clare gripped Andrew's arm. "Oh, we must be on the road leading to the house. We have nearly arrived." She began to cry, and Andrew pulled out his handkerchief and handed it to her.

"Why are you crying, Ma? I thought you were supposed to be happy to be here."

"She is crying," Andrew said, "because she is remembering how in a carriage much like this, on a day when the skies pounded down with rain, the man who was to be her husband came house by house, seeking to find his princess."

"And Uncle Davin and Aunt Cait were young, and they were with me." Clare dabbed her eyes. "We were all terrified because we thought it was robbers when your father pounded on the door."

"You know how many times I've heard this story?" Garret raised his eyes.

Andrew gave his son a playful look. "We're in Ireland, son. You better get used to hearing the same stories over and over."

The carriage stopped and Clare let out a yelp and clapped her hands. "We're here. Oh my, Andrew, we're here." She leaned across and gently shook her daughter. "Ella darling. We've arrived."

"Are you sure we're in the right place?" Garret was glaring out the window.

"We gave good directions to the driver," Clare said. "Why?"

"There are all these people out in the fields. It would seem . . . the whole village."

"What?" Clare went to look, but the carriage man opened the door.

"Welcome to Hanley Farm," he said, with a sweep of his arm.

Clare stepped out the door and then took the man's hand as he guided her down the step.

"What are you doing here?" The voice in front of her was forceful.

She looked up and Garret was right. This was Hanley Farm, but dozens of people were on the property, scrambling about, laboring with hoes, shovels, and wheelbarrows. Others were on ladders against the roof, while still more were walking inside and out the door of their shanty.

"You are two days early, and have all but ruined my surprise." The man before her was wearing priest's clothes, and his face was quite familiar, although his head was as bald as an egg.

"Father Quinn?" Clare was overwhelmed with all of the activity before her.

"None other. And who are these young ones?" He glanced back to those working behind them. They had begun to put down their tools. "Keep at it, all of yous, until we get the job complete, and not a moment before." He bent down to Clare's daughter and held out his hand, which she shook meekly. "And who is this little flower?"

"Ella." She leaned up against Clare.

"Ella. Is that so? You must have been named after your grandmama. Actually, your great-grandmama. And a finer woman there's never been. And you, sir." He held out a hand to Garret.

"This," Clare said dramatically, "is Garret Connor Hanley."

Father Quinn perked up. "Well, I'll be. And I don't suppose you know my full name is Father Quinn Connor. I must have been named after you, then."

Andrew laughed. "Why the man who married us deserves some honor."

"Shhhh!" Father Quinn put his finger to his lips and looked behind him. "Don't share a word of that around here. They'll string me up for marrying the two of you before having you properly converted."

"What is all of this?" Clare started to recognize some of the faces, although it had been so long since she had seen so many of them.

"Come. Let's have you see it with your own eyes." He cupped his hands to his mouth. "Tommy, Angus, come and fetch this luggage. Margaret, you'll need to get some ladies together and start the stew. It's time for the fatted calf. And tell your sons to bring their fiddles, and we shall have song and dance." He clapped his hands. "Today is a day of celebration. Our dear Clare has come home and brought these treasures with her." He put his arm around Ella, who had already warmed up to him.

Father Quinn pointed to the fields. "When I got your letter, I knew this land needed a good turning." He gave a mock grimace at Andrew. "And we remembered what a fine farmer this fellow was the last time. So we gathered a few friends around the village, and your spring tubers are just about planted. The folks were more than pleased to help out the famous reporter for the *New York Daily*."

"Oh, Father Quinn, they don't even know what the *New York Daily* is." Clare tucked her arm under Andrew's.

"They don't, do they?" Father Quinn winked at Ella. "Well, you shall see about that. There, we re-thatched the roof and reset a few of the stones. The chimney had a few breaches, but we mudded that well. Now inside."

Clare took a deep breath before she entered. The entire stone hovel was the same size as the living room in their New York home. She gave Garret a glare to keep him from saying anything that would embarrass them, but he seemed as captivated by Father Quinn's charisma as she always had.

When she entered, Clare covered her mouth with her hands. "Oh my." They had laid wooden boards along all of the walls and painted it a bright blue. The chimney looked as clean as the first day it was built and was already burning two logs of peat. She took in the smell as if it were perfume of a rose and with it poured in memories of her youth.

They somehow had managed to extend the loft so there were two beds and a new larger one against the wall.

"And here is the best part of it all." He held his hand out to a desk against the wall. "This is where you'll write your novel, Clare. And if you need any stories for inspiration, we'll be sharing them around the fire tonight. Here is some paper, and we even got you your own quill and ink."

Clare started to sob and Andrew pulled her in tightly.

Father Quinn lifted a black leather portfolio off of a small table leaning against the wall. He unwrapped the string around it and opened it up. Then he flipped through the pages. "Do you know what these would be?"

"Those . . . those are my stories."

"Not all, but many. We had as many clippings mailed to us as they would. Most of us have taken our turns reading them." He leaned forward. "And regarding a few of them, we'll have some serious questions for you later."

"Clare? Clare?" A woman entered the door tapping her cane, her eyes clouded.

"Is that you, Fiona?" The woman had lost most of her weight since Clare had last seen her, and she obviously could no longer see, but the joy in her face remained. Clare embraced her.

"Child. You came home. You came home."

She introduced her family to Fiona, who touched them each on their faces with the tips of her wrinkled fingers. After a few minutes, Father Quinn intervened.

"You all are mighty weary to be certain. I am going to chase all of these folks away so you can have your peace, and we'll meet a couple houses down for our welcoming feast. You take your time and get acquainted with your new home. I hope it suits well."

Andrew grabbed his hand and shook it firmly. "How could we ever thank you properly?"

Father Quinn looked to Clare. "By bringing her home. You already did." He looked at all of them. "We are truly, truly happy to have all of you back in Branlow."

He turned to go but then paused at the door. "There is something I did want to ask, and you can be kind to the old priest by giving him an honest answer."

Father Quinn narrowed his eyes. "We must . . . we must look backward to you, after all you've seen."

Clare smiled. "You are right, my dear friend. We have seen

large cities. And met with presidents and dignitaries, even kings. But I can tell you plainly. There is nothing backward about this place. In fact, you may be the only ones who have it all right."

"Ah." Father Quinn pondered this for a moment, nodded to them, and then turned and left.

When the door shut, they were alone, their luggage piled up and taking up a good portion of the room. Clare looked to Garret and expected to see the cynicism in his face. But instead there was something else. "Garret. What is it?"

"These people." He looked to her and his eyes were glazed. "They are so kind. No one has ever treated us this well."

"Welcome to Ireland, son." Clare put her arm around him, and he didn't pull back. Instead he was her little boy again.

They pulled chairs around the fire, and Clare explained how the turf was dug out of the peat bogs, and what a tinker was, and how every Irishman fancied himself a singer and a dancer, and the difference between blarney and blather. They laughed and listened, even nearly forgetting about the feast being prepared in their honor.

And when they arrived, they were cheered and people wrestled for the opportunity to speak with the Yanks. When the fiddlers played, two of the local girls taught Garret how to step dance, and Ella befriended cousins she never knew she had.

Then, in the wee hours with their children asleep, Clare and Andrew spilled outside like restless thieves, laid a blanket on the dewy grass, and stared at the moon peering out of the low-lying fog, listening without words for a long time to the bellowing of the frogs.

Finally Clare spoke. "Andrew?"

"Yes, my love."

"Seamus. Caitlin. Davin. Do you think I'll ever see them again?"

"I believe you will."

"And why is that?"

"Because Ireland is in their hearts, and America is in ours. We will all meet again. I am quite certain of this."

"I would like that very much. Very much."

Then Clare curled up against Andrew, comforted by the idea she was close to the soil that had been tilled by so many of her forefathers, as if she was being held by the arms of the Emerald Isle.

And as she drifted, a sweet melody arose, and she recognized it as the hymn from her music box—a beautiful song, and one accompanied by the sound of Andrew's heartbeat.

Discussion Questions

1. What did you enjoy most about *Songs of the Shenandoah*? Which were your favorite characters? Why?

2. Was there a character in particular you most closely identified with throughout the story? How so?

3. What do you see as the central themes in the novel?

4. Which characters in the novel went through the most emotional, physical, and spiritual changes throughout the course of the story? How did they change?

5. When the Hanleys and Royces first reunited for Christmas at the beginning of the book, what were some of the struggles each were facing? Were those initial struggles resolved by the end of the novel? How so?

6. Seamus was disillusioned at the beginning of the book. What had caused him to be discouraged?

7. In what way did Pastor Asa help Seamus rediscover his ministry purpose?

8. What was your understanding of the "songs of the Shenandoah" as Pastor Asa described them?

9. Are there times in your life when you've felt out of touch with God? When it doesn't seem as if you can hear His voice clearly in your life? What does that feel like?

10. What are ways you have used to reconnect your relationship with God?

11. Of all of the characters in the novel, the life of Colonel Percy Barlow was the most tragic. What were his shortcomings?

12. John 8:47 reads: "Whoever belongs to God hears what God says. The reason you do not hear is that you do not belong to God" (NIV). What does that say about hearing God's voice in our lives?

13. Jeremiah 33:3 reads: "Call to me and I will answer you and tell you great and unsearchable things you do not know" (NIV). What does this passage say about the role we play in hearing God?

14. How would you describe the marriages of Clare (Andrew) and Seamus (Ashlyn)? What made them persevere despite facing such difficult times?

15. Ecclesiastes 4:12 reads: "Though one may be overpowered, two can defend themselves. A cord of three strands is not quickly broken" (NIV). How would this verse apply to marriage?

16. What role does the Holy Spirit play in a marriage?

17. Have you read all three books of Heirs of Ireland series (*Flight of the Earls, In Golden Splendor,* and *Songs of the Shenandoah*)? How would you describe the separate themes of each novel? What about overall message for the series?

18. Have you ever wished to have a stronger relationship with God? To be able to hear His voice clearly? Have you ever asked for forgiveness through His Son Jesus Christ? Would you like to do so now? If so, follow along with this prayer (or something similar in your own words):

Father, I believe You are an awesome God and that You always have the best in mind for me. I want to hear Your voice clearly in my life. But I also know I have made mistakes that keep me separated from You. I have tried to find my way out of the despair and darkness through my own strength and know now that this path only leads to conflict and loneliness. I know that Your Son, Jesus Christ, sacrificed His life so we may all be saved and that He is the only true eternal path to forgiveness. It is only through surrendering my life to Him that I can be forgiven and spend the rest of my days with You. So I ask now to receive Jesus Christ in my life, not only for the purpose of forgiveness, but also so He will guide and lead my steps for all eternity. Amen.

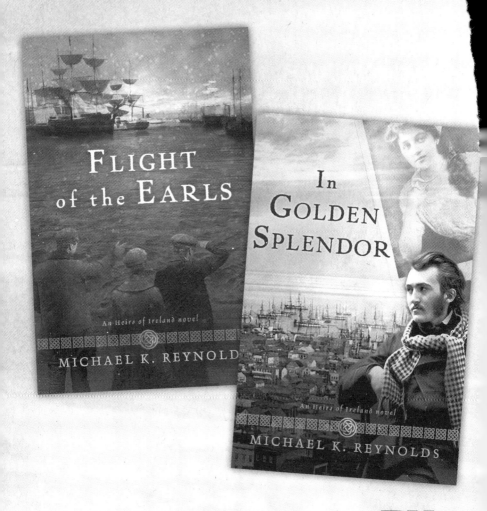